As We Peer Out From Under Our Rock

By Peter L. Campo

plc

The Table Of Contents

Introduction   6
CHAPTER 1 Setting The Challenge   8
CHAPTER 2 Assending The Mound   11
CHAPTER 3 Mr. Moe At The Rock   18
CHAPTER 4 Mr. Moe, Where Are You   25
CHAPTER 5 Another World   30
CHAPTER 6 The Cottage   36
CHAPTER 7 Looking For Hope   43
CHAPTER 8 The Gas Station   46
CHAPTER 9 Driving Into The Uunknown   53
CHAPTER 10 Arriving At Miss Mary's Home   64
CHAPTER 11 Moe And Mary's Relationship   74
CHAPTER 12 Entering Bluetropolis   81
CHAPTER 13 Imprisoned   85
CHAPTER 14 The Great Escape   92
CHAPTER 15 Learning About The World   96
CHAPTER 16 Enteing The Wild Zone   103
CHAPTER 17 The Frighting Confrontation   110
CHAPTER 18 Moving On   119
CHAPTER 19 To Stay Or Go   125
CHAPTER 20 The Preparations   131
CHAPTER 21 ArrivingiIn Bluetropolis   136
CHAPTER 22 Discovering The Rebellion In Bluetropolis 143
CHAPTER 23 Preparing For The Worst   151
CHAPTER 24 Learning About Education   155
CHAPTER 25 Confronted By The Sentencer   161
CHAPTER 26 Ike Jions Us In Our Journey   167
CHAPTER 27 Arriving In Dotsville   175
CHAPTER 28 The Great Disruption   182
CHAPTER 29 Arriving In Redtown   186
CHAPTER 30 Staying With Ike's Family   191
CHAPTER 31 In Yellowton   201
CHAPTER 32 Sorting Out The Events   215
CHAPTER 33 Arriving In Stripepost   220
CHAPTER 34 MEETing The Chiefs   226

CHAPTER 35 The Purple People   233
CHAPTER 36 Interpreting What Had Happened   242
CHAPTER 37 Passing Through Orangestop   245
CHAPTER 38 Troubles In Greenhinge   257
CHAPTER 39 Arriving In Blackside   269
CHAPTER 40 Decolorizing Blackside   277
CHAPTER 41 On The Road To Mechanicburg   283
CHAPTER 42 Arriving In Mechanicsburg   287
CHAPTER 43 Chair And Mate Are Told Of The White
Light   293
CHAPTER 44 The Factory Tour   297
CHAPTER 45 Coming To Terms Wth Chair And Mate 302
CHAPTER 46 Taking Charge   307
CHAPTER 47 Getting Back On The Road   312
CHAPTER 48 Approaching Warland   316
CHAPTER 49 Captured By The Soldiers   326
CHAPTER 50 Learning About Warland   328
CHAPTER 51 Captured By The Reds   332
CHAPTER 52 Finding Freedom   338
CHAPTER 53 Hoping To Reach The End   347
CHAPTER 54 The Hot And The Cold   353
CHAPTER 55 To Step Off The Cliff   360
CHAPTER 56 In The Cloud   365
CHAPTER 57 The Farewells   372
CHAPTER 58 Heading Home   375
CHAPTER 59 What The Future Holds   381

Dedication

To my divorced wife, Ann, mother of my children, who once was an avid reader and has since passed on. Ann, thank you. I will always love you. Perhaps, without your inadvertent influence, this book would not have come to fruition.

INTRODUCTION

Since humans first appeared on Earth, stories have been transmitted from one to another to enlighten us. Stories, whether truth or fiction, come in many forms, such as fairy tales, fables, myths, folklore, and by stating historical facts as seen through spiritual or secular lenses. Old or new in their origins, they have served us well in shaping who we are.

The imaginative side of our brain sparks storytelling. If we gave up that natural resource and lived only in the external world, we would be in danger of losing the very essence that defines as human beings. Although I believe most of us secretly seek adventure, yet only find it vicariously through the telling and retelling of our stories. Limiting ourselves to only reading or listening to those stories expose us to little risk and is a safe place to learn how to navigate our culture and make good choices. However, we each live a personal story to tell. How one lives their story is an individual's choice. It can be bold and daring, or it could be timid and safe.

Civilizations rise and fall, and many are remembered only through the quality of their stories. Unfortunately, since the beginning, *Good and Evil* have existed in the world, leaving each of us with the hard choice of choosing right from wrong.

What stories intrigue and motivate you? The characters in this story are unwilling pulled into an adventure. As in all good stories, there is a cause and a purpose. If one never experiences difficult, unpredictable, or perhaps risky adventures, it could amount to tragedy, for that's where one's true character grows.

Each life, in essence, is an adventure, a story that should be embraced with all its joy and pain, for each of us has only one chance to live it. Don't listen to those that try to limit your imagination by stifling the natural or spiritual side of your story. As you travel through life, no matter what's thrown at you, make sure your response is written on the good side of the mythical ledger. In the real world, at one time or another, all face complex situations to overcome.

In this story, the kid's experiences are in the supernatural realm, but if one thinks about it, the universal question being asked is when faced with obstacles and injustices, do you passively submit, or do you stand against it? This implies one has a moral compass with a purpose. Finding one's purpose is a uniquely human trait. To pursue it can be exciting and fulfilling, making life worth living in spite of the obstacles and dangers it might entail.

I hope you will read and enjoy this tale.

CHAPTER 1 Setting The Challenge

When I allow reflection, my memories flood in. It's still hard for me to believe how, at the age of twelve, in the mid-nineteen-fifties, my life took an extraordinary sharp turn.

In those days, a child's life was believed to be safe and predictable. However, on extremely rare and unpredictable occasions, a young person's life would spin out the ordinary, propelling them into the extraordinary.

Our incredible adventure began the day we met with Mr.Moe Smart, the eccentric nighttime school janitor under the large ominous legendary rock, only days before he mysteriously disappeared.

It was an ordinary summer's day, and by midday, I was sprawled out on my belly, exhausted and breathing heavily in our favorite spot in the center of our town's public park under the shade of the prominent, and distinguished old oak tree.

I was feeling good about myself, for I just beat my twin sister, Lucy Peterson, and our two best friends, through the hilly park in another of our energetic, playfully competitive bike races.

I was hardly able to hold my head up to keep my nose from touching the ground and smelling the fresh-cut grass, which wafted in the dry air. The hot sun beat down, casting a thousand shadows of the leaves from the hefty branches above as they danced in the light breeze. I forced myself to roll over on my back, letting out a sigh of relief in a much needed moment of rest along with my boisterous companions.

My sister Lucy caught up and flopped next to me on the grass. Lucy was small for her age, but she made up for her size with the attitude of a giant and sometimes the stubbornness of a mule. She could be full of energy when in the mood, and for her to sit still for any length of time was not her thing. Both of us were naturally athletic, but neither cared to work at it, we preferred to play games which took little thought or preparation.

Our best friends Matt and Marla arrived and plopped down by us. Matt was tall for his age with a laid-back and lackadaisical personality. He wasn't an innovator, always waiting for others to lead the way. Most times, I took the lead or at least struggle with Lucy for that position.

Marla was a beautiful girl with eyes so blue they blended with the blue of the summer sky, and her blond hair ran down her back like a golden waterfall. At that age, I must admit I took little notice of those qualities of hers.

Marla, or Mar, as we called her, just wanted to please. She would tag along, hoping to accomplish just that in her gentle way. Although, at times, she did exercise her own will, along with her many youthful uncertainties.

In those early years, the town's park was our favorite refuge. It wasn't a large park. However, to our adventurous young eyes, it seemed as vast as the African savanna. In reality, it covered not much more than a few hundred acres.

Other than school, in good weather, the park was the place we spent most of our days—a place we spent our idle time thinking up things to do and keep out of trouble. At twelve, little was expected of us beyond our school work, allowing us, especially during the summer's school break chasing after fun in an endless pursuit.

Looking back, even with all our energy, we were just average kids with no special abilities or direction. However, we were outspoken and exercised a bit of mischief, although obedient to adults. Of course, we had no idea of the adventure about to begin, which would shape the rest of our lives.

Once recuperated from the race, Lucy ordered, "Johnny, so let's do something."

"Let's go swing on the swings," Matt suggested.

"No, we did that yesterday," Lucy said with little enthusiasm.

"We can go boating on the lake? I love doing that," Mar suggested.

"No, that cost too much, anyway we did it not long ago," Lucy said, rejecting that idea too.

"Let's go for a walk," Matt suggested.

"Oh, boo-hoo," Lucy responded with her usual contrarian attitude.

"We did that not long ago," Mar added.

As always, I knew it was going to be my job to figure out what to do to satisfy our youthful appetite for adventure. I racked my brain. Suddenly, a bold idea struck me, perhaps, the most daring idea I ever came up with, at least up to that point. Therefore, I challenged Lucy, Mar, and Matt, saying, "I'll bet you can't make it up to *The Rock of Woes* with me?"

Lucy protested, "Johnny, who in the world wants to go up to that spooky place?" The quiver in her voice gave away her apprehension, which betrayed her fragile, tough persona.

"You know no one is supposed to go there on their own," Mar said.

"You know what happens to those who try?" Matt added.

"Oh, come on, don't be spoiled sports. It might be fun. Anyway, you know no one believes the legend anymore," I insisted, knowing Lucy always said no before she said yes. She maintained control by being the one we had to convince to join in.

Matt never wanted to appear to be scared, especially in front of the girls, and Mar just wanted to please, so they both sided with me.

Matt poked, "Come on, Lucy, don't be a chicken.".. Calling her a chicken was the number one thing she never liked. Although I must confess, in those days, we called her that all the time, and it usually got her to do what we wanted. Being restive, as we teased, it didn't take long before she gave in and agreed to go, of course, she dragged it out as long as she could.

I'll go too," Mar bravely chimed in, successfully masking her misgivings. I was sure she was trying to please me.

Wow, it was done! However, unknown to us on that day, the wheels of our future were set in motion. The four of us jumped on our bikes and courageously sped towards the infamous *Rock of Woes.*

CHAPTER 2   Ascending The Mound

On our bikes, we arrived at the edge of the set-aside wooded acreage in the center of the park. We hesitated for a moment to catch our breaths and bolster our courage before entering the area where the mysterious *legendary Rock* sat atop a massive ancient man-made dirt mound. We stashed our bikes in the bushes, even though in those days, no one in town would have thought to touch them.

I must admit, it took an act of determination to walk through the thick growth to reach the foreboding entrance in the disintegrating ten-foot-high ancient stone wall that surrounded the mound. Short of climbing the wall, the only access was a locked dilapidated wooden gate.

We glared up through its slats to see the mound, said to be the size of a football field. It reared up some twenty feet high and with the added height of the spindly young trees on top; it was like looking up at a five or six-story building, taller than anything else in town, except for the church's steeple.

I was beginning to feel, perhaps, in this challenge, I had bit off a little too much. Seeing the clenched teeth and fists of the others, which revealed their doubts, I wondered if I should reconsider… However, in those days, I would've rather died than to admit to making a mistake and believed they were just as determined not to back out before I did. I guess kids are kids, no matter the circumstances or how smart they think they are.

We found the gate to be decayed and rickety, too risky to climb. Fortunately, there was a space barely deep enough to squeeze under. I ordered Lucy to crawl in. As usual, she said, "No, you go first."

Surprisingly, Mar took it on herself, and bravely said, "I'll do it." She was inches taller than Lucy, yet more slender and quickly slipped through. I thought it was brave of her.

Not to be outdone, Lucy, in a huff, followed her. Matt, with his beanpole build, quickly slipped through. Being stouter, I had to wriggle, twist, and turn. Finally, with their help pulling me in, I also made it.

As expected, once within the walled-in area, all the plant life was straw-colored as if it were dead, although alive and flourishing. A deafening silence greeted us, which eerily lacked all the sounds usually heard in the woods. These elements only increased our misgiving, making me think it might not be as much fun as I hoped. It felt as if we were very much alone in this strange, forbidding place, even though we spent our lives around it.

Early on, the town set aside the mound and protected it in fear of it being desecrated. As the population grew, the people eventually surrounded the small walled-in three-acre parcel with a much larger public park. The park not only served the people but also purposely hid the mound right out in the open if one could imagine that.

Back then, the settlers gave some leeway to the indigenous people who once dominated this part of the country, by allowing them to keep ownership of that small parcel, which was sacred to them. About a hundred years ago, as the settlers multiplied, the original indigenous people became vastly outnumbered.

Many of the old cultures in the Americas constructed numinous mounds for ceremonial or burial purposes long before the Europeans arrived. We believe our mound was a ceremonial one, although it was never proven one way or the other. Due to the forbidding legend, no one ever dared to excavate it.

Back then, many superstitions prevailed. Most thought it would be taboo to touch it, and to this day, that view still holds. Therefore, the town never allowed an archaeological dig.

"Do you think we ought to do this?" Lucy asked.

I figured, if I backed out now, I would lose my credibility. The truth was I no longer wanted to go up there any more than the others. However, as my back stiffened, pride forced me to say, "Come on, Lucy, you wanted to do something different. You're not afraid, are you, you know what I mean?" I challenged. However, I tipped my hand by saying, "You know what I mean," for she knew I only used that phrase when I was unsure of myself.

"You're really a dummy," she said, knowing me better than I would've liked.

However, not willing to admit anything that made me look weak, I again asked, "You're not afraid, are you?"

As usual, her stubbornness couldn't let my challenge go unanswered. Although just as hesitant as I was, nevertheless, she stepped forward and said, "No, of course not, let's do it." Unfortunately, in so many ways, we were just alike. Matt and Mar went along with it, never wanting to be left out.

So... with a facade of courage, as if we were in control, we continued on our way in the waist-high straw-colored wild growth. In spite of it being summer, even the blooming flowers were colorless. However, we knew it would be so for we visited the *infamous Rock* twice before on class trips in the company of several protective adults, which were always guided by a decedent of the original native people from whom the legend originated.

Those guides were the only ones who possessed the original and only gold key to the gate, along with their knowledge of how to properly approach the *Rock*. Everyone understood that no one should ascend the mound and approach the *Rock* without a Shaman guide. Strangely, a fact lost on us that day.

At one time or another, all the children of the town visited this place in small groups. Always in connection with a particular event as part of their education of our town's history. However, every time a class went there, even the guides were visibly uncomfortable as they monotonously recited the legend and quickly led them away.

Through the years, all the town's children took that excursion. Parents accepted it as being a rite of passage. I was just a little kid the first time I did. I still remember being scared out of my wits. An attitude justified, for all experienced the same unexplained feelings, which were potent chills up and down everyone's spines raising the hair on their arms and the back of their necks, which spooked everyone.

Parents warned their children never to play on or near the mound without supervision. However, once in a great while, that rule was not obeyed by an unwise young soul who attempts to go up there on their own without a guide. Perhaps, out of curiosity or more likely having been dared, as we had done on this day. In those days, goating each other was a large part of our childish interactions.

After those attempts by those misguided youngsters, they always came away rattled and confused never to tell anyone what they experienced, never entirely being the same or willing to go near the *Rock* again. As if there was a sinister factor in play, yet they never questioned or understood that experience. However, I felt no one ever made it up to the *Rock* without a guide, regardless of what anyone might have claimed.

With just enough courage, or perhaps foolishness, as not to give those elements as much thought as we should've, we continued on our way. The *Rock* was so close, yet it was so far, almost alien. Looking back to that day, it seemed to have an extra allure, drawing us in as if it was our destiny, although contrary to knowing there might be consequences.

We reached the ancient stone steps embedded in the steep incline leading up to the top of the mound. I remembered the terrain from our previous trips. However, it's been a couple of years since our last visit, so I led with caution. It wasn't easy to keep our balance while climbing the steps. It was scary, like climbing to the top of a twenty-foot ladder. I never liked heights.

Once on top, we knew we had to follow a barely distinguishable foot trail in a zigzag pattern, marked only by ancient chiseled stone four-by-four-inch and four-foot-tall totem-like posts. In a way, it was like playing a game.

The posts were set along the path about twenty feet apart. As the legend instructed, everyone had to touch each post as they passed them. Over the years, through erosion, the posts had sunk a bit, causing them to tilt, which perhaps took a thousand of years of wear and tear to accomplish. For some unknown reason, lost in history, the legend instructed the posts were never to be reset, especially by outsiders, so not one of their people was ever brave enough to straighten them.

The original Indian tribe was active until a couple of decades ago, before which they kept the mound clear of trees and foliage, leaving the posts and the massive *Rock* the only objects up there.

The legend said if an unwelcome visitor, not led by a

Shaman, attempted to follow the ritual path, they would become disoriented and confused, never to reach the *Rock*. It seemed illogical for one not to find their way in that unobstructed open space. A fact hard to believe, but that's what the legend said.

Consequently, those elements were never put to a scientific test, and those youngsters who secretly tried never spoke of it. Even adults believed the mound was an enchanted place, thereby not always explainable.

Being kids with short attention spans, we easily overlooked those fundamentals. However, I did realize it was going to be much harder to find our way in the now neglected dense woods, which now engulfed the mound.

Over time the town's people became modernized, leaving many today to doubt the legend. Yet, they remained leery because of those unexplained intense sensations this place still evoked. They suffered from the contradiction of believing and not believing as they lived in two worlds, the old and the new. Even today, only the fool-hearty, I guess like us, attempt to go up there without a Shaman guide. Even the most potent legends in time fade, and *The Legend of the Rock* was in jeopardy of that fate.

The posts were hardly recognizable encrusted with dirt and weeds, only spotted because we knew to look for them. With the aid of the faint footpath and touching each post, we cautiously worked our way along, with Mar and a reluctant Lucy purposely trailing behind. I marked our way with the piece of chalk I always carried with me in my youth, with pointed arrows on surrounding surfaces to help the girls follow us and to find our way back.

The mound was crowded with young, thin close-knit trees entwined with dense weeds and twisted bushes, all with the same unexplained straw-color. The trees formed a canopy overhead blocking most of the sunlight giving the impression of being in a dark, gloomy grotto. I must say, this place was unnerving, especially for us being so young and inept.

The indigenous people once ceremonially walked this same path in their rituals. I imagine they only wore animal skins, crowns of feathers, brightly colored beads, and painted faces. Over the centuries, those countless processions carved out the footpath, which was incredibly still visible, although faint.

The tribe uniquely lived in peace for eons before they melted into the current population, leaving only the mound and *Rock* as evidence of their ancient existence. Eerily, we could almost feel their presence as a mysterious, unexplained force that appeared to be moving us along, for it made little sense to be doing this on our own.

It seems childish now, but back then, we always played imaginary games in our activities. I envisioned being an explorer in the jungle bravely hunting for buried treasure under the *Rock* at the end of the path. I know Matt invented his own fantasy, allowing him the courage to go on. Imagination can be a powerful force.

In a contrary mood, lagging behind Lucy said to Mar, "Hold on, it's dark in there; let's stay here and let the boys do their thing."

Since we were little kids, Mar always followed me a couple of steps behind." With some urgency, she insisted, "Come on, Lucy, let's not lose them," as she grabbed her hand and pulled her along.

In a sense, Lucy and I were fused to Matt and Mar almost from birth. The four of us were fortunate enough to be close neighbors. Our moms shared their pregnancies with each other, which all took place within months of each other.

Since our infancy, we played together and were in the same classes at public school number seven. Inseparable, in spite of our playful teasing of each other. We were popular with our peers, and it was no surprise when they nicknamed us, *The Bookends*. It was a good fit for the four of us until we inevitably grew out of our childish ways.

At one time, *The Rock of Woes* was a popular tourist attraction. The Shamans regularly led tours up to it. However, with the development of automobiles in the early twentieth century, which allowed people to travel further afield, it sadly was to end. By the late forties, tourists chose more commercial and appealing places to visit. And with the building of the super-highways, which bypassed our town, it compounded our loss. Main Street had become a secondary road, not often traveled by outsiders. Those conditions led to the loss of its appeal to attract tourist's dollars.

The Shamans, who once guided numbers of people to *The Rock,* have since moved on to more lucrative endeavors. Just one family was left willing to conduct the class trips once or twice a year. To support themselves the rest of the time, they grew and sold produce at the market, plus making and selling Indian curios connected to their tribe and the legend to those who occasionally stop in town.

No longer were there enough local tribe members willing to work at preserving the once carefully groomed site, which resulted in it becoming a neglected, overgrown wooded area. Our town being frugal by nature, wasn't willing to pick up the cost of maintaining it. Consequently, over time, the outside world had mostly forgotten the legend. The mound now being covered with dense woods was a challenge to penetrate. In spite of the surrounding park having been well used and maintained.

We continued on our way...

CHAPTER 3 Mr. Moe At The Rock

As Matt and I worked our way towards the *Rock*, the silence was suddenly broken by what we thought was someone talking. The mound was void of the usual sounds, for the wild creatures felt those unnerving vibes and kept away. We never expect anyone to be there. Other than the guided excursions, people avoided coming here like the plague. Nervously, Matt and I proceeded, forgetting the girls for the moment.

In spite of the supernatural elements, the surrounding modern world convinced many in town to accept the legend as only a myth, a fairytale. Yet, up to this day, no one has been able to explain away the eeriness one feels when being there. Most reject, even thinking about it.

However, the town capitalized on the legend. Keeping it alive by teaching it to their children, promoting it on the road signs, and symbolically, it always had a place in our parades, special events, and was pictured on the town's souvenirs. Why, because it remains the only noteworthy historical event our town can claim as its own. And of course, it still has some monetary value, not to mention people being mesmerized by the supernatural elements. For those reasons, the town's counsel successfully denied those who wanted to bulldoze and develop the site for other usages.

Reaching an opening in the brush, we found ourselves within sight of the *Rock*. Incredibly we arrived safely without getting lost or confused. An act that blew away the belief no one could make it up here without a guide.

However, before we were able to give it much thought. We were stunned to see a man on his hands and knees in the hollowed-out space under *The Rock*.

Baffled, Matt could barely say, "I don't know about this."

Hearing him, the man spotted us. Jogged out of our game playing, we froze where we stood. The man quickly rose, dusted off his knees, and called out, "Well, hello boys. Don't be afraid."

To our great relief, we saw it was only Mr. Moe Smart, the nighttime school janitor. A lanky elderly white-haired man, who we knew to be harmless. He was dressed, as always, in his wrinkled maintenance-man outfit.

Contrary to the gloomy mound, the much larger surrounding public park was usually bathed in sunshine, and its pure air filled our nostrils with the sweet smell of nature. A place where the birds, insects, and animals were not only seen and heard but flourished and roamed freely. To this day, the park remains a safe and tranquil place. A place where people stroll, jog or run along the many paths, smell and picked the flowers, picnic, play games, go boating, or swim in the small lake fed by the many streams, sit on the old wooden benches or stretch out on the manicured grass spaces. However, it is not to be confused with the eeriness of the mound.

In the summer months, before television consumed much of our time, people spent their unhurried hours in the park with its gently rolling hills to unwind, interact with others strengthening relationships, or engaged in the many outdoor activities. The summer band concerts and competitive sports remain the most popular events. Everyone enjoyed the summer activities, regardless of the mound and the ominous *Rock* sitting right in the middle. Oddly, it was not considered a threat, as long one kept their proper distance.

Before Moe became the nighttime school janitor, he was the welding and shop teacher at the high school. Due to his previous position, everyone still respectfully referred to him as Mr. Moe. As the story goes, well before I was born, he began to act in strange ways, which eventually led to his dismissal as a teacher.

It started with him hitting his head against the wall for no apparent reason. Later, he would lose his temper over small things. In time, he would occasionally fall on his hands and knees and bang his head on the floor, as he spewed out a diatribe about life and society, which no one understood. That behavior not only embarrassed the school but upset the students, although they never considered him a threat.

Nevertheless, it forced the school board to remove him from his teaching job. Fortunately, due to his many years of satisfactory service, and with many on the board once being his students. They kindly offered him the nighttime janitorial job, which, fortunately, was open at the time. However, they tied one condition to it. Due to his strange behavior, he had to submit to counseling.

In those days, they understood little of what he suffered from. Back then, counselors weren't as commonplace as they are today, so the local Pastor counseled him. The janitor's job didn't pay him as much, yet it was enough to meet his needs. He graciously accepted it, not having a better option, especially at his age. Most important to the board was it kept him out of sight.

In time, and always behind his back, the youngsters who didn't know him, referred to him as Mr. Moe, the strange nighttime school janitor. I must confess, in hindsight, not knowing any better, we called him that too. Since he took that job, he has not exhibited any odd behavior. However, people paid less and less attention to him. Now accepting, he is just an old man who recently retired and quietly shadows around town still wearing his work uniform. Those who remembered him as a competent teacher, such as my father, always spoke of him respectfully.

In our preteens, with our many friends, we played games in the park such as cops and robbers, cowboys and Indians, even war games, and of course, knights slaying the dragons, which was my favorite. In those games, most kids wanted to play the good guys. To avoid disputes, we used several methods to choose who played the different roles. Those who lost their choice were doomed to play the villains. Lucy was one of the few who enjoyed playing the bad guys. I never understand that in her.

In those games, with our youthful imaginations, we acted boldly and bravely, not having anything real at risk. Although, in my secret heart, I wished to live a life of adventure, defeating the evil ones, and bathing in glory. That was our childish mentality back then in our protected little world.

However, at the moment, I felt ascending the mound was no longer a game. Moe invited, "Come and see *The Rock*. It won't bite you." Having seen it before, Matt and I move towards it, staying close to each other, for it was a little unnerving. The huge legendary slab of granite jutted up out of the ground. It had a highly polished gleaming jet-black surface and measured two to three feet thick at its center and thinned out on both ends, about twenty-five feet wide, arching over an eight-foot-high cave-like space underneath it. The cave's ceiling tapered back a short distance until it hit the ground leading nowhere. It unmistakably resembled a giant clam with its mouth wide open waiting to slam shut if anyone entered.

In the shadows of the canopy, it helped to present that forbidding image, which even gave the sturdiest of the adults' chills. As we peered at it, an extraordinary thing occurred as a white cloud rose from behind it. It left us speechless as it hovered just below the treetops causing it not to be visible from any other spot in the park.

Moe quickly reassured, "Boys, don't be afraid. I think it has something to do with the humidity. Hey, most are too scared to come up here. What brought you, boys, here today, and where is your guide?"

"Mr. Moe, we just wanted to see if we could make it up here on our own, and as we came near, we heard someone moaning or talking. Was it you, you know what I mean?" I asked, not seeing anyone else.

He didn't answer me, he just asked, "Boys, did you really come up here on your own, without a guide?"

"Yes, sir, we did."

"Why, that's amazing. I never heard of anyone else achieving that. Good for you youngsters."

"There was nothing to it," I boasted with little thought, although I sensed something unusual was going on. I wondered who guided him, then realized he implied he must have also come alone.

He said with a tone of sarcasm, "Well, then I guess there's nothing here to be concerned about like some people want you to believe. Now that you're here, why don't you sit and keep me company for a while."

In spite of the spooky tales about this place, and since tourism-ended years ago, the town adapted to having *The Rock* by acting as if it didn't exist. Except for those special events still carried around it. Later I realized how the people in my town weren't an inquisitive lot for how easily they blocked the unexplained out.

"Johnny! Matt! Where are you?" the girls called out.

"Who's that? Are they with you?" Moe asked, somewhat alarmed.

"Yes sir, that's my sister Lucy and our friend Mar."

"Well then, get them up here before they lose their way. They shouldn't be out there alone."

"Yes, sir." I yelled as loud as I could, "Lucy, we're up by *The Rock*. Mr. Moe is with us. Hurry and get up here." Hearing me and being surprised, Lucy ordered Mar to get going as she now pulled her along, taking charge as she usually did only when she decided to do so.

They quickly followed my chalk marks touching each post along the way. When the girls spotted us from a distance, Lucy yelled, "Why did you leave us?"

"Mr. Moe, that's my sister," I apologetically said.

The girls arrived, and we introduced ourselves. Moe said, "Nice to finally meet you, youngsters. I've always known who you were, for I once taught your fathers."

Acknowledging, we knew he had. In the past, we only nodded to him as we occasionally passed him on the street. We were too timid to have ever spoken a word to him before. However, we couldn't help but notice how disheveled he looked and how bloodshot his eyes were.

Along with seeing him and the white cloud, Lucy and Mar reflected their concerns as they looked at me. Moe said, "Now that we're acquainted, I must tell you because you made it up here safely in spite of the legend, it makes you kids special?"

"Oh, we're not special," I said.

"Someday, I believe you'll find out you are, whether you appreciate it now or not. Now, girls, sit and make yourselves comfortable," Moe invited. "I find it relaxing here, and you're the first ones to visit with me up here."

Being together, the four of us felt safe in spite of what the legend said. Consequentially, we were entirely comfortable in giving this lonely old man our company.

Up until that day, we lived a charmed and carefree life

without a real worry. Not yet knowing what the future held for us, and probably not mature enough to handle it. It was a slower-paced and simpler time period. The world was at peace after the Korean War. The economy was booming, and decency was still highly valued, even on television. At that time, a child's future was safe and offered an easily found, comfortable place in society.

Moe softly asked, "Would you kids like to hear *The Legend of The Rock of Woes*?

"Mr. Moe, we've heard it many times. Hasn't everyone?" I answered. Being in this place, as spooky as it was, none of us were interested in hearing it again. But despite our lack of interest, he proceeded to recite it. He illustrated and animated it by dramatically changing his voice from a whisper to a loud bellow to highlight his words, and added the waving of his hands, arms, legs, and even rolling on the ground.

He recited, "*The Legend of The Rock of Woes*, tells of the people of old who once occupied this land. They were a brave and proud people who believed when a person of their tribe started to engage in acts of evil or corruption, causing mayhem, it brought dishonor to the whole tribe. If those individual's bad behavior continued, they would unwillingly gravitate towards *The Rock*. As long as they held onto those wrong thoughts or actions, they were slowly drawn closer and closer to it, as if it were magnetic, not allowed to break free.

"However, if they became remorseful and willing to give up their dark ways, they would be set free. Unfortunately, being corrupted and lacking sincerity few ever repented. Consequently, as they reached the mouth of the cave, they would cry out profanities and express their personal woes. That's why it was named *The Rock of Woes*. Their woes were cries filled with justifications and excuses for their bad behavior.

"Each day that followed, their moans grew louder as they were pulled deeper into the cave, being sucked in by that mysterious unnatural force. Tragically, they would disappear on the seventh day. Never to be seen again.

"No one dared to help them to get away during those seven days. Although, some brave family members of the condemned, while avoiding eye contact, tossed them bits of food and jugs of water and then just as quickly would run away.

"On the seventh day, everyone stayed away and even covered their eyes when they looked in the direction of the mound. Strangely, they did this, no matter how far away, in of fear of disappearing along with those condemned ones. Having to accept there was nothing more they could do to save them; they kept away until it was over. Therefore, no one ever witnessed what happened to those poor souls. It was believed they were sent to a place of torment. The indigenous people never knew if the spirits inhabiting this place were delivering judgment or even if they emanated from *Good or Evil*.

"When a loved one in the tribe was taken, the people were most distraught. However, they believed this unsolicited supernatural ritual purified the tribe, at least until the next time one of them gave into corruption.

"Kids, as you know, no settler has ever been pulled in, which is a blessing for some who live around here."

Moe ended the tale seated deep under *The Rock* with just enough space to sit up. We found his telling of the story with his amplified gyrations to be fun. We laughed and clapped our hands as he performed what we thought was a show just for us.

Then he began to expel a list of woes and regrets about life and society intermixed with groans. The truth was, at that time, we were too young and lacked the knowledge to understand much of what he was saying. We just listened, mistakenly thinking it was part of his performance.

Oddly, back then, I never tried to figure out why I was comfortable with him. I knew he was strange, but I felt sure he was a good and kind person by nature, as my father always said he was.

At that point, knowing it was getting late, Moe ordered us to head home. So, at the end of that first day, we left Moe sitting by himself under *The Rock*.

CHAPTER 4 Mr. Moe, Where Are You

The following day, the four of us return to *The Rock* to be with Mr. Moe. We quickly followed my caulk marks to find him peacefully sitting there, and incredibly not getting lost this time either. Fearing our parents would have forbidden us to go there, we didn't tell them. It was most unusual for us to keep a secret from them, although if asked, we would have been truthful. Not to excuse it, but it was almost as if we were under a spell.

The cloud rose again, confounding us even more so. Behaving a little odd, Mr. Moe quietly began to lament about life telling unrelated stories. Still, at the time, we assumed he was simply trying to entertain us. To us, it was just another game. Looking back, I realize how genuinely naive we were.

On the fourth day, we'd become used to the fact of getting there safely and seeing the cloud rise each time. He had worked his way so far back under *The Rock* he could no longer sit upright. He laid on his side with his head propped up on his hand. He seemed to take pleasure in telling us stories. When we stayed long enough, he sent us home knowing our parents would worry.

Another day passed, and to our disappointment, he no longer was there, and just as baffling, the cloud didn't appear either. Hoping to see him again, we nervously and quickly visited it for the next couple of days in spite of experiencing those creepy vibes. Secretly, we even looked around town for him. We kept silent about having seen him, thinking we might have gotten into trouble for being there with him, although it was a childish notion.

We ask ourselves, "Could the legend be true?" This was the first real situation we ever faced on our own. Because of the ease of making it up to and back several times, we concluded the legend couldn't possibly be true.

I've come to understand we should have told our parents. With our vivid imaginations, we agreed most likely he had gotten sick and was secretly whisked away in the dead of night. Of course, it was another unreasoned and naive assumption. However, it wasn't unusual for Moe to stay out of sight for days at a time. Understanding his state of mind, he was allowed that option.

However, when he was not seen for more than a week, the authorities became concerned enough to conduct a search. We even helped in the search, along with many others. In fact, on our own, we checked out the mound several times. With no known relatives or close friends, no one knew what happened to him.

Not knowing how to explain our concern, we placed ourselves in an awkward position by not speaking up right away. With some guilt, we remained tense and in doubt. For us, the most stressful day was when they dredged the lake, which conjured up such unpleasant images, we had to stay away. Thankfully, he was not there.

It took weeks before they ended the search unsuccessfully, and things became normal again. However, a mini-legend emerged, called, *What Ever Happened to Mr. Moe Smart the Strange School Janitor?* With some humor, the people dreamed up many different scenarios in what they imagined happened to him, some humorous, others unbelievable. Not knowing he was ever at *The Rock,* no one came close to guessing the truth. It became one of the topics often vigorously discussed at the local gathering places. Nevertheless, it troubled us when they joked about his disappearance, knowing how serious it was.

He was never seen or heard from again. We felt some guilt but realized there was little any of us could've done. We understood it was a mistake not to tell what we knew for our own peace of mind. I learned children should always tell adults of any strange occurrences. In hindsight, if we had obeyed that rule, maybe we could have saved some distress, although the truth would've confused many.

Choosing not to believe the legend had anything to do with it, we preferred to think he quietly left town, willing or not, leaving no trail for reasons only he knew. Eventually, the episode faded, to give it little more than an occasional thought as we went about our lives.

However, the experience unnerved us, so we stopped going anywhere near the mound. That was until five years later, on our high school graduation day, at the age of seventeen.

Our teen years passed slowly. By then, Mr. Moe's disappearance was no longer mentioned. On our high school graduation day, the June sky was clear of clouds with unnatural streaks of red, orange, and blue, as if a giant hand, in celebration of our graduation lightly brushed stroked those colors across the sky, maybe not. Anyway, my young heart was pounding a little harder, as was with all the graduating students, for a significant change in our lives was taking place.

The purple-robed and capped officials, along with the guest speakers, sat on a raised platform set up on the ball field behind the school. All were excited as the sweat built up under their caps and gowns in the heat of the day. In the bleachers, Lucy, Mar, and Matt sat among their fellow students as they listened to me giving the valedictorian speech.

It was an honor I looked forward to and thought I deserved, as overconfident and childish I was. In light of that, I finished with these inspired words, *"We now have the whole world in front of us and must choose the right road to follow for the rest of our lives."* I held my hands high and shouted, *"So let's get to it!"* The applause filled the school grounds, intermixed with cheers from the students, undoubtedly led by my *Bookends*. I must say, hearing that sound gave me a feeling of pride to a height I never experienced before.

After all the speakers had spoken, Mr. Upright, the school's principal, stepped up to the podium with the tassel swinging from side to side on the square cap atop his shiny bald head. He looked out through his thick black plastic eyeglass frames and smiled as he began the traditional passing out of the certificates. With a beaming pride, each graduate walked across the stage to receive his or her diploma.

Afterward, they teased me in that no one looked as proud as I when I marched across the stage with my chest puffed out almost to the breaking point, looking much like a peacock ready to take on a world of dragons. At least, that's what they mercilessly teased me about. I knew it was their way to keep me humble.

At the close of the festivities, we made our way to our families through a throng of well-wishers. Everyone was relieved this part of the day was over as the men loosened their ties and took off their suit jackets. With our parents, Lucy and I worked our way to our family's 54 Chevy and headed home to change into casual clothing for the celebratory picnic in the park.

As planned, we joined Matt and Mar and their family's. Along with all our fellow students and their relatives to enjoy the picnic and the good company. The park was filled with a festive mood.

Later, after we had eaten our fill, and wearied of running around playing games, it was a moment for leisure when the four of us were alone off to the side. Suddenly, out of the blue, I again was struck to challenge Matt, Mar, and Lucy to go up to *The Rock of Woes*.

We were older and hopefully wiser, for five years was a long time. However, to this day, I still don't understand how I blocked out what happened years earlier and was willing and even eager to go up to the *Rock* again.

"Oh, I don't know about that," Mar said, most reluctant.

"Hmm, I'm not sure either," Lucy, mumbled, uncertain.

"You're not afraid, are you?" Matt challenged, touching the right key.

Lucy answered with little thought, "Okay, but you'll have to give us a head start," as she took up the challenge to beat both Matt and me up there. We told our parents we were going for a walk, which was shamefully accurate, but not specific. We quietly slipped away.

Cleverly, Lucy, with Mar in hand, stepped out, starting to walk fast, then yelled, "One, two, three and go!" and both took off. Reaching the wall, still slender, the girls had little trouble in slipping under the gate and quickly rushing up the steps. Having grown some, Matt and I had more difficulty getting under it. By the time we mounted the steps, the girls had found their way well into the zigzag path, remarkably accomplishing it due to my caulk marks, which were amazingly still as vibrant as the day I'd placed them.

Reaching *The Rock* first, Lucy and Mar began to laugh

hilariously and shouted to Matt and me, who were not far behind, for we couldn't catch up with them, and not for the lack of trying.

"You lost. You lost. We beat you!" The girls were able to outsmart us more times than I would like to admit.

"You cheated!" I responded as we teased each other as we'd always done. Exhausted, we fell limp to the ground to catch our breaths.

Laying there, we could almost sense Moe's presence as the hair on our arms and necks rose. In spite of that feeling, I said, almost apologetically, "I know Mr. Moe was a strange man, but I liked him anyway. I can't believe he's been gone for five years. I wonder whatever happened to him. I hope he's still alive."

"I hope we did the right thing by not saying anything?" Matt said.

"Well, we'll never see him again, so let's not think about it," Lucy said, not ready to deal with the feelings of guilt and uncertainty about what happened.

I couldn't resist jumping up and with mischief chanting in Lucy's face, *Mr. Moe, where are you? Mr. Moe, where are you?* I raised my voice louder with each repeated exhortation.

Not wanting to miss out on any fun, Matt joined in, followed by Mar. Lucy rose to the challenge and screeched even louder, *Mr. Moe, where are you!* We continued trying to outdo the other until we reached our limit. Raucously laughing, we landed breathlessly on the ground.

Our energy exhausted, we laid there silently for a moment. Then, without any warning, the ground began to shake violently. Thinking it was an earthquake or even worse, we all screamed in horror as we tried to hold onto the ground for dear life. Then an even more frightening sight appeared as the back wall of the cave under *The Rock* opened, and a blinding white light shone through the opening, which contained a force sucking us in. Once all of us were pulled in, the opening closed, and the light dissipated. The ground stopped rumbling.

(We were gone!)

CHAPTER 5 Another World

Rather than being pulled, it was a sense of floating into the supernaturally opening under *The Rock*. It lasted only seconds, although it seemed longer until we were unceremoniously spat out and sprawled on the ground stunned and dazed.

Stuttering, Lucy exclaimed, "Wha-what just happened!"

"Wow!" I responded. "I-I-I don't know. It was something, yy-you know what I mean."

It took a moment before I could collect my thoughts, to ask, "Hey, is everyone okay?" Answering, they were unharmed, although being disoriented and rattled.

"I thought it was the end of the world, and we were going to die," Mar said. None of us ever felt such a frightening experience.

"Was it an earthquake? It certainly felt like one," Matt said.

Lucy sat up, shook her head, getting back into focus. As she looked around and asked, "Where are we?"

I said, "We are in front of *The Rock*."

"Really! Don't you see the colors of the grass and trees?" she asked with alarm. "Or is it just me?"

It was not just her, looking around with our eyes opened wide, we saw the previously straw-colored grass and foliage now had a variety of bright colors, many times sharper than it should've been with a strange yellow aura. The leaves were more massive, with an abundance of huge rainbow-colored flowers. We were speechless.

Mar said, "An earthquake couldn't have caused this. This is not right. I'm scared."

Attempting to make sense of it, I could only say, "There must be a logical reason for this. There's a logical reason for everything. Wait, I know. Maybe the bright light affected our eyes?"

"That's right. If we close our eyes for a while, everything will go back to normal," Matt suggested.

"I'm not going to close my eyes for one second!" Lucy declared. Panicky, she turned to me, "Come on, Johnny, what's going on?"

Trying to figure it out, I stood up and said, "Hold on a minute, let's see." I found the opening that appeared under *The Rock* was now closed. Perplexed, I slowly took in the lushness, touching the surrounding growth. Unfamiliar vine-like plants twisted up and around *The Rock* embracing much of it. It all seemed so unreal, yet it was all too real. I didn't know what to think, say, or do.

"Hey look, there's something wrong, isn't there?" Lucy asked.

"What's wrong?" Matt asked.

"Can't you see how the right is on the left, and the left is on the right. It's backward!"

Studying it, Mar said, "You're right. I see that."

"It's not the same *Rock*," Lucy declared.

"You mean there's more than one?" Mar wondered.

"I don't think so." Speculating, I could only say, "This doesn't make sense, could it be we're on the backside of it?"

"Yes, we did come through a hole and are now on the other side. Aren't we?" Matt asked.

"I think so. Could this be a mirror image or something?" I said in a desperate attempt to grasp what happened.

Not appreciating any of this, Lucy said, with more than her usual skepticism, "Wait, this is too weird, and it frightens me."

We heard a rustling sound in the near distance. With great apprehension, we peered in its direction. A voice called out, startling us, "Hey, how in the world did you kids get here?"

I exclaimed, "Wait, isn't that Mr. Moe's voice!" not quite believing. Overwhelmed and relieved when we saw him stumbling through the tangled vines towards us. When he reached us, we crowded around him as if he were a savior, for he was the only familiar sight.

We bombarded him with questions as he carefully examined the cave…

"What's happened?"

"I'm scared."

"Are we going to be all right?"

"Can you get it back to the way it was?"

"Can you help?"

"Please help us."

Not finding what he hoped would be there, he said, "Hold on. Wait a minute, please, please calm down so I can answer all your questions." When quiet, he breathlessly said, "I heard an enormous roar and saw the burst of the *White Light* and knew something was up, I ran here as fast as I could. Whew, kids, wait a minute I have to sit down and catch my breath. I haven't run that fast since I was a youngster," he said as he sat on a large rock.

We waited as he took deep breaths. I was glad to see him. However, instead of being dressed in his maintenance man outfit, he wore grease-stained coveralls, which made him look even more disheveled than usual. But most striking were his eyes, for they no longer were puffed and were clear of those bloodshot veins, and they even had a twinkle in them.

After taking several deep breaths, he asked in his well-worn raspy voice, "Now tell me how in the world you kids got here? I must say I'm glad to see you.

My-o-my, how you have grown, I hardly recognize you. Ah—I see by your expressions, you have no idea what's happened to you. I think this might be a big problem."

"A big problem!" Lucy repeated.

Trying to wrap his brain around it, he could only say, "I don't like this... Well, it's a long story, and you're probably not going to believe it right away, so let's go to my place first."

"Your place, Mr. Moe? Where have you been all this time?" I asked.

"Yes, where? We've looked everywhere for you," Matt said.

"Well, kids, I've been right here," he said with a smile. "But first, before we go anywhere, I need a couple more minutes to rest and steady myself, and then I'll take you to my place where I'll explain what I can.

We sat around him on the ground, hoping he was going to be all right for he looked so much older, but I guess after five years one does age. We could hardly believe it was him since we had come to believe he was likely dead all this time.

He took deep breaths as we looked at each other curiously,

not knowing what to think, say or do. I know we all shared the same feelings in knowing he was our only link back to the way things were. We waited as patiently as we could while fidgeting.

Recovered from his run through the woods, he led us through the thickets as we huddled close behind. Our heads twitched around in all directions for everything we saw was, without any doubt, unlike anything we ever saw. The trees and plants were tropical, almost artificial-looking, with brilliant colors and an embellished beauty as opposed to the straw-color they should have been.

I asked again, "Mr. Moe, what happened to you? And where are we?"

"Kids, I've been right here in this other world since I last saw you."

Unsettled, Lucy said, "Otherworld? Oh—I don't like this" and whispered to me, "Johnny, what are we going to do?"

I saw the same expressions on Mar and Matt's faces, and answered in a hushed tone as we trailed behind, "Everything will be all right, we're with Mr. Moe now."

"I'll believe it when I see it," Lucy whispered back.

"I'm sure we'll be all right. You know what I mean," I whispered in the hope of tossing off their fears, even though I felt the same.

As we came off the mound, there was no wooden gate. Just beyond where the wall should've been, there was a snake-like road paved with pea-sized lavender-colored pebbles. Where the park should've been was now a jungle-like forest of trees wrapped in vines. It was too much for us to grasp.

"My place is just up the road," Moe said.

As we walked along, suddenly out of nowhere, a car appeared. It roared by, billowing smoke with a loud engine that rumbled and shook the ground. Everything about it was unfamiliar, the sound, the shape, its entire look. It was painted in brilliant colors with a design looking like a large bold modern art painting. Multicolored fireworks were shooting out of its tailpipes.

"Wow, look at that!" I exclaimed. It was a sight to see, built higher, shorter, and narrower than any car I ever saw. It looked more like a full-size toy than a real automobile.

Moe seeing how overwhelmed we were, explained,

"Everything here is different. Everything will be new to you, so don't let it upset or confuse you."

"You're not kidding," Lucy murmured.

"Look, there's my place around the bend," Moe said, trying to divert our attention away from our anxiety.

Mar excitedly exclaimed, "I see it! I see it!" only able to see the top of a slate roof that had splashes of blue, orange, and brown, among other colors as if an assortment of paints were accidentally spilled on it.

"Yep Mar, that's it. We'll be there in no time," Moe said, with a touch of pride.

Another car roared by at a speed that seemed too fast for safety on this road covered with loose pebbles, pelting us with dirt and stone dust the tires kicked up.

As we walked on the soft shoulder, another car whizzed by from the opposite direction. Neither of them painted with the same design. It seemed each was decorated by a different artist, yet all in the same crude style. "Wow, those are weird cars. Who makes them Mr. Moe?" I asked.

"I'm not sure. But as you can see, they are not Ford's or Chevy's," he jokingly said. Then added, "Kids, I honestly don't know? What I do know is most of the creatures around here aren't very artistic. Look, kids, you're going to find unbelievable things here."

Reacting with alarm, Lucy said, "Creatures!"

He lacked confidence in his answers, "That's right, Lucy. It took a while for me to get used to all this. Some people here act in ways, which make me think of them as creatures, not all of them. Let's get to my place and have something to eat. Then I'll explain what I can." He quickened our pace.

His place was a small building set some fifty feet back from the road with a dilapidated tiny gas station out front. All painted in the same makeshift manner as the roof, looking more like a mishap than a planned design. The structure wasn't built in the same proportions, dimensions, and angles I could relate to.

It was captivating like being in Toyland or as we might have envisioned in one of our make-believe games in the park. An extra-large canopy stood over four gasoline pumps, which looked similar to those used decades ago in our world with a colorful Art Nouveau flair.

"Mr. Moe, do you sell gas here?" I asked.

"Yes, Johnny. But, it's not gas as we know it. It's their own concoction made from grass, which they call fuel, not gasoline. Isn't that something?"

Standing alongside one of those cars at a pump, we saw a man with a bright yellow face, dressed in yellow cartoon-like clothing. He was turning a sizable rotating crank on the side of the pump, apparently filling his tank. If that wasn't bizarre enough, a man at another pump had a chalk-white face. He yelled out, "Moe when are your prices coming down?"

"Never again, I hope," Moe shot back, apparently disturbed.

"Moe, you have not lost your gouging ways," the patron said, who seemed to be enjoying provoking him.

"If you don't like it, you can go someplace else," Moe said.

Now worked up, the patron yelled back, "Someday, you will pay for your stinking prices."

Moe just grunted. His behavior surprised us, for until then, we'd only seen his gentle side, although we heard tales about this other side, which helped in losing his teaching job. Seeing how tense we were, he quickly ushered us towards the house, as he said, "Don't worry about that creature."

Small bushes surrounded the house bristling with sharp thorns and an assortment of large colorful flowers that measured almost a foot across. We might have thought it was charming if the situation wasn't so extreme.

Parked out front was one of those unrealistic cars, looking as if it had been in a demolition derby. The front door of the house was much larger than it should have been. To better describe his place, it looked like an unusual fairytale cottage.

Uneasy, we entered his place as if entering a different world. Actually, it was just that.

CHAPTER 6 The Cottage

Moe's home consisted of just one large room, which included a mixture of a kitchen, living, and bedroom with no order to it. It was clean, yet was in a state of disarray slightly out of proportion to our eyes, in size and shapes.

"Sit at the table and make yourselves at home. If you need to, the john is out back," Moe invited. "I'm famished. I'll bet you kids are hungry too?" As I learned later, eating always gave him comfort, especially when stressed, and at that moment, we all were.

As he fumbled with the cooking utensils that cluttered the wooden counter, he asked, "How about having what might be like sausages and home fries only different?"

The food he described sounded weird, but, in spite of eating at the picnic not long ago, we were extra hungry and game to try anything.

He ordered, "Lucy, the sausages are in the icebox. Mar, the potatoes are under that pile over there. You girls can help me cut them up." They followed his orders, as he filled a large pot with water from a hand-pumping faucet over the extra-large sink by energetically pushing and pulling the handle up and down, priming it until the water flowed on its own, much as it was done in the old days. Still, in a state of bewilderment, Matt and I just sat there watching as the pot filled, each trying in our own way to sort all this out.

He placed the filled pot on the massive cartoon-like potbelly cast iron stove. Striking a match as he turned a knob on its front, igniting an explosive orange flame that shot little sparkles out a couple of feet. The fire covered the entire top and rose about three inches high, sending out a dense billowing puff of colorful smoke to the ceiling. As we reared back, he explained, "It's something like kerosene." As the blaze settled down, it was a further hint of how far from the ordinary this place was.

"Hey, the potatoes are green," Mar, said.

"And the sausages are black," Lucy added.

"Kids, they're not like the potatoes or sausages as we know them. It'll take time to get used to how different things are."

"I hope we won't be here that long," Lucy mumbled.

"Hmm... Well, try the food before you reject any of it, you'll find it might not taste like you think it should. However, I guarantee, overall it tastes pretty good, that's if you like sweets," he said.

Mar asked, "Mr. Moe, how come those people paint their faces?" as she awkwardly cut up the potatoes, or whatever they were, never having been required to do food preparation before.

"They're not painted. It's their real colors," he answered, amused as he cut up other unfamiliar looking food.

"Really?" Lucy quizzically said, still finding it all hard to believe.

"Yes Lucy, the people in this world have different skin colors, more colors than we have in our world, you'll see, and don't ask me how come, for I haven't figured that out yet."

"Wow! Mr. Moe. Do you work here?"

"Johnny, I not only work here, but I also own this place," he boasted. Seeing our interest, he continued, "When I came into this world, I only had loose change in my pocket."

Lucy gulped, and with a wavering voice, said, "Into this world. O---kay."

Without hesitation, he went on, "The first place I found was this station. A fellow called McCloud owned it. He was a white fellow like us; in fact, he was the only other white person I've seen in this world. At the time, I was as confused as you are now. Anyway, he filled me in on everything the best he could. I must admit it floored me. As I'm sure, it has done to you.

"However, once over my initial shock and able to think, I was so hungry, I asked him if I could get something to eat, explaining I had little money showing him my loose change. He told me my money was of no use here. However, he said he would feed me this one time. Warning, hereafter, I'd have to pay for it. Naturally, I asked, how would I do that? He suggested he could use some help around here, and I could pay for it by helping him. Not knowing what else to do, I decided to do just that, at least until I could figure things out."

"Couldn't you just go back through *The Rock*?"

"Lucy, that's the first thing I thought of. And I tried, only to find the opening I came through was no longer there. It had closed, just as it did when you came through, leaving no trace of it ever being there. I'm sorry to say, that way is impossible."

He put the supposed sausages, potatoes, and vegetables in a small pot of water, adding strange spices and placed it on the stoves, blazing fire.

"You mean, we can't go back the way we came."

"Nope, Johnny. I tried and found no way back. I searched and searched. I poked, pushed, pulled, pounded, and kicked every inch of *The Rock* and found no way to open it," he said, with a sense of failure as he stirred the pot.

"Isn't our world just on the other side?"

"It would seem so Lucy. Isn't it amazing? Theoretically, we might only be a foot away from our world, but it might as well be a million miles."

"If it's only a foot away, couldn't we just breakthrough," I asked, with more than a glimmer of hope.

"Johnny, I also thought that. I tried with a cold chisel and hammer. The fact is I couldn't even scratch its surface. I even used a pickaxe, but it just bounced off without making the slightest mark. That *Rock* has the hardest surface I ever saw. Kids, I guess I could've used dynamite if I could've found some. Anyway, I figured if I blew it up, for sure, I'd never get back. Look, kids, if you think about it, we might be in a whole other dimension and not just a foot away. I'm sorry, you can forget about breaking through to our side, which might not even be there."

"In another dimension, how in the world are we going to get back home?" Mar exclaimed.

"Kids, I even drove up the road in an old car McCloud fixed up, hoping to find a way back, only to fail at that too."

"Mr. Moe, there must be a way out of this place, right?"

Not answering Lucy, he went on, "Well, when I came back from my trip, sadly, McCloud confessed he was sick and dying. So, all I could do was to stay and help him the best I could until he passed away two years ago.

To my surprise, since there was no one to leave his belongings to. He willed it all to me as payment for taking care of him in his last days. However, there was just one catch. He made me promise I'd keep the station open after he was gone. Since I still had to eat, I just stayed here."

With the meal ready, Moe opened a wooden box on the counter and took out what looked like a deformed loaf of orange and yellow striped bread. He cut it up and passed the pieces around. Turning off the stove, he dished out a bowl of his homemade stew to each of us and gave us each a sizeable scoop-like spoon to use. Fascinated with the utensils, we mimicked each other to see who used them best. It was awkward but amusing even to Mr. Moe.

I asked, "Mr. Moe, if this world is not ours, where are we?"

"What's this place called?" Matt asked.

"Kids, this might be hard to believe, but it has no name."

"Wow! Can we get things back to the way it was?" I asked.

"Are we going to be all right?" Mar asked.

"Hold on kids. Let me tell you more. Look, without any doubt, we're in some other parallel world or something. I don't understand it, or even begin to comprehend why we're here."

"Hey, this food is not half bad."

"Why, thanks, Matt. See what I mean... Now tell me what happened on the other side just before you were pulled through?"

"We were just playing around," I explained.

"We did nothing to make it happen," Lucy said.

"At least, not that we know of," Matt added.

"Weren't we calling Mr. Moe's name?" Mar remembered.

"Hey, that's right, we were," Lucy agreed.

"You were calling my name. Why?"

Feeling foolish with my mischief in chanting his name, I said, "We were just fooling around."

"We were wondering what happened to you," Matt added.

"Yes, everyone was upset when you disappeared. You just vanished. No one knew what happened to you."

"Gee, Johnny. I never thought anyone would miss me. My-o-my, that's interesting. Well, kids, I've been trapped in this world since I saw you last. And I can't imagine why you would be pulled through simply by calling my name. Although five years ago, when you made it on your own up to *The Rock*, I knew you were special. However, I have to think about why that's so."

"There is a way back, isn't there?" I asked again in an attempt to get a positive response.

"If we're special, can you get us back?"

"Mar, I tried to get back, but failed."

"Why? How?" Lucy pressed, wanting answers.

"As I said, it's all a mystery to me." Seeing our disappointment, he said, "Well… I can only tell you what I know. You see, I've found some answers, and is what they are; it has to do with that road outside the door. The one we just walked up with the lavender pebbles?"

We all went to the windows and looked out. "Well, to get back home, one must travel up it. It's called *The Road of Understanding*. It's not just any old road. It's the one *Road* whose end must be reached. And not only that, but along the way, one must acquire a certain understanding, an understanding I don't understand. I was told it is the way to get back home."

With a glimmer of hope, Lucy said, "Well then. Let's go up that road."

"Good, let's go now!" Mar said, as robust as she's ever expressed anything.

"Look, kids. It's not that easy. There are obstacles to overcome that will stop you, things that will prevent anyone brave enough to try. There's a scary world out there, where strange things happen. There are weird people and creatures you've never seen before. Things you couldn't even imagine. A person has to be strong, and I didn't have the strength. It was impossible for me. I'm not going to try again. I should just stay here. I just can't do it again. Nope, not ever again."

Lucy appealed, "Then, can't we at least try?"

"Yes, can't we just go up that *Road* on our own?" I asked.

"Well, I'm not going to try again, nope, not ever again." Seeing our anguish, he said, "However, let me think about the possibility of you going. Well… First, I have some chores to do when we're finished eating. Boys, you can give me a hand."

When ready, he asked the girls to clean the dishes using the leftover heated water in the big pot and marched Matt and me out the door.

When the girls were alone, Mar frantically said, "I'm scared. This place is creepy."

"I know what you mean. Let's hope the boys can figure it out. That's with Mr. Moe's help."

"And if they can't?" Mar worried, finding it hard to be positive.

"They'll just have to, it's their job, and with our help, they will."

"You know Lucy, if the rest of this world is any weirder than what we've seen so far, I'm not sure if I want to go up that *Road.*"

"Don't be a wimp, we'll go and get back home," Lucy insisted, as they cleared the table and washed the dishes the best they could, never having been asked to do chores before.

When the work was done and the evening darkness was falling, Moe lit a type of old kerosene lamp, which looked like it might've belonged to Aladdin.

"Mr. Moe isn't there any electricity?" Mar asked.

"Nope, as you can see, everything is hand operated."

"You mean, no TV!"

He smiled, "Nope Lucy, there are no radios, no telephones either, and as you can see, ice is needed to keep things cold in the icebox. Since I don't have much fuel for the lamp, we'll have to turn in early. Anyway, it's been a long day, and I know we all could use some sleep."

"How can anyone live without TV?"

"You'll see Lucy. It's possible you know, not too long ago in our world there was no such thing," he said to our groans, even though we remembered as little kids it was so, but by now we had become addicted to such luxuries.

"Now, girls, you can sleep in the big bed. I'll sleep on the sofa. Boys, it looks like you'll have the whole floor. We'll hang a blanket for the privacy of the ladies. Tomorrow, after a good night's sleep, we can figure out what to do." Rummaging through a small closet, he mumbled, "Let me see if I have enough pillows, sheets, and blankets."

At that point, we were exhausted from the long graduation day and the shocking events of this most extraordinary adventure. When comfortably bedded down, with the lamp out, our eyes peered into the dark, wondering what was going to happen to us. In time, sheer exhaustion allowed us to doze off.

CHAPTER 7 Looking For Hope

In the morning, the light of the new day streamed in through the windows. Moe was the first to wake. He quietly got up and dressed not because he was rested, but instead, he had his daily work to do. He ate breakfast while an oddly-contrived pot silently perked away on the stove.

He poured the purple brew into a large mug and took a swig. At dinner, he told us it wasn't a drink for us, for it took him a while to develop a taste for it until its addictive qualities took hold. Much the same as some beverages do back in our world. Perhaps, our worlds weren't so different.

On his way out, he saw me looking at him and whispered, "No need to get up this early, get some more sleep. When rested, eat, help yourself to anything, there's a shower outback, I have work to do." He silently slipped out the door with a mug in hand.

Unable to get back to sleep, I lay there for a while, grappling with the fact of still being in this incredible place. Suddenly, I sat up as I met the reality of the moment. My eyes searched the room, attempting to grasp the situation better.

Most of the objects were familiar, although the order and dimensions threw me off. Sitting there quietly and uncertain for a time, I saw Matt's eyes open. He wasn't coping any better than I was, as he said, "I didn't want to open my eyes, hoping when I did, we would be home. Johnny, what's going to happen to us?"

"I don't know. Let's get up and see if we can find out."

As we fumbled, Lucy's voice came from the other side of the privacy blanket, "It's too early to get up."

"Hold on. Stay there. Give us a chance to put our pants on," Matt, modestly called out with panic in his voice.

She said, "Take your time. I don't want to get up anyway," never having liked getting up early.

Come on, Lucy, wake Mar, we have to get going. You know

what I mean," I ordered.

"Okay. I know." She shook Mar, saying, "Wake up! Then in her early morning grumpy way, she said, "I need something to eat."

"Mr. Moe said we should help ourselves to the food, and there's a shower out back."

"Please, let's eat first. Hey, are we going to be able to brush our teeth?" Lucy asked.

"I saw him brush his teeth with this stuff, it smells different than toothpaste and its powder, and I guess we'll have to use our fingers," I answered, as I searched the icebox.

"Oh, no, our fingers and to use powder," Lucy said, as Matt and Mar grimmest in unison.

"Then don't clean them. Hey, I don't see any eggs or anything I recognize, only those sausages things we ate last night and some other strange looking stuff."

Snatching an unmarked box from the shelf above the counter, Matt said, "This looks like corn flakes."

"Oh yeah, I saw Mr. Moe eating that stuff." Taking a single flake out of the box, I chewed it, and said, "Hey, it tastes like pure sugar."

"Great, I guess it'll be okay if Mr. Moe ate it. Is there any milk?" Lucy asked.

Looking, Mar said, "Could this be milk in this bottle? It smells like milk; only it's yellow and has black dots in it. What do you think?"

"Yes, that's what Mr. Moe used," I said, as I dipped my finger into the bottle and licked it. Mar groaned with disdain.

I looked at her a little embarrassed and could only ask, "What?" then said, "Ha, it tastes like milk, only much more buttery."

"Johnny, why didn't you just tell us what Mr. Moe ate in the first place!" Lucy complained.

"Right… Okay, who wants what might be cereal with buttery yellow milk or whatever it is?" I asked, trying to ignore her, which was the best way to deal with her in the morning.

"I'll have some, it sounds good," Matt said.

"Okay, I'll take a chance, too," Lucy said. With a little urgency, she ordered, "Come on, let's get going."

"This is all too much. I'm still scared. What are we going to do?"

"Mar, we'll figure that out as soon as we're dressed. Don't worry, we'll be all right," I said, being protective of her and again feeling I was the one to take the lead.

"This is no joke. You better figure something out, and soon," Lucy insisted. "Hey, this cereal is not bad and is really sweet in a different way."

"Hmm... It is good. Well, anyway, Mr. Moe is outside; I'm sure he'll help us."

"But he said, he'll never try to go back home again," Lucy reminded me.

"I'm sure he didn't mean it."

"He sure sounded like he meant it?" Mar said.

"Well, what if he won't take us back?" Matt asked.

"He will. You'll see," I assured him, feeling with a naive certainty he would.

"Well, nothing is going to happen until we get dressed," Lucy concluded.

Later, when Matt and I were showered and dressed in the same clothing we wore the day before, we felt uncomfortable in putting on our grungy clothing on our clean bodies. Despite it, the warm showers refreshed us, and with a burst of self-assurance, I turned to Matt and said, "Let's go talk to Mr. Moe."

"Sounds good to me."

I yelled to Mar, who was primping herself behind the hung blanket, "We're going out to talk to Mr. Moe."

"Okay, I'll wait till Lucy is ready." Matt and I went out of the door.

CHAPTER 8 The Gas Station

Outside, we approached Moe, who was busily sweeping around the pumps. "Good morning, boys. Feeling any better today?"

"We're okay, Mr. Moe," I said. Then with some buoyancy, I asked, "We're ready to head back home, when can we start?"

"Boys, as I said, it's not that easy. I've given up trying."

"Why, Mr. Moe?"

Speaking rapidly, as his eyes darted around as if he was visualizing something unpleasant, he said, "Because, along that *Road*, there're things you wouldn't believe, things that'll stop you in your tracks, things that aren't pleasant."

"But Mr. Moe, what else are we to do?" I asked.

"We have to get back home," Matt added.

As we spoke, those strange cars were moving in and out of the station. Each driver slipped a card into a slot on the side of a pump. A purple-skinned man who was grudgingly pumping fuel suddenly yelled, "Moe, why are you charging so much?"

Annoyed, Moe responded, "If you don't like it, go someplace else."

Compelled I defended Moe, exclaiming, "Yeah, do you think fuel grows on trees!" having forgotten this fuel comes from grass.

Boldly jumping in, Matt added, "Yes, and if you don't like it, you can go someplace else."

Hearing the commotion, a fearful Mar slipped out of the cottage to see what was going on as the purple man said, "Why you little pink-skinned xyc's!" Calling us a name I didn't recognize, although, by his tone, I could tell it wasn't complimentary. He jumped into his car, and in a burst of speed, he drove off.

In his haste, he hadn't removed the nozzle from the tank. It ripped away from the hose, causing fuel to spew out in all directions. The hose jumped and jerked around like a snake out of control. In desperation, Moe grabbed the bucket of sand sitting by the pumps for just such an occasion. He tossed it on the spill to little avail as he pinched the hose with little success to stop the flow of fuel as it flowed under another car with its engine still running. The sparks these cars naturally generated instantly ignited the fuel as the flames engulfed it.

Moe grabbed Matt and me, pulling us away from the flames. I shouted out to Mar, "Run! Run!" Meanwhile, the other patrons scattered and drove off. Unbelievably, the person whose car was burning escaped the flames without attempting to put out the fire and quickly left in another vehicle, leaving us alone to deal with the situation.

Matt yelled, "Lucy, run!"

"Where's Lucy? Lucy run, run!" I yelled frantically, looking for her as Moe led the three of us into the woods.

The burning car exploded, followed by a second tremendous explosion, which blew up the pumps, sending out a blast, knocking us off our feet. We screamed in horror as a third catastrophic blast erupted as the fuel storage tanks blew up with such force it sucked the air from around us. It sent out a plume high up looking like a small atomic blast, causing a gigantic deep hole in the ground where the station once stood. At the same time, it lifted the canopy and burning car high in the air spinning them around.

Horrified, we watched those two objects rise and fall as if in slow motion. Inconceivably, the canopy landed squarely on the cottage entirely demolishing it. The burning car landed on the parked car sitting in front of the cottage scattering car parts in all directions. Stunned, we pressed as close to the ground as we could, petrified.

When sure no more explosions would occur, I jumped up and, in a panic, called, "Lucy, Lucy!" As I looked at the others with my heart in my throat and fright in my eyes, I screamed, "Where's Lucy?"

"She was in the shower!" Mar shrieked.

I ran towards the cottage, followed by the others, all intermittently shouting, "Lucy! Lucy!"

When the canopy landed, it kicked up a cloud of dust so thick we couldn't see through it.

As the mist quickly settled, it looked like no one inside could have survived. At that moment, I felt as if my heart dropped to the ground, and my life ended, it was the most horrific moment I ever experienced.

In our terror, Moe had a thought, "Wait for a second, the shower is in the back." He ran as fast as his age allowed leading us around to the back of the cottage. Arriving breathlessly, we found the shower room, which once protruded from the main structure, was now missing. Choking on the remaining dust and smoke, I called out as best I could, "Lucy! Lucy!"

In despair, I dropped to my knees. Moe put his hand on my shoulder to console me. After the longest few seconds of sheer emptiness I'd ever felt, miraculously, we heard a barely audible groan. With renewed hope, I called "Lucy! Lucy, is that you?" A muffled voice was heard coming from the woods, "Get me out of here!"

I turned to the greatest sound I ever heard and asked, "Lucy, is that you?

"Who do you think it is!" her voice sounding far away as she weakly screeched.

Bewildered, I yelled back, "Where are you?"

"I'm in the shower, where else. What happened out there?"

Confused, I said, "The shower room is gone. Where are you?"

"What!" also confused, she responded.

"Wait, keep talking, Lucy," Moe instructed.

As she babbled, we moved towards the sound of her voice. It was coming from the dense woods well behind the house. Frantically searching, Matt was the first to find something and shouted, "The sound is coming from over here."

"The sound is me!" Lucy spouted.

We rushed over to find what was left of the shower room, which laid collapsed and fragmented in a pile hidden in the dense bushes. "Lucy, are you in there?" I loudly asked.

"Of course, where do you think I am?"

"It's a miracle," I said, rejoicing in my heart.

"Yes, it is… Lucy, are you okay?" Moe asked, much relieved.

Disoriented, she answered, "I guess I'm okay. I don't think anything is broken. What happened out there? Get me out of here!"

We furiously began to pull away the rubble trapping her. Fortunately, she was in the sturdy metal shower stall lying on its side. It had a metal door that protected her from serious injury in her projected flight like a missile propelled by the force of the canopy's impact. As we worked, she bellowed, "I'm in the shower. Get the picture! Don't you dare uncover me!"

Frustrated, I asked, "Well then, what are we suppose to do?"

"Listen. My clothes were in this room. Find them." As we searched, she added, "Guys, don't you dare touch my clothes. Mar, when you get them, please would only you give them to me." Her modesty amused Matt and me in spite of the dire circumstances.

We found her clothing under some debris undisturbed in a neat pile. Mar passed them through a small opening in the rubble at the top of the stall. She dressed in the cramped space as quickly as she could. The rest of us sat on the ground to catch our breath and recover from the disaster.

Shortly, she announced, "I'm ready," We cleared away the remaining wreckage freeing her. She emerged from the top of the stall, a little shaken, disheveled with her hair messed and still wet, coated with dirt, dust, and having suffered some minor bruises.

When I looked at my twin sister, I couldn't help but burst into hysterical laughter. Not because it was funny, instead I was so joyous and relieved to see she was okay. An emotion I couldn't contain. Matt and Mar joined in the joyful laughter, also relieved to see her.

Annoyed, Lucy declared, "It's not funny."

I was so thankful I hugged her and said, "Oh, yes, it is."

Surprised by my reaction, she characteristically asked, "What's wrong with you?" Looking around and seeing the devastation, she asked, "Hey, what happened here?"

After we described it the best we could, a low wailing sound caught our attention. It was Moe, who had slipped away. He was in front of the cottage kneeling by the two smoldering burned-out cars, one piled on the other. He was banging his head on the ground and groaning, "What have I done wrong this time? Why do things like this always happen to me? What are we going to do without transportation? Why-o-why," expressing a deep bitterness.

Not knowing what else to do, I knelt by him and said, "I'm sorry, Mr. Moe. We didn't mean to cause any trouble by saying those things to that purple guy."

He looked at me quizzically, then slowly at the others. He pulled himself up onto his feet, dusted himself off and stood at attention like a soldier taking charge of his wits, and said, "Yes, yes. Johnny, he deserved to be told off. Don't worry. I'll take care of it. I know it wasn't your fault, that creature caused it."

"Mr. Moe, can't you sue that purple man, or something?" Lucy asked.

"Why don't you call the police or fire department?" Mar asked.

"Girls, I'm afraid it can't be done. There are no lawyers, police, firefighters, or even phones in this world. People are pretty much on their own." He then admitted, "Oh well. I guess I wasn't cut out to run a place like this anyway. I never did fit in."

He looked up towards the yellow sky and yelled, "Sorry, McCloud, I hope you know I tried my best." He turned to us and ordered, "Let's see what the damage is." He led us around the still burning property, periodically repeating, "Oh my." "Oh, my." We looked at him when he spoke, then at each other, not quite sure what to think.

Lucy asked, "Mr. Moe, what are we going to do now?"

He stopped in his tracks, closed his eyes, and said, "Hmm. What to do?" Then as if an idea popped into his head, he said, "Wait, there might be a way out. Yes, of course! Kids, come, follow me."

Grabbing a pry bar, conveniently laying nearby, he led us to a dirt mound concealed deep in the woods. He pried the lock off the door that was built into the side of the mound. Swung it open to reveal a vehicle the size of a minibus. Chuckling, he said, "Ha! I always wondered what McCloud kept back here."

It was unlike any vehicle I ever saw before. It had oversized curving fenders and a massive high bumper, looking like it was made to ram. It had five rows of three seats and more than ample cargo space. There was a full set of spare tires strapped to its roof, and of course, it looked like a full-size toy.

However, even more extraordinary was the way it was painted with more than a simple design. It had a picture of a fiery dragon wrapped around the car's entire body. Its colors were so vibrant and painted on a raised texture molded right into the sheet metal, making it look almost real. Painted flames shot out of its mouth, coming to a point like a spear in front looking quite fearsome. It was magnificent, and I was so impressed. I let out a, "Wow!" Lucy wasn't impressed at all."

"I'd forgotten about this place. It's unbelievable. McCloud would come out here late at night, keeping what he was doing a secret, even from me. He told me he was just tinkering with some old junk cars, like the one he gave me. I mistakenly believed there was only a pile of junk out here, how stupid of me to have never looked. Now, in seeing what he was working on, I can't believe it! I knew he was a great mechanic, but this is fantastic.

"Kids, this is our transportation, and it's more than I could've ever hoped for. And look! Its fuel tank is even full. How fortunate can we be?" He looked up at the sky and shouted, "Thank you, McCloud." Then he said, "Kids, this is going to take us away from this forsaken place. First, let's salvage what we can and load it into the Dragon."

The Dragon!" Matt exclaimed.

"Yes, I just named it. We'll call it the Dragon. Kids, don't you think it's appropriate?" We smiled and nodded in agreement. He ordered, "Let's get cranking," as he marched us around the property.

Expeditiously, Moe selected a few tools and supplies from the mound and property that survived the blast. When satisfied and everything was loaded into the Dragon, he ordered, "Get in and let's get going."

"Mr. Moe, where are we going?" Lucy asked, almost demanding.

"Relax. You'll see." He turned the crank with confidence as if he knew it would start. It flared up with a mighty roar, which immediately filled the inside of the mound with thick white smoke choking us. He quickly pulled it out into the open air, and ordered, "Open the windows and stick your heads out and breathe."

He slowly drove it like a tank onto the pebble *Road*. Once

there, he carefully shifted the unfamiliar gears. Then stepped down on the accelerator, and we sped away, disappearing around the first curve, leaving the smoldering station behind.

Still choking on the fumes, Lucy, with her head out the window, shouted, "I definitely do not like this!"

CHAPTER 9 Driving Into The Unknown

Roaring away from the station in the Dragon, as colorful sparks flashed trailing behind from its exhaust pipes. Amazed at how it negotiated curve after curve at a speed too fast for reasonable safety. Yet it tightly held the *Road* as Moe handled it quite well. It was a noisy beast, too loud to exchange ordinary conversation at the slower speeds necessary to ride out the sharp snake-like curves.\

Recovered from the smoke inhalation, Lucy and Mar nudged, urging me to ask the big question. Complying, I loudly asked, "Mr. Moe, where are we going?"

"You'll see, you'll see," he answered, with a gleeful edge. Not satisfying the girls with his reply, never the less, they had to be content for the time being.

"Mr. Moe, did Mr. McCloud build the Dragon?" I asked.

"Well, it looks like he might've, but I'm not sure. I've never seen one like it. Even being an expert welder, I don't think I could've designed and accomplished this work. In his own way, I believe he created it, maybe with the help of stock parts. It also looks like he kept it in tip-top condition, ready to go at all times. I only wonder what his purpose was, for I never saw him take it out for a drive. Why he kept it a secret from me and only worked on it in private late at night is a mystery. I guess I'll never find out. In many ways, he was a strange fellow."

With his voice tiring, due to the difficulty of talking over the loud sound of the engine, he said, "Now kids, sit back and enjoy the ride. We have a ways to go."

"How much farther, Mr. Moe?"

"You'll see Lucy. Be patient." Again, his answer didn't satisfy her at all. However, she knew she wasn't going to get a straight answer.

In time we came out of a curve to where The *Road*

straightened out across a flat plain as far as could be seen. It allowed Moe to drive faster, which left the loud roar of the engine behind, enabling us to relax for a more comfortable journey. It was incredible how its speed seemed to be greater than cars would be capable of in our world, especially on a pebble-covered road.

Enthralled with the landscape, we expressed our wonder with phrases like, "Wow," "Gee," "Look at that," "I see it," "What's that?" and "I don't know." All said in low tones as not to disturb Moe, who was concentrating on his driving, not yet familiar with all the Dragon's many controls.

In the far distance, to the right and left, were rolling hills, however, immediately surrounding us were meadows filled with large flowers, which contained a sprinkling of tiny sparkling objects looking as if diamonds were growing in the far-flung fields. Over-sized leafless trees, separated by hundreds of feet, looked like giants ready to move. The bright sky had an astonishing luminous yellow aura.

Mar asked, "Hey, where's the sun? I can't see it."

"It should be right up there," I said, with certainty as I pointed straight up.

"Maybe it's behind a cloud," Matt speculated.

"Wait! There are no clouds, and there's no sun!" with anxiety, Lucy said.

Overhearing her distress, Moe calmly said, "That's right. There're no clouds, and there's no sun. I told you things were different here. It just gets dark and light without the sun. And, believe it or not, the day is only about eight hours long and the night is another eight hours, some sixteen hours in a full day. Isn't that something? This proves we are not in our world. I discovered that when I first arrived wearing my watch, which is no longer of any use. By the way, you'll find no watches or clocks in this world, as if time didn't exist."

"How do they tell what time it is?" I asked.

"It's like these people have an internal clock or something. Anyway, they don't worry about it. Neither do they count in years, four hundred of their days are called a cycle. I'm taking you to someone who can explain it better than I, be patient."

Lucy, never having been patient, had to do her best as not to appear rude, so she slammed her back against her seat in a huff crossing her arms in frustration, not at all content with his vague answers.

We continued to zoom along mystified in this cartoon-like world. It was like taking a ride in a wacky amusement park or in one of those cartoon movies we so enjoyed. Our surroundings hadn't changed for some time, but suddenly it dramatically changed to a desert-like terrain with sparsely scattered bushes. "Mr. Moe, "How come it changes like that?"

"Matt, I don't know. I guess it's just the nature of this world. You'll see more changes as we go along. And, I don't know if any of these places even have names. For some reason, many things here remain unnamed. I asked the same questions, but their answers weren't adequate, or maybe they didn't want to give me that information. I'm afraid you'll have to figure a lot out for yourselves."

"I know what you mean," Lucy muttered.

We passed expansive meacows followed by vast wooded areas and miles of rocky outgrowths, among other configurations.

Later, still on the straight stretch, Mar and Lucy had dozed off while Matt and I remained fascinated with sightseeing. Moe asked, "I can hear my empty stomach speaking. Kids how about stopping for something to eat, I'm hungry, aren't you?"

"Yes, let's eat," Matt said.

I woke the girls, "Do you want to eat?"

"Of cause I'm hungry," Lucy said.

"Okay, Mr. Moe, let's eat," I said, also feeling hunger pangs.

"Yes, but is there any place out here to eat?" Mar asked.

"There is, it's not far ahead, in the grasslands."

In time, the terrain changed to fields of tall grasses. We couldn't see over the plump blades of grass that were no less than two inches wide and twelve feet high. In relationship to the grass, it felt as if we were tiny insects.

We passed cars parked here and there with flatbed platforms built on top of them. People were loading bundles of harvested grass.

Lucy was the first to notice. "Hey, look, those people have green faces?"

"Is that their real skin color?" Mar asked, still finding it hard to believe.

Moe chuckled, "As I said, they're not painted. You're going to see people of many different colors. And, for the life of me, I cannot understand how they all descended from those who originally came through *The Rock*."

I asked, "What are they doing with the grass?"

"That's where their fuel comes from. I often thought we should've done the same in our world."

"Wow!" I said.

"Hey, look over there! Those people have red faces," Matt said, pointing to a group of four loading grass.

Smiling, Moe said, "See what I mean. I promise you'll get answers to your questions, but for now, I have to pay attention to my driving."

"We'll wait, Mr. Moe, we'll wait," I said.

Shortly, we approached several buildings looking like business establishments where active people were coming and going. A big sign on a roof came into view, which read, "Food." Moe pulled up to the fuel station in front of the building.

I nervously said, "Mr. Moe, I don't think we have enough money between us to pay for food."

"Don't worry, kids, remember, our money is no good here."

"You mean we don't have to pay anything?"

"No. Mar, we'll have to pay."

"How can we?" Lucy asked.

Moe took one of those cards out of his pocket and held it up, "I have this," as he tapped his index finger on it. "That's how they pay for things in this world. It somehow knows what my balance is. Incredible, isn't it?" (At the time, in the fifties, in the kid's world credit cards were almost unknown.)

"But, Mr. Moe, none of us have those cards," Matt said.

"Don't worry kids, we'll use mine."

"We'll pay you back, Mr. Moe," Lucy said, wanting to do the

right thing.

Moe could only smile as he stepped out of the Dragon. He slipped his card into a slot on the pump, and said, "Look at those prices, what gougers." Thinking back to what he said earlier at his station, we were amused and attempted to suppress our smirks.

With the tank filled, he suggested, "Hey kids, we better use the johns, we still have a ways to go, and we might not get another chance. They're around back." Huddle together, as we walked among the strange people of assorted colors, and they didn't give us any special notice.

To Lucy and Mar's surprise and discomfort, instead of finding men's and women's restrooms, there was a row of colorful rundown wooden booths, covered with gross artwork or better described as potty graffiti. "Take your pick kids," Moe said. "We'll meet out front."

"Oh, my!" Mar exclaimed. She and Lucy never had to rough it before, for back in our world, they were treated like princesses.

"I don't believe this," Lucy said, "I know I can't wait until the next stop, we better take care of it. Come on, Mar," as she pushed her into the closest stall and entered the next one. Inside, the walls were splattered with gross unspeakable hand-drawn pictures, which stunned them as they did their best not to look.

A large armchair, with an enclosed bottom and around hole cut in the seat leading down into a deep pit with no running water. Much like the outhouses, which we knew of, but never had an occasion to use. There were no tops on the stalls exposing the inside to the elements. A pile of soft paper-like tissues sat on a shelf next to the chair. Lucy, grit her teeth and did what she had to do, knowing there was no choice. "Mar, are you okay?" she called out.

"I'm okay. Isn't this just awful? Is everything going to be like this?"

"I certainly hope not."

Matt and I were doing better, having been Boy Scouts. And shamefully, we were pitifully fascinated by the artwork in our innocence.

When finished, we all met out front. Moe rubbed his hands together, saying, "Time to eat."

Entering the building, we were thrown off balance with everything being a little out of proportion. What should be larger was smaller, and what should be smaller was larger is the only way to describe it. It was interesting to see how those little changes affected our sense of balance.

The place was crowded and noisy. Each group of people sitting together at a table were wearing similar clothing and had the same skin color distinguishing them from the groups at other tables. In the many different segregated skin-colored groups, noticeably, there was no mixing of people of different colors.

Their clothing ranged from bright colors with flowers or abstract shapes to depressing solid drab colors. An individual's dress closely matched their particular skin color along with the others in their group. The styles and combinations were all strange to us. Within the crowded space, it was hard to focus on any particular one or get an accurate count of how many separate groups there were.

Moe ordered, "Let's wash up and find a table." There was one large shared washbasin with continuous water flushing by. It was like washing in a cold-water stream.

When seated, a waiter appeared and asked, "What is your choice?"

"What do you have?" Moe asked with a noticeable glimmer of mischief in his eyes.

"We have our special," the waiter answered unenthusiastically.

"What's the special?"

"It is hamburgles with fats."

"What else do you have?" Moe asked.

"That is all we have," the waiter answered.

Moe seemed to enjoy seeing the confused looks on our faces. He smiled and quickly ordered, "Okay, we'll all have the special," knowing all along, there was only one choice available.

"Five specials," the waiter said. "What do you want to drink?"

"A Coke," I said, as Lucy, Mar, and Matt quickly nodded in agreement.

"A what?" now the waiter was confused. "Come on. I do

not have time for jokes. What do you want?"

"We'll all have a coolly," Moe ordered.

The waiter held out his hand, "Your cards." Moe gave him his card, and the waiter left.

"Mr. Moe, what's a coolly?" Mar asked.

"As I said, things are different here," he reminded us. "Try it. If you don't like it, you don't have to drink it."

"What are hamburgles and fats?" Lucy asked.

"Well, it's their version of hamburgers and french fries only sweeter with an entirely different taste. They taste like nothing you've eaten before. Don't worry, kids. You'll like them, just don't pay attention to their colors. You'll have to eat, so do your best."

Waiting for the food, I continued to look around the room in awe. Most of the patrons were wolfing down their food over the clamor of conversations. It was as if each group came from a separate world, showing no connections or relationship to the others.

"Why are the people not mixing?" Lucy asked.

"That's one of their hard rules. They're not allowed to mix."

"You mean, like segregation? I asked.

"I guess, only worse."

The waiter arrived with the food in a time, making fast foods seem slow. The hamburgles were black with white streaks and still smoking, served on hard green rolls. The drinks were an effervescent green. He placed the tray on the table and left. "Okay, kids, let's dig in," Moe ordered as he took his card off the tray and passed the food around. We looked at the food hesitatingly. To encourage us, Moe bit into his hamburgle and said, "Hmm, that's good."

Lucy looked at her's and said, "I don't know about this," not wanting to say yes just yet.

I bit into mine, knowing it was going to be up to me to take the lead. Chewing it some, I smiled and said, "Hmm, it's not bad. You know what I mean."

"No, what do you mean, is it good?"

"It's good, it's good. Come on, Lucy, let's eat and get out of here."

Matt followed my lead and took a bite, saying, "Hey, he's right. It's not half bad."

After a groan, Lucy took a bite, followed by Mar. Then said, "It's different, you're right; it tastes not as bad as it looks, in fact, it's good." She picked up a fat, which looked like a fry only; it was green, twisted into a single spiral shape about a foot long. She held it up high, and as it dangled, she took a bite off the bottom. Tasting it, she acknowledged, "Hmm, I don't know what it tastes like, but it's sweet like candy."

Mar giggled and took a sip of her coolly. Regardless of its name, it was served at room temperature. She giggled and said, "It's bubbly, and I don't know what it tastes like either, but it's good." We all chuckled, sharing the humor of the moment as we dug into the food, not having eaten for much of the day.

While eating, I examined the people in the room. Halfway through the meal, my eyes met the eyes of a man sitting across the way. Awkwardly, I quickly looked away. He stood and peered directly at me. His skin was a dark purple, and his head was as bald and shiny as a bowling ball. He was wearing a long purple coat that hung down to just below the tops of his high purple boots. His bulging, bloodshot eyes looked quite fearsome. He was obviously annoyed, and yelled, "Boy...what are you looking at!" which brought an eerie hush over the room. I was speechless and didn't know what to do.

Moe stood and, with mischief, said, "Sir, the boy was just saying, how well dressed he thought you looked." Followed with, "And, the boy wondered why those men at the next table were making faces at you."

At first, the big man was flattered, his face then flushed with a tinge of red as he turned to the next table and asked those seated there, "Did you made faces at me?" None of the six green men could admit to something they hadn't done. Bewildered, they sat there in silence. Infuriated, the purple man violently turned their table over, tossing their food in all directions. It upset them so much, all six jumped on him, pounding away. Spontaneously, fights burst out of nowhere all around the room between the different groups.

"Grab your food, and let's get out of here," Moe yelled. Fearful, we followed his orders and clenched on to his coveralls as we ducked, pushed and bumped our way through the mayhem and out the door, luckily without injury.

We piled into the Dragon and sped off as fast as it would take us. Safely away and traveling at the Dragon's high speed, Moe began to laugh. "Mr. Moe, I didn't think that was funny," Lucy said. "I thought we were going to get hurt."

"Sorry, Lucy," understanding her feelings. "I think soon you'll see how it could be funny."

"Mr. Moe, I didn't see those green men making faces?" I asked, in my innocence.

With the same mischief in his voice, he explained, "I know Johnny. You see, in a place like that it's not wise to make eye contact with people of other groups, it could be especially hazardous with the Purple people, which was why I used a divergent move to take the attention off you. Now, sit back and finish your food, we're safe now."

"Gee, Mr. Moe, that was something. Thanks."

"No problem," he said, as we looked at him with wonder, not knowing what to think.

"Are all the people in this world going to be like that?" Lucy asked.

"Heavens, no! Yes, there are some mean creatures here, but there are a lot of good people too. You'll meet some of them soon."

"I certainly hope so."

"We'll be there before long. Now kids, get some rest, you'll need your full faculties later."

"Where are we going, Mr. Moe?" I asked again.

"You'll see, you'll see. For now, finish eating and relax," he ordered and turned in silence to focus on driving.

Later, the *Road* was now a combination of straight runs and occasional sharp turns. Growing dimmer, with no sun, the uniform light in the sky just darkened.

Large strange-looking houses set back in the woods began to appear. As time passed, the houses became more frequent, although still separated by many acres.

"Kids, we're almost there."

"There is where Mr. Moe?" Lucy asked, with a slight touch of sarcasm.

"You'll see, just wait," he said, with that unmistakable look of glee on his face. We settled back in our seats.

With no stars or moon to light the sky, it evoked an eerie feeling of being under a blanket, not able to see our hands in front of our faces. We were only able to see ahead in the glow of the Dragon's fuel-burning headlights.

In time, he slowed down and turned onto a narrow dirt road as we stretched our necks, trying to see where he was taking us.

At long last, he pulled into a long twisting paved driveway. At its end, illuminated in the headlights, we saw a sizeable unusual house with an impressive circular tower at each corner, looking like a miniature castle.

Moe expressed a "Ha" as he applied the brakes and turned the engine off, blowing the horn three times. In a moment, fuel lights on each side of the front door turned on automatically. It was incredible how they came on without striking a match or having an electrical spark.

The front door opened, and a head peered out into the glare of the headlights, a feminine voice loudly called, "Who is there?"

Turning the Dragon's lights off and jumping out, he answered, "Miss Mary, it's me, Moe."

"Mr. Moe, is that you? Is it really you?" the voice asked.

"Yes, it's me," he answered, obviously pleased. She opened the door wide and rushed up to him as if she was going to hug him, but stopped just short of doing so. She was an elderly aristocratic-looking woman with her white hair swirled up and around her head, wearing a light blue full-length frock, which highlighted her tall, slim figure. But most startling was her stark chalk-white skin.

"What are you doing here?" she asked. "I did not expect to see you for another three segments. What has brought you back so soon?"

With an extra sparkle in his eyes, stumbling over his words, he said, "Yes, well. I'm back and… It's good to see you, Miss Mary. The thing is… We have a problem."

"What do you mean, we?" she said.

"Oh. Yes… Well, Miss Mary…" He ordered, "Kids, come on out." We disembarked and huddle around him. "Kids, I like you to meet Miss Mary Right. Miss Mary, I'd like you to meet Lucy and

Johnny Peterson, Marla Carter, and Matt Davies." I must say, seeing her chalk-white skin up close gave us some pause, as if we were in a creepy movie, a feeling that took a while to get over.

"Children, I am pleased to meet you," she said with a welcoming smile. "Lucy and Johnny, you must be brother and sister?"

"We're twins," Lucy answered.

"Ah... Twins, I have never known twins, how exciting."

"Miss Mary, they're from the other side. We're going to need your help."

"Quick, inside, inside," she said, grasping the significance of the situation as she shuffled us into the large house.

CHAPTER 10 Arriving At Miss Mary's Home

We entered a large circular foyer covered with dark wood paneling and a high glass dome overhead. An extra-wide center staircase led to the upper floors. It was fabulous, something we've only seen in movies. Except for the oddly shaped doors along the walls, none of which were rectangular as a door should be. Neither did they match each other, painted with different bright colors that clashed with the wood paneling.

"Children, make yourselves at home. You must be hungry. My people are gone for the evening. However, I will see if I can get something together."

Lucy asked, "Miss Mary, could we use the bathroom?"

"Bathroom, hmm?" she wondered.

Miss Mary, she means the private room," Moe said.

"Yes, of course. You will find it behind the staircase, behind the red door. The washroom is next to it, behind the white door where you can wash up. When finished, come to the cooking room, which is behind the orange door."

"Thank you, Miss Mary," I politely said, and led the way as the others followed with a sense of urgency. As we moved along the darkened space, the fuel lights lit up ahead of us, and when we passed, they shut off automatically. That fascinated us, for, at that time in our world, we knew of no such mechanism able to turn things on and off by our movement.

The cooking-room had odd-looking commercial-size stainless steel fuel-burning appliances. The top cabinets were a little higher, the bottom ones a little lower than they should've been. A wooden block counter surrounded the space. An expansive work island sat in the middle with a large number of odd-looking pots and pans dangling from hooks over it. Again, everything was slightly out of proportion. However, it was evident that serious cooking took place there.

Alone with Moe, Mary fretted. "What is going on?"

"Miss Mary, in a flash of the *White Light,* they showed up at the *Rock.* I remember them from the other side."

"Mr. Moe, why are they here?"

"Miss Mary, they don't know or understand why, and neither do I. They unwilling were pulled through just as I was."

"Oh my Mr. Moe, I see why you brought them here?" she said, as she poured him a goblet of juice. "And who is taking care of the station?"

He first took a sip of the juice, then reluctantly replied, "Oh, the station... Well, Miss Mary, that's a long story." He then blurted out, "It's gone! It's gone!"

"It is gone? How? Why? Mr. Moe, what do you mean, it is gone! Would you please tell me what is going on?"

"Miss Mary, it blew up along with the transport you lent me," he bemoaned.

"Mr. Moe, it blew up, just like that? How?"

He awkwardly turned away and washed his hands to hide the tormented expression on his face in admitting his failer. He described what happened. She nervously listened while vigorously chopping the food instead of taking her anxiety out on him. Then suddenly, a peace came over her, and she said, "I guess it was not your fault. The transport was a wreck anyway, and I know the station was a burden to you. Where did you get the transport you came in?"

"That's the unbelievable thing. I'd forgotten McCloud had a storage mound in the woods. He kept the Dragon there in secret. When I saw it, I couldn't believe it, and the good news is, it now belongs to me.

"The Dragon?"

"Yes. That's what I named it. When you see it in the light of day, you'll understand."

"Oh, how nice."

Meanwhile, Lucy was the first to use the private room as we waited in the hall for our turn. She called out through the door,

"This place is a lot nicer than that awful restaurant. Isn't it crazy how the lights go on and off by themselves? Hey, there's a cord hanging from the ceiling over the toilet. Do you suppose it is…?

"Pull it," I suggested.

"I don't know about that."

"Go on Lucy, pull it," Matt urged

A gushing sound was heard behind the closed door. She yelled, "It works!"

"That's great. Now, come on, others are waiting out here. You know what I mean."

"I know. I know. Give me a minute."

"Where do you think we are, and who is this, Miss Mary?" Mar asked.

"She must be rich to own a place like this," Matt guessed.

"Yes, and she's Mr. Moe's friend. I'm sure he brought us here for help. I don't think we have to worry. Everything will be all right, you know what I mean," I speculated.

As Mar took her turn, Lucy said, "Mom and Dad must be going crazy by now, we better get home fast. Do you understand?" she said, giving me the look of; you'd better do something about it. Then said, "I'm going to wash up."

Matt shamefully admitted, "Gee, I didn't even think of that."

"As soon as we're finished here, we'll ask them how to get back home," I said.

Back in the kitchen, "Mr. Moe, what are you going to do now? How are you going to take care of yourself?" Mary asked as she continued to ready the food.

With a look of despair, he said nothing. "You know there's always a place for you here. The garden needs care, and the roof leaks," she reminded him.

"I know Miss Mary, but the immediate question is, what in the world are we going to do about the kids? They want to go up the *Road* by themselves."

"Mr. Moe, I do not know what we could do for them."

"Miss Mary, I don't know either. I have no idea what to think or do."

"Well, Mr. Moe, I know you will figure it out. You know

well what my world's like," she said, trying to encourage him.

"I will, Miss Mary. I'll find the solution," he said, not wanting to disappoint her, knowing he hadn't been able to find any answers and was hoping she'd come up with something.

We entered the kitchen huddle together as Mary was finishing the food preparation. I said, with determination, "Mr. Moe and Miss Mary, we must get back home. Our parents don't know where we are. When can we leave?"

"Kids, I don't know. I tried to get back before and failed. However, I think you should first understand where you are and what obstacles there are." Knowing in his heart, he had given up trying to get back. Yet, he now felt conflicted. He looked to Mary for help.

She said, "Children, let us sit in the eating-room and have some nutrition. We can talk better there." She ordered, "Girls, help me bring the food into the eating-room while the boys get the silverware out.

The eating-room contained a large round table built a little lower than it should be — twelve ornately carved high-backed wooden armchairs, built lower to compensate for the table. Sitting on them was disorientating as if they were made for short, robust people or perhaps for tall, thin people.

A chandelier hung low over the center of the table, not quite bright enough to illuminate the entire room. The walls were a deep violet color reflecting little light. The extra-large window allowed sunlight to shine in during the day. During the night, the dim glow gave the room a gloomy austere atmosphere.

Matt and I searched the credenza for the silverware, not finding any. Puzzled as Moe entered, he beckoned us over to a carved wooden vase sitting on a pedestal. He lifted the top, which slid up on a shaft, revealing the silverware nestled in basket-like compartments. That illusion fascinated us. Under his direction, we laid out the knives, spoons, and forks on the table.

As we began eating, Mary said, "Johnny, in answer to your earlier question. Mr. Moe and I can only tell you what we have learned so far, which amounts only to pieces of the puzzle in how to get back to your world. Children, I am not from your world; my world is here. We are different. Sadly, I must tell you, I have never heard of anyone successfully going back to your world. Now, that does not mean it cannot be done. Do not get discouraged, for I know little."

"Are you different? Aren't you just like us? I mean… Aren't you human?"

Struck by Lucy's question, we all began to wonder. In spite of her skin being chalk-white, we hadn't thought she could be anything else but human. She thought carefully before answering, "Lucy, honestly, I do not know. That is physically speaking. Some of us are quite different in our behavior. However, others are very much the same. From what Mr. Moe has told me, our ancestors came from your world, which I believe makes us almost if not the same."

"Kids, Miss Mary, is human. Let's not forget that," Moe ordered.

Relieved, Mar then asked, "Miss Mary, will we be able to go home?"

"Children, I understand how much you want to return immediately, and I do not blame you. I will try my best to help you accomplish that. But, you have to show patience and gain a certain understanding."

"What are we supposed to understand?" I asked

Moe jumped in, "Kids, Miss Mary is going to tell all she knows, so first listen to the whole story. Then you can ask questions." We accepted that point for the moment.

"Thank you, Mr. Moe. Children, as I understand it, all the people in my world descended from the ones who crossed over from your world. They were called *Rockers*. No one has come through for more than a lifetime. Consequentially no *Rocker* remains alive. That was until Mr. Moe came, and now, you."

Mar raised her hand. "Yes, child?" Mary patiently asked.

With a queasiness, she asked, "Does that mean we are now part of your world?"

Moe motioned for us to be calm. "It is all right, Mr. Moe, let them ask questions. Their youthfulness is hard to contain," Mary softly said. He nodded in agreement.

"Children, I do not believe you are to be part of my world. However, I only understand what I have seen. The immediate question is not why or how you got here, but rather how to get back to your world. Mr. Moe told me he explained that you must travel up *The Road of Understanding*. Children, do you understand that much?"

"Yes, Miss Mary, we know we must take that trip," I answered and asked, "How long will it take?"

"Again, I can only tell you what we know, for we understand little about how the *Road* functions. In how long it might take, I can only say, we don't know. Mr. Moe, it might help if you tell the children how far we got."

"Yes, I think so." He took a deep breath and cleared his throat before he spoke, "After working for McCloud for a while, I became so melancholy he fixed up an old junk transport and urged me to drive up the *Road* to see if I could find my way back home. Later, I learned what must be done from one of *The Men in White*.

"*The Men in white?*" I asked.

"Yes, and all I can tell you about them is they are dressed in white suits and have skin much like ours with a full head of white hair. They appear at different times and places answering my questions. I believe they are trying to help in the understanding. I think for you to appreciate them better you'll have to see them for yourselves.

"Well, then… McCloud turned a transport over to me, and off I was with a full tank of fuel and a money card in my pocket, for I spent little of the money I earned. In a cloud of dust, I left him behind, hoping I was on my way back home. Shortly I realized how much I would miss him, for he became a good friend. Anyway, I followed the *Road*, just as we did today.

"Several miles along, I saw the first *Man In White*. He was standing on the soft shoulder with his thumb out, indicating he needed a ride. Glad for the company, I picked him up. Being the first time I saw one of them, I'd no idea of his significance. At first, he said nothing much, so I explained my situation, hoping he might be of help.

I was delighted when he went into detail. He explained I was to travel the *Road* to its end, collecting bits of understanding in each city to gain a true understanding of my purpose. He was the first person who seemed to know anything and spoke with authority.

Although, at the time, I understood little of what he was telling me. He went on to say there would be painful and challenging obstacles in my way, attempting to stop me. I had to be strong with determination and have a pure heart to gain success.

"He then asked me to stop the transport. To my surprise, he opened the door and stepped out, telling me to go on my way. I pointed out we were in the middle of nowhere. He assured me he would be just fine. Still unsure, I asked, "What should I do next?"

He instructed me to continue traveling up the *Road*, stopping in each city to learn as much as I could until I reached its end. He ordered, "Now get going, Moe," and stepped away, waving me on.

"I took off. Then I realized he called me Moe. It was strange since I hadn't given him my name. I quickly looked in the rearview mirror and found he was nowhere in sight. He had disappeared in the middle of nowhere. I was startled, not knowing what to make of it.

"Well, kids, that was my first experience with a *Man in White*, and I must admit it was mystifying. Nevertheless, since they are the only ones who seemed to know anything, I now treat them with a great deal of respect and listen carefully to every word they say."

"Who was he, and are there more than one of them?" I asked.

"I don't know who he was or how many of them there are."

"Do they appear and disappear like magic?" Mar asked.

"Kids, I don't know, I never actually saw them appear or disappear, they were just there, and when I turned away, they were gone.

"Anyway, I continued to speed along, wanting to get to the end as fast as possible. However, later, disaster struck as the engine began to sputter, making clunking sounds. Fortunately, I came upon the side road that leads here. Desperate, I pulled off the pebble *Road* onto it hoping to find help. Before I could, the engine with a loud bang stopped working. Fortunately, I found myself at the bottom of Miss Mary's driveway. With little choice, I walked all the way up to this house and jingled the doorbell."

Mary jumped in, "Yes, my Slop Janis answered the door, and then came and told me there was a sorrowful-looking man at the door asking for help. I ask my Slop, Samuel, to go and see if he could help the poor fellow."

"Miss Mary, a sorrowful poor fellow!" Moe Indignantly exclaimed.

"Yes, Mr. Moe. It is what you looked like. The same way you all looked like when you arrived tonight."

"What's a Slop?" Lucy asked.

Collecting himself, he explained, "Kids, it would be like household help, a cook, a servant, or an employee in our world. You'll meet them in the morning." (Janis and Samuel, an elderly married couple who worked in this house since their youth, well before Mary arrived as a young bride. They resided in a separate cottage on the estate.)

We looked at Mary even more impressed by the fact she had servants, for we never knew anyone who had servants.

"Kids, after Samuel studied the transport, he concluded it was serious and suggested we tow it up to the house. I agreed, and by using a thick rope and one of Miss Mary's other transports, we pulled it up to the house. By the way, kids, in this world, they call their cars, transports."

Mary added, "Yes, and it was getting dark when Samuel came to me and told me nothing could be done until morning. I could not send a poor old man out into the night, so I asked Janis to put another plate on the table and told Samuel to prepare a guest room."

"Old man? Miss Mary, please!" Moe exclaimed.

"Come on, Mr. Moe, continue the story."

"Err. Okay. Okay." Swallowing his pride, he continued. "Well, not knowing what else to do, I accepted Miss Mary's hospitality, at least until the transport could be fixed.

"After a sumptuous dinner, we sat in the great-room where I explained my situation. We talked well into the night. Finally, Miss Mary showed me to a guest room, leaving me to a sleepless night, wondering if the transport was fixable, and most of all, wishing McCloud was here."

"Children, I also had a little sleep that night, understanding his predicament and wondering how I could be of help," Mary added.

Moe continued, "Well. The next morning Samuel knocked

on my door. He instructed, everything I would need was in the washroom, including a fresh set of clothing, and when ready, Miss Mary would be waiting in the eating-room for breakfast. I quickly got up, washed, shaved with the straight razor placed there for me, and dressed in the clothing. I wondered where the clothing of such high quality came from, which included underwear and socks that fit so well.

"I remember at breakfast Miss Mary commented on how I looked better washed and dressed in the clothing. I couldn't help but ask about the clothing."

Mary interrupted, "Children, he did look better, and I told him they belonged to my husband. I could not help being amused by seeing the surprised look on his face and quickly explained, Mr. Right, my deceased husband, who died ten years earlier.

"I also remember the disappointed look on his face when Samuel entered and described how the engine was no longer repairable. With despair, he moaned. Oh my, I knew I had to think fast."

"Hmm… Yes, Miss Mary, then you suggested, perhaps I could help around the house until the motor could be replaced. Well, with my janitorial background, I said, "I could. I'll clean this place like it's never been cleaned before." Kids, at that moment, I didn't know what else to do."

"Mr. Moe, is this as far as you got?" I asked.

"Oh no, not by any means, there's a lot more to tell," Moe responded.

Mary said, "Children, it is getting late, and it is a long story. We should get some sleep. Tomorrow we will continue." When finished with the meal, she ordered, "Children, follow me." Disappointed not finding out when we could head home, Lucy gave an almost audible "Err" in frustration, but we obediently followed her.

She gave us instructions, "I will get fresh night clothing, that will be a little large. However, place all your clothing, including your undergarments, outside the door. My Slopes will clean them before you wake." She placed Lucy and Mar in one room and Matt and me in another.

After getting the pajamas and in bed, wondering if we would

ever get back home, we talked ourselves to sleep.

CHAPTER 11 Moe And Marys Relationship

Early the following morning, Mary leisurely soaked in her bathtub before we woke. When dressed, she settled in the great-room to read a book, as was her custom while waiting for things to get started. The great-room was a spacious room with overstuffed plush couches, armchairs, and hassocks surrounded by bookshelves.

However, since this was such an unusual morning, she was unable to relax and concentrate on reading. It was a significant break from her daily routine of tending to the gardens and house, seeing to it everything was functioning smoothly, including her finances. All made possible by the hard work of Janis and Samuel.

Relieved when Samuel entered, she ordered, "Wake Mr. Moe. Let the children sleep on. When he is ready, have him come here. When he arrives, please have Janis prepare breakfast for two."

She successfully ran her life in an orderly manner, when finished giving the marching orders she turned back attempting to read her book, again with little success. The books in her culture lacked inspiration. However, since her husband passed away, she lived this lonely secluded life on the estate. Reading books gave her some comfort and contentment but lacked fulfillment.

Other than the books, she used her imagination to keep her mind active. Living in this strange world, and being elderly, she had long ago lost any hope of real stimulus. That's was until the day Moe arrived on her doorstep.

Samuel entered Moe's bedroom, ringing his little bell. A bell he carried hung around his neck at all times to announce his presence when necessary. "Sir, the Madame, asked when you are ready, as usual, she will receive you in the great-room."

"Tell her I'll be there," Moe said, knowing the routine.

Samuel said, "Sir, as always, I laid out a fresh set of clothing and have run your bath," and then left.

Moe thanked him and slid off the edge of the bed, taking a big stretch, only able to sleep on a soft mattress during his visits here. He was limited to visiting Mary just once a month, or more specific, a period of forty, sixteen-hour days, or one-tenth of a cycle. These people had no written calendars, yet they divided their months were into four segments, similar to our weeks. Somehow, even without anything written, they were able to track the passage of time. Moe needed to mark off the days to keep track. He stuck to this schedule due to honoring his commitment to McCloud.

When McCloud's illness reached its critical stage, Moe had little time away from the station. With his passing, Moe was restricted to spending even less time with her. He couldn't find anyone to fill in for him while away, due to the strict rules of not being allowed to work for someone of another color. This caused him to leave the station unattended when gone, having to trust his customers with being honest. Most were, occasionally, one was not although minimally. However, he was willing to take any losses to see Mary that once each month.

It took him a day to drive from the station. Spending the evening together, they enjoyed dinner and talked late into the night before retiring to their separate bedrooms. The next day they rose extra early and had breakfast in the garden. After an early evening dinner, he would head back to be at work the following morning, having had little or no sleep.

After McCloud's death, life at the station became a lonely existence. His only reason for keeping it open was his promise to McCloud. Although he never understood why McCloud made him promise that, for he honestly couldn't see a good reason to do so? (In retrospect, if he wouldn't have remained there, the kids might never have seen him again.) Now, the realization of never having to go back to the station was beginning to sink in. He felt that heavy load on his back was lifted, freeing him.

With it gone, and not directly by his doing, he was beginning to think about spending his time with Mary. For an outsider to find employment in this world was impossible, leaving him only with Mary's generous unorthodox offer. Yet, conflicted about being her employee, so to speak, for he had an independent or macho streak indicative of the times he grew up in.

After shaving, he settled into the tub. The water was almost too hot, and with the floral fragrance of the added softening agents, it was most relaxing, a pleasure he so enjoyed only when here. Soaking for just five minutes, not really wanting to get out. However, he quickly scrubbed down and dressed, knowing Mary was waiting.

Checking himself in the mirror, he thought, "I don't look like a pitiful old fool. Where does she get that from? I guess people see what they want to see." When dressed and satisfied, he looked just right, he headed downstairs to join her.

She was sitting in her favorite overstuffed chair, which faced the large set of oversized ornate misshaped French type doors, which opened out onto an expansive garden. While sipping her morning juice with a book on her lap, he entered and said, "Good morning Miss Mary."

"Good morning Mr. Moe. Sit, have your juice. Did you have a good night's rest?"

"Yes, Miss Mary, I feel completely renewed. How was your night?" he asked, as he plunked himself into the posh over-stuffed chair he always sat in.

"Mr. Moe, you know what happened on the first trip up the *Road*. I would not want anyone to go through that. It troubles me concerning the children traveling by themselves."

"Yes, Miss Mary, I feel the same way. I've been trying to figure out what else could be done."

"Mr. Moe, have you come up with anything?"

"I'm sorry, Miss Mary; so far, I've only drawn a blank."

After a thoughtful pause, she said, "Mr. Moe, the children have families on the other side, which will be lost if they stay here. We are old and alone, things matter little to us, but they have long lives ahead of them. We are just old fools who perhaps can do nothing. Maybe, we should not think about it and just keep them here. I do not know what...

As she said that, out of nowhere, SUDDENLY, an unexpected gigantic explosive bolt of White Light struck just outside the French doors. The flash left them stunned and blinded for a moment. When their sight recovered, they saw the old oak-like tree, which stood there for many lifetimes, was now split right down its center, charred and still smoldering.

Moe jumped up, rubbing his eyes, he asked, "Do you know what that was?" Answering his own question, "It was the same *White Light* that brought us through the *Rock*. Do you know what that means?"

"Maybe… But, I am not sure. What does it mean, Mr. Moe?"

He excitedly paced back and forth in front of the glass doors that framed the split tree, and exclaimed, "No, I must do something!" with a burst of energy. "I might be an old fool, but I'm going to get these kids back home."

Samuel and Janis had rushed into the room in a reserved panic, having heard the thunderous sound of the lightning bolt. Recovering from the miraculous occurrence and seeing his resolve, Mary ordered, "Wake the children. Get them washed, dressed, fed, and in here."

Still shaken, Janis announced breakfast was ready. Mary ordered, "We will help ourselves, go with Samuel and help the girls."

"Wait, if the kids ask, tell them it was only a lightning strike," Moe added. They both moved into the eating-room with their glasses of juice in hand.

The strike shook and rattled everything in the house, waking Matt and I. We ran to the windows trying to see what it was. Upon seeing nothing, we went into the hall meeting Lucy and Mar, who also woke. At the same moment, Mary's Slopes emerged up the staircase. Realizing who they were, we rush to them, wanting to know what happened.

Ever calm, Samuel said, "Children, it was only a lightning strike, do not be concerned, everything is just fine," as he reassured them, even though he had no idea what a lightning strike was.

"My name is Janis, and this is my husband Samuel," she said. We introduced ourselves, and she instructed, "The Madam wants you to wash, dress and come down for breakfast. I will run baths for the ladies. Your laundered clothing will be found in the bathing rooms."

"Boys, I will run your separate baths upstairs. Now, please get on with it, the madam wants to see you as soon as possible," Samuel, ordered.

Moe and Mary finished breakfast and moved back into the great room. Still stunned, they collapsed into their chairs in reaction to the perceived sign Moe believed was given. Silently, they stared at the split tree for a long moment, perhaps picturing what was experienced in the first attempt to reach the end of the *Road*.

Saddened, she reflected, "Mr. Moe, it was a beautiful tree."

"Miss Mary, you know all things have a finite time to live."

"Yes, I know, and the children should not lose their limited time by staying here. They should be with their family's in their world. I wonder what would happen if we told them what awaits them out there? If they knew, they might not want to go."

"Hmm. Miss Mary, I would think if we didn't tell them in advance, they might not be prepared for what they'll have to face."

"Yes, it would not be fair. We must tell them everything and allow them to choose whether to go or stay. Mr. Moe, I hope we are ready for this?"

Deep in his heart, he was now convinced he must do this, accepting to no longer live in the shadows of life just coasting along, avoiding any responsibilities beyond himself, as he had done for so many years. The strike of white-light affected something deep inside him. He conceded, "I don't have a choice, do I? I must do what I know must be done, and I'll not fail this time."

Mary smiled.

When we entered the great-room huddled together, Mary said, "Good morning, children. Come… sit by us. Have you had enough to eat?"

"Yes, Miss Mary," I said, as we found comfortable spots at their feet.

"Can we start home today?" Mar asked.

"Now, children, before anyone goes anywhere, we must first tell you about our prior trip," Mary instructed. "After which you must decide whether you want to go or stay. You will have to understand every step as you go along. Do you understand that much?"

"Yes, we must travel up *The Road of Understanding* to its end, and along the way, there'll be obstacles that'll try to stop us. Is that right, Miss Mary?" Lucy asked.

"Yes, as far as it goes. However, we believe the most important element will be to gain a certain understanding."

"What certain understand? I'm not sure I understand?" I asked, confused.

"Kids, we're not sure either," Moe said. "It's still a mystery, which I believe is something to be found along the way, I suppose."

"Now, children, Mr. Moe and I have agreed to take you to the end of the *Road*." Hearing that news took us by surprise, making us so thrilled and excited, we let out a cheer. I was pleased with myself as I looked at the others with the look of; see I told you he would help. A fact Lucy didn't appreciate having gotten that same look from me so many times.

Mary, in her calm way, continued, "First before anyone goes anywhere, you must understand as much as we do."

We keenly listened as Moe started where he left off the night before. "After I worked here for a time, having cleaned as much as could be cleaned around the house and garden, I felt as if I was spinning my wheels, so to speak. I became impatient and was determined to travel up the *Road*. I told Miss Mary, it was time for me to head home…

Three years earlier, while in the great-room, Mary asked, "Mr. Moe, how will you travel without a transport?"

He was already stumped and said with little thought, "Well, I'll just have to hitchhike, I guess."

"Now Mr. Moe, you do not know what to do next, do you?" she asked, trying to be of help.

After a brief pause, he admitted, "Nope. I don't, Miss Mary. All I know is I must get back to my world."

"Mr. Moe, I do not think you are going to get very far with that plan, are you?"

"Miss Mary, I don't know what else to do. I can't just stay here and forget my past."

After thinking for seconds, she concluded, "Well, I see you

are determined. As much as I would like you to stay and help with the maintenance. If I cannot persuade you to stay, I will join you. Tomorrow we will take one of my transports and head up the *Road.*

"Miss Mary, I can't ask you to do that," he said. "Couldn't I just borrow one of your transport?"

"Mr. Moe, I am offering you transportation, and with that offer, I go with you. Anyway, you will need my Merchants Passport to gain safe passage. Is that clear?" she said firmly.

Thinking it over quickly, having no alternatives, and realizing having Mary's company might be quite pleasant, and without knowing what's ahead, he declared, "That's clear, Miss Mary, but I'll have to do all the driving."

"Mr. Moe, I would not have it any other way," she agreed, never telling him she never drove a transport.

Ringing for Samuel, she instructed, "Please make ready my best transport and pack it with sufficient supplies for an extended road trip starting early tomorrow." Then she asked Janis to bring a tray of tea.

Sitting back satisfied, she said, "Well, Mr. Moe, tomorrow morning, we will start on a most exciting road trip up *The Road of Understanding.*"

The next morning when ready, Moe and Mary were filled with the kind of enthusiasm one might have when starting on a vacation trip. Sitting in her new shiny elegantly decorated transport, jammed packed with supplies, Mary thanked Samuel and Janis for getting everything ready on time. It was quite a feat, for the two of them having to do everything in triple time. That was a miracle in itself. Mary handed them the necessary papers and charged them, "The place is yours until I return."

"Yes, Madam," they said in unison.

Moe turned the starting crank, shifted the gears and stepped on the accelerator, and off they went down the driveway headed towards the pebble Road.

CHAPTER 12 Entering Bluetropolis

On the first day of their trip, things went smoothly until they reached a checkpoint manned by a group of Bluemen, dressed in blue military-type uniforms, although not carrying weapons. "Miss Mary, do you know who these guys are?"

Visibly tense, she said, "Mr. Moe, I believe they are the Blue enforcers. Do everything they tell you to do. I will explain later."

One of the officers circled the transport as another approached and asked, "Your papers." She quickly handed him her family's Merchant Credentials.

Moe, not knowing who these men were, wasn't yet concerned. The Blues examined the papers, and after a consultation, one of them returned and handed them back to her and asked, "Who is this with you?"

Thinking fast, she said, "He is only my driver."

"You are forbidden to enter Bluetropolis." The officer ordered. "Stay on the *Road* until you are out of our domain. Do you understand?"

"Yes, sir. I understand. We will not leave it," a compliant Mary, said.

"All right, go on your way," the officer ordered.

As they took off Mary breathed a sigh of relief, "Mr. Moe that was frightening, I thought we were in some sort of trouble."

"Miss Mary, what's it with these Blues?"

She explained, "Bluetropolis is a strict city, which does not tolerate people from other places. No one is allowed to enter without permission. They severely punish those who do not obey their rules."

However, in the stress of the moment, they both forgot about collecting bits of understanding in each city, which they would come to terms with shortly.

"Miss Mary, many Blues stopped at my station. I know little about them, except that they are a little strange, for they never talked much. However, they don't seem to be dangerous."

"Yes, but those are the merchants. As you know, they are only allowed to mix for trade and are forbidden to speak of their city. And if caught doing so, they would face harsh punishment."

"Oh well, tyrants exist everywhere."

"Mr. Moe, do you have that sort of conduct in your world?"

"Yes, we haven't solved that either." Glancing down at the dashboard, he said, "Miss Mary, I think we might have a problem."

"Mr. Moe, what might that be?"

"We're almost out of fuel."

"What are we going to do?

"We passed a station not long ago."

"But, Mr. Moe, that station was in their domain, and we were told not to leave the *Road* while in their domain. Do not disobey their rules."

"Miss Mary, it's not that far off it, and it'll only take a couple of minutes. We'll be gone before they could do anything. It's either that or run out of fuel."

Without another word, he sped back to the station, jumped out, slipped his card into the pump as the Blues in the station stared at them motionless. He filled the tank, took his card, jumped back in, and took off. Back on the *Road*, he said, "See Miss Mary, nothing to it."

"Old man, you frightened me," she said, not at all impressed with his actions.

Suddenly, out of nowhere, sirens wailed around them coming from all directions as blue transports encircled them. Blocked off, Mary exclaimed to Moe in desperation, "What have you done!"

One of the blue officers, ordered, "Step out of your transport,"

"Sir, I just got off the *Road* to get some fuel," Moe feebly said.

"You have broken the law. You are under arrest," the officer declared.

Mary started to cry as Moe protested, "We just needed some fuel." The officers didn't respond.

"What are you going to do with us?" Moe asked as they shuffled them into one of their transports. "Where are you taking us?"

"We are going to The Sentencer."

"What about our transport?" The officers gave no more answers. They headed towards the city of Bluetropolis with Mary sobbing and Moe trying to console her.

Back in the great-room in Mary's home, as they told us of their arrest, Mar asked, "Miss Mary, where both of you really arrested?"

Moe, still feeling the guilt of his bad judgment, said, "Yes. They took us to a place that might be called a courtroom in our world, only with a big difference. The guy in charge was not a judge. They called him *The Sentencer.*"

"*The Sentencer!*" Lucy exclaimed, beginning to feel stressed about what might be ahead.

"Yes, *The Sentencer*. There was no trial. There was no defense on our behalf. We were not considered innocent until proven guilty. Kids, we weren't given any of the rights we have in our world. There was no justice, only sentences."

"Yes, that is true. I was so displeased with Mr. Moe for getting us into such serious trouble," Mary said.

"Miss Mary, I know you were mad at me, and I'm still sorry about causing you that pain."

"Hmm," she muttered, showing the acceptance of his apology in her feminine way.

Awestruck, I asked, "Gee, what happened then?"

"Well, let me tell you… We arrived in front of that so-called *Sentencer* surrounded by a nasty bunch of Blue thugs. He was sitting on a high platform, on what looked like a throne. There was no bench or desk. He appeared to be more like a king than a judge. Dressed in a long blue robe that hung down to the floor, covering the entire top of the platform. A silly blue cap looking like a mangled crown sat on his head. It might have been amusing if it wasn't so serious."

"Mr. Moe, nothing was amusing about it. It was a frightening experience in that horrible, dimly blue-lit room."

"Yes, it was…"

Three years earlier in the courtroom, "What have they done?" *The Sentencer* asked a little blue man who was seated to his left at a little blue desk at floor level.

He answered with his little squeaky voice, "Sir, they have crossed over without permission."

"I see." Without any further deliberation, he proclaimed, "The sentence is one cycle." The little man at the desk struck a bell one time.

As the officers started to lead them off, Moe yelled as they restrained him, "I only needed some fuel. That's all I did,"

"Two cycles," the *Sentencer* ordered. The little man struck the bell two times.

"Is this justice? I want a lawyer," Moe responded.

"Three cycles," the *Sentencer* decreed. The little man struck the bell three times.

"Mr. Moe, would you please SHUT UP! Mary screamed. The two of them were dragged off bewildered.

CHAPTER 13 Imprisoned

The guards forcibly led the two of them across a stone bridge into a formable stronghold, which resembled a fortress from the Middle-Ages. Taken down a narrow spiral stone staircase, which cantilevered out from the wall, with steps about three feet wide. It had no railing to keep one from falling into the pit it encircled, which was about thirty feet across and at least that deep with no roof, open to the elements. With Mary softly weeping and Moe's knees shaking, due to his fear of heights, they were terrified.

After an arduous descent, they reached the bottom. Two guards led them through one of the locked doors that circled the bottom level into a narrow corridor leading to a smaller circle of doors. Stopping at door number six, a guard peered into a slot in the five-foot-high door. Unlocking it, the guards opened it wide and pushed them into a darkened space. Having to bend over to clear the doorway, Moe could only say, "Hey, watch it!"

The door slammed shut and was locked behind them. To find themselves in a pie-shaped room, which was more than twenty-five feet deep, that widens out from the six-foot width at the door to about twenty feet across at the far end. There were two tiers of sleeping cots hung from the rough stone walls. The only light came from a barred opening high in the ceiling, out of reach, which allowed air and a shaft of light to enter, leaving much of the room in the shadows.

"Oh, Mr. Moe, what is going to happen to us?" she asked, hardly able to speak.

"Don't worry, Miss Mary. We'll get out of here."

A voice came out of the shadows, startling them, "There is no getting out of here."

"Who's that?" Moe asked, as his eyes searched the darkened area to see who it was. "Where are you?"

"I am back here," the voice answered.

"Come out into the light. Show yourself," Moe ordered.

"No, you come into the dark. I was here first."

They looked at each other distressed. Mary cautiously nudged Moe in the direction of the stranger's voice, as it said, "Do not be afraid, I will not bite you."

"Who said I was afraid," a defensive Moe said, as they moved towards whoever it was. As their eyes adjusted to the dim light, they saw the silhouette of a man sitting on one of the cots.

Mary introduced both of them, then asked, "And who are you, sir?"

"I am no, sir. My name is Inge. What brought you, unfortunate people, here?"

"We just stopped for fuel. That's all," Moe said.

Inge let out a "Ha-ha!"

"It is not funny. And Inge, why are you here?" Mary retorted.

He didn't want to upset her any more than she was. He sadly said, "I just wanted to visit my lady friend. That is all I did."

"You mean a gentleman cannot visit a lady friend in Bluetropolis?" she asked.

"If the gentleman is not blue, no, I could not court my Ofeela," as he stuck his head out into the light.

Seeing his red skin, long red beard, and hair, she blurted out, "You are a Redman!"

"Yes, and you are a white woman."

"Oh no, you must have known they do not tolerate mixing," she said.

"Aren't you a white woman and Moe is a pink man, isn't that the same? Besides, you must have known not to stop for fuel. I afraid, under their rules, you have a weak case."

"Unfortunately, you are correct. I have always heard about the Blue's bitter discrimination and unreasonableness, but had no idea it was to this extent."

"Well, we now know," Moe said, not ready to accept the circumstances and began to focus in a crisis mode, he asked, "Now, how do we get out of here?"

Before he could answer, Mary asked Inge, "How long did The Sentencer give you?"

"So far, twelve cycles." Seeing their shock, he sorrowfully added, "Yes, it is a long time, Blues are not a forgiving people."

Moe asked, "Why that's about nine years, my time, isn't it? Okay, now tell us how do we get out of this place?" Moe pleaded.

"There is no way out. I have been here for almost a cycle and have tried to find a way out, and every time I attempted to escape and failed, they gave me more time to serve. There is no way out."

"Mr. Moe, you must find a way out of this awful place."

"Yes, Miss Mary, I'll find a way," accepting it was going to be his responsibility as he continued to rack his brain.

Seeing them staring at him, he pleaded, "Just give me a little time."

"Yes, you will figure it out. I will just wait right here until you do," Inge quipped. Then with a serious tone, he asked, "You said, nine years your time? What does that mean?"

"Yes, he did say that. You see, Mr. Moe is a *Rocker*."

"How could that be? I thought all *Rockers* were dead?"

"Not the newly arrived ones."

"You mean they are coming through again?"

"Only Mr. Moe so far."

"That is unbelievable. Do you know a way out of here?" Inge asked, not knowing what to think, hoping for a positive response."

"Just let me think," Moe said.

"Okay, go ahead and do your thinking," Inge said, backing off in silence.

Moe sat on a cot in quiet thought. After a moment, he asked, "Is there a private room outside this room? And if there is, how do we get to use it?"

"Mr. Moe, of all times," Mary retorted.

"Yes, and it is quite convenient. All you have to do is to pound on the door and wait until those blue critters are willing to take you there. Moe pounded on the door.

"Mr. Moe, I have to use the facilities too," Mary said.

"Miss Mary, let me check it out first," satisfying her for the moment.

Pounding and pounding for some time, the guards eventually

came to the door and peered into the slot, grumbling, "What do you want?"

"I have to use the private room."

The guard ordered, "Step back from the door." When he did, they opened it and hustled him out, locking the door behind, leaving Mary alone with Inge.

Inge asked, "Are you afraid to be alone with a man of a different color?"

"I do not think so. I have never been alone with a Redman." Thinking about it, she said with courage, "No, I am not. But, if you come near me, I will kick you."

He chuckled, then said, "I am sorry, I was just wondering." She indignantly sat on a cot impatiently waiting for Moe's return.

He was back shortly. Eyes glared into the slot, and the door opened. As they pushed him in, he yelled, "The lady needs to go too."

The door slammed shut. Again, eyes glared in, and a voice ordered, "Lady must step into the light, away from the others."

As she passed him, he quickly whispered, "Miss Mary, try to remember everything you see and be careful."

"Lady, indeed," she whispered back. Once taken out, the door slammed shut. Moe plunked down on a cot in a state of thought. Inge asked, "Have you figured out how to get out of here yet?"

"I will. I will. Just give me a little time and let me think."

"I do hope you can find a way out. I have been here way too long." After a pause, Inge asked, "Do you special powers?"

"No, of course not. I just need to think."

"Thinking is all yours." There was silence until Mary returned.

Moe quizzed her, "Miss Mary, what did you see?"

In a huff, she exclaimed, "What did I see! Mr. Moe, what do you think I saw. I saw the private room. That is what I saw. It had no door to keep prying eyes out, and was not in the least bit sanitary."

"No. No. Miss Mary, I mean how many doors, how many people, and a way out?"

"Oh. I see what you mean. All right, Mr. Moe, let me

think… Yes, there were several tiny doors in a small circle with numbers on them, which I guess lead to other rooms just like this one. A big locked door was at the other end of the passageway we came in. Let me see what else… Oh yes. Out by the stairs, I saw several doors around the walls, which I believe led to corridors like the one we came through, which I assume contains many more rooms. I saw no one other than the two guards who brought us in. They were the only ones I saw."

"Yes, that's what I saw. There's got to be something more?" Moe mumbled to himself.

"Oh yes, Mr. Moe, there was. One of the guards was carrying a key ring with enough keys that perhaps unlocked all the doors. He seemed to be the one in charge."

"Good. We'll have to lure both of them in here, knock them out, and get those keys."

"Yes, then we just walk out through all the doors while passing all the Blues along the way," Inge quipped.

"No, we'll just stay with you for three years, I mean cycles."

"Now, Mr. Moe, do not lose your track. How will we get past those obstacles?"

"Miss Mary, I must think. I need more time."

Just then, the sound of a tray pushed through a slot at the bottom of the door was heard. Inge ran over, picked up one of the three bowls, and said, "Come and get it. It is mealtime."

"Without hesitation, Moe got his bowl and brought the other to Mary, saying, "Let's eat."

Thank you, Mr. Moe." She looked at the thick lumpy substance, which appeared to be a blue slime with tiny objects of different colors in it. She said, "What in the world is this?"

"It is all there is on the menu, day in and day out, and if I told what was in it, you might not want to eat it, so do not ask." He chuckled as he dipped his fingers into it and licked the food off them.

"Are we supposed to use our fingers without even washing them?" she asked, with a sickening look on her face.

"I don't think we have a choice Miss Mary, we'll have to suffer with the way it is," as he dipped his fingers in the guck and licked them off. Tasting it, he said, "It's not as bad as it looks."

"Are there any napkins Inge?" she asked as she hesitantly, in a lady-like manner, licked her fingers.

"Please, the service here is not what it should be. However, they do occasionally give a jug of water to drink and wash up with."

"I am sorry, Inge. I guess I should not expect any kindness from these hateful Blues."

"You have got that right."

"Look! Look!" Moe exclaimed, waving his hands.

"Look at what Mr. Moe?" Then she answered her own question, "You rubbed the food all over your hands."

"Yes, Miss Mary, I rubbed the food on my hands, making me look blue, and the color stays there. I'm Blue. Get the picture?"

"I would guess you mean if we cover our skin with the food we might pass as a Blue, and then again we might not," Inge theorized.

"Mr. Moe, I am not going to rub that substance all over my body."

"No, no, Miss Mary, we'll just put it on our face and hands and wash it off afterward" Then he spewed out, "Or perhaps, you prefer to stay here for three cycles."

"Most certainly not, Mr. Moe!" she rebuffed. Then thinking, "Well, if it is only on my face and hands, and it will come off afterward, I guess I could manage that. But, how do we get through those doors without being caught?"

"Miss Mary, give me a little more time to figure it out. Right now, let's save some of this food."

"How does this look?" Inge asked, after smearing some food across his forehead.

"My, it does not cover your red skin," Mary said.

"Wait a minute, if it does not make me blue what am I going to do?"

"Don't worry, Inge. I'll figure that out too."

"Mr. Moe, I hope so. I am beginning to feel sick with fear."

Back in the great-room, Lucy asked, "Mr. Moe, did you figure it out?"

"Of course, I figured it out," he boasted.

Mary added, "Yes, he did, with help, and a great deal of luck.

"Wow, Mr. Moe, what happened next?" I asked.

"Well, what happened next was...

In the jail cell, after some thought, with exuberance Moe jumped up, using animated hand motions as he spoke, "We'll lure the two guards in here. That's after we rub the blue food on."

"But that stuff does not cover my skin," a dejected Inge said.

It doesn't have to. You'll be the lure to get the guards in here. Then we'll knock them out. Miss Mary and I will put on their uniforms and make-believe you are our prisoner, and with their keys, we'll walk right out of here."

"Mr. Moe, we will knock them out? I am not sure I can do that. And, if I could, what would I use?"

Beginning to feel hope again, Inge enthusiastically leaped on a cot and with an "HA-HA!" he jumped up and down on it and motioned for Moe to join him. They both pounced on it until the wooden frame ripped away from the wall, both crashing to the floor. Inge jumped up, broke off a bat size piece of the wood frame, and swung it like an ax in a chopping motion with delight.

"Good. Good. Now, Inge will get the guards in here. Then, Miss Mary, you and I will knock them out."

"Mr. Moe, I do not know about that. How would I be able to do that?"

He took the piece of the frame and showed her how to swing it, "Miss Mary, like this." He handed it to her and showed her the motion again. After she swatted it a couple of times like a giant fly swatter, he said, "Miss Mary, remember these Blues are going to keep us in here for many cycles. Swing it with all your might." Understanding, she swung it with a vengeance and a grunt.

"That's it, Miss Mary, you've got it."

He explained the whole plan, ending with, "We'll have to wait until the next time they come to the door as not to make them suspicious."

CHAPTER 14 The Great Escape

Unfortunately, they had to wait until the next day when the guards brought their one daily meal. While waiting, Moe spoke of his exploits and what his side of the *Rock* was like to satisfy Inge's curiosity. In turn, Inge told more of his situation as they got to know each other better.

After a restless night and more talk, shortly before Inge figured the guards would bring the meal they prepared for their daring planned escape. As Moe rubbed the blue food on his face from the day before, he said, "Do it this way, Miss Mary."

She grimaced, "This is not only sticky, but it smells. Mr. Moe, is there any other way?" Knowing the answer, she gently rubbed it on.

Inge acted as a mirror as he pointed out the bare spots on their faces, saying, "There. No there!"

When ready, they grabbed their makeshift clubs and took their positions. Moe stood on the lock side of the door and Mary on the hinge side, both in the shadows.

Inge sat on a cot in the beam of light to be seen by the guards. Apprehensive, they waited for the right moment. Finally, they heard a rattling at the door, alerting them. Eyes peered in, and a tray slid in through the lower slot. Inge took his cue and began to yell, "They are gone!" Not hearing a response, he continued, "They have escaped! They ran away!"

The dimwitted guards feared they might have failed in their duties. The upper slot opened, and a commotion was heard. The door swung open, and the two guards rushed in stooped over to clear the doorway. Before they could straighten up, Moe struck the first one with a quick blow to the head, knocking him out cold.

He yelled, "Miss Mary hit him!" She closed her eyes and swung her club, hitting the other confused guard on the back of his head. He straightened up and began to reel in an erratic circle. They watched him as he strayed near Moe. Without hesitation, he struck him squarely on the head. However, instead of falling, the guard just stood there with glazed eyes. Inge circled him, and with his index finger pushed him, incredibly, he collapsed like a bag of potatoes.

Immediately, they stripped the guards of their uniforms. Moe began to undress as Mary exclaimed, "Mr. Moe, I am not going to undress in front of both of you!"

Realizing he wasn't as considerate of her as he should've been, he thought for a moment, then offered, "Miss Mary, if each of us goes to a different dark corner with our backs to each other." She thanked him.

They dressed quickly, carefully concealing their white hair under the guard's caps. Moe breathlessly grabbed the keys and peeked out the door. Seeing no one in the corridor, he ushered them out and locked the guards in the cell.

Inge stopped at the next door marked number five and looked into the viewing slot, and said, "There are Reds in there. Moe, unlock this door."

"I don't know about that. It's not in the plan."

"Plan or no plan, most of these people are here for the same unjust reasons we are. We must not leave them behind."

"I don't know? It might risk our chances of getting out of here."

"To leave them behind would not only be selfish but immoral."

"Mr. Moe, I think he has a point."

"Oh, boy… Okay, I guess I'll have to unlock all the doors."

Inge said, "Yes, we do, and it can be done quickly, perhaps having a crowd might be of help."

"Please let us get on with it. I am getting nervous," Mary said.

"Inge, I'll unlock each door, you go in and tell them to come out while I unlock the next one. We'll repeat it with all the doors as fast as we can, hoping all will come out about the same time.

Now, at the count of three and go. One - two - three and go." He unlocked the first door and moved to the next one as Inge opened it and yelled in, "You are free, come out, you are free." When finished, they looked back, expecting to see the prisoners, but none came out. They were dismayed.

"We must go," Moe said.

"No, we must not leave them. Wait." He went back into room five, grabbing the arm of a Redman pulling him out, yelling, "You are free. You are free." With Moe and Mary's help in urging, the prisoners began to overcome their disbelief as the realization of freedom took hold.

Slowly they filed out into the dark corridor, looking like the poor souls they were. When all crowded in the passageway, there were more than a hundred, and they were becoming vocal. Inge said, "Now's the time to leave."

Unlocking the main passageway door and not seeing anyone, they lead the horde out and up the precarious staircase motioning for quiet. Reaching the top, Mary asked, "Mr. Moe, what do we do now?"

"Miss Mary, we'll go on with the plan. We'll hold Inge by his arms as if he were our prisoner. Hey, maybe if we let the prisoners rush out ahead, they might confuse whoever is out there."

Before opening the door, Inge asked the prisoners, who of them will dare to unlock all the doors in the building? Without hesitation, several willingly volunteered.

It was a risky move. However, Inge knew which colored individuals were the boldest, strongest, and best to carry it off. Handing a bunch keys to each of those he chose, urging them on. Opening the door, they pushed the mass out while repeating, "You are free, run for your lives." A stampede erupted with a roar as they spilled out into the courtyard.

Holding Inge's arms, the three of them mixed into the middle of the chaos as a large force of Blues confronted them. In the swarm of confusion, their deception fooled the Blues, who allowed them to pass through to find Mary's confiscated transport parked in the courtyard.

Moe turned the crank over without it starting. Nervously, he tried again, and to their relief, on the third try, it flared up in a cloud of smoke. Driving slowly through the bedlam, they fooled the Blues by holding their blue hands out the windows as Inge crouched down in the back seat.

They reached the large wooden entrance door, which was

barred shut. Left with only one choice, Moe yelled, "Hold on," as he crashed through it and drove off, leaving the entire hullabaloo behind. He asked Inge, "Which way?"

"I know a shortcut. I used to sneak around here to see my love. Turn right here!" They soon reached the pebble *Road* and freedom.

Back in the great-room, Lucy asked, "So you turned around and came back here?"

"No, of course not! You see at the time we thought that would be the worst of it," Mary said as she rang her little bell.

"Then, what happened next?" I asked.

"It was only the beginning of our troubles," she said, as Samuel entered carrying a refreshment tray. "Children, let us take a break. You might like to have your refreshments out in the garden. We will continue the story when finished with our snacks."

"Yes, Miss Mary," I said.

Lucy, disappointed in having to stop, whispered under her breath, "Oh, rats," as each of us grabbed a bun-like treat and coolly and headed out.

CHAPTER 15 Learning About This World

Entering Mary's garden, the four of us poised at the split and scorched tree, wondering what caused it, not yet knowing. We rushed along the cobblestone walkway, which evolved into a competitive race to get the best seat on the oversized wrought iron settees, placed around a high coffee-like table in a protected patio area some fifty feet from the house.

Being captivated by what they were telling us, we were almost oblivious to the cartoon-like flowers and plants around us. Actually, it was beautiful, but it wasn't the right time to enjoy it.

"How are we going to get to the end of the *Road* if we're going to be arrested or even killed? I miss my mom and dad so much. We just disappeared. What must they be thinking?" Mar said.

"I'm not sure we'll ever get out of this place. In any case, I'd rather be dead than spend the rest of my life here," Lucy added.

"You're right. We must get back no matter what it takes," I said.

"Maybe we should make a Pact," Matt suggested. It being one of our childish practices we used all the time in our game playing.

"Good idea, let's do it," I said as I held out my hand. One by one, we placed our right hand on top of the others. I recited, "I promise to get back home no matter what it takes."

"I promise," Matt followed.

"I promise," Mar said, holding back a sob.

Lucy said, "Oh, please. Okay, I promise too."

Back in the house, Mary said, "Mr. Moe, do you think the children understand the dangers there will be? It still gives me the terrors when I think of what we went through," She took a sip of her tea, a brew not what Moe would call tea, for it tasted entirely different, more like honey, but had the same soothing effect.

"Yes, Miss Mary, I also have concerns. However, they're young and probably won't fully appreciate what they'll face until they're there."

"Mr. Moe, I am not sure we should tell them the rest of the story?"

"Miss Mary, you surely know if we didn't tell them now when we're out there, they'd ask why didn't we tell them before. What would we say then?"

"Of course you are correct. Mr. Moe. We must tell them all we know, and let them decide if they are willing to take the chance," Mary concluded, as she sat back and took another sip of tea.

Out in the garden, as I took the last gulp of my coolly, I observed, "Hey, I haven't seen any bugs. Has anyone, you know what I mean?"

"You're right, there're no bugs," Mar said, looking around.

"So? Who wants bugs anyway?" Lucy said.

"I don't know, aren't they needed to pollinate or something?" Matt wondered.

"It's like everything else here, weird," I said.

"I don't like this. It's too creepy. Let's get back to the house," Lucy said.

"Okay, they must be done by now."

We rushed back, looking in all directions as our movements evolved into another competitive race. As Moe heard us scrambling back, he said, "Miss Mary, I guess the time has come."

"They are so young. What are we to do, Mr. Moe?"

He shrugged his shoulders as he opened the double doors. "Come on in kids." As we poured in, he said, "Sit and get comfortable."

"Mr. Moe, how come there are no bugs around here?" I asked.

"You know, I noticed that right away too. I think Miss Mary can explain that."

She cleared her throat, searching for the right words, "I can answer that question only with what I understand. You see, as a child, I learned the history of my group. All children are required to learn the history of their color group, no matter how distorted or misleading it has become. I was taught that only those who came through the *Rock* populated our world. It was said, insects were also sucked through, likely carried on the bodies or clothing of the *Rockers*."

"Am I a *Rocker*?" Mar asked, perplexed.

"Yes, kids. I guess we're *Rockers*," Moe said, amused.

"Wow!" I exclaimed.

"Yes, it is true. However, the original *Rockers* were contentious and unruly. They were hateful, spiteful, and highly suspicious of one another. They resisted any form of order. They were a most troubled lot who couldn't get along. Mr. Moe has told me those were the very character flaws that drew them through in the first place, men and women alike."

"Do we have those flaws too?" Mar asked, feeling unsettled.

"Of course not. Right, Mr. Moe?"

"Why, that's right, Johnny? That's interesting. I haven't given that any thought. Yes, and it brings up a good question, why were we pulled through? Miss Mary, what do you think?"

"My, I cannot even guess why. However, one would think there must have been a reason.

"Maybe it's what we must learn to understand?" I said.

After a slight pause, Moe said, "Miss Mary, maybe we should continue telling our story."

"Yes, indeed, Mr. Moe. Well then, as you can see, our population multiplied over thousands of cycles. However, for some reason, a couple of lifetimes ago, fewer and fewer came through, until the flow completely stopped.

"Of course, that was until Mr. Moe arrived, being the first time in at least a cycle the portal opened. However, at first, no one knew of his arrival, except for McCloud and those in this house, which was not public knowledge until we traveled to Bluetropolis. I do not understand why it has started up again. Especially now, with you who lack those dreadful character flaws. It is most curious.

"In any case, among the first arrivals, strong leaders arouse banding together those who were like-minded. Each group pitted themselves against the opposing groups, which caused conflicts, ranging from simple arguments to outright fighting.

"Sadly, it took generations before the children of the children of the children grew weary of the strife. Then one day, the strongest and meanest leaders mysteriously began to disappear, which brought fear to those who took their place, so those new leaders decided to declare a truce, in which each group was to live separately, except for trade, which was necessary for the survival of all.

"Therefore, each group carved out an independent city, and to this day, the truce still holds, except for those who live in the outer parts, who we know little about."

"What happened to those leaders who disappeared?"

"Lucy, in my youth, they never spoke about what happened to them. As we studied our history, our teachers made it clear we weren't to ask about them. However, I do believe no one living today knows. I am afraid, by not speaking of it, that knowledge has been lost."

"Do you think it had anything to do with the *White Light*?"

"Mr. Moe, when I was young, I tried not to think about it. However, some secretly whispered, it was the work of assassins, which brought a greater fear to the new leaders."

"I can see how it would."

"Yes, Mr. Moe. Then, as if miraculously, over an extended period, those who lived in each city incredibly took on similar characteristics and began to resemble each other. The most significant was in how their skin color gradually changed to all the variations marking each person as a citizen of their particular city."

"Is that true? You mean the color of their skin changed to look like the others in their city?"

"Yes, Johnny, with each succeeding generation, the change in color slowly became more pronounced. More important was how an individual's thinking also came into line with those in their city. I believe it happened due to their enforced separation and perhaps inbreeding over many lifetimes."

"Yes, evolution can act in strange ways," Moe said.

"Why couldn't they just communicate and end all the separation?" Matt asked.

"I can see how you would think it to be the solution.

However, communications with other cities concerning what was happening were outlawed, "Mr. Moe told me about your televisions, telephones, radios, and newspapers in your world, which allows everyone to communicate. We do not have such things to help us. I have little idea of what is happening elsewhere. Inge was the first person I ever met who spoke freely of other cities." Most do not dare to break those laws in fear of punishment.

"But, Miss Mary, what about all the books on these shelves?"

"Mar, let me clarify. Communication within a city is allowed, but not between cities. What is written in the books here is only legal if it's about Inbetweeners with no mention of others."

"Inbetweeners?" Lucy wondered.

"Is that the city you live in?" I asked.

"I don't live in or belong to a city, so to speak, I am an Inbetweener. A free person who lives in-between the domains in unclaimed territories. The laws or rules of any of the cities do not bind us, as long as we remain in the area between the cities."

"You mean there are no laws or rules here?" Lucy reasoned.

"Oh, to the contrary, we also have laws and rules, which in most cases are just as stringent, except there is no one to enforce them."

"Are the laws and rules like ours?"

"Well, Johnny, let me tell you what they are. What is most important is one must not interfere with another's business or intentionally do unnecessary bodily or monetarily harm, and of course, we must not employ or marry someone of another color. Each of us knows the rules and follows them without question. Although I guess I violated them by helping Mr. Moe, however, at first, no one knew."

"That's kind of like the things we try to do in our world, except for the not mixing."

"Johnny, from what Mr. Moe has told me, it seems so. The Inbetweeners are the descendants of the first successful merchant families who traded with all the cities. We are permitted to live in peace as long as we remain businesslike and neutral. I believe to live in my zone is the safest."

"Mr. Moe told us all the people on the *Road* were merchants. They're of different colors. You are White. You know what I mean?"

"Yes, Johnny, I believe I do. My father and husband were Inbetweeners and were pure white, as I am, along with our helpers and Slops who work for us, for we could not have those types of relationships with those of another color. Those you see on the *Road* are licensed merchants, chosen by each city to be sent out to do the trading only for their city.

"Of course, there are also those who like to travel, like Inge. However, one needs approval to enter another's city. As Inbetweeners, we deal with all the cities but only through their merchants."

"Miss Mary, don't forget the Finders. And kids, let's not forget a person's color is only skin deep."

Oh, yes, the Finders. They are the ones who travel in secret to find out what is taking place in other cities."

"You mean like spies?"

"That's right, Lucy. They're like spies in our world. They work in secret."

"Yes, Mr. Moe, it seems some in my world think it is important to know what others are doing. And, from what I understand, those caught finding face punishment," Mary added.

"Maybe, our worlds aren't so different."

With a sigh, she concluded, "Maybe not Matt... Children, getting back to the question of where the insects are. The legends tell that the insects became numerous growing in size and stinging people to distraction, being a danger to all, for some even died from their stings. It became so bad the people banded together and drove the insects out into the wilderness, where they now live and apparently flourish in their isolated territories. I have never seen an insect and can only imagine how dreadful they are."

"Yes, and with them being so fierce, I can't imagine how the people were able to run the insects off permanently," Moe said.

"Wow!" I exclaimed.

"Don't they have to pollinate the plants?" Matt again wondered.

"What is meant by pollinate?"

"Miss Mary, I think we should get back to telling the story of what happened after our escape."

"Yes, let's," Lucy added.

"Oh well… Let me see where were we?"

"You were driving out of the Blue's zone after escaping from jail."

"That's right, Johnny, I remember. Once back on the *Road* and had driven for a short distance, to our alarm, several Blue transports came up behind us. Mr. Moe sped up to get away when all of a sudden, there were transports in front, heading straight towards us. Coming at us from both directions, it was a most dangerous situation…

CHAPTER 16 Entering The Wild Zone

Three years earlier, during their jail escape, Moe, Mary, and Inge realized they were being pursued by Blue transports from behind. As they sped up, they saw others in front, heading straight towards them. Mary yelled, "They are going to crash into us!" An unbelievable occurrence.

Moe abruptly made a sharp right turn onto a dirt side-road, which fortunately just happened to be there at the right moment. That move caused the dimwitted Blue drives to run into each other head-on as the sounds of metal and glass colliding erupted. How stupid they were.

Inge, who was wedged in the back seat among the supplies, stuck his head up and gave out a "Ha-ha," Dumbstruck and relieved, they drove on with no one following. Further along, the side-road became more like a trail than a road. Inge said, "Moe, I do not think you made a good choice by turning in here."

"Why not, we got away, didn't we? They're not following us anymore."

"And they are not going to follow us."

"Why not, Inge?" Mary asked.

"Why not! Because we are in a Wild Zone! That is why not."

"So, what's wrong with being in a wild zone?"

"Mr. Moe, I know what he means. A Wild Zone is a place people should not go."

"Miss Mary, they're not following us anymore. We're safe now."

"Of course, they are not following us. Nobody with any sense would come into a Wild Zone where wild, dangerous creatures live."

"Inge, you're frightening me."

"Yes, please stop frightening Miss Mary."

"I am not trying to frighten anyone. I am just saying, you should be frightened of being in here."

"Come on, you know we can't go back, you know what faces us there. So, our only option is to go around. Don't you agree?"

"I guess I have to agree, but I am not sure coming in here was the best thing."

"Please, Inge, you are frightening me even more with this talk."

"Okay, Miss Mary, I'll drive as fast as I can to get out of here."

Back in the great-room, recovering from the Blues episode, we were thrust into the hearing of another scary situation.

"Gee, the Wild Zone sounds frightening to me," Mar said.

"It really does. What happened then?" Lucy asked.

"You took care of any danger, right, Mr. Moe?" I asked.

After a pause. Matt asked, "Didn't you, Mr. Moe?"

"Mr. Moe, I think you should continue with our story."

"Yes, Miss Mary, I think so… Let me see where we were? Okay… We were driving in the Wild Zone when we came upon a large group of animals crossing the trail. Creatures I'd never seen before. Kids, none of the creatures in this world are anything like the animals where we come from. Only parts of them would be recognizable. I believe they were here long before people arrived, for I don't think they came from our side of the *Rock*, for they're too weird and were never mentioned in any of our legends or history.

"However, the only way to describe this bunch was they looked like a cross between a buffalo and a zebra. Yes, that's it. Their faces were similar to Buffalos, only with long orange hair and three menacing horns resembling Unicorn horns only shorter and twisted like corkscrews. Their bodies were zebra-like, only much larger with orange and blue stripes oddly running horizontally. They were most unusual. However, I wasn't yet concerned, and being left with little choice, we were forced to wait until their countless numbers moved on. Only…"

Mary interrupted. "Yes, except Mr. Moe was impatient and blew the transport's horn causing the creatures to look at us. It was evident the piercing sound agitated them. Yet, Mr. Moe continued to sound the horn as their rage swelled.

"Suddenly, they approached us, butting their horns against my transport. Then, to our horror, they began to push us until they flipped us over, causing us to tumble down the embankment just off the trail, inflicting considerable damage to my poor transport. Thankfully, if it was not for the safety ties holding us in place, I'm sure we would have been seriously injured."

Still feeling the guilt, remembering it was his doing, Moe meekly said, "Yes, Miss Mary, but we did survive, didn't we?"

"Barely, Mr. Moe."

"I know… Kids, fortunately, the transport landed upright. However, we had to sit there until the creatures moved on into the jungle."

"And children, it took forever. However, finally, with them gone, it was a miracle the engine was able to start, even though my beautiful new transport looked like a wreck."

"You know, Miss Mary, it could have been worse."

"Oh, really?"

"Was that the car that was in front of Mr. Moe's house?" I asked.

"It certainly looked like a wreck?" Lucy added.

"Yes, children, and it was my favorite one."

"Right… Anyway, I was able to drive up the embankment and back onto the trail."

"Yes, Mr. Moe, we were most fortunate to travel safely for some distance, although an occasional creature would dash across our path, keeping us on edge. That was until we encountered the next sickening dilemma. I must admit, we had no idea of what lay ahead, and without much thought, we continued on our way. How could we have known?"

"Yes, Miss Mary, that's right. "Kids, you wouldn't believe what came next?"

Enthralled, we shook our heads side to side, not knowing what even to guess.

"Well, let me tell you… We came upon the biggest snake I ever saw, which was slowly undulating across our path."

"Wow," I said as the girls gasped in revulsion.

"Kids, only I don't think it was actually a snake. You see, its head looked more like a dog or a dragon with a long nose, pointed ears, and fearsome looking k-9 teeth. It was black with red and white stripes spiraling around the full length of its snake-like body.

"It was more than two feet thick at its middle and perhaps a hundred feet long, for we couldn't see it from head to tail. Therefore, this time, I stopped, not wanting anything bad to happen. I turned the engine off, and we sat as still as possible in the hope it would just pass us by."

"Yes… Only children, instead of leaving it turned its big ugly head towards us and slithered in our direction. If that was not sickening enough, it had a large forked tongue that moved in and out of its big drooling mouth. We were petrified as it slowly started to wrap its body around my transport, and in doing so, it prevented us from opening the doors and running for our lives. It squeezed tighter and tighter until the metal of my poor transport began making noises as if it was going to collapse in on us."

"Yes, Miss Mary, that's right. Kids, I had to think fast. I remembered Samuel packed knives in the front storage box. I grabbed one, opened a window, and frantically jabbed its underbelly. However, its skin was so tough the blade couldn't penetrate it. Although, I could see it reacted to my jabbing. In desperation, I kept doing it with all my strength countless times until it started to wiggle away from the knife.

"Seeing that, Miss Mary and Inge joined in with the other knives Samuel wisely packed. We jabbed and jabbed wherever we could. Thankfully, the creature couldn't take any more agitation and gave up and glided off, disappearing into the brush."

Mary jumped in and said, "Children, the three of us were so exhausted we collapsed in our seats, for it was one of the most unpleasant experiences any of us ever had. It still gives me chills thinking about it. I wouldn't want to go through it again. However, at that point, we had little choice but to continue on our way…

In the Wild Zone, Mary said, "Mr. Moe, I do not think I can take much more of this, could we please get out of this awful place?"

"Nor can I. But until we are away from here, we will not be safe," Inge added.

Stopping, Moe banged his head on the steering wheel,

confessing, "I'm sorry I got both of you into this. I guess I'm just an old fool."

Mary, seeing him weakening, said, "Oh, Mr. Moe, you are a fool if you think you are a fool. You did get us out of that dreadful jail, did you not?"

"Why, yes, Miss Mary, I did. And, I'm going to get us out of this place too."

"There you go, Mr. Moe."

"We will see," Inge mumbled.

They drove on.

Back in the great-room, Lucy asked, "Miss Mary, after the creepy snake thing went away, were you able to get out of there?

"Oh, no, child. The story is not over."

"Are we going to have to go through that place too?"

"Not at all, Mar, all one has to do is not to turn onto that dirt road," Moe said.

"Wow! Then what happened next?"

"Well, Johnny, things went fine as daylight started to dim, so we decided to stop and eat in the hope of getting some sleep. I remembered hearing in our world if you build a fire, it'll keep the animals away. So…"

Having built a blazing fire in the Wild Zone as darkness closed over them, Mary asked, "My Janis packed our meals in packets, would you like them hot or cold?"

"Well, Miss Mary, since we have the fire, let's heat them up."

"I have not had a real meal in over a cycle. What is in them?"

"Inge, I do not know. They must be opened to see what they contain." She fumbled with a tray still shaken from the events of the day.

Hey, why don't we heat up three of them and take potluck? We'll have to eat them all, no matter what. Is it all right with you, Inge?" Moe asked.

"It is all right with me. Food is food, and potluck is something else."

Moe took the tray, "Let me handle this, Miss Mary. "Thank you, Mr. Moe," glad to be relieved of that chore and able to relax. Her emotional wear and tear were showing.

He placed some rocks around the fire to support the tray. When ready, Inge took his first bite, relishing it, "Hmm, real food, yum, that is good."

It wasn't easy for them to relax as they sat around the fire, for the sounds of the jungle surrounded them. The yelps, yaps, howls, baying, meowing, bellowing, growling, and other unrecognizable sounds of the night became louder as they ate.

Also, out of the dark, shining sets of eyes began to appear in the near and far distance. There was one set, then another followed by more. Mary abruptly stood, with food in hand, and said, "Let's eat in the transport."

"Yes, Miss Mary, but first, let's each choose a piece of wood we can use as a club if it becomes necessary."

"Oh my Mr. Moe," she said. Filled with anxiety, they quickly selected a club from the fallen branches lying around. With the help of Inge, Moe threw more wood on the fire before they piled into the transport.

With the doors locked and windows up, they finished their meals and then tilted the seats back, attempting to make it as comfortable as possible. They sensed movement outside, and the numerous sets of eyes staring at them, "Let's get some sleep, so we'll be ready to get out of here at first light," Moe said.

"Are we going to get out of here, Mr. Moe?" Mary questioned.

Inge said, "Who knows? For now, I am going to get some sleep. Goodnight."

"Don't worry, Miss Mary, things will be all right. Now, please try to get some sleep."

"I will try Mr. Moe," as she pulled her blanket over her head as not to see any of those staring eyes, not knowing if she would be able to sleep...

Back in the great-room, Mary said, "Children, it was most difficult to sleep under the circumstances. None of us wanted to disturb the other, so we laid there in silence for some time listening to the sounds around us, hoping the creatures would not break through the windows and attack us. Thankfully, out of sheer exhaustion, we were able to finally fall asleep."

"How did you get out of there?" Lucy asked.

"Wow, what happened then?" I asked captivated.

"Mr. Moe, do not keep the children in suspense, continue the story…"

"Moe continued the story…"

CHAPTER 17 The Frightening Confrontation

In the Wild Zone, the next morning, Inge shook Moe and Mary, awakening them from a deep sleep, saying, "It's time to get going." They roused themselves and looked around to find not a creature in sight, thankfully. Inge handed out packets of breakfast food, suggesting they eat on the way, all too glad to get out of there.

"Hoping nothing else dreadful would happen, they drove on. Moe made every left-hand turn looking to find a way back onto the pebble *Road*."

Mary asked, "Inge, do you have any idea of how much longer it will take? I mean, when do you think we'll be out of this zone?"

"We'll be out when we are out."

"Miss Mary, I don't think he knows."

"I don't think you know."

"You got that right, Inge. Anyway, I don't like this," Moe said, as tensions grew.

Still rattled from the day before and feeling most vulnerable, Mary lashed out, "What do you mean, you do not like this? I do not like this either, at all. Mr. Moe, I want to go home." It was a clear sign of her weakening, causing Moe's concern.

They approached a rise in the trail where a luminous glow radiated from the other side. Reaching the crest, Moe hit the brakes jarring them all. Staring straight ahead with his jaw dropped Mary following the line of his gaze and let out a gasp as she saw stretched across the valley a vast number of creatures. A herd so massive, there was no visible way around them. Stunned, she asked, "Mr. Moe, what are we going to do?"

He stepped on the accelerator, blurting out, "Miss Mary, we're going to get out of here." Unfortunately, the hard stop stalled the engine. He turned the crank several times to no avail as the horde slowly moved towards them. He said, "It seems to be flooded or something, we'll have to wait until they pass."

Inge took hold and said, "Let us hope they are harmless. If not, we better defend the transport," grabbing his club, he boldly stepped out into the open. His move was most uncharacteristic and didn't make much sense, why he did it was a mystery, even to him.

"Mr. Moe, we are not going to be able to fight them off, are we?"

Also sparked with unjustified courage or perhaps an underestimation of the possible consequences, he said, "Inge is right, Miss Mary. We must keep them from damaging the transport any more. Grab your club and let's follow him." She meekly followed, although terrified, not knowing what else to do.

Moe guarded the front end while Inge stood on the left side of the transport, and at a loss, Mary stood on the right side, saying, "Mr. Moe, I think we could die."

By this time, Inge had apparently gone too far, as he said, "To die is to die."

With his knees shaking, Moe mustered up as much courage as he could manage, "Miss Mary, we're not going to die, we must be strong. Everything will be all right. I hope."

"Easy for you to say," Inge mumbled.

"Oh my, oh my," Mary said, trembling hardly able to compose herself.

Moe took a big gulp. Suddenly, they were possessed with a spirit of courage, which defied reason when considering the fear they felt. Waiting for an expected attack, what seemed like forever, they held their clubs like baseball bats ready to hit a home run.

The creatures slowly and quietly moved in around them as they walked erect on their hind legs. They were about six feet tall with bodies similar to hyenas, only larger. Instead of having hoofs or paws, they had feet resembling a human's foot, and their long arms had hands with three opposing articulated fingers. Their faces were akin to chimpanzees, only rounder with cartoonish-like expressions. But, the most striking feature was their long mixed yellow and white curly hair that had a subtle luminescent glow that bedazzled the three of them.

Surrounded by such strange beasts almost overwhelmed them

as the creatures moved to within a couple of yards of them, to where they stopped and just stood there staring at the three of them in silence…

Back in the great-room, we were utterly taken up in the story, Lucy asked, "Mr. Moe did they attack you? Did you have to kill them?"

"Well, not exactly," he said, as he sheepishly looked at Mary.

She said, "Children, you could not imagine how frightening it was being surrounded by those creators, not knowing what they might do."

"Mr. Moe, I'll bet you chased them off," I said.

"I guess you got away; otherwise, you wouldn't be here now, right?"

"That's right, Lucy. Although, at that moment, we felt it was going to be our end. However, it is hard to believe what happened next. Mr. Moe, would you please get on with the story."

"Yes, Miss Mary. Well, we stood face to face with them as they examined us. Then…"

Confronted in the Wild Zone, Moe held his club at the ready as the creatures came within arm's reach. Suddenly, one of them poked him, followed by a menacing snarl. He held back as the unpleasant thought of having to strike one of them gripped him. Then another nudged him as others advanced.

Inge yelled, "Hit them! Whack them!" As he said that, one of them pushed him to the howl of the throng, seemingly to be challenging or testing him. Without hesitation, Inge landed a blow squarely on its head, knocking it out cold, which brought a stark silence among the throng. Sickened by Inge's action, Mary and Moe froze, waiting for a strong reaction to such a deed.

Then another one pushed Moe. Inge yelled, "Whack him!" Although fearful, Moe believed he must now act and swung his club in a circle knocking several of them down. Although terrified, Mary was able to shake her club in a menacing manner keeping them away from her. However, instead of attacking, the creatures backed off and just stood there staring at them as if confused.

The trio held their ground with that unnatural courage that

kept them above their dread — holding their clubs at the ready, as they tried to anticipate what was going to happen next.

After a tense moment, far back in the Horde, a commotion ensued. A path cleared through the throng, allowing a small procession of creatures to pass through approaching them. It took a while before they were close enough to make them out. One of them was noticeably larger than all the others. After the long walk, they stopped only feet away, as those who were clobbered hobbled back, disappearing into the horde. None of whom seemed seriously injured.

The big one was more than a foot taller than Moe. It came right up to the three of them, sniffing, studying, and mesmerizing them with its luminescent glow. Then without warning, it grabbed Moe and lifted him above its head. It turned in a circle holding him as high as it could to the loud whooping sounds from the horde.

Mary, believing the creature was going to harm Moe, reacted in a state of total panic. Screaming, she rushed up to it from behind and stuck it solidly on the head. It collapsed in a lump with Moe landing on top of it. A tumultuous moan rippled through the horde. Thankfully, instead of attacking the creatures backed off and just stood there stunned as they expressed mournful whimpering sounds. Clearly, the creatures were just as horrified as the three of them were. Not knowing what to make of the situation.

Moe jumped up, pulling himself together, and said, "Let's get out of here." As he did, the big creature let out a whimper.

Mary said, "Wait, it is bleeding. I split its head open," Overcoming her fear and collecting her wits, she said, "We cannot leave it in this condition, it will die."

"Miss Mary, we better go," Moe said, although not sure if the Dragon would start.

"Mr. Moe, I am not going to be responsible for this creature's death. They did not harm us, did they?"

"She is right, Moe. They did not harm us."

"Oh no, Miss Mary, what do you think it was going to do with me?" However, he was unable to resist the plea shown in her eyes and quickly gave in, saying, "Okay... But let's hurry."

Mary ordered, "Inge, would you please get the aid box from the transport, it should be under a back seat."

She knelt by the unconscious creature, who incredibly had lost its glow. Inge rushed and handed her the box. She took a cloth pad out of it and placed it on the wound, ordering, "Mr. Moe pressure is needed to stop the bleeding. Please hold and press it in this way."

"Miss Mary, where did you learn how to do this?"

"Oh well, Mr. Moe, I have done more things than you know about."

"I guess you have. Miss Mary, that was courageous of you to save me from getting hurt."

"Mr. Moe, I know you would have done the same for me." Flustered by her confidence in him, he humbly thanked her.

Back in the great-room, I asked, "Did the creature die?"

"Did you kill it?"

"Please, Lucy. I just thought it was going to injure Mr. Moe. I only did what I had to do, as I saw it at that moment."

"Did the creature die?"

"Oh, my. Mar, we assumed when it lost its glow, it was dying. Mr. Moe, would you please get on with the story."

"Yes, Miss Mary... Well, as we helped the Big One, as we named it, the rest of the creatures backed farther away and just stood there watching. Fortunately, we were able to stop the bleeding. Then..."

Kneeling by the Big One in the Wild Zone, Moe asked, "What's next, Miss Mary?"

"Mr. Moe, if we do not close the wound, I believe it will not survive."

"Yes, I see its light has gone out," half-joking, to no one's amusement.

She ordered, "Inge, please get the sewing box from under the seat."

Taken from the aid box, she sprinkled a powder on the wound that was open down to the bone. Then she took a threaded needle out of the sewing box. Dipped it a tiny bottle of liquid, then proceeded to stitch the wound. Watching, Moe felt weak in the knees and had to turn away.

When finished, she asked, "Mr. Moe, please hold this cloth in this way while I tie it around its head." With the creature still unconscious and having done all she could, they sat back and noted how still and quiet the horde had become looking like statues.

Moe speculated, "This creature must be significant."

"It might be their leader, their king, the dominant one, or just the biggest," Inge said.

"Oh my, if that is so, what might they do if he dies?"

"I'll try to start the transport." They watched him with hope. It ignited a couple of times, then stalled. He pumped the accelerator a few times and turned it over again, however, it wouldn't ignite. He again banged his head on the steering wheel.

Mary, knowing how to deal with this side of his temperament, kindly said, "It will be all right, Mr. Moe. Soon it will start." Not knowing if it would.

"Miss Mary, I'm so sorry for getting both of you into this," as he banged his head again.

"You are an old fool. It was my idea to come with you."

"Come on, Moe, give it more time. Eventually, it will start, Inge said. Anyway, we're safe for the time being, at least as long as the Big One is still alive."

The Big One let out a painful moan. Understanding the need, Mary ordered Inge, "Get a cup of water," asking Moe to help her sit it up." Mixing a different powder in the water, she slowly fed it to it, "I hope this will help with the pain." She covered the creature with a blanket and put a pillow under its head, that Inge retrieved from the transport.

After doing as much as could be done, and only then, she let out a sigh. They looked around to assess their situation further. The horde was watching their every move as they backed off some thirty feet. Moe said, "Since we're going to be here a while, let's build a fire, I'm famished."

"Mr. Moe, is this a time to eat?"

He said as he picked up some fallen branches, "Miss Mary, if we don't eat, they won't have to kill us, we'll die of starvation."

"Well, you are correct, Mr. Moe. Then I will help with the wood too."

The horde backed off as they allowed the three of them to

move out and collect arms full of kindling. As Moe lit the fire, the creatures expelled a soft sound, which was an indication they had never seen a fire before. It was interesting to see the creature's reaction, as the dancing flames captivated them.

As the food heated up, Mary said, "I do not think they want to harm us."

"Maybe not. Not as long as we have control of the Big One. Right Inge?"

"Yes, I think we better stay close to it,"

"I agree. We might have to stay until he is well enough to survive on his own."

"Miss Mary, we could turn the transport around and speed back to where we came from. I think we can outrun them."

"Yes, Moe, let us go back through the dangers we barely escaped. Good idea," Inge said.

"Let us keep our eyes on the task at hand and nurse the Big One back to health."

"Miss Mary, how long do you think it'll take?"

"Mr. Moe, I believe when and if it gets its glow back. Do you not think so, Inge?"

"I never heard of that glow. However, what makes sense, makes sense."

"Okay, Miss Mary, we'll help the Big One."

Just then, the Big One let out a weak grunt, followed by making chewing motions, being most sympathetic. "What's it doing?"

"Why, I think he wants something to eat."

Moe tried to feed it some of their food. It spits it out in disgust. "It does not eat our food. Look out there?" Inge said.

Seeing some of the creatures busily chewing big leaves, Moe using his imagination, stood and articulated with exaggerated hand motions, indicating the Big One needed to eat. The creatures watched his gyrations of crewing, pointing, and waving his hands, which he continued until he got a reaction. A few at the parameter seemed to communicate with simple grunts to each other. Astonishingly, one of them ran halfway towards them with an armful of leaves, dropping them as close as it dared, and just as quickly running back.

"They are not so dumb after all," Inge said.

"Oh, my."

Moe scurried out, picking up the leaves, bringing them to Mary. She slowly fed the Big One as it devoured the leaves as if it hadn't eaten for some time. "The poor thing, he probably needs some water."

Inge volunteered, "I will get the water. I will do whatever you say. Just keep it alive."

When it had eaten its fill, she gave it another cup of the medicated water, saying, "This will help it sleep," as she fluffed up the pillow and tucked the Big One in as if it were a baby.

With little hope of relaxing, they were only able to sit back watching the Big One and evaluating the mood of the horde. It remained that way for a time until exhaustion took its toll on Mary. She said, "I cannot do this any longer, I must rest."

"Please, Miss Mary, lie down for a while. I'll do the watching."

"Then I will take a nap too so I could relieve you later," Inge added.

"Okay, the first watch is mine."

Once Mary and Inge were nestled in their sleeping bags, it wasn't long before they were asleep, for their stress level exhausted them. Moe sat there, feeding the fire while watching the Big One.

As darkness fell, the creatures began to coil up in fetal positions facing the three of them as they watched every move Moe made until one by one sleep overtook them. Amazingly, as each creature did so, their luminance glow turned off, eventually leaving him in total darkness except for the fire.

His thoughts ranged from being in charge of his destiny to being a hopeless failure, devoid of any chance of doing anything right. In his world many years ago, he had given up trying to feel good about himself, accepting he couldn't live up to his own expectations. However, at times, he had renewed hopes of redemption, especially with the help of the Pastor's counseling. Those hopeful episodes only lasted long enough to save him from slipping into a permanent internal world, lacking reality.

In this alternate world, McCloud and Mary treated him with a measure of respect, allowing him to feel good about himself. A feeling he hadn't felt for many years. They gave him a sincere regard without recriminations about the miss-steps he too often took. However, now he wasn't only concerned about himself, but also for Mary's well-being. He felt he must protect her at any cost, determined to get her safely out of the Wild Zone as soon as possible.

As he sat there, he cycled those ruminations in an attempt to make sense of what was happening.

Sometime later, Inge awoke and said, "I will watch now. You get some sleep." Moe jokingly pointed out, "It looks like their lights shut off when sleeping."

Inge smiled and said, "Yes, indeed. Now, get some rest."

Moe packed himself into his sleeping bag and, just as fast, fell asleep.

CHAPTER 18 Moving On

Back in the great-room, Lucy asked, "Mr. Moe, you mean you had to sleep with those creatures all around you?"

"Yes, we did. There was no choice. We didn't know what was ahead, and we well knew what was behind."

"Oh, Lucy, you couldn't imagine how frightening it was. At that point, we did not know if they would attack us, or if we would ever get out of the Wild Zone alive. However, I knew one thing; we had to help the Big One. I could not have his death on my conscience."

"I know what you mean, Miss Mary. Did it live?" Mar asked.

"And how did you get away?"

"Well, Johnny, believe it or not, there was an unexpected outcome…"

Back in the Wild Zone, Mary awoke suddenly in the full light of morning. Reconstructing her thoughts, she looked around and asked, "Inge, you did not wake me for my turn?"

"You needed the rest."

Getting out of her sleeping bag, she went over to the Big One and put her hand on its forehead. "It seems to be all right," she said, relieved. Having felt her touch, it opened its eyes and embraced its head, moaning in pain.

After applying an ointment to the wound, the only other thing she could think of doing was to pet it, an act which miraculously calmed it. It let out a soft yelp as it moved its mouth in the now-familiar chewing motion. "The poor thing is hungry again."

Again, they looked towards the horde for help, who were busily chewing those leaves. Inge used the motions Moe used the day before to indicate the Big One was hungry. After some commotion, one creature came towards them with a bunch of leaves in hand, dropping them and quickly running back. In seeing that, Inge let out a "Ha!" Then said, "It is most amazing," as he gathered up the leaves.

Feeding it, she said, "It is almost like a person. How can I tell it how sorry I am?"

"Maybe, you can just say, you are sorry."

"Yes, of course… I am very sorry, Mr. Big One." It looked at her almost as if it understood what she was trying to convey. She asked Inge, "Do you think it understands?"

"To understand is to understand."

"Thank you, Inge," she genially replied, correctly interpreting Inge's language.

Moe awoke and said, "Good morning Miss Mary."

"Good morning Mr. Moe."

After a moment, Inge said, "Good morning, me too," for no one greeted him.

They both chimed in with, "Good morning, Inge."

"Inge, would you please get a cup of water." Adding some powder, she fed it to the Big One and said, "I hope this will help."

"Miss Mary, can we leave now?"

"Please, Mr. Moe. Someone has to take out the stitches."

"I guess that someone is us?"

"Inge, I am afraid so, if they are not removed infection might set in and out here, it will not survive an infection."

"Miss Mary, it's only a creature."

"Yes, Mr. Moe, it is only a creature whose head I split open. I am not going to be responsible for it dying because of what I did." Not wanting to cause her any unhappiness, he backed off.

Able to sit back and evaluate their situation, Mary said, "They seem to be calm. They do not appear to be as fearsome as we thought they were yesterday. They are going about their business peacefully. I believe we misjudged them. Mr. Moe, what are we to do?"

"Well, Miss Mary, yesterday they did seem quite hostile, and we did what we had to do to defend ourselves. Perhaps, they should've been nicer to us."

"Yes, Mr. Moe, but they are just simple creatures. How could they have known how to treat us?"

"You are right, Mary, and come to think of it, you are right too, Moe."

"And you are also right, Inge," Mary added.

"I don't understand. I never did understand. How am I supposed to gain an understanding if I don't understand it from the outset?"

"Mr. Moe, with all this stress, I had not given that enough thought. We must gain that understanding to get you back to your world. I must now give it more attention."

"Understanding is sometimes beyond understanding," Inge said, summing it up.

Later, unexpectedly, a group of seven creatures emerged from the multitude and approached them. Two out front with the others huddled behind. They cautiously moved up close. The two-out front carried armfuls of leaves. The others held a variety of small melon-like fruits. Stopping a few yards away, the five behind pushed the two ahead, urging them to move even closer. They nervously went right up to the Big One and dropped the leaves. The others quickly placed the fruits at the feet of the three of them and nervously indicated they were for them to eat by using primitive broad motions and grunts. Then all seven scurried back to the horde.

"Oh my, they want to help us. It is their way of thanking us?" a disarmed Mary could only say.

"Most interesting, we hurt them, and they want to thank us," Inge quipped.

"Well then, let's eat breakfast. I'll start with these fruits."

"Oh yes, of course, Mr. Moe," Mary said, with a soft understanding chuckle...

Back in the great-room, Mar asked, "Did they really start to feed you?"

"You bet, and those fruits were the tastiest I ever ate. Not only that, but they brought more every few hours."

"I'll bet they became your pets."

"Lucy, don't make fun of those creatures."

"Johnny, I'm not making fun. I just feel sorry for them," she retorted.

"That's right, Lucy. At that point, we also felt sorry for them. However, it confused us even more so in trying to understanding what we were supposed to do. Was that not so, Mr. Moe?"

"Yes, that's right, Miss Mary. However, what was even more interesting was later in the day Miss Mary had little trouble in coaxing one of the females who brought more leaves to help feed the Big One. And then, to our surprise, the next time they brought food, three of them boldly surrounded the Big One."

"Oh my yes, then to our astonishment, one of them began to lick the Big One's wound. I quickly realized it was their way of nursing it, and relieved to have them take that burden. In fact, the healing power of the licking was miraculous, and within hours the wound was healed almost enough to take out the stitches. By then, the Big One was fully awake and looked better, and amazingly its coat was regaining its radiant glow as it calmly sat there watching us."

"Yes, Miss Mary, it did like being waited on. Anyhow, after seeing its remarkable recovery, we were able to get some rest and had a chance to discuss what to do next…"

In the Wild Zone sitting around the fire as darkness fell, the time had come to make some decisions. In the now calmer environment, Mary was able to bring up the big question on her mind, "Mr. Moe, do you really want to go back to your world?" perhaps, expressing a secret wish.

"Yes, I have things there," he answered.

"Mr. Moe, what do you still have there?"

"Well, Miss Mary, I have… Then I have… After a moment of reflection, he admitted, "I guess whatever I'd had died in me when I was still young enough to care—when I was young, I had such a zeal for life and cared so deeply about the world and those around me. I wanted to be perfect. I wanted to contribute. I wanted to believe in something good. However, I found I wasn't perfect. I fell into the same corruption most people allowed into their lives. I was unable to cope with that contradiction, which led me into a state they called depression.

"Unfortunately, in my world, if one behaves differently,

people are likely to shun them. Oh, how I regretted that rejection. As a result, it allowed me to fall deeper into a dark pit, which tried to close in on me, although it took many years to see that in me, it made me believe I was a hopeless failure. Miss Mary, maybe that's the reason I was pulled through the *Rock*. I don't know?"

"Mr. Moe, do you really want to go back to that?" she asked, with sorrow.

After some thought, he gave in, saying, "No, I guess not Miss Mary. There's nothing left there for me, although there is little in this world."

"Now, Mr. Moe, there is our friendship, is that not so!" she said indignantly.

"Oh yes, Miss Mary, it's the most valuable thing in my life. What I meant was, as far as a career goes," he said, as he quickly and apologetically back stepped.

"Mr. Moe, I want to go home," she pleaded. "Could you please take me home?"

Not at all sure, he felt a sense of confusion deep in his heart. He could only say, "Yes, all right, Miss Mary, I'll take you home." He then quickly realized if he were able to make it back to his world, he probably would have to leave her. That thought easily allowed him to embrace the decision to stay.

Pleased, she smiled as Inge let out an almost audible "Irk" in reaction.

She turned to him, as he sat there, feeling a bit awkward and asked, "Inge, what do you think?"

Also, after some thought, he understood and lamented, "I guess I only want to go back to my love Ofeela. I do miss her so. I have not seen her since my imprisonment."

Taking charge, Moe said, "All right, as soon as the Big One is well enough, we'll all go home. For now, let's get some sleep."

"Yes, but before we do, help me take out the stitches," Mary concluded.

When they awoke the next morning, they were astounded to find the Big One along with the entire herd was gone, and in their place stood a *Man in White*. So shaken by his presence, it took several long seconds for Mary to ask, "Sir, would you like something to eat?"

"No, thank you, Mary, I must go."

"Sir, What are we suppose to do now?" Moe asked.

"It is said; To successfully travel *The Road of Understanding* to its end, one must truly want to gain the understanding that is to be understood. One must dedicate themselves, giving all their strength and wits to that end. One must become a hero, a soldier, and a person of high integrity. To seek the end of the *Road,* unprepared is unwise. I must go now."

"But, sir, where would you go out here?" Moe asked, knowing he wouldn't get an answer.

"I will be just fine, Moe. Until the next time," he said, as he walked around the transport.

"Who was that!" a dumbfounded Inge exclaimed.

"It was one of *The Men in White.* I was hoping you could tell us more about them, for I wish I could find out who they are."

Inge quickly ran around the transport to see if he was gone. Then said, "I never heard of them, nor do I know anything about them. However, that was incredible. Do things like that happen in your world?"

"Nope, not at all. Okay, let's see if it will start." To their delight, the transport ignited on the first try. They packed their sleeping bags and changed into fresh clothing. Moe gave Inge one of his outfits to wear, replacing his filthy worn-out jail garb. Since it was quite large, Inge had to roll up his pants and sleeves to fit and used a piece of cord to draw in its waist. They smiled at seeing him dressed like that, for it was a comical sight.

Moe revved up the engine and asked, "Which way?"

"Mr. Moe, where else? Back home."

"Back to Bluetropolis, back to my Ofeela."

By now, Moe understood and accepted he wasn't prepared to go back to his world, and said, "Okay, let's go." Turning the transport around and without fear, they headed back. After what they had been through, it seemed unwise, yet they sped back with unjustified hope.

CHAPTER 19 To Go Or Stay

Much to their relief, without incident the three of them reached the intersection where the trail met the pebble *Road*, Moe said, "We're going to need fuel."

"There is a station a little farther out on the *Road*, and not to worry, for it's not in the Blue's zone," Inge said.

"Oh my, are you sure it's safe?" Mary asked.

"It's a merchant's station, it is safe."

"That's good enough for me," Moe said as he pulled out and headed in its direction. Mary let out a sigh.

Arriving there, they saw a large Food sign atop a dinner-like building. "Oh good, let us have a real meal," Mary suggested.

Moe filled the tank and parked in front of the dinner. Mary excused herself, pointing to the back of the building. Then added, "Mr. Moe, please do not leave me alone." All three scurry around back.

When finished, they enter the dinner to find the usual mix of people. After washing their hands, they sat at a table in the corner, hoping not to be noticed, although it seemed impossible. However, no one paid them any attention.

A waiter asked, "What is your choice?" Knowing the answers to any questions he might've had, Moe ordered, "We'll have three specials with Cooleys.*"

When the waiter left, he asked, "Why don't they just say there's have only one meal?"

"Maybe they want to give a choice."

"Inge, the trouble is I'm beginning to understand that kind of thinking."

Inge chuckled. He spotted some Redmen across the room and excused himself to join them. As Inge spoke with the Redmen, Moe and Mary could only wonder what was being said.

Occasionally the men glanced towards them, making them

feel uneasy. When Inge got up, to their surprise, instead of coming back, he headed across the room to join a couple of Bluemen. It was an unprecedented and possibly dangerous move.

Just then, the food arrived, "Miss Mary, let's eat and get out of here."

"Oh yes, Mr. Moe, I want to go home so much."

When Inge returned, Mary asked, "What did you find out that allowed you to speak with the Blues?"

"It is incredible." He first took a bite of his food, and then continued, "It seems days ago there was a jailbreak causing a rebellion in Bluetropolis."

"You mean our jailbreak?"

"What else. It led to the people rebelling. I must get back to protect my Ofeela."

"That's incredible. Well then, let's eat and get out of here," Moe said.

Later, when they reached the side road leading to Bluetropolis, Moe stopped and said, "There's no sign of those Blue officers."

"Yes, it is most unusual. What they told me must be true."

"And, I hope we never see those ruffians again," Mary added.

Inge said, "I am getting out. This is as far as you need to take me."

"It might be dangerous to go into the city? You might need help. Let me drive you there."

"No, I always sneak in this way. Moe, you must get Mary home safely. I will be all right," he said.

Accepting it was best to do, they exchanged hugs and wished him well. "Till the next time, old friend, take care of yourself and Ofeela," Moe said.

"Now be careful. We will miss you, and, by the way, get a new outfit," Mary said, tearful, but smiling.

Inge said, "Thank you for my freedom. I will never forget you. Goodbye," he started to walk towards Bluetropolis.

They watched him for a moment, then she said, "Mr. Moe, take me home.

"Yes, Miss Mary. They sped off.

Back in the great-room, after being told of their experience in

the Wild Zone, Lucy asked, "Mr. Moe, is that as far as you got?" with a feeling of disappointment.

"Under the circumstances, we went as far as we cold," Moe answered, a bit taken back. "At that point, we had no idea of what dangers were ahead. In going any further, something might have swallowed us up."

Thinking his defensive talk might scare us, Mary said, "Yes Lucy, but you must understand I am from this world. This is my home, and Mr. Moe had nothing left in your world. He was not treated well there."

"I can understand that, but what about us getting back?"

"Don't worry, Johnny. I'll get you back."

"Children, Mr. Moe and I will do our best. Now, we know almost nothing about what lays beyond the point we traveled. As you can see, due to the lack of communication, I know little about the rest of my world, and what I think I know might only be a myth.

"We've been told. So we must do."

"Mr. Moe, you've been told?" Lucy asked.

"Children, it remains to be seen," Mary said.

I could see Moe saw the dilemma of explaining what he hardly understood himself, especially concerning the *White Light and the Men in White*. At the time, their significance remained well beyond our knowledge. *The Men in White* seemed to be the only ones who knew what was going on with any certainty.

"Mr. Moe, have you been told we'll get back home?" Mar asked.

Not knowing how to explain, Moe tried to put the answer off and could only say, "I think so. Kids, at this point, you'll have to trust me. Miss Mary knows more than I do."

"Please, Mr. Moe, I know little. Children, the day before we turned around in the Wild Zone, we talk about the reasons for being out there."

"Yes, Miss Mary, we did do that. We did come to an understanding."

"Mr. Moe, can you please tell us why this is happening to

us?" Mar pleaded.

Seeing the more he spoke, the more we became anxious. He looked at Mary with such a pitiful look she felt she had to take charge for the moment. "Children, I think the key to it all is in gaining knowledge. I do regret, at this point, we do not understand much more than you do. You certainly must see that?" She turned to Moe, wanting him to stand on his own two feet, "Mr. Moe, please explain all we have learned."

Uncertain, he took a deep breath and slowly expelled it, then said, "Well, kids… When we were out there waiting for the Big One to heal, we concluded we were supposed to gain an understanding of each encounter, a sort of a learning process, kind of like being in school."

Standing behind his words, Mary added, "Children, our rationale is not the same as yours. What we did has little to do with what you'll do. Mr. Moe, tell them why we came back."

"Yes, Mr. Moe, please tell us?"

"Please, Mr. Moe. Tell us what we must do so we won't fail?"

"Look, kids, at the time, we believed it would get harder if we traveled on."

Mary injected, "Yes, and I am very comfortable here, and we did not know what would happen to me if and when we reached the end." She looked painfully at him, "Sorry, Mr. Moe, please continue."

"Right… Kids, you see, the main thing was, we were having trouble finding what we believed was the most important element, which was why it was so hard for me to grasp what was meant by the understanding? We kept asking ourselves, was it this, or was it that, or were we not suppose to hit a person or creature on the head with a club? Were we to avoid people of other colors? Were we expected to stay in jail? Were we not to enter the Wild Zone?"

With a sense of defeat, he admitted, "Since we couldn't figure it out to our satisfaction. We thought we might reach the end without the needed understanding. Fearing what might happen if not prepared; it was just easier to come back here."

Mar teared up, and Mary asked, "What is wrong, child?"

"We're never going to get back home, are we?" she said.

"Don't worry, Mar. We'll get back. I promise, you know what I mean," I said, trying to reassure her, not yet able to even imagine what was going to take place.

"Yes, don't worry, kids. *The White Light* told me to help."

"Mr. Moe, the *White Light,* told you that?" Lucy asked, a bit edgy.

Realizing he said something he didn't want to bring up, he had to think fast. Then, suddenly, an epiphany struck him, which was; instead of fudging this time, as he often did, he must be forthright and honest if there was any chance of finding success. Following that insight, he said, "Look, kids, remember the *White Light* that brought you through the *Rock.*" We nodded a yes. "Well, I think that same *Light* will guide us to where we have to go."

"Mr. Moe, the *Light* told you that?" Lucy pressed.

Mary answered that daunting question, "Remember yesterday when you were told of a lightning struck." We nodded a yes. "Well, Mr. Moe did not want to confuse you, so he suggested you be told that. You see, in my world, we do not know what lighting is. It was a flash of the *White Light*, and as you can see, it split my favorite tree just outside these doors."

We went to the door and look out at it. She continued, "It was something I heard about in my youth, but never saw it until that moment. I had come to believe there were no longer such occurrences. Mr. Moe believes it was a message telling him to help you."

"Oh, yes, Miss Mary, it told me what to do."

"Are you sure, Mr. Moe?"

"Yes, Miss Mary, I'm sure, although I don't understand it."

"Well then, Mr. Moe, I am sure too. Children, we will take you to the end of the *Road.* That is if you still want to go."

"Miss Mary, remember how frightened you were? You don't have to come. I can take the kids myself."

"Nonsense, Mr. Moe, if you go, I go. Now, with that settled, children, it will be up to you. You must decide whether to go or stay." Ringing her bell, she instructed, "Let us have lunch. Children, I think it would be better if you had lunch in the garden where you can discuss it amongst yourselves."

"Kids, remember whatever you decide, we'll honor it," Moe

added.

"And be assured, you are welcome to stay here if you so choose," Mary instructed. Samuel entered, she ordered, "We will have lunch now. Please serve the children in the garden."

"Yes, Madam, I'll let you know when it's ready."

"Now children, go out into the garden and enjoy lunch. Stay there until you have thoroughly discussed it. Is that understood?"

"It's understood, Miss Mary," I answered for all. We exited into the garden, leaving Mary and Moe alone as they looked at each other with uncertainty.

CHAPTER 20 The Preparations

With the two of them left alone in the great-room, Mary said, "Mr. Moe, I hope we are doing the right thing," as she settled back in her chair.

"Miss Mary, I hope so. I certainly hope so."

The four of us having flopped on the settees to have lunch out in the garden, Lucy said, "It seems they don't know very much about getting back."

"There's no one else in this world to help us. They're the only ones here who care about us getting back."

"That's right. Johnny is right. Who else here cares about us?" Mar said.

They've been kind to us. I know we can rely on them," Matt added.

"Okay. I agree. Now, we're supposed to decide if we're staying or going," Lucy said.

I proposed, "Let's take turns and say what we should do."

Just then, Samuel appeared with a large tray placing it on the table as we sat there watching him in awkward silence until he disappeared back into the house.

Lucy blurted out, "This world is creepy. Let's get out of here as fast as we can."

"This isn't our world— we don't belong here. Anyway, we already made a pact," Matt added.

"I want to go home," Mar said, with a tear.

"You know. I also think I rather die than stay here," I said and held my hand out, saying, "Let's re-confirm our pact." We each place our right hand on the others. I recited, "We promise to get back home no matter what it takes."

Each followed with a, "I promise."

I said, "Let's eat, I'm hungry, You know what I mean."

When we finished eating, we quietly filed back into the eating-room as Moe and Mary were still eating, and awkwardly stood there. Mary asked, "Children, have you eaten already?"

"Yes, Miss Mary, we have," I answered for all.

She slowly asked us, "Children, have you made your decisions?"

"Yes, Miss Mary, we have."

"Well then, what is it?" Moe pleaded.

"We want to go home!" Mar exclaimed. Thinking she spoke out of turn, she said, "Oh, I'm sorry."

"It's okay, Mar," I said. Then stated with certainty, "We all want to go home."

Mary took a deep breath and said, "Well, it is done. Okay, now we must make plans and prepare. Children, first go into the great-room and allow us to finish our meal."

"Yes, Miss Mary," I said, as I led Lucy, Mar, and Matt out.

Left alone, Mary said, "Mr. Moe, my stomach is turning."

"Miss Mary, remember we were told to be strong, and this time we will be. And I'll not make any mistakes," Moe said, hoping to pacify her.

"Mr. Moe, I know you will not. I know you will do your best," she said, trying to help him to feel better about himself.

The next morning things began to accelerate as Mary dressed, and Samuel rang his bell in Moe's room, waking him. While he readied, Mary sat in the great-room checking over a list she jotted down of the items she thought might be of use on the trip. She ordered Samuel, "When Mr. Moe arrives, ask Janis to serve breakfast for two. When I am finished with this list of supplies, would you start collecting them?"

"Yes, Madam," he left.

She collapsed back into her chair and took a deep breath as she pondered in what the future would bring. She wondered if she was going to have the strength to complete the journey this time, or if they would even survive it. She knew deep in her heart, she had to do this, not only for the children but for the sake of Moe as well.

Moe said as he entered with a perky attitude startling her out of her ruminations, "Good morning Miss Mary."

"Ah, good morning Mr. Moe, sit, have your juice. I have listed the items we might need. Please go over it. Add or subtract as you see fit."

He quickly studied it, and then warned, "Miss Mary, we'll need clubs and knives for all."

"I was afraid of that, Mr. Moe."

"Miss Mary, you know what it's like out there. In my world, we would bring even more lethal weapons."

"Mr. Moe, you know those abominable contraptions were outlawed because of the danger. If they were not, I am sure it would have caused disastrous results. However, I do understand, at times, there is a need for them. Please, let us not resort to the use of violence unless it becomes absolutely necessary."

"Yes, Miss Mary, only if necessary, although I must say, if it were not for weapons in my world, we would still be an oppressed people just as they are here. The rest of the list looks fine. I'll select the necessary tools."

Samuel, announced, "Breakfast is served,"

Meanwhile, in the girl's bedroom, Lucy and Mar were awake, having slept little. "I can't wait to start back home," Mar said.

"Yes, however, we must first travel that *Road*, and I'm not sure about collecting the understanding the *Men in White* talked about."

"Yes, I think that too. It's too confusing. Do you think we'll find it, whatever it is?"

"We have no choice, we must get home. And Mar, when we get back, don't you think we'll have a tale to tell," Lucy concluded.

"I guess...

In my and Matt's bedroom, I said, "I'm not clear about the understanding we're supposed to find."

"It seems Mr. Moe and Miss Mary aren't either."

"It looks like it's going to be up to us to find out what it means. And I've been thinking...

"Well, what?"

"You see, so far, it might be something like this; first, one must not be segregated by color. Second, one must not judge others. Third, one can defend themselves against danger, but must also love their enemies. You know the same things our parents taught us."

"I hadn't thought of that. You might have something there."

"I hope so. I hope we'll find out soon," I said.

Samuel entered ringing his bell and gave us the instructions for the morning and left. We jumped out of our beds, eager to start today's preparations.

Mary and Moe had finished breakfast and were in the storage room, choosing their clothing. She was saying, "Let me see, I picked out several changes of clothing for both of us. We will have to buy additional clothing for the children. Enough food for several days is being prepared. And you are still to pick the necessary tools and equipment."

"Good, Miss Mary, but you know I can't help but wonder how long it'll take to get to the end of the *Road*?"

"Mr. Moe, I wish I could even guess. I do not have the slightest idea. I am afraid we cannot know what the future holds for us. It might take days, or even worse, it might take cycles to reach the end."

"Well, Miss Mary, isn't that what life is all about. I mean, we don't know what tomorrow holds in store, do we?"

"I suppose not, Mr. Moe. Being out there living by our wits has been new to me."

"Don't worry, Miss Mary. I'll protect you."

"I know you will, Mr. Moe."

Flustered by her blind trust, he said, "I'll go and check out the tools with Samuel."

Dressed and having finished breakfast we joined Moe and Mary in the great-room where he spread out a batch of papers on the library type table, which included written directions and a makeshift map, Moe said, "Okay kids, let's go over the travel plans. Now… We'll start early in the morning, and first on the agenda will be to stop and buy new clothes for all of you." Hearing that prospect delighted us, especially Lucy and Mar, who I always thought worried way too much about what they wore.

"That'll be the easy part. The first obstacle will be when we enter Bluetropolis," as he pointed to it on the map. "When we passed it coming back, there was no sign of those Blue gangsters. From what Inge told us, there was some sort of trouble taking place, so we'll have to be extra careful when we enter that city."

"I hope we will be able to find Inge there."

"Yes, Miss Mary, it'll be great if we could. After our return, I tried to find out if what Inge told us was so from the Bluemen who stopped at the station, but they were closed-mouth. I didn't want to ask outright about an upheaval thinking it might cause trouble. Therefore, we know little about what to expect in Bluetropolis. Now, when we arrive at the last point, we had traveled to...

Mary jumped in, "Yes, and Mr. Moe has promised not to turn down the road leading into the Wild Zone," as she pointed to it on the map.

Kids, I promise not to. So, from that point, it will be uncharted territory," as he pointed to the blank spot on the map. We must write down all the directions, and draw our route on the map, just in case we have to backtrack. Kids, do you think you're ready for this?"

In unison with conviction, we said, "Yes sir, we are!" as we slapped each other's hands with Moe joining in.

Mary ordered, "Children, we will rest for the remainder of today for tomorrow will be one of the most important days of your lives."

CHAPTER 21 Arriving In Bluetropolis

Early the next morning, Janis rang her little bell in Mary's room, waking her. Abruptly, she got up and ordered, "Wake everyone. We will all have breakfast together. Now get on with it." She quickly stepped into her bath. Janis and Samuel went through the ritual of ringing bells, running baths, seeing to it we had everything needed. They rushed the process to please their mistress.

Mary reached the great-room with her and Moe's glasses of juice. Sitting in her chair, she tried to read a book to divert her mind away from her concerns, again with little success as she waited for us to arrive. Finally, Moe entered, "Good morning, Miss Mary."

With a sigh of relief, she said, "Good morning Mr. Moe, sit, have your juice."

He took a swig of juice, then said with a bounce in his voice, "Miss Mary, isn't it a beautiful morning? Why today, I feel like I was young again."

"Oh, Mr. Moe, to be young again, would it not be magnificent, she said.

"You know Miss Mary when I was young I had such high hopes. I wanted to do great things. I wanted to make the world a better place."

"Mr. Moe, I think you have made your world a better place just by being there."

Sorrowfully, he said, "No, Miss Mary, I'm afraid I was just excess baggage, so to speak."

Not wanting to dash his vitality, she changed the subject, "Is it not glorious this day has once again arrived?"

With more positive energy than she's ever seen him exhibit. He said, "Oh, yes, Miss Mary, to be free, to go out on the *Road*; to be on the great quest; to fell the foes; to right the wrongs; to travel in the Dragon on the high road and perhaps the low road too. It's almost magical?" She chuckled with delight in seeing him like this.

Samuel announced, "Breakfast is served, the children are waiting."

"Let's go, Miss Mary," as he offered his arm. Like a young girl going to her first prom, she held his arm as they sashayed into the eating-room.

When finished with the plentiful, but rushed breakfast, we were filled with high expectations and ready to depart. Moe asked, "Has everyone used the facilities? It might be a while before you have another chance."

"Yes sir, we're more than ready to go," I answered for all.

Mary charged Samuel and Janis, "Now, the place is yours until I return, and if I do not return, here are the papers stating everything belongs to you." (It must be noted, to leave real estate to a Slop was unprecedented and would break the unwritten rules and if successful would positively change their world.)

A teary-eyed Janis impulsively hugged Mary. So taken by the show of affection, Mary looked at an uncomfortable Samuel and impulsively hugged him as a young girl might with her father as his face turned pink. She then said, "Goodbye, take care of everything. Goodbye." We boarded the Dragon as Moe turned the starting crank.

With wet eyes, Samuel and Janis waved, saying several times, "Goodbye, Madam." (Although they served Mary in an austere manner most of their lives not being much older than her, the truth was they quietly protected and cared for her as if she were their own child. They allowed her to think she was in charge, but in fact, they actually ran the household. It was a sad departure, for they served her well and feared they would never see her again.)

We drove down and out the driveway. Reaching *The Road of Understanding*. Moe stopped for a second, and then with a loud "He - Ha," he turned onto the pebble *Road*, and with the roar of the Dragon's engine, we sped off to the high spirits of all.

In a while, Moe turned off onto a side road. "Children, we're stopping to get your new clothing," Mary said and ordered him to stop at the next building, a building looking more like a mansion than a store.

We entered what Mary called, The Clothing Place. Inside, it looked like a warehouse outlet filled with racks of clothing for all the different groups. Many people were shopping.

Two chalk-white female clerks greeted us and led us to the section containing clothing for Inbetweeners. There was a large assortment of styles, mostly for girls. Mary ordered, "Children, pick out four outfits each."

Full of glee, we searched the racks to find clothing that appealed to us, aided by the clerks. The styles were most unusual, with a variety of colors. It was more like picking out costumes for a party than regular shopping.

"We must try them on," Mar said. A clerk pointed to a changing room.

"I see this is going to take some time," Moe wisely observed. The other clerk quickly brought him a chair. "It's going to take longer than a while," he said under his breath. The clerk also brought Mary a chair.

Matt and I tried on a half dozen outfits each. We chose four in a reasonable amount of time, for the styles for young men were more straightforward, lacking the large variety the girls had to choose from.

Moe sat there, twirling his thumbs. Mary reminded him, "Remember, Mr. Moe, the girls are females."

"Yes, Miss Mary - females."

Matt and I also were given chairs as we waited for the girls to finish. With the help of Mary, for every three or four outfits they tried on and displayed, they would pick one. After a painfully long wait, while Lucy and Mar indulged themselves, we were ready. As we were leaving, dressed in one of our new outfits, the management surprised us by presenting each of us with a gift of a sweater-like pullover. We thought that was cool.

Back on the *Road*, as we sped along, we spent much of the time dozing, exhausted from the excitement of the morning and the little sleep we had gotten the night before.

On the second day, we began to encounter traffic, which was

more substantial than Moe and Mary expected as they showed concern in seeing the hustle and bustle. Moe drove with caution. Off in the far distance to the left, only indicated by the blue aura it gave off, we saw Bluetropolis. "Kids, from here on in, we must be careful," Moe instructed.

"Mr. Moe, see those Bluemen walking along the *Road*. They look harmless; do you think it would be wise to ask them why there is all this activity?"

"Miss Mary, I think it'll be okay." He pulled up and jumped out. As they curiously looked at him, he asked, "Sirs, could you kindly tell me what's causing all this traffic?"

"Traffic? What is traffic?" one asked.

"Oh… I mean, why are there so many transports on the *Road*?"

With her head out the window, Mary warned, "Be careful, Mr. Moe."

One of the Bluemen answered, "It is the citizens of Bluetropolis, who are now allowed to travel freely."

Mary overheard and wondered, "Travel freely?"

Another Blue said, "Have you not heard? Since the jailbreak rebellion, we are now free to come and go as we please, and everyone is allowed to enter our city."

Moe was a little befuddled and tinged with some delight, as he said, "No, I hadn't heard." He then asked, "Would you know a Red fellow called, Inge? He's a friend of ours."

"Do you mean, Sir Inge, the son-in-law of The Exalted?" a man asked.

Another man, having overheard Mary calling Moe's name, asked with amazement, "Is this The Moe?" He turned and said to the other Blues who had gathered, "It is The Moe, is it not?"

"Yes, it is The Moe. It is The Moe!" the crowd excitedly echoed.

A man jumped up on the sideboard of the Dragon and looked in the open window and yelled, "And it is The Mary!" Several in the crowd ran out, stopping traffic. Not knowing what to make of this strong reaction, Moe jumped back in the Dragon in the hope of getting away. It was too late, in seeing the heightened activity, many transports stopped, trapping us.

"Oh, my. Oh my," Mary muttered.

Several other Blues jumped on the sideboard, waving to those transports blocking the way to open a path leading directly to Bluetropolis. A man pointed to the cleared path and urged Moe, "Go! Go!

Mr. Moe, what is going on?" Mary asked, in a contained state of panic.

"Are we going to jail?" Mar asked.

"They said, Sir Inge. Don't worry. He'll help us," Moe said.

"Yes, Inge will help us. You know what I mean," I said, not knowing anything.

Out of the turmoil, the transports formed a caravan following us. With no choice, Moe slowly moved along the path. Entering the city, we were welcomed with unexpected cheers from the people along the way, as those traveling ahead were yelling out who we were.

As things calmed a bit, Mary said, "Mr. Moe, they seem pleased to see us, do you think it's a good thing? Could it be that Inge has indeed become a Sir?"

"Miss Mary, the man said, "Sir Inge, the son-in-law of The Exalted and how else would they know our names, but through him?"

This impressed her, "The Exalted, and a married man, perhaps, he will be able to help us."

"Miss Mary, they also said jailbreak and free travel. I wonder why I never heard about it at the station."

"Now, Mr. Moe, you know the Blue, and Red merchants who travel south are extremely secretive. Even though they seem to have more freedom now, they may still hold to their old ways."

"I can't believe it, Miss Mary. Do you think we're part of effecting this change?"

"Mr. Moe, you are perhaps more effective than you think you are."

"Imagine that." He turned to us and said, "Don't worry kids, we'll be all right." I could see in his expression he was hoping so, but not at all sure of it being so.

It seemed it took forever to reach the center of the city as the crowds had to part along the way for us to pass. It gave us comfort in seeing the multitude of enthusiastic people smiling and waving. Finally, we arrived at the foot of a massive bronze gate deep in the city.

Those in the stirred up armada told the guards who we were, at which point the gate swung open. We entered an expansive walled-in area as the guards cut off the crowd following us. Directed to an imposing building, I said, "This must be the King's place."

"Are you sure it's not a jail?"

"No. Mar, it is not a jail. However, I do not know what it is," Mary answered.

The impressive sound of bugles filled the air along with the cheers of the many already in the compound. We arrived at the foot of the steps leading up and into the palatial building. Moe and Mary were helped out of the Dragon. A path was cleared leading up to the set of massive double doors, which flew open, allowing a small group of distinguished-looking people to exit and quickly head down towards us. Lucy, Mar, Matt, and I remained in the Dragon frantically trying to see what was going on.

Dressed in a finely decorated red robe, a man led the group. When close enough to Mary and Moe they recognized his now shaven red face and the pounds he had gained, Moe yelled, "Inge, is that you?"

"My friends. Yes, it is me!" he said, much to their relief and delight as they exchanged hugs.

Moe asked, "It's good to see you. What's happened here?"

"We have lots to talk about. But first, come, I want you to meet my Ofeela."

"Wait for a second," Moe said, as he motioned for us to come out of the Dragon. We expeditiously got out and huddle around him, as he said to Inge, "These are our friends."

Inge smiled and eagerly said, "Come, my friends," as he led the way into the building to the delight of the highly charged crowd.

Once inside the quiet of a grand marble entrance hall, away from the sounds of the crowd. Waiting in the center of the large space, an attractive petite Blue woman wearing a finely decorated gold-laced blue robe stood along with two small children. Inge said, "Mary and Moe this is my wife Ofeela and our next generation, Hinge and Ginge."

Ofeela held an infant girl as a two-year-old boy gripped her thigh. She said, "I am so pleased to meet you finally. I have heard so much about you."

"As we have heard about you. Congratulations, Inge, your children are beautiful," Mary said.

"Yes, congratulations, my good man, I see you have been most productive," Moe jokingly added, as Inge beamed with pride.

Mary introduced us. "Your friends are our friends," Inge said. We will have a feast in your honor. First, you must freshen up and change your clothing. We will talk later. I am most interested in hearing what you've been doing." He snapped his fingers, and several humble-looking ladies appeared and led us off.

CHAPTER 22 Discovering The Rebellion In Bluetropolis

In the palace, as we called it, the ladies led each of us to a separate dressing room where baths were being drawn. The woman in charge of my care, instructed, "Everything you will need is being laid out for you. There is no rush, for there is ample time before the meal will be served. When ready, you can meet your friends in the waiting room. If you need anything additional, pull the cord hanging by the bath."

After a long much needed relaxing soak in the tub, filled with fragrant water almost too hot, I dried off, to find in that short time an elegant robe and soft moccasin-like shoes were laid out in the adjacent dressing room. Surprisingly they matched my skin color. How they were able to come up with those garments that fit so well, so quickly was incredible. We were grateful the ladies didn't come in to dress us, allowing the privacy we needed at that age.

When ready, one by one, we were escorted to the waiting room. Mary was the first to arrive with Moe being next. As he looked around the room, he said, "This is something, isn't it?"

"Yes, Mr. Moe, I see Inge has done quite well for himself. Who thought little Inge could have gained all this. And, Mr. Moe, look at these clothes, are they not splendid?" she said as she spun around, showing off her white outfit.

"Yes, and Miss Mary, you look quite fine in yours," he said, pleasing her as her face showed an orange blush.

"And, so do you, Mr. Moe."

When we all arrived, I said, "It looks like you and Miss Mary are heroes."

"Oh, we're no heroes," Moe responded.

"I was told that too," Lucy added. "The lady said it was

because of your jailbreak. And look at the way they're treating. Inge must be an important person."

"Mr. Moe, it does look like our actions caused something exceptional to take place. And, whatever it was, you were the one who started it."

In wonderment, he said, "Yes, I guess I did. Maybe I did do something special this time, didn't I?"

"Yes, you did, Mr. Moe, you're a real hero," I added.

Moe could hardly handle that much praise. He settled into one of the cushioned chairs and changed the subject, "Hmm, I wonder what's going to happen next."

After having been indulged, pampered, and being together for a time, the Blue ladies led the six of us out into an extra-wide hallway where uniformed guards were conspicuously posted along the walls a dozen or so feet apart. Seeing such a large force, we were impressed.

We arrived in front of a tall set of ornate misshapen double doors, for all the doors in this world were oddly shaped as opposed to being rectangular. The guards opened them to reveal a large room packed with people. The ladies nudged us to enter what appeared to be a banquet hall. Overhead, some thirty feet above were blue-tinted glass skylights, which allowed blue light to shine down lighting the room.

Almost all the people were Blues, who were noticeably shorter than us, none taller than Lucy. However, there was a sprinkling of taller individuals of other skin colors, which was unprecedented before the rebellion. All dressed in similar finely decorative robes made of cloth matching one's skin color with embroidered designs of silver and gold threads. They wore headpieces tightly wrapped around their heads, which spiraled up to a point, looking much like the cartoon wizards we had seen in the movies. It was an impressive sight.

Although we felt a little shy and awkward in facing such a large crowd, yet, at the same time, it was exciting to have all these people staring at us as if we were movie stars. Still, we couldn't help to feel apprehensive about why all this pomp and ceremony was necessary.

A low large V-shaped table sat in the center of the room,

seating about fifty people on pillows, for there were no chairs. Elsewhere, in the room, most sat on the bare floor away from the table, while others stood against the walls among uniformed guards, now conspicuously posted six feet apart. The table was about two feet high and four feet wide and covered with a blue tablecloth, which hung down to the floor. In front of each person sat a blue plate, a blue cloth napkin, and even a blue knife and a two-pronged fork.

As we stood there, the room became silent. A little Redman motioned for us to follow him. The crowd began to clap their hands, strangely by holding one hand in a palm-up position and slapping the other down on it, as if in slow motion. Those sitting on the floor scurried out of the way to make a path. We weren't sure how to react to the honor we were obviously being paid.

Standing inside the V space of the table, we faced a blue aristocratic elderly couple who were sitting on the outer side at the very point of the V. Both were seated on pillows somewhat thicker than all the others, placing them higher than everyone else. We knew they were special, as indicated by a large impressive sparkling blue stone pinned to each of their headwear, and a larger one hung around their necks. They also wore rings on several fingers with imposing blue stones mounted in them.

Seeing Inge and Ofeela sitting there reassured us, everything was going to be okay. Inge stood, followed by everyone else in the room, except for the elderly couple, and announced in a loud voice, "Your Exalted Ones, It is my honor to present my good friends, Mary Right and Moe Smart and their friends, Lucy and Johnny Peterson, Mar Carter and Matt Davies."

The Exalted Ones were the elderly couple. He said, "I have heard of what you have done for us, and we are most pleased to meet you finally. Please sit and break bread with us." Everyone obediently sat as Inge motioned for us to come and sit on the pillows in the reserved spots next to him.

When seated, The Exalted One snapped his fingers, causing a stream of servants to pour out of several doors that slid open along the walls. Huge trays of food were carried out and served to those at the table.

The food was cut into bitesize gelatin-like cubes of different shades of blue. We found each shade had a distinct taste. Some tasted like chicken; some a bit like beef, some like bread, and others like nothing we've ever eaten before. It was fun in discovering what each shade tasted like. As we ate, the chatter in the room was loud enough, so what we said to each other wasn't overheard."

"What in the world has happened here since we left?" Moe asked Inge.

"My friends, it has been a struggle. It all started when we let the prisoners out of jail. Which included those in all the other wings, amounting to more than a thousand. As you remember, they all ran out into the streets yelling: We are free! We are free!"

"Yes, we remember. But how did that change anything?"

"How! Why that phrase caught on like wildfire. Soon people all over the city were exclaiming, '*We are free, We are free!*' The enforcement guards tried to stop the momentum, but the movement became so massive it overwhelmed them. It led to a wave that brought down the whole oppressive system that has always been."

"How wonderful. So now you are all free?" Mary asked.

"Well. Not exactly, there is still a problem. I will explain later."

Partway through the meal, The Exalted One stood and held up a glass half-filled with a blue liquid. A hush came over the room, and he said, "Friends, we finally have among us the two people who so profoundly changed our lives. I honor them, and so shall we all." Everyone gulped their drinks down, which tasted like fruit juice only with a slight kick, it was a drink the four of us never tasted before. I feel our parents would've been upset with us drinking it, but we didn't know it might be alcohol until we swallowed it.

Suddenly! Without warning, a loud crashing sound erupted, followed by bits of glass raining down from the skylights. Masked Bluemen began propelling down ropes they'd dropped through the holes they made. Inge yelled, "Quick, get under the table!" as he pulled up the tablecloth and pushed us under it.

In total darkness, we crouched on our hands and knees under the table as Lucy asked, "What's going on?"

"Are we going to be killed?" Mar couldn't help but ask.

"No, I don't think so," Moe yelled, clumsily trying to

reassure her.

"Mr. Moe, I certainly hope not!" Mary scolded.

Inge joined us, saying, "Do not worry. Everything will be all right. It will only take a short time." To our horror, there were sounds of crashing, breaking, exertion, and screams of turmoil. The table rattled, caused by people either jumping or being tossed on it. Along with the sounds of dishes and glasses being smashed. This activity continued for a short time. Finally, the rumbling stopped. After a moment or two, Inge ordered, "Stay here," and left us.

"Are we going to be arrested?" A tearful Mar asked.

"Come on, Mar, everything will be all right," I said.

"Oh, please," Lucy said.

Just then, the tablecloth was lifted up and away by Inge. He said, "Come out, my friends, it's safe now." We crawled out to find the room in shambles. Most of the people were gone, except for those injured by the falling glass and being treated. The guards were dragging off the unconscious assailants by their feet.

Inge ordered, "Come this way." Encircled by guards, he and Ofeela led us to a small plush room as we huddle close to Moe and Mary. The guards didn't enter, closing the door behind, leaving us alone with Inge and Ofeela. "Make yourselves comfortable," Inge said.

Ofeela said, "I apologize for the meal being disrupted. We will be brought fresh food,"

"Could you please tell us what just happened?" Mary asked, still shaking as she dusted off tiny bits of glass from her clothing.

As Inge began to answer, several servants entered. Each carried a tiny table, one for each of us with drinks and dishes filled with those cubed foods. Having to eat seated on pillows was a little awkward and took some adjustment.

In response to Mary's question, Inge explained, "What is good for all is not always good for everyone."

"You mean, not every Blue wants to be free?" Moe interrupted.

"What I see, I see."

"Inge, what do you see?" Mary asked. We listened with great interest.

"The people of Bluetropolis have never known freedom.

They are finding it hard to learn how to exercise it," Ofeela said.

"You mean people have to learn how to be free," I asked.

"That is it! That is it! The Blues are slowly learning about freedom for the first time in their history. It is those who held the old dictatorial power since our beginning who are causing the problems," Inge said.

"Gee, you would think everyone would want to be free," Lucy said.

"Those who were in control are trying to regain that power. Sadly, they are using those who they once oppressed to accomplish it.

"Inge, that's incredible. Although I can understand it, for it also happens in our world," Moe said.

"Ha! That is interesting. You must tell me about that. However, our enemies exploit the ignorance and fears of some. Offers of bribes to others, causing confusion in the hearts and minds of the people."

"Inge, it is most bewildering," Mary said.

"You mean those who oppressed you before, want to do it again?" Matt asked.

"Yes, yes. It has been difficult to convince the people it is better to be free. As you saw, they send their followers out on senseless raids only to instill fear. We have been trying to show the people how freedom works with the little knowledge we have," Inge added.

"How awful. However, I can see how freedom is a learned behavior," Mary contemplated.

"Isn't it natural to want to be free?"

"I guess not, Lucy. Remember, we're used to being free. The Blues have never known it," Moe instructed.

"Yes, yes, and the same jail cells where the rebellion started are now filled with those who want to enslave us again."

"Oh, my. Will you win?" Mary asked.

To win is to win. We will be free. However, we must first overcome the evil ones, the corrupted ones who use terrorism to enslave."

"Yes, we will be free. Although, it will be a struggle until the day comes when all our people will appreciate and practice freedom," Ofeela added.

Lucy said under her breath, "Good luck with that," not fully understanding what she just said.

"I wish we could stay and help, but we are on a mission," Mary said, almost apologetically.

"Mission? A mission?"

"Yes, Inge, the kids are from my world; they are *Rockers*. They came through unexpectedly without knowing why. We must get them back before they lose the opportunity to do so."

Surprised, Inge said, "Moe, you never cease to amaze. This is almost too hard to believe, but everything about you is unbelievable."

"Yes, and the children miss their world, and their parents undoubtedly miss them," Mary added.

Being sympathetic, Ofeela said to us, "How awful it must be for you? It is most remarkable the *Rock* has opened again. What could be the reason?"

"It's a mystery to us."

"Regardless, you must get them back. But, is it not true no one has ever gone back?" Ofeela said.

"As far as getting back, there's a first time for everything, just as it was for your people to find freedom," Moe said.

"You make a good point, and it is almost beyond belief it opened again, I wonder if there will be others? And to what end?" Inge said.

Ofeela offered, "But, first, you must rest here tonight and spend at least another day with us before you go. You can stay as long as you like. Leave when you are fully prepared, we will help you as much as we can."

Later, after reminiscing and talking about many things, Inge said, "It is late, tomorrow we will talk more. He snapped his fingers, and several ladies entered. After bidding our good nights, we were taken to guarded guestrooms. Mary and the girls placed in one room and Moe, Matt, and I in another.

In the lady's bedroom were six beds, and to no one's surprise, all decorated in dark blue. "Miss Mary, how come everything has to be blue?" Lucy asked.

"I guess it makes them feel comfortable."

"It makes me feel uncomfortable."

"Me too," Mar added.

"Children, I guess different people have different feelings."

"We were taught all people had the same feelings. And we all have the same needs, and the most important was peace and freedom," Lucy said, remembering that concept from school, but not yet fully understanding it.

"That is interesting. In my world, it is all about separation. It is about not mixing."

"What about the mixing of Inge and Ofeela?" Lucy pointed out.

"Yes, it is most extraordinary. I do not know what is happening, for my world is definitely changing."

"And you and Mr. Moe are causing that change," Lucy added.

"I guess it is so, but I still do not understand it. Children, I wish I did. Now, let us choose a bed and get some rest. We will need to be rested for what tomorrow will bring."

In our guest room, settled on individual beds, Moe's feet hung over the end of the bed. He said, "I wish the blues weren't so short."

"Mr. Moe, I don't understand what's going on. Aren't we supposed to understand it?" I asked.

"Kids, I don't understand it either."

"We're supposed to understand it, right?" Matt asked.

"Yes, I think we're supposed to."

"I understand being a bigot and wanting segregation is not a good thing. Do you think that's what we're supposed to understand?

"Johnny, I never thought of it exactly in that way. You might have something there. I have to think about that."

After some seconds, Matt asked, "Is it as simple as that?" We waited for Moe to respond. Instead, we heard a snoring sound coming from him.

"I guess he's exhausted," I said.

"You know he's very old," Matt said.

"Yes, he is, and it's been a long day. I guess we better get some sleep too."

CHAPTER 23 Preparing For The Worst

The next morning, as usual, Mary was the first to rise, she moved slowly as not to disturb Lucy and Mar. Eager to start the day, she asked the little Blue lady who sat just outside the door waiting to serve, if it was possible to get fresh clothing from the Dragon. The woman explained, "Madam Ofeela has chosen new clothing for all." Again, Mary was impressed.

Bathed and dressed in the provided clothing, the lady led her to the waiting room. She couldn't help but noticed the guards were doubled. When asked if she would like anything, she replied, "Could I please have a glass of juice of any flavor?"

"Juice? Yes, madam."

Moments later, Ofeela entered, "Good morning, Mary."

"Good morning, Ofeela," she replied, pleased to see her.

"Did you have a restful night? Ofeela asked.

"The best I could. What happened last evening was most distressing. Does that sort of thing take place often?"

"All too often. I am sorry you had to witness it. Our people are most resistant to change. However, Inge is stubborn. He will not give up until we are all free."

"I see he will not. You must be quite proud of him. By the way, thank you for the clothing, they are beautiful."

"You are most welcome. It is our honor. We will help you as much as we can. Yes, I am proud of Inge. And you must be very close to Moe?"

"Oh. We are just good friends."

"You must be very close friends to be willing to travel to the end of the *Road* with him, with all its dangers. You are of our world and have nothing to gain by doing so."

"Well, we are just good friends. Anyway, the children must get back to their world." Mary said as a final answer.

With a smile, Ofeela agreed, "Yes, of course, the children must get back. I must tend to Inge. We will meet you in the eating-room when Moe is ready. If you need anything, please ask one of my ladies."

"Thank you, Ofeela." Left to herself, she asked the attendant who brought the juice, "Would you have a book?"

"A book, madam?"

"Yes, a book I could read to pass the time."

"Oh, yes. I will see if I can find one, madam."

"Thank you."

Meanwhile, Moe was startled out of a deep sleep by a nondescript dream. Taking some seconds to recognize where he was, he saw daylight streaming through the cracks around the closed window shutters. Assuming Mary would be up by now, he quietly slipped out of bed as not to disturb Matt and me, leaving us to sleep. He soaked in the prepared tub for a short time, then quickly dressed in the clothing provided, eager to be with Mary for breakfast.

Once with her, they were led to a small intimate eating-room where Inge and Ofeela joined them. After exchanging greetings, the meal began, served by a different attendant who stood behind each occupied chair. Mary expressed an, "Oh my."

Moe just said, "Thank you" as he dug into the variety of small cubes with the two-prong fork specially designed to pierce and pick up the soft cubes. A variety of fruity tastes delighted his taste buds.

"My friends, tell me of your plans to get the children back?" Inge inquired.

"Well, it's as simple as this; we're going to drive to the end of the *Road*," Moe answered.

"Have you prepared for the worst?" Ofeela asked.

"What do you mean the worst?" an unsettled Mary responded.

"You know the problems we had in Bluetropolis and the Wild Zone. I think that was only the start of what you might encounter," Inge said, and asked, "Are you prepared for even worse?"

"Well, we brought bigger clubs, knives, and a good supply of food and whatever else we thought might be needed. We prepared the best we could for any contingencies. But, as you know, we have no idea of what to expect," Moe explained.

Not sure where the conversation was going, Mary asked, "You know how most groups are so secretive, how could we know what is ahead and what plans to make?"

"Along the way, you will find friendly groups and also hostile ones. It might be wise to only rest in the friendly cities and take care in avoiding the hostile ones," Ofeela added.

"I was told by a *Man in White* to enter every city along the way," Moe informed.

"I see." Ofeela understood.

With a smile, Inge said, "Yes. And what must be done must be done. I-a-a, we suggest you take as much information with you as possible."

"We agree, but it's not easy with information being so scarce? We didn't even know what happened here until we arrived. No one who stopped at the station spoke of it."

"Having someone to travel with you with the knowledge of the different cities might be of great value," Inge suggested.

"It is a good idea, but we know of no one like that, except for you," Mary acknowledged.

"That is precisely what Inge is getting to," Ofeela said."

"Yes, dear… As you know, I would like nothing more than to join you in your quest, but as you can see, I am needed here. However, my closest and most trusted friend, who is also an experienced traveler, would be proud to join you. That is if you have room for him?"

"You mean to travel with us?" Mary asked.

"Yes, he could be of value in dealing with the hostile groups and to seek help from those who are friendly," Ofeela added.

Mary now understood, and said, "I think that is an excellent idea. Do you not think so, Mr. Moe?"

As he was about to take another tasty cube in his mouth, he answered, "Oh Yes, Miss Mary. Yes, of course, it's a good idea, and there's plenty of room in the Dragon.

"Good. His name is Ike. Now, with that is settled, let us finish breakfast," a pleased Inge concluded.

CHAPTER 24 Learning About Education

Dressed in our new clothing, the four of us were together in the waiting room. The new robes appeared to swirl around rather than hanging on us. It gave me a funny feeling as if I weighed less. Mar asked, "How do I look in my outfit?"

"You look good to me," I replied, not yet knowing the best way to answer such a question from a girl.

"I think these outfits are a little silly," Lucy said. However, I was beginning to understand my sister's feelings and answered, "You look good in yours too."

"Oh, really?" she said as she looked at herself in the mirror, being pleased by my compliment. In time, I realized back in those days compliments from me were in short supply.

Ofeela's teenaged sister and brother, Olivier, and Ofrado joined us for breakfast. After introducing themselves, Olivier asked, "Are you really from the other side of the *Rock*?"

"We are," I said, with unjustified pride.

"Why did you come to our world?" Ofrado asked.

"I wish we knew. We were just pulled through the *Rock* by The *White Light*, and to our surprise, here we are," Lucy answered.

"*The White Light*? Oh my," Olivier said, glancing at her brother, who was also startled.

"What about the *Light*?" I asked, intrigued by their reaction.

"Can you tell us where the *Light* comes from?" Lucy asked, in the hope of finding out more.

"We know nothing. Anyway, we are not to speak of it," Ofrado quickly said, as the two of them stiffened.

"Can I ask, who said, you weren't supposed to talk about it?" I pursued.

"It is against the rules. Can we please talk about something else?" Ofrado pleaded.

Seeing their discomfort, after a slight pause, I changed the subject, "Are you still in school?"

"School, what is school?" Olivier wondered.

"School? No, we do not have anything like school," Ofrado added.

"Who teaches you? I mean, how do you learn things?" Lucy asked.

"Oh, yes, we have personal toots who teaches us all we must know."

"You mean like Home Schooling? I asked.

"Homeschooling? What is meant by that?"

"It means; your parents teach you at home. It's the way it was done a long time ago in our world."

Olivier thought for a moment, then said, "This is what we do; we go to the learning room upstairs where our toots, directed by our parents, teach us what we must know. The only trouble is due to the revolt, we must now relearn many things. It used to be we were supposed to obey our leaders. Now we are free and must think for ourselves."

"Yes, it has been most difficult. We now have to learn how to be free," Ofrado added.

"Isn't it easier to be free? Lucy asked.

"Why no, it is much harder to be free and do our own thinking," Ofrado said.

Olivier said, "We are told we must accept the new way," Then she asked, "And, how do you learn in your world?"

Lucy answer, "Okay, to explain it simply, it's like this; when we were very young, they sent to a place called a school, where we spent much of the day in classrooms being taught by teachers what we must know."

"Classrooms? Is that like our learning room?" Olivier asked, fascinated.

"I guess. The only difference is there are a lot of other kids in the classroom with us," I added.

"Yes, and our parents never came in or got involved," Matt added.

"You mean you spend all that time away from your parents?" Olivier asked.

"Our parents have little to do with our schooling, except for sending us there," Lucy said.

Ofrado could only say, "How strange?"

After a reflective poise, Olivier asked, "And you want to go back to that school place?"

"No, we want to go back to our parents and families," Mar said.

"We already graduated that school anyway," Matt added.

"Graduated? What does graduate mean?"

"It just means we completed our time there."

Olivier thought, and said, "Oh... Now you are on your own."

"Not yet, we plan on going to college."

"College, what's that?"

"It's a higher form of schooling, where we go away for four years to learn more important things," attempting to explain it as simply as I could.

"You mean you have to go away from your parents to learn things?" Ofrado asked, with alarm.

Olivier found all this confusing, "Why is that? We learn everything from our parents. Is there something wrong with them?"

Giving it some thought, Lucy answered, "Why no. I don't know why they can't teach us? I guess our schools believe it's better to separate us from our parents for us to learn."

Beginning to see something I never thought about, I said, "Now that you bring it up, I wonder why they separated us? There were many times I wish I could spend more time with my parents."

Matt remembering the gut feeling he had as a child, said, "I was so upset when they first left me at school. I didn't want to be there, and I don't think I ever fully got over that feeling."

"And you still want to go back to that college place?" Olivier asked, unsettled.

"I just want to get back to my family," Mar, again said.

"I can understand that. But, I do not understand your system," Olivier said.

"Yes, your way of learning is strange to us. I feel sorry for you," Ofrado added.

"And your ways are weird to us, too," I said.

Changing the subject, Ofrado asked, "Do you expect to go back to your world soon?"

"We certainly hope so," I answered.

"Hope so! We better!" Lucy jumped in.

"Sir Inge will help you," Ofrado said.

"Yes, he certainly will," Olivier added.

After breakfast, we parted from our new friends and joined Moe and Mary in the waiting room. Mary asked, "Children, did you have a good night's sleep?"

"We tried to. But your world is a funny place. It makes me feel uncomfortable," Lucy said.

Moe said, "Yes, kids, this place is different than our world. The way they do things could easily make one feel that way. It's too formal for me. Kids, you'll have to keep reminding yourselves everything here is out of the ordinary. I probably wouldn't feel safe if it wasn't for Inge being here."

"Do you know they don't even have schools? They don't even know what a school is," I said, still perplexed.

"Yes, from what Mr. Moe has told me, our way of learning is different than yours," Mary said. "It is most interesting, and each of our cities has its own system. I do not know what to make of it."

A young Blue couple entered. The man said, "My name is Olook, and this is my companion Olooker."

"I am Mary, this is Mr. Moe and Lucy, Johnny, Mar, and Matt."

"Of course, we know who you are. Everyone knows who you are. Sir Inge asked us to give you a grand tour of Bluetropolis if you would like?" Olooker asked.

"Well, since we are staying the day, it might be interesting. But is it safe out there? Mary responded.

"The guards will be with us. It will be perfectly safe."

"Children, would you like a grand tour?" Mary asked.

"We would like that, but do you always need guards with you?" Lucy asked.

"Yes, those who cannot give up the old ways are a threat to the new ways," Olook answered.

"Why's it so hard for your people to accept freedom?" Matt asked.

"Why can't people just get along?" Mar added.

"We do not know. We have little experience with freedom. We were never allowed to think for ourselves," Olook said.

"Kids, our world isn't the same in many ways, although it seems our human nature is much the same. Maybe, if we didn't fight for our freedoms a long time ago, we would be more like these people."

"Mr. Moe, I guess it is so. Even Inbetweeners never fought for our freedom; we were just allowed to be."

"You told me if someone didn't tow-the-line, they would be treated differently."

"Mr. Moe, what is meant by tow-the-line?"

"It means to obey the rules."

"Oh, I see. Yes, if someone does not follow the rules, causing disruption, they would be dealt with in a way that forces them to stop their unruliness. Most treated in that way soon comply, which allows them to continue to live among us. If not, they were banished from trading."

"You mean they are given the old snub, so to speak," Moe said.

"What does that mean?"

"Miss Mary, I guess it means, to shut them out if they don't obey the rules until they behave better," Moe answered.

"Yes, it is our way."

"I always thought freedom was just there," Lucy said.

"Remember what we learned in history class. How all those wars were fought to gain our freedoms," I added.

Matt agreed, "Yes, we even had to kill each other, so all would be free."

"Does that mean they'll have to kill each other here too?" Mar asked.

"I hope no one has to be killed for our freedom?" Olooker said, horrified.

"Not if we can convince our people that freedom is best," Olook said.

"Famous last words."

"Mr. Moe, what does that mean?"

"Oh, sorry, Miss Mary. It's just another one of my sayings."

"Don't you think the main thing is whether we'll ever get

back home?" Lucy said, reminding us.

I was beginning to get tired of that being said, "We're-going-to-get-back-home. You know what I mean," I articulated.

"Oh, foo."

"Yes, Lucy, you know what he means, and we're going to get you there," Moe said.

A little puzzled, Olook changed the subject. "Well, shall we begin the grand tour? The transports are waiting."

"Yes. Are you ready, children?" Mary asked.

We acknowledged we were. In fact, I was more than ready, even at that age, I didn't like sitting around and waiting for things to happen, neither did Lucy.

CHAPTER 25 Confronted By The Sentencer

In a small caravan of transports, we headed out on the grand tour. On our flanks, were a protective contingent of transports manned by officers. Arriving in the center of Bluetropolis after having seen several sites of interest through the windows, Lucy asked, still not understanding, "Why does everything have to be blue? Can't you use other colors to liven things up?

"Liven things up, what does that mean?" Olook wondered.

Moe explained, "It simply means to make things more interesting. In our world, we use all the colors, and by doing so, it makes us feel better."

"Yes, I remember in class, we learned how the use of colors affected the way we felt," I added.

"That's what I mean. I don't think everything being blue is good," Lucy offered.

"Everything has always been blue. We do not know why. It is just that way."

"Olooker, I think what Lucy is saying is that part of being free is for a person being able to choose the colors that comforts them."

"Exactly, Miss Mary."

"Interesting. We will have to ask Sir Inge about that."

"Hey, look, there's the courthouse," Moe excitingly said.

"Oh, that dreadful place where that awful Sentencer was," Mary recounted, remembering the fright he caused.

"Yes, The Sentencer is thought to be the leader of the resistance," Olook informed.

"Some even say, he is hiding somewhere in the city," Olooker added.

"You mean that terrible person is still able to cause harm!" Mary exclaimed, feeling a chill.

"I am afraid so. Sir Inge believes the resistance would

collapse if he were captured," Olook added.

"Oh, my."

"Hey, could we see the inside of the courtroom?" I asked.

"I believe we can?" Olooker said, turning to Olook for confirmation.

"There is no reason we cannot."

"Do we have to?" Mary pleaded.

"Miss Mary, it'll be all right," Moe said, reassuring her.

Lucy looked at Olook and Olooker and enthusiastically stated, "Then let's see it?"

Ill at ease, Mary asked, "Could I stay outside while you go in?"

The head officer said, "Of course, my men and I will remain with you."

Stopping at the courthouse, a couple of officers led us up the marble steps and opened the doors, leaving the others outside with Mary, who remained in the transport.

Moe, Lucy, Mar, Matt, Olook, Olooker, and I, along with the two officers, entered the intimidating room where the sentencing took place. It was dim, cloaked in a drab blue color as everything else was. Large tall windows with blue glass dulled the daylight that was able to penetrate, giving the room a spooky foreboding atmosphere.

However, the light of the day shined in through the wide-open entrance doors allowing us to see the platform with the ornate chair where The Sentencer sat. To its side was the small desk with the bell and the stool where the little man sat, just as it was on the day the sentencing took place as Moe described it.

"I don't like this place," Lucy said, feeling its coldness.

Olook said, "We have never been here. It is a place no one ever wanted to enter."

"I don't remember those windows," Moe said. Suddenly, without warning, the doors slammed shut. Metal plates slid down, covering the windows leaving us in total darkness. Moe quickly concluded, "That's why I don't remember those windows."

"What's going on!" Mar exclaimed with fright.

"I do not know!" Olooker answered, also frightened as we all were.

To our horror, many hands grabbed us from behind as we all shrieked. Blue-tinged spotlights suddenly illuminated the Sentencer seated on his throne on the raised platform, along with the little clerk at his little desk. The room was now populated with many of those unwholesome blue-uniformed thugs restraining us. All casting long spooky shadows, just like in a scary horror movie.

Fearful, Olook asked with subdued confidence, "Sir, what is the meaning of this?"

"Justice! That is what," The Sentencer proclaimed.

"You mean the same kind of justice you used on us?" An unsettled Moe accused.

"Ah. The Moe! The very one who caused all the disorder. The very one who so disrupted our lives," The Sentencer said, with morbid delight.

"Sir, your days of power are over," Olooker bravely said.

Olook added, "You are an outlaw."

"I am not an outlaw! My power will always be. Now with The Moe in custody, our way will be restored."

Lucy collecting her thoughts, stated with courage, "You're a has-been. Your days are numbered." Turning to us, she ordered, "Let's get out here."

"That's right, let's go," I said, as we tried to break free without success.

"Who are these little people?" The Sentencer asked.

"Who are these little people, who do you think they are? Why they're *Rockers*, you dimwit. You'll be sorry you messed with them." Moe's statement brought ripples of alarm through the pack of thugs.

"Ah, this is even better." The Sentencer said. He turned to the little man at the desk and ordered, "Send this message to that Exalted pretender. If you want no harm to come to The Moe and the little people, you must return my power."

"You cannot do that," Olooker proclaimed. "Sir, Inge will make you pay for this."

"Yes, he will, you maniac," Lucy added.

"Maniac! You will see who the maniac is."

Meanwhile, outside, Mary, greatly distraught, watched as the officers worked desperately to pry the doors open. The Sentence's message was slipped under the door where the head officer picked it up and read it, then ordered one of his men to speed and bring it to Sir Inge."

"What does it say?" A distressed Mary asked.

"Mary, Sir Inge will be here shortly. Please be patient," the officer replied.

"Oh, my! Oh, my! Would you please keep trying to open those doors?" He assured her they would, as he ordered more men to help.

Inside the courtroom, The Sentencer was speaking, "You think you were able to destroy our order just by your presence. You are mistaken. The people of Bluetropolis need to be controlled. They are like children who need strict supervision. When I put down this rebellion, things will return to the way they were."

"Yes, back to your hateful, oppressive, tyrannical, evil ways. Never!"

Moe's words infuriated The Sentencer even more so, as he responded, "Evil Ways! We will see who is evil."

"You don't even know you're evil, you pitiful evil creep," Lucy said, with unwarranted confidence.

"Yeah, you pathetic evil creep," I added.

"Yes, now open those doors," Moe, ordered.

The Sentencer became so infuriated by our accusations, he could hardly contain himself, "You worms, just like all the others, you are of no value. If it were not for me, there would be no order. There would be no meaning. The feebleness of the Blue people would lead to chaos and the downfall of our society. I am the keeper of the rules and laws, which protects us from unworthy commoners who do not understand unless they are dealt with harshly. My intellect and understanding make me infinitely qualified to be The Sentencer."

"Yes, that's if someone wants the bad guys to be in charge, you overblown idiot," Moe said.

"Idiot! Bad guys! You will see who the bad guys are. You will never see the light of day again."

Emboldened, as an unnatural strength in this dangerous situation, grew in us, which even surprised us. Olook threatened, "Your days of terror are over, and unless you open those doors immediately, you will pay the highest price."

His arteries bulged out of his neck as his face turned almost black, The Sentencer yelled, "Why you insignificant specks of nothing. The highest price, if you mean the *White Light*, I am above that. I am of the highest rank." The moment he uttered those faithless few words, his head began to swell until a bolt of *White Light* exploded around him blinding us.

When able to see again, there lay only a heap of his clothing where he sat. All the thugs, including the little clerk, were frozen in place. Astonished, we looked at his now empty clothing, the thugs, and then at each other.

Then…a speck of *White Light* appeared at the head of the room, and in spite of the glow, we were able to see a *Man in White* standing among us. He said, "Johnny, Lucy, Mar, Matt and you too Moe, there is always a lesson in what one experiences. It is most important to understand your purpose in all that takes place. If one tries hard enough showing great courage, as you just did, one gain's that understanding."

"Sir, what happened to The Sentencer?"

"Lucy, there are some who are so opposed to goodness they believe they are worthy of challenging the *White Light*, which causes true justice to take place. He no longer can harm anyone."

Before any of us could ask anything more, a thunderous cracking sound was heard. A beam of *White Light* began to cut through the wall, at a point behind The Sentence's seat traveling up and around the ceiling and down through the entrance doors. It split the building-wide open like an eggshell fully exposing the inside. As this took place, we couldn't help but scream at the top of our lungs.

When the *Light* dissipated, the *Man in White* was gone. Before we could collect ourselves, a distraught Mary dashed through the mangled doors, followed by the officers. She exclaimed, "You are alive! You are alive!" She hugged us, then turned to Moe and asked with tears of relief in her eyes, "Mr. Moe, are you all right?"

"I think so, Miss Mary. You wouldn't believe what just happened. There was The Sentencer, there was the *White Light*, and there was a *Man in White*."

"I thought we were going to die," Mar tearfully said,

trembling.

"What did that man mean when he said, to understand our purpose?" Lucy asked.

"I think he meant there's a lesson in all this," I speculated.

"Miss Mary, the Sentencer, just got a taste of real justice."

"Mr. Moe, I want to hear all about it, but please let us get out of this dreadful place."

The head officer ordered his men to round up the dazed thugs. Then led us to the transport and we sped us back to the palace.

CHAPTER 26 Ike Joins Us In Our Journey

Arriving in the palace's courtyard, we found Inge readying a regiment to rescue us. They were carrying wooden spikes or short spears, which surprised Moe, for he told us the deadliest weapons he ever saw the Blues carrying were clubs. He wondered if he had influenced this change by speaking of it when first here.

However, an extremely concerned Inge, asked, "Are you unharmed? What happened, my friends?"

"Sir, it was The Sentencer," Olook said, as a hush came over everyone.

"Yes, he trapped us in the courthouse and tried to sentence us to jail forever," Lucy recounted.

"Yes, I thought we were going to die," Mar said, stressed, yet relieved.

"Then there was the *White Light* and a *Man in White*," I said.

"The *White Light*, a *Man in White*, where is The Sentencer now?" Inge asked.

"He's no more, at least I hope so," Moe said.

"Yes, it is so, and the *White Light* split that awful place in two," Mary said, with satisfaction.

"The *White Light*? Well, I see you have been through an extraordinary experience. Let us go inside where you can relax and tell the whole story." He first ordered some of his men to go and help with the prisoners.

In the comfort of a plush room, we related what happened along with Olook and Olooker, who both for unexplained reasons not only saw the White Light but the Man in White as well. After Inge heard the whole story, he said, "It looks like you have done it."

"Done what?" Moe asked.

"Why you have rid us of our most sinister enemy," Olooker said.

"We didn't do much."

"Moe, you must admit you did something that caused the demise of the Sentencer," Inge said, then admitted, "We have been looking for him since you were here last without success."

Proudly, Mary turned to Moe, "Yes, Mr. Moe, you did something great."

"What about us? We were there too," Lucy said.

"Yes, it is true, they all stood up to The Sentencer with great courage until he exploded," Olooker testified.

"Olooker and Olook also spoke up to him," Lucy added.

With a smile, Inge said, "I see you all did. Now you are all heroes." I must admit, that recognition made us all beam with pride beyond anything we ever felt before, but at that point, we didn't yet comprehend where that remarkable courage came from.

Ofeela said, "My father must hear the whole story from your lips. Tonight you must tell him at a celebration of this great victory. Now, would you like something to eat?"

"I'm famished," Moe said, as he rubbed his hands together.

"Yes, please. We would like that very much," Mary added.

"Well then, come this way," Ofeela ordered, as Inge excused himself to take charge of his men at the courthouse.

That evening we gathered with Inge, Ofeela, Olook, and Olooker and were led to the great hall packed with hundreds, which overflowed into the courtyard and out into the surrounding jam-packed streets.

To the sound of bugles announcing our arrival, we moved through the gathering to the center of the large room. It was comical to see The Exalted One and his wife seated on those huge pillows on a portable raised platform. Wondering if they lived like that all the time for they remained distant, like cardboard characters, never having socialized with us.

Ofeela motioned for us to sit with her and Inge on cushions in a semicircle facing her Exalted parents. The Exalted One raised his hand, and the room became silent. He said, "I have heard of the miracle you have performed. However, I want to hear the whole story in your own words."

Bolstered by all the adoration, we flamboyantly described the events, along with Olook, and Olooker. Our embellished descriptions delighted everyone.

When finished, the Exalted One said, "We forever will be in your debt and grateful to all of you for eliminating the evil one. Now with The Sentencer gone, there is no longer a resistance. We would like you to stay in Bluetropolis to be honored."

Moe stood up and said, "Thank you, but sir, the kids must get back to their world. Their parents surely are frantic by now. We must get back on the pebble *Road* as soon as possible."

"Certainly, I understand. Please stay the night and rest with us tomorrow so we could show our gratitude. We will fill the Dragon with additional provisions for your trip," The Exalted proclaimed.

"Yes, we will be grateful to rest and appreciate all the help you can give us," Mary said, thanking him. Mary and Moe understood, in this world, to rush off and not accept the hospitality when invited could amount to an insult.

"So be it," the Exalted One declared. The people cheered and moved in on us, lifting us over their heads, honoring us as they paraded us around the hall to the enjoyment of all.

Later in the evening, while the celebrating and honors were still going on, Mary said to Ofeela, "After this, we will need tomorrow to rest."

With a sigh, Ofeela said, "Yes, so shall we all. Tomorrow, please sleep as late as you like." Shortly we exchanged good nights with Inge and Ofeela and slipped away, for I must say was a well-earned night's sleep, leaving the people to continue their celebrating.

The next morning, after an uneasy night and sleeping late, we were more than eager to continue on our journey. However, we agreed to stay the day. We spent part of it trying to interpret the momentous events of the past few days. We could only come up with simple conclusions, such as; there is *Good and Evil,* in both our worlds.

However, a fundamental understanding was all too simple for us to accept as the answer to what we were to look for. (At that age, our emotional and intellectual depth was shallow, yet we looked for deeper and more profound forms of knowledge we assumed was to be grasped.)

What we clearly knew was in order to get back home, we must continue the journey. The great mysteries remained, like where does that *White Light* come from, and who are those *Men in White*? So far, we found little help in finding answers, except for a simple suggestion from Inge and Ofeela, those answers might only be found at the end of the *Road*, or perhaps forever remain unanswered.

We knew Moe and Mary's knowledge was limited, and they weren't entirely sure what their part in all this was. However, in turn, they knew how awful young and inexperienced we were. These factors were building tension as the trip became painfully slow in our view, although it's only been days since we arrived in this world.

Our frustration in not quickly returning home was growing as we faced each new situation, although, we strangely were enjoying the adventure of being among these people. However, on the other hand, we wished we could drive straight through to the *Road's* end. Yet, we couldn't dismiss making contact with the inhabitants of each city. Those requirements only added to our guess in how much longer the journey would take.

Instead of getting any rest that day, the Blue people actively celebrated us. For good reasons, they couldn't stop rejoicing in the demise of the Sentencer and their newfound freedom. The Blues were only beginning to taste freedom. They didn't yet realize how drastically their lives had changed forever. They just felt the good feelings they were experiencing, which was permissible before the sobering up necessary for them to accept the responsibilities of good governance, which would come into play soon enough, hopefully with Inge's guidance.

In hindsight, we tried to figure out why it was so easy to topple The Sentencer. For it only took words to unleash the power of the *White Light* and The *Men in White*. It made us feel uneasy about all the credit they were giving us. We accepted strange powers were enabling us. This fact alone added to our desire to get back on the *Road* and away from the confusion innocently being heaped on us.

By order of the Exalted One, the Blue people washed and

packed the Dragon with as many provisions as possible, including several cans of fuel.

Inge introduced us to our new traveling companion, a little Redman looking very much like Inge. "My friends, this is Ike, my oldest and most faithful friend, a person you can put your full trust in. I believe he will be most helpful."

"Glad to meet you, Ike," Moe said, as he shook his hand.

"Yes, we so appreciate your willingness to come with us," a pleased Mary added.

"It is my honor to be your guide."

"Good. Tomorrow morning we will see you off," Inge concluded.

Later, due to the sheer exhaustion of the people, to our relief, the festivities slowed and finally ended. After our last time alone with Inge and Ofeela, we retired to our rooms in anticipation of what tomorrow would bring.

The next morning we were up early and ready to leave. After breakfast, Inge cleared the emotions out of his throat before saying, "Well, the time has come, let us get on with it." He and Ofeela led us out into the plaza where countless numbers of well-wishers were waiting to see us off. When we exited the building, the throng let out a thunderous cheer.

The Exalted One and his wife were waiting, as always on their platform, seated on their throne pillows. We worked our way through the adoring crowd to the sound of bulges, which was awe-inspiring.

Reaching their platform, The Exalted One stood and raised his hand, silencing the crowd. He said, "Our gratitude will last forever. You will always be welcomed in Bluetropolis. May your trip up the *Road* be safe and triumphant. Farewell, our friends," followed by more cheers.

Inge gave Moe a manly hug, "Be careful, my friend." Mary hugged Ofeela with a tear in her eye. She then hugged Inge as Moe shook Ofeela's hand.

Turning to us, Ofeela said, "It was so nice to meet you, Lucy, Johnny, Mar, and Matt, may you reach the end of the *Road* and your dreams of getting back home be fulfilled.

We gave her a modest nod of appreciation and looked to Moe and Mary as young people might when not sure how to act.

Moe ordered, in the biggest voice he could muster to be heard by all, "Let's get back on the *Road*!" Exciting the crowd as we climbed into the Dragon. We waved and yelled our farewells over the roar of the Dragon's engine and slowly drove by the masses along the streets until we were out of the city and once again alone and on our way home

CHAPTER 27 Arriving In Dotsville

Back on the *Road*, Moe accelerated to get the roar of the Dragon behind us. He asked, "Ike, what's next?"

"What is next is what comes next."

Mary, seeing how similar to Inge he was, rephrased the question, "Ike, what is the next realm we will be driving into?"

"I will be Dotsville, the land of the Poke-a-Dotted people."

"Mr. Ike, the Poke-a-Dotted people? What kind of people are they?" Lucy asked.

"I'm not a Mister. Just call me Ike."

"Yes, Sir."

"I am not a Sir either. Unless they are bestowed on us, we do not use such titles. Just call me Ike."

"Sorry," Lucy said, a bit embarrassed. Then with a grin, she blurted out, "Ike."

"Anyway Ike, what are the Poke-a-Dotted people like?" I asked.

"They are a harmless people. The only thing is if you ask them a question, you cannot believe their answers."

"As a child, I heard about them, but now I can only wonder if they cannot be believed, how are we trust them?" Mary asked.

"They are not capable of giving truthful answers just as they're not able to ask questions."

"Are they liars?"

"Liars, not so Johnny. They just do not ask or answer questions."

"If you don't tell the truth, isn't that lying?"

"Lucy, it's true in our world. Remember, this is a different world."

"Yes, Mr. Moe, we know everything is different here, right?" I said as I looked into Lucy's eyes, correcting her.

"Yes, I remember. I remember," she grudgingly said.

"Ike, how many cities must we go through to reach the end?" Mar asked.

"I do not know. No one knows. No one has ever reached the end."

"Do you mean there's no end?" Mar asked, confused.

"No, of course not. It just means no one known has ever reached it. We might well be the first," Moe said.

"Do not worry, children. Mr. Moe and Ike will get you there. Now, let us rest, for it is going to be a long ride."

"Yes, Miss Mary," Mar said, as we sat back and tried to relax as the Dragon sped on.

Driving on, we passed a variety of terrains, fields of large flowers, thick and tall grasses lands, heavily wooded areas, rocky or entirely barren spaces. Driving for almost a full day, we only stopped for picnic-style meals. There was no pattern to the changing landscapes, which seamlessly rotated from one to the other.

In spite of the terrain being unusual, it remained just something of curiosity not to spend time analyzing. It seemed our young minds hadn't yet developed to the point of concentrating on details. We simply longed to get back home. However, we did spend some time on the *Why Us* question. We tried to analyze what we might have done to deserve this adventure, not yet knowing if it was a blessing or a curse.

The only people we saw since leaving Bluetropolis, were speeding by in their transports so fast we weren't able to unrecognize who they were or their color. When our questions were exhausted, we spent time either sleeping or being mesmerized by the scenery, hoping the end of the *Road* would soon appear.

In time, we began to see people in the distance along the roadside. Mar, the first to notice, saying, "Hey, look at those people," with puzzlement in her voice.

"I see them. So?" Lucy asked.

With a chuckle, she said, "Don't you see? They're poke-a-dotted."

Speeding closer and able to see them clearly, "Hey, that's right, they're poke-a-dotted," Lucy agreed.

Closer yet, Mar pointed out, "See they have red, blue,

orange, and yellow dots on their chalk-white faces and clothing."

"I see some black and purple dots too. Hey, don't they look like clowns." Matt said.

"Yes, they do," I said. Turning to Ike, "We must be near Dotsville, right?"

"Yes, we are approaching Dotsville." We will soon be there."

"So, these people can't tell the truth, right?"

"Well, Lucy. When you ask them a question, you cannot believe the answers they give, and they will never ask questions. However, they are not liars, as you might think. It is because they are not capable of dealing with questions and answers."

"Having known of them all my life, I must admit I never gave it much thought, but now, I only wonder how they function without asking or answering questions. By the way, what are clowns?" Mary asked.

"Clowns are people who work in the circus to entertain us. They paint their faces and wear brightly colored clothing with lots of dots, looking very much like these people.

"Mr. Moe, that is most interesting," Mary said.

"Yes, but clowns are funny, honest, and are make-believe, who use makeup on their faces," Lucy said.

Mary said, "That is very interesting."

Ike explained, "You must remember, these people are not dishonest in spite of their misleading answers and never asking questions. Sometimes the truth is in the ears of the listener. They have developed a way of communicating the real answers without saying it. They know how to ask questions without expressing them as questions."

"Kids, I guess it's like in our world when things are seen differently. When people disagree with each other, each side believes they are truthful, and their opposition was not, and they start to accuse without understanding where others were coming from. They do this instead of trying to find how to communicate in a way that could resolve their misunderstandings. Kids, let's see what they're like before we condemn them."

"Mr. Moe, you mean like in politics?" I said.

"Yes, I guess something like in politics, where people don't always ask or answer questions straightforward and sometimes lack honestly. Yes, in those circumstances, one must learn to interpret what's actually being said," Moe, instructed.

"Mr. Moe, how strange your world is. Ike, how does one know when the Dot people are telling the truth?" Mary asked.

"You must understand they are honest when spoken to correctly. The trick is not to ask questions. One must rephrase a question, so it appears not to be a question. And, if you should ask them a question, you must understand what they say is probably the opposite of the correct answer."

"That's complicated. Can't we just skip this place?" Lucy asked.

"I am afraid not. We must pass through all the city centers."

"Can't we just drive around it?"

"There're no roads around them. The only way to get past them is right through their center. And, as I understand it, the way to gain understanding is by going to the heart of each city." Ike again explained.

"That's correct, we must enter all the cities," Moe added.

"Yes, I agree, if understanding is found in the cities, then we must go into each one. The *Road* runs right through some cities, and others are far off it, like Bluetropolis. No matter who lives in or where each city is located, we must drive into each one." Ike reasoned.

"Ike, I guess we'll have to leave no rock unturned," Moe said, with humor as Ike almost smiled. "Kids, we must remember what the *Men in White* instructed us to do."

"We're never going to get back home, are we!" Mar exclaimed.

"Children, yes, you will, everything will be all right. We will do just fine," Mary again reassured.

"Yes, kids. Now sit back and relax. Let's enjoy your ride back home."

Before long, we entered the city. The density of the population increased as we drew closer to its center. "Are you sure we're going to be all right?" Mar asked Ike.

"As I said, Dotes are harmless. There is no need to worry."

The city was colorful, filled with bright poke-a-dotted patterns covering all things. Even the pebbles on the *Road* were poke-a-dotted, which was amazing. Just seeing the variety of colors and the high energy of the people going about their daily activities could only help to cheer one up. Even Ike seemed stimulated.

At its center was a large square, which looked like an open market. However, tables piled high with goods blocked our way. The overflowing crowd seemed to be shopping. Unable to drive through, Moe stopped and stuck his head up through the hatch on the roof of the Dragon and looked around.

After a moment, he yelled down, "There are so many tables covering the *Road*, it's impossible to see where it is."

"Oh, my!" Mary exclaimed.

"What do we do now?" Lucy asked.

"Where did it go?"

"Nowhere, Mar, it is under the feet of the people," Ike said.

"Does that mean we have to stay here until they go away?" Lucy asked.

"I guess we'll find out," Moe said, as he sat back down.

"It's time to stretch our legs," he opened the door and stepped out.

A little child exclaimed, "Look!" as he pointed his little chubby finger at us, upon which everyone within hearing stopped what they were doing and stood there staring at us. "In which direction does the *Road* go?" Moe asked. Hands went up, pointing in every direction except straight ahead.

"See what I mean. Questions do not work," Ike said, with a sigh.

"Why are they looking at us like that?" Lucy asked, feeling all eyes were on her.

"I believe these people have never seen a dotless person."

"Yes, Mary, and especially pink children," Ike added.

"Will they hurt us?"

"No... Mar, as I said, these people are not dangerous."

"Kids, we'll be all right," Moe reassured.

"What do we do now?" I asked.

To our surprise, a voice came from the crowd, "Welcome to Dotsville." A short, thin man with a smile on his face approached.

He was wearing a tightly fitted poke-a-dotted suit with a poke-a-dotted fedora on his head. "You are tired and hungry, come this way," He ordered.

"Where is the *Road*?" Lucy asked, forgetting. Again, hands pointed in every direction except straight ahead. Puzzled, she mumbled, "What are they doing? I think they're crazy."

Ike quickly placed his hand on her shoulder to hush her, saying to the crowd, "She thinks how good looking you all are. I know you have never seen pink children before, but these children are your friends. We're on our way to the end of the *Road*." A loud-soft "Ah" rippled through the crowd.

Curious and non-threatening, the people closed in on us. Uncertain, we looked back at them as Ike said to the man with the fedora, "Sir, to be hungry and tired is not good."

The man cheerfully volunteered, "I will show you a place to eat. It would be best to drive there." He directed the crowd to part, and quickly, the tables and goods were moved off the *Road*.

Moe started to ask, "Do we follow...?"

Ike quickly whispered, "Do not ask questions." Moe understood and nodded.

Once in the Dragon, without being asked, the man ordered, "Follow the *Road*." We poked each other, calling attention to the looks of this strange man, who had a frozen smile on his white poke-a-doted face with the corners of his deep red lips pointed up.

"Will we be all right?" Mar whispered to Mary.

"We must trust Ike."

Moe followed the man's directions, turn here, turn there, and so on. Meanwhile, Ike cleverly held a conversation seeking information without questioning. "My name is Ike, this is Mary, and this is Moe," followed by introducing us all.

"My name is Patrued," the man said without being asked.

"The houses out here are built of exceptional quality," Ike said.

"This is where the High-pokes live," Patrued said.

"These are beautiful houses to live in."

"I do not live here. Only the High-Pokes do."

Mary picked up the twist, "I would have guessed you to be a High-Poke."

He responded cheerfully to her non-question, saying, "I am just a Middle-Poke, the go-between the High-Pokes and everyone else." Shortly, he ordered, "Stop here" alongside a set of massive iron gates and said, "Wait here," he jumped out and jerked a chain hanging by the gates, which rang a loud bell. Someone appeared on the other side, Patrued announced, "I have travelers with me." The gates swung open. He jumped back in, and with that permanent grin of his, he ordered Moe to drive in."

Inside the gates was a walled-in area. Patrued pointed to a large stately building across the open plaza. We drove to the foot of the massive marble steps leading up to its entrance doors. The twenty-five steps were about forty feet wide. Patrued jumped out and ran up the steps to the set of massive doors and rang the bell. He said something into a small slot in the door we couldn't hear.

"Wherever he is taking us, I hope everything will be all right," Mar said.

"Not to worry," Ike reassured. Patrued motioned for us to come out and up the steps. Halfway up, the doors flung open, and a short, robust poke-a-doted man popped out, followed by a cluster of poke-a-doted men and women of all shapes and sizes. They quickly moved down the steps to greet us. The lead man enthusiastically invited, "Come in, my friends."

He led us into a large room where several semi-circle tiers filled with poke-a-doted desks, poke-a-doted chairs with poke-a-doted people seated on them. And up onto a raised platform, he said, "I am Sir Patrin, the leader of the High Council."

After an awkward pause, Ike introduced himself and then indicated for us to do the same. The council members were delighted to hear and react to each of our names. Then, Patrin said, "It is a great pleasure for the council to meet you," as all the members stood and bowed in acknowledgment. He then said, "We would like your story to be told," not quite a question.

"Sir, they are tired and hungry," Patrued said.

"Yes, yes, it must be so. It is late in the day, and they must be refreshed. Patrued, take our guests to the residency. We will all rest tonight and hold a grand meeting early tomorrow."

"Come this way," Patrued directed us.

At the residency, we were served dinner on a poke-a-doted table with a poke-a-doted tablecloth, sitting on poke-a-doted chairs, eating off poke-a-doted plates with poke-a-doted utensils. We enjoyed the make-believe feeling, quietly making many silly poke-a-doted jokes to each other as we ate.

After dinner, in a room with couches clad with plush poke-a-doted fabric, we waited for our sleeping accommodations being prepared. We curled up, getting as comfortable as possible. Moe asked, "Well, kids, what do you think?"

"Isn't that a question, I thought we couldn't ask questions?" Mar asked.

"That's only when talking to the poke-a-doted people," Lucy said as she shook her head from side to side.

"Oh, yes, I knew that."

"I still wonder how we are supposed to gain understanding from these people if asking or answering questions can't be done," Mary said.

"Aren't we to rephrase questions into non-questions?" I asked.

"I think that's it."

"Yes, Moe, it is as right as right could be," Ike said.

"It's ridiculous, why can't they just ask questions," Lucy said, as she again shook her head from side to side.

Still puzzled, I asked, "How do they get along with each other and communicate if they can't ask questions or give answers?"

"In my world, there are different cultures with many confusing ways to communicate. I do not fully understand why it is so."

"Miss Mary, I think you've touched on something. These people seem to be doing okay."

"You are right, Moe. The Poke-A-Dotes seem to do just fine in their way. They appear to talk in code or something only they understand. However, I believe the real question is, what are we supposed to do while here?"

Mar changed the subject, "When are we going to get back on the *Road*? We're never going to get out of this world at this rate."

"Yes, I'm feeling the same way," Matt added.

Just then, seven poke-a-doted young ladies entered, followed by Patrued. "The dots will show you to your sleeping places. Please follow them," He instructed.

As we stood, Moe whispered, "We'll try to find those answers tomorrow."

In the glow of their lanterns, each of us was led by a personal dot to a private room with a bed with poke-a-doted sheets, pillowcases, and a set of poke-a-doted pajamas laid out for us. We felt a little fearful of being isolated from each other, but it was another exhausting day, and it wasn't long before we were all asleep.

CHAPTER 28 The Great Disruption

After spending several short sixteen-hour days in this world, things weren't making any more sense than when we first arrived. We seemed no closer to getting home.

Alone in Dotsville at breakfast allowed us to speak freely; I asked Ike, "What do you think this meeting is all about?"

"The High Council is the ruling body of Dotsville."

"What do they want with us?" Lucy asked Ike.

"That is simple, they are fascinated with you. These people want to know all about you."

"How in the world are they going to find out about us if they can't ask questions so we can give answers?" Lucy wondered.

"I am thinking the same thing, and it seems to be most difficult," Mary concluded.

"Oh, how are we ever going to get home?" Mar asked.

"Don't worry, we will," Moe reassured.

"Yes, we will, you know what I mean," I added.

"What-do-you-mean?" Lucy articulated.

"Now, children, let us stay positive and spend our time trying to gain more of the understanding," Mary instructed.

"Yes, let us deal with each step as it comes. We will reach the end of the *Road* when we reach the end of the *Road*," Ike added.

Just then, Patrued entered, "The High Council will greet you when you've finished eating and freshened up."

"Let's eat," Moe said as he took another full, helping with a sense of urgency.

"Children, do not rush your eating," Mary added.

We entered the high council's meeting room full of misgivings. It was crowded with chattering Poke-A-Dot men and women. A silence abruptly came over the hall. "Ah, they are here. Welcome. Please, come up and sit with me," the leader Patrin invited.

As we moved onto the platform, the gathering applauded, taking us by surprise. We sat on straight-back chairs lined up facing the audience. Prancing around in front of us, Patrin declared, "It would be wonderful if your travels could be told," again not a question, but rather an invitation.

We looked at Moe to speak first. "Be truthful," Ike whispered.

As he stood and cleared his throat, Patrin said, "Please, stay seated. You do not have to rise for us."

A little taken back, he sat and started to speak with the highest volume he could muster, "Well, my friends, we took to the *Road* to get these kids back to their world."

The crowd let out a soft-loud, "Ah..."

"Members, he means the world on the other side of the *Rock*," Patrin clarified. Turning to Moe with anticipation, he pleaded, "Please, please continue."

"Well, days ago, we started on our journey." The crowd listened intensely to every word as he told of our trip. However, he didn't say anything about the *White Light* and the *Men in White* in fear of what it might invoke. Ending with, "And now we are here," to the delight of the audience as they applauded.

"Yes, and there are adventures ahead," Patrin said as if it were a boast causing ripples of excitement through the room. He looked to Moe for a response. Ike motioned, urging Moe to continue who was puzzled, being unsure of what they expected of him.

Dismayed at that point, Lucy, in her frustration in seeing the Dots unusual behavior, allowed her natural feelings to well up from deep inside her as she asked, "Why can't you just ask questions so we could give answers?" to the chagrin of Mary and Ike.

"Oh, my."

"No, Lucy."

In a quandary, also frustrated and being protective of Lucy, Moe said, "Yes, yes, why can't you just ask questions so we can give answers?" This caused an excited commotion among the council members.

"Here we go," Ike mumbled.

"Oh, my. Oh, my."

Patrued, who'd been silent, asked, "What is meant by questions?" Suddenly, he realized he asked a question and was horrified, he clasped his hands over his mouth.

With that one slip, the council was thrown into a frenzy as we watched their bizarre behavior in wonderment. Extremely troubled, Patrin raised his hands and called for order. As silence came over the room, he said, "Patrued made a mistake, a big mistake."

"Why is it so wrong to ask questions?" Lucy sincerely asked without hesitation, still baffled.

Seeing the developing problem, I came to the defense of my sister, "Yes, what's wrong with questions, you know what I mean?"

"Oh, my."

"Please, please, we must get back to the story," Patrin pleaded.

Patrued, conflicted, asked with gusto to everyone's surprise, "Yes, what's wrong with questions?" His brow wrinkled as his eyes darted around as if trying to see what was going on inside his own head.

Moe stood and asked, "Yes, what's wrong with that?"

Amidst the shock and disorder, some of the councilwomen fainted. Patrin tried to stop the pandemonium and appealed, "Please, no more questions."

Patrued, who had now lost all inhibitions and his sense of conformity, blurted out, "I want to ask questions, and I would like to get answers!"

At that point, the council members began to scream and run for the exits. We looked at each other in awkwardness and a bit amused in seeing their more or less comical behavior. It was like watching clowns in the circus carrying on in their silly larger-than-life skits.

When the room was almost empty Patrin, asked, "Patrued, what have you done?" Realizing he asked a question, he placed his hands over his mouth and fainted.

In shock, Patrued asked, "What is going on? What has happened to me?"

Immediately an enormous clap of thunder with a flash of *White Light* struck, blinding us for seconds. When able to see again,

Mar pointed to Patrued, "Look!"

We looked at him and gasped. "What is wrong?" he asked.

"Your dots!" Mar exclaimed.

Rubbing his face, "What about my dots?"

"They're gone. You're white like Miss Mary," Lucy answered.

Patrued said, "I am White. I am White," letting out a shriek of horror.

"I think it is time to move on. I believe we have done all there is to be done here," Ike said, with a sense of urgency.

"I think that's a good idea," Moe agreed.

"Let us go, children," Mary ordered.

"Where are we going?"

"To the Dragon Mar, if it is still outside."

"Let us not hesitate," Ike ordered.

We quickly moved out into the plaza where the council members were prostrate on the ground lamenting, not in pain, but in fear. Hesitating, not knowing what to think or do as we saw a loud vocal crowd streaming through the entrance gate, Ike again urged, "Let us go."

The Dragon was where we parked it, "Keep moving children," Mary said as she herded us along.

As Moe started the engine. he realized Patrued was among us, "You can't come with us."

"Why not, I am white now, and you caused it. I cannot stay here."

"He might have a point," Ike said.

"Well… Okay." He stepped on the pedal, and off we went blowing the Dragon's horn as we cut a path slowly through the crowd. Since the people didn't recognize us through the tinted windows, there was no attempt to stop us in spite of the undeniable appearance of the Dragon. We exited the gate, and Patrued directed us to the quickest way out of the city.

We sat in silence, filled with high anxiety until we were well beyond the city's limits.

CHAPTER 29 Arriving In Redtown

Back on the *Road*, driving away from Dotsville. "What went wrong?"

"Who knows Mar, Lucy innocently said."

I accused Lucy, "You said the wrong thing."

"All I did was to ask a question. That's all."

"And, that was the wrong thing."

"Wait! I do not think it was wrong. I always wanted to ask questions," Patrued said.

"Why didn't you just ask them?" Matt asked.

"We were not supposed to. It was not to be done. We were taught if asked a question, we were to give wrong answers. It has been our way."

"Why that's crazy," Lucy said.

"Children, remember in my world people do not have the freedoms you have in your world," Mary instructed.

"Maybe, I did what I was supposed to do. Ha!"

"Lucy, you might be right. It certainly was effective. Hopefully, your actions will cause Dotsville to change for the better and never to be the same," Ike speculated.

"There was a strike of *White Light* back there, and I'm beginning to see a pattern. Now kids, let's keep our eyes on the prize to get you back home. I think if we add everything up, no matter how or why it happens, it might lead to the understanding. And, I think something in Dotsville must be understood."

"Yes, Moe, it does seem the *White Light*, which I never saw before, is at the center of this understanding."

It makes sense, Ike. I heard of the *Light* all my life but never saw it until the day it split my beautiful tree. Mr. Moe, do you think it will remain with us until we reach the end?"

"Miss Mary, I do believe it will."

"And it seems from my understanding when the *Light* strikes it is time to move on," Ike added.

"You see, I wasn't wrong," Lucy said with a smirk.

"Oh Lucy," I said, although I had to concede that win went to her.

"Now, kids, we're on the *Road* again, which means we're closer to its end."

"Yes. Yes," I said as I pumped my fist in the air.

"Yes. Yes," as we all join in, repeating it several times, getting our attention back on our quest.

"This is thrilling," Patrued said. "You know I have never been outside of Dotsville. Where do we go next?"

"To now be a free man must be exciting for you?" Moe asked.

"It is. And I do not understand why this has happened to me? What is this *White Light* anyway?" he asked.

"We're not sure. Would you like to join us in finding the understanding?" Moe asked.

"Oh, yes. I would be honored to join you."

Moe asked Ike, "Well then, what's next?"

"What comes next is what comes next."

"Oh, Ike, please tell us what's next," Mary pleaded.

"I will, I will. It is my home city, Redtown. It has been most exhausting traveling with you, let me rest awhile, and then I will tell you more," he said as he sat back in his seat. Moe floored the pedal, and we sped on our way.

The next day, we approached a populated area with red people. "Ike, are these your people?" Moe said, asking the obvious to stir him from his nap.

"Ah yes, we are approaching Redtown," he said, rubbing his eyes as he looked out the windows.

"Is everybody going to be red in Redtown?"

"Yes Lucy, red is red," Ike, answered.

"Ike, how long have you been away?" Mary asked.

"This time, I have been away for almost a cycle."

"You must be homesick?" Mar asked.

"Homesick, what is meant by that?"

"It means, to miss your home a lot," Moe said.

"Ah, I guess I am homesick."

"Then you must be happy to be back?" Lucy asked.

"Happy?" Ike didn't know how to apply that feeling to this situation.

"It means you are pleased," Mary said.

"Ah, yes, I am pleased."

"I'd be really pleased to get back home," Mar said.

"Ike, tell us about Redtown," Mary asked.

"I will... It is a quiet place. Not much happens here. We find most of our excitement in reading about other places, and in traveling to see them, for we are travelers."

"I thought you were printers, for all the books I have read were printed in Redtown," Mary said.

"Yes, that is what we do for a trade. We do all the printing for the cities."

"I thought you said you were travelers?" Lucy asked.

"Yes, that is also true. You see, as a result of our printing, we have access to all the reading material from all the cities. Reading about other places, we could not help but become curious and wished to see those places. Therefore, some of us have also become travelers."

"So you're a painter too?" Moe asked.

"Yes, all Redmen work in printing in one way or another. Fortunately, we are also able to satisfy our desire to travel from the profits made from printing. Many take advantage of that opportunity, as Inge and I have. My father is a master printer, as well as a great traveler. If you would like, I will take you to my family's home to meet him?"

"Oh Yes, I think it would be very nice," Mary said.

"That'll be fun," Lucy said.

"Yes, it would be," I added.

"Then, I will direct you there."

"Just tell me where to go?" Moe said.

"I shall. It is still a distance up the *Road*. When we get there, I will direct you."

"You got it."

"What have I got?"

"Sorry, it's just an expression in my world."

"I see," Ike said, although not understanding.

Later, Ike said, "Turn right at the next intersection."

"Okay," Moe said and headed towards the city as the rest of us focused on watching where we were going.

"Everything is really going to be red, right?"

"Yes, Lucy. As I said, red is red."

"Lucy, I guess that's why they call it Redtown. You know what I mean," I said and poked her.

"We all know what you mean. It seems most things in this world exist only in one or two dimensions," Moe said.

"Are things not like that in your world?"

"Ike, everything in their world is mixed all together, which is most confusing," Mary added.

"And your world is confusing to us," Lucy added.

"I guess what one knows is what one knows," Ike said.

"It must be true; it's all in the eyes of those who see it," Moe added.

"You mean whatever we become accustomed to, becomes normal, right?"

"Right, Johnny, something like that."

"Turn left at the next intersection," Ike directed.

"You got it. I mean, okay. I mean, I'll turn here."

Driving deep into the city, along streets that appeared to be residential neighborhoods, built in a style of construction unfamiliar to us. The streets were lined with tall, extremely narrow detached red houses, separated only by a few feet. They were surrounded by dense dwarf bushes and sparse trees with trunks only about two inches thick, yet forty feet tall, reaching above the rooftops and laden with stunted branches as not to touch the buildings, carrying an abundance of red leaves.

The people were leisurely walking up and down the streets. Each house had a small veranda out front, where people were sitting on benches or the steps. They looked relaxed and were apparently were enjoying the sociability of the community. Traveling for several blocks, Ike ordered, "Stop at the third red house."

"All the houses are red," Lucy mumbled.

"Now Lucy," Mary scolded.

In front of Ike's home, several youngsters were sitting on the steps. They greeted him with much delight, for they hadn't seen him for such a long time. He marveled at how much they had grown as they glared at us in wonderment and excitement, for it appeared they never saw a person of another color. Ike knocked on the door. In a moment, a female voice called from the other side, "Who is there?"

"Mother, it is Ike."

"Ike, is that you?"

"Yes, mother, it is me."

The door swung open, and a small squat woman burst out. She had red hair piled high on her head and wore a red dress that reached down to her red shoes. She clasped Ike's left hand with her right hand and with her left hand his right hand giving their arms several bold pumping actions. Obviously, it was their strange way of greeting. She turned away and called, "Father! Father! Ike is home."

A little thin red man, who looked like an older Ike, excitedly surged out the door and said, "Welcome home, son," as they clasped and shook his hands in the same manner.

"These are my friends," Ike said.

Somewhat overwhelmed, for it was evident his mother also never saw a person of another color, "Well then, everyone, please come in," welcoming us with genuine delight. Even though their skin was red, it looked like this was going to be our first opportunity to mingle with the ordinary people of this world as we entered their modest home.

CHAPTER 30 Staying With Ike's People

In the cramped quarters of Ike's twelve-foot wide family's home, he introduced us to his mother Ieed, his father Idge, sisters Iedaly and Iedela along with all the uncles, aunts, cousins, nieces, nephews and other members of his extended family who all lived in this one narrow dwelling.

Idge said, "Well, well, we have heard of your great deeds in Bluetropolis. It is an honor to have you in our home."

"You must be hungry? I will prepare something to eat," Ieed offered.

"Mother, we will be grateful," Ike said.

"No, mother, stay with your guests. We will do the cooking," Iedaly and Iedela insisted.

"Thank you, daughters," then invited, "Please, let us all go to the sitting-room."

The sitting-room took up most of the second floor. It was a barren space except at one end; there were slender high-backed wooden chairs neatly stacked up to the ceiling. They were half the width of the chairs in our world. Another space-saving measure in these cramped quarters. Lacking enough seating, youngsters sat on the floor. After a moment of awkward silence, Moe said to Idge, "Nice place you've got here."

"Thank you, Moe. What brings you to Redtown?"

"Father and mother, brace yourselves for what I am about to tell you," Ike said.

"Tell us, son."

"Father and mother, everyone knows Moe is a *Rocker*. What you do not know is Johnny, Matt, Lucy, and Mar are also *Rockers*, and we are on our way to get them back to their world."

This news astonished everyone, even though it was plain we were the same color as Moe. Ike proceeded to tell the story of our travels, thrilling them. They asked many questions, and we did our best to satisfy their curiosity. It wasn't long before Iedela announced, "The food is ready."

"Please, let us go to the eating-room before the food gets cold," Ieed ordered.

Back on the first floor, they led us through the narrow house, which was at least seventy feet deep, but only twelve feet wide and four stories high. There were no hallways, so we passed through all the rooms along the way to reach the eating-room, which was the last room at the back of the house.

The dining room table was only two feet wide and about twenty-five feet long with a stationary bench on either side. It seated more than twenty-five comfortably at one sitting, which was necessary to accommodate Ike's extended family, although it would take more than one sitting to feed everyone.

It was interesting to see the kitchen or cooking area was just outside the back door in the large open communal yard. Out there, they cooked the food over a blazing open fire pit, which made it feel more like a picnic than a formal meal even though it was served inside. The yard overflowed with awestruck neighbors peeking through the doors and windows, hoping to see what they could see.

Once again, the food was strange. We asked about each unfamiliar food as we ate. The red meat tasted similar to beef only much sweeter, and amazingly, although singed, it melted in our mouths, much like ice cream. Not much else tasted like it looked or what we thought it should've. However, we were getting used to the fact of experiencing the unexpected. Fortunately, almost all the food was tasty enough to enjoy.

Idge asked, "Moe, what is your plan?"

"Our plan is to get the kids to the end of the *Road*."

"Yes, sir, we must get home as soon as possible," I said.

"Our parents must be really worried by now," Lucy said.

"And I miss them so much," Mar added.

"I see what your goal is," Ieed concluded.

"What brought you to our world?" Idge asked, still in a state of wonder.

"We don't know. It's a mystery," Moe answered.

"So far, it makes little sense," Mary added.

"My father has traveled farther than anyone I know."

"Please, sir, tell us as much as you can about what we will encounter as we travel on," Mary asked.

"I am afraid if I tell you, it might make you reconsider your goal."

"Oh no sir, we must get home," Mar said, with determination.

"Sir, we'll get home no matter what it takes," I said.

"Father, you see what is, is."

"Yes, we are all resolute in that quest," Mary said.

"Very well, I hope I can be of help."

"Before we talk about such things, please let us finish the meal," Ieed said.

"Yes, let's," Moe said, as he took another helping.

We finished eating, and gathered in the relaxing room, a room that took up the entire third floor. Piled high at one end was what looked bean bags. Each person grabbed one and sat in a circle around us, filling up the entire space, which now included many neighbors who had to sit on the floor eager to be involved. It was fun. It felt as if we were in one of our childhood games, and we were the heroes.

We then understood why there were so many people roaming the streets. It was to get away from the overcrowding inside their homes.

After some small talk, Ike asked, "Father, please tell us what you have learned in your travels?"

"I will, son… When I was young, I traveled the *Road* as Ike and Inge have since done. It is our nature."

"Did you ever reach the end?" I asked.

"I traveled only as far as I thought safe."

"How far did you get?" Lucy asked, impatient with the slow pace of the talk.

"If you mean how close to the end, I do not know. I found no one in my travels who knew where that point was, or even if an end existed."

"Father, I think it would be helpful to tell us all you did see."

"Yes, it would be useful," Moe agreed.

"Yes, we are most interested in what you can tell us," Mary

added.

"I learned many things on several trips to the outer reaches throughout many cycles. I will try to put things in proper order. Let me see... When you leave Redtown and travel on, you will find one domain after another."

"Sir, how many domains are there?" I asked, hoping to get more information.

"Sir, will things be any worse than they were with the Blues?" Lucy asked.

"Sir, is it going to be any scarier?" Mar asked.

"Those are good questions. I am afraid there will be some trouble spots along the way. I was only a traveler and did my best to keep from having trouble. I tried not to say too much, and just asked questions when necessary. I was more interested in seeing the landscapes than in dealing with the people. However, I was able to see things that might discourage you.

"You mean, like what the Bluemen did before Inge reformed them?" Mary asked.

"You are too modest, it is known that you and Moe caused the rebellion," Ike noted.

"It's amazing how so little can do so much," Moe modestly said.

"You accomplished what seemed impossible for countless lifetimes."

"Ike, there were higher powers involved," Moe said, ever humble.

"Yes, there were higher powers that came to our aid," Mary acknowledged.

"I believe you are going to need additional help from those forces to reach the *Road's* end."

"Father, to do so, we are going to need all the information you can give us."

"Yes, son, you are correct. As you know, you will encounter many groups with different skin colors. You have seen the Whites, the Blues, the Poke-a-Dots and, of course, the Reds like us. When you travel farther out, you will find people of many other colors. And, it is believed there are also Pinks like you out there, although, until today, I have never seen one colored like you."

"Sir, what are those people going to be like?" I asked.

"Sir, will they help or try to hurt us?" Mar asked.

"Some will help, some will not. As far as being hurt, much depends on whether you respect their laws, rules, and customs, and in turn, they respect you."

"Sir, if we would've followed the Blue's laws, we'd still be in jail with Inge."

"Mr. Moe, if you had not disobeyed their laws and stopped at the fuel station, we would not have been put in jail."

"Yes, Miss Mary, but it's a stupid law."

"Yes, and by disobeying it, it led to the downfall of The Sentencer giving freedom to their people."

"Ike, that is true. However, it was terrifying," Mary said.

"We were taught in our history classes how we had to fight for our freedoms," I said.

"Yes, in our world, freedom didn't come easy. And to maintain it is still a challenge. We had to rebel against bad leaders and laws used to control us. Sadly, many people had to give up their lives for the sake of our freedoms."

"Moe, that concept is most interesting," Idge said. "In our world, the original *Rockers* were not nice people and did many bad things. However, after we split into different groups, most became loyal citizens who adhered to the rules of their leaders."

"Sir, you mean when everyone followed what they were told to do by force?"

"No matter how dumb it was?"

"What Mr. Moe and Lucy are saying, is why we so readily obey harsh and unjust rules?" Mary clarified.

"In our world, we don't accept cruel leaders," I added.

"It is true. There have been unjust rulers. Perhaps, we complied out of fear of those all-powerful leaders. Fortunately, in Redtown, we became so prosperous in our printing enterprises our leaders allowed us to become readers, thinkers, and travelers. That is, as long as we did our sizable share of work as printers."

"But, sir, everything is red?" Lucy wondered.

"Yes, everything is red. Is there something wrong with that?" Ieed asked.

"What Lucy is saying, your rules seem restrictive to our way of thinking. You see, in our world, each person chooses the colors they like and are comfortable with," Moe said.

"You mean you are not comfortable with red?" Ieed asked. "I like red, but it's only one color. Have you ever tried other colors? Or is there a rule against it or something?" Lucy asked.

"Why no, it is not against the rules. I have seen all the colors in my travels, but I accept everything being red in Redtown as being just the way it is."

"Yes, we never questioned it. It is what gives us order and peace? We just obey the rules and go along with the way things have always been," Ieed said.

"You mean you gave up your freedom because someone told you to?" I asked.

"I can see how, from your viewpoint, that might be possible," Idge said.

"You mean using other colors is part of being free?" Ieed wondered.

"Yes, that's it," Lucy said.

Amazed, Ike watched his family's reaction to what they were hearing and asked, "Are you telling us if we choose other colors, it will bring more freedom?"

"Why yes, I guess that's part of what we're saying," Moe said.

"But we do not have other colors to use," Iedela stated.

Lucy impulsively pulled off her gifted blue sweater and offered to her, "Here, try this on."

She asked, "Mother, may I try it?"

"Gracious. I guess it will be all right. What do you think, father?"

"There is no rule against it."

"Yes, it is not forbidden," Ike, conceded.

Lucy helped her put it on and stepped back and said, "Hey, it looks great on you."

Mary saw the pleased expressions on their faces and slipped off her white sweater, and offered it, "Iedaly, try mine," and helped her put it on.

"Mother, how does it look?"

"It looks very nice, daughter."

"Yes, it highlights your skin, which is most attractive," Mary said.

"Father, I think I would like to try a different color too," Ieed meekly asked. Not knowing what to think, he nodded in acceptance.

"Please try mine," Mar offered her light green sweater, and when she put it on, the woman exhibited them to all. Idge looked at the women and said, "This is most stimulating."

"Yes, father, I too find this exciting," Ieed said.

I offered my sweater to Idge, who was fascinated. Matt gave his sweater to Ike, and they strutted around the room to the delight of all.

"I believe you are once again working your magic," Ike said.

"No, it's not magic, we are just saying there's more than one way to do things," Moe said, and then slipped off his sweater and asked the gathering, "Who would like to try mine on?" Hands went up all around the room. He said, "Why don't you pass it around so all can have a chance."

"I am beginning to understand what happened in Dotsville," Patrued said.

"Father, the next time the merchants come around, do you think we could order things of other colors," Iedaly asked.

"I see Ike is correct. I believe you have just changed our lives," Idge said.

"Yes. I am beginning to understand how infectious freedom is," Mary said. Then she offered, "Children, do you not think they should keep the garments?" Of course, we all nodded in agreement, knowing it was the right thing to do, and it was most satisfying to do so. In their excitement, they were overwhelmed and most thankful.

"Yes, there is not only red but many other colors to be used. If you only knew how revolutionary this was, I believe you would see how magical you are."

"Ike, it is true. Mr. Moe and the children cannot see that yet," Mary agreed.

"Please, you're too generous. However, what I think would be magical is getting the kids back to their side of the *Rock*. Now, tell us more about the other cultures we must face to accomplish that?"

"What can you tell us about the understanding we must

find?" Mary asked.

"I only heard of its existence in my youth. As an adult, I had no contact with anyone who spoke of it or read anything about it. It seems as we became adults, we lost much of the curiosity we had as children. I am sorry, but I have no information concerning it."

Somewhat disappointed in not being able to help more so. However, he told of many other experiences in his travels. He ended with this little story, "We came to the boundary of a land thought was called Warland, where we heard loud sounds of bangs and booms in the distance that shook the ground. We read tales about how they killed each other with instruments that blew people apart. I must admit, because of the fear that picture instilled, we decided to go no farther."

"So, you have wars here too?" Moe asked.

"You also have deadly struggles in your world?"

"Oh yes, we wouldn't have our freedom if there were no wars."

"That sounds dreadful. I thought it was peaceful where the *Rockers* came from, and they were expelled because of their unruliness."

"No, Miss Mary, it might have been so with the native tribe with whom the legend originated, but with most others, we still have to fight for peace and freedom."

"Do you think you will have to go through Warland?" Idge asked.

"Yes sir, we will, if it'll get us back home," I added.

"We must get back home," Mar pleaded.

"Ike, will you be going with them?"

"Yes father, I will guide them to the end of the *Road*. I have given my word to help them in that quest."

"Son, that is good. You must allow us to give you additional supplies," Idge said, as he motioned to another man, who immediately left to carry out that task.

"Thank you, sir, it'll be most helpful, we must get on our way as soon as possible," Moe added.

"Son, please spend the night," Ieed invited.

"You must, everything will be ready by morning," Idge said.

"Yes, father. We will if it is all right with Moe, Mary, and the children."

Mary spoke for us, knowing it was best, "Thank you, Sir. It will be an honor to stay the night."

We continued to discuss the different groups and the elusive understanding through the evening. Wearied from the events of the day, we retired to the fourth floor, which contained many bunk-type beds and closets to accommodate the large household. There was one interior wall that separated the males from the females.

It was a new experience for us to have such little privacy, especially for the girls. It was hard to understand how these people could live like this. However, there were many youngsters near our age, who did their best to make us feel comfortable. Their curiosity and excitement kept us awake for a time before we were able to get some sleep.

In the morning, after breakfast, we all gathered around the Dragon in front of Ike's home. Idge, Ieed, their daughters, along with their extended family, including the entire neighborhood, filled the street, all wanting to be involved in sending us on our way

Idge spoke, "We wish you well in your quest, and we will miss you."

"Thank you for visiting us," Ieed added.

"Thank you for your kind hospitality," Mary graciously said.

"Yes, and thanks for the information and supplies," Moe added.

"It is our honor," Idge said. He turned to Lucy, Mar, Matt, and me, "May you gain the understanding that will get home."

"We will, no matter what it takes," I said.

"You better be right," Lucy muttered.

Ike bid his farewells, exchanging those hand pumping actions with his people. "Please remember to come back home for a while when you have finished your obligations," Ieed said.

"I will, mother."

Moe ordered, "Let's pile in kids." Seated and tied in the restraining ropes for safety, he turned the crank with a flare, and we drove through the quiet crowd who were moving their arms in that now-familiar pumping action.

Directed by Ike away from the crowds, the neighborhoods,

and back to the *Road*, Moe asked, "What's next?"

"As my father said, it will be the city of Yellowton."

CHAPTER 31 In Yellowton

In hearing Yellowton was the next city, Lucy said, "I never liked yellow."

"We'll see Lucy," Moe chuckled.

Sensing from Lucy's tone, Mary empathized, "Lucy, I am also afraid." Lucy realized her deep ambivalent feelings, which she always attempted to cover up, were showing.

Ike asked Patrued, "You were quiet at my parent's home. Were you uncomfortable?"

"Certainly not, I was just afraid someone would ask me a question." He amused us as we chuckled to his dismay.

Later, driving through the vast unoccupied lands, the only people seen were those unrecognizable ones speeding by. Darkness closing down over us. To avoid arriving in Yellowton in the middle of the night, Ike suggested we stop and camp out. Finding a clearing just off the *Road*, we quickly build a fire. We carried out these stops in an expeditious manner, which by now, were routine. Finished with the evening meal, we crawled into our sleeping bags in a tight circle with our heads pointed towards the fire.

"It's awfully quiet out here, isn't it?" Mar said.

"Yes, child, it is soundless." Mary agreed.

"Quiet is good," Ike added.

"Remember, kids, there're no insects."

"Hey, that's right. In our world, insects make most of the night sounds," Matt said.

"Yes, they do. You know what I mean."

"We know what you mean. What I like to know is how in the world can we find the understanding if no one knows what it is?"

"Lucy, that's a good question, and I don't know the answer either. Wait a minute... Could it be something we're learning without even knowing it."

"Children, perhaps Mr. Moe, has stumbled on the answer. What have we learned so far?"

"Well, anyone can see people shouldn't allow the bad guys to be in charge, like the Sentencer," Lucy thought.

"Then there's; we should be willing to ask and answer questions even if it's painful," I added.

"And, it is painful," Patrued said.

"Yes, sometimes doing the right thing can be painful," Mary agreed, understanding Patrued's pain. "Now, children, what else have we learned?"

"A sign of freedom is the right to use any that surround us," Lucy said.

"Yes, I guess it is not good to live life only in one or two dimensions," Ike said.

"Gee, I believe we are gaining some understanding of things, especially in making better choices," Moe said.

"Mr. Moe, do you think that's all there is to it?"

"Johnny, I don't know."

"Remember, we might have to get to the end of the *Road* before we find out for certain," Ike said.

We talked until one by one, we fell asleep as the fire burned down, not sure of the things we discussed.

The next morning, as the sky began to light up, the sound of a crackling fire awoke me. I opened my eyes and was astounded to see a *Man in White* tossing wood on the fire with his back to me. Motionless for a moment, I shook Moe, who was sleeping next to me and whispered, "Mr. Moe, Mr. Moe."

He opened his eyes to see the *Man in White* with his back still turned to us, who said, "Good morning, Moe and Johnny."

Moe responded, "Good morning, Sir." Immediately all of us were wide-awake, although we found we were unable to speak. We moved our lips, but no sound came out, it was a most mystifying and exasperating experience. However, a calming peace filled us, and then we were able to speak.

Moe asked, almost as if the words were put in his mouth, "Sir, what are we supposed to do now?"

"you are to keep following the pebble *Road*. Go into every

city you pass, and the understanding will come. If you keep seeking it, it will bring you to where you need to be," he instructed.

Mary asked, "Sir, would you like to join us for breakfast?"

"No, thank you, Mary. I must go," he answered as he walked around the Dragon. I clumsily squeezed out of my sleeping bag and ran around the Dragon, followed by Lucy, Mar, and Matt to find him nowhere in sight.

Moe called us back, "There's no use looking for him, he's gone. Let's have something to eat."

"Mr. Moe, where did he go?" I wondered.

"I wish I knew."

"Mr. Moe, who do you think he is?"

"I don't know, Lucy."

"Why couldn't we talk?"

"I don't know, Mar."

"What did he mean?"

"Matt, I think we just have to do what he told us to do."

"Mr. Moe, you are confusing the children."

"And, I am confused too," Patrued said.

"I am sorry. So far, I don't know who any of the *Men in White* are. Or fully understand what they're telling us."

Also stunned, Ike suggested, "They seem to speak in riddles. We must study what they say and follow their instructions."

"Yes, I do believe they're guiding us, and as this one said, to where we need to be," Moe said.

"Didn't he say if we keep following the *Road*, and to go into every city, we will find the end," I said.

"It sounds correct to me," Ike said.

"Why do not these Men just travel with us?" Patrued asked.

"I have the feeling they are not part of either of our worlds; they are more like spirits as strange as that might sound," Mary speculated.

"Oh my, what is going to happen to us?" Patrued said.

"I think we'll be just fine. Now let's eat," Moe, ordered, as he proceeded to heat the food over the fire the *Man in White* prepared. After finishing the meal, we packed our sleeping bags and headed towards Yellowton.

In time, we began to see people along the *Road*, "Look, they're yellow. Ike, we're near Yellowton, right?"

"Yes, Mar, yellow means Yellowton."

"Again, the *Man in White* told us to go into all the cities, didn't he?" Lucy asked.

"I am afraid he did."

"Ike, didn't your father say we should not be concerned about the Yellow people."

"Yes, Mary, however, he also said, they suffered from Yellowism.

"Yellowism, what's that?"

"Lucy, it means they are not a content people, they always expect the worst side of everything. However, they are a sensitive and gentle people. In fact, it is discouraging to be among them. So far, no leader has been willing to rise up and take leadership to help them feel better about themselves. We must do our best not to hurt their feelings, adding to their woes," Ike instructed.

"I can understand that," Patrued said.

"Yes, children, the lesson is one must never intentionally hurt another's feelings."

"My parents always taught me not hurt anyone's feelings," Mar said.

"Ours did too," Lucy agreed.

"Mine too," Matt added.

"Unless they try to hurt you first," Moe injected.

Mary scolded, "Now, Mr. Moe, I expect you to be on your best behavior."

"Not to worry, Miss Mary."

"Hey, there's Yellowton," I said, just able to make out its yellow aura to the left in the far distance. It was extraordinary how, from a distance, the cities emitted a glow the same color of its people, although close up, it was not visible.

"Oh no, I see everything is going to be yellow?"

"Yes, Lucy, yellow is still yellow."

"Maybe we need more sweaters?"

"Now, Lucy," Mary scolded.

Moe turned onto the side road leading to the city, and Ike directed us to its center having been there before. Parked on a busy street, we sat silently for a long moment watching the people go by.

"What do we do now?" I asked.

"I'm not sure?"

"Moe, why do we not just get out and stretch our legs, as you would say," Ike said.

"That's right, let's do it," I said.

"My-but-My," Patrued expressed, being new to this.

"We seem to have little choice. Here goes." Mary said, as she bravely stepped out onto the sidewalk.

"There you go, Miss Mary," Moe said. We all followed.

"Everything is so yellow," Mar said, blinking her eyes, adjusting to its glare.

I said, "Mar, remember yellow is yellow."

"Where have I heard that before?" Lucy muttered.

As usual, the people gathered around. "Why are they looking at us like that?" Mar asked as they peered at us through their squinty little eyes. Their eyes appeared to be, just slits, similar to the Orientals in our world only different, and their skin was an effervescent yellow like nothing I'd ever seen before. Their color and looks had little relationship with any group of people in our world. Their facial features were more like their native ancestors, and their eyes were not like the Orientals we knew of.

"Remember, they are just as curious about us as we are about them," Ike said.

"Just as they look different to us, we look entirely different to them," Mary instructed.

"It is true," Ike said.

"Hello, how are you?" Mary asked the gathering crowd.

They just stood there, as Ike whispered, "They do not want to be asked that, for feeling good is something they will never admit."

"How depressing," Lucy muttered.

"Depressing?" Ike asked.

"It kind of means; to be down, to be negative, to be on the dark side, well it means to be stricken with like you said, Yellowism," Moe said, attempting to explain.

"Moe, the trouble is I am beginning to understand you," Ike said.

Moe smiled and then asked the gawking crowd, "Hello

everybody. Where would we be able to get a good meal around here?"

A squat woman appeared out of the crowd and unemotionally directed, "There is an eating-place just up the street. Come follow me." Without another word, she led us to where we assumed was an eating establishment. However, it was a drab building with no sign indicating it was a place of business.

We entered a room containing several small tables surrounded by chairs. Two women came in from an interior door. They quickly evaluated the situation and moved several tables together so we could all sit at one. Without a word, they brought in dishes filled with a stew-like food.

Moe asked, "No, menu?"

"They have no selections. It is their way. One has no choice but to eat what they have ready."

"Ike, I guess that makes life easier," Moe said, jokingly.

"And they're not very friendly, are they?" Lucy whispered, not hearing a word from them.

"And, they don't seem to be very excited about seeing us," I said.

"Remember, they do not allow themselves good feelings," Ike reminded.

"That's probably why their skin turned yellow," Moe said, jokingly.

"How come our skin didn't change color to fit our feelings?" Mar asked.

"I am sorry to say, we do not understand or have ever questioned why our skins turned different colors. Consequently, there are no satisfying answers," Mary could only say.

"Maybe, long ago, our skin did change color to suit our feelings. Perhaps, that's why there are different races in our world. You know, having pale pink skin doesn't say very much for us, does it? Kids, think about that? Anyway, let's eat," Moe ordered.

The women served us while a crowd gathered in and around the doorway and watched through the windows. Eventually, a tasty dessert was served. Although, since every dish was on the sweet side, it was hard to tell which was dessert and which was not. When finished, the little woman reappeared, and Moe asked, "How do we pay for this?"

"There is no need for that."

Ike wondered, and said, "It is most generous, thank you."

She nodded and ordered, "Come this way." We obediently followed as she led us out the back door and up a rickety outside staircase.

Apprehensive, we entered an unpretentious room over the eating-place to find three elderly Yellows seated on a couch. The oldest looking man stood up and said, "My name is Ick, and this is Ock," and then introduced the old woman who was the third person, "And this is Uck."

Ike introduced us, and then Ick said, "Welcome, we are the Elders, please sit and make yourselves comfortable." When seated, he asked, "What do we owe this honor to, and how can we be of help?"

Ike explained our journey. As they listened, oddly, they did not exhibit any reactions. With our story told, Ick asked, "Why would you want to do that?"

"Do what, sir?" I asked, not understanding.

"Why do you want to go back to your home?"

"Because, we miss our moms and dads, and all our friends," Mar stated, at a loss.

"I see," Uck said.

"What we cannot understand is why you would want to do something that cannot be done?" Ick said, without any intonation.

Even Ike was taken back a bit, "Sir, what cannot be done remains to be seen."

"Sir, just because it hasn't been done, doesn't mean it can't be done," Moe added.

"Sir, where we come from, if someone tries, anything is possible," Lucy said. Her statement came from a place beyond her own experience.

"Unless one tries, how can one know what's possible," my answer also came from that place beyond myself.

"Sir, in their world, they are positive in their thinking," Mary said.

Still unmoved and without expression, Uck said, "That is most interesting."

"To do something that cannot be done is truly most interesting," Ick said.

"Are you saying that in your world, it is possible to do things that are not possible?" Ock asked.

Beginning to get a sense of these people's strange temperament, Moe said, "Yes, it's true, in our world we are always finding things that are not possible to be possible."

As we talked, a stream of young people quietly flowed into the room, eventually crowding us in. They listened intently, although not showing any signs of emotions. It was almost like talking to statues.

Still not comprehending, Ick asked, "Is it true in what you say, things not possible are possible?" This time, that question caused a noticeable stir among the youngsters.

A mischievous Moe seized the opportunity, and with his limited knowledge of psychology, he answered, "Yes, more things are possible than you can imagine. To feel right and good about something is the key to accomplishing an impossible goal."

"Oh, here we go," Ike mumbled.

Hearing him, Ick asked, "Ike, what do you mean?"

"Sir, I suggest you listen to them."

We sensed something was beginning to happen. Mary said, "Sir, in their world, there is a significant difference in the thinking."

"I can see that," Ick said.

A young girl asked Ick, "Grandfather, could we ask questions about their world?"

"I guess it would be all right," not knowing what to think he turned to the other elders, "Would it be all right if my granddaughter and others asked questions?" They passively complied, also not knowing what to think.

"Little do they know," Ike, mumbled under his breath, unheard.

"We will be honored to answer any questions," Moe said.

"What do you mean when you say, positive?" Eck asked.

"Mr. Moe, doesn't it mean to have an uplifting attitude on the light happy side, instead of the gloomy dark side?" Lucy said, trying to be of help, not knowing a better way to express it.

"Yes, it also means to feel good about yourself, able to look at the bright side. On the good side of the things around you," Moe added, as he looked for any reaction.

"Sir, do you mean feeling good is a good thing?" A youngster asked.

"Yes, child, in Mr. Moe's world, they seek good feelings," Mary answered.

"What are good feelings?" An even younger child asked.

"It means to be pleased with yourself," Moe answered.

"To feel things are okay," I said.

"Yes, and to smile, to laugh," Lucy added.

This perked up Patrued, "Yes, it is like in my situation, once I was a Poke-A-Doted person, and now I am a white person. I can only see it as a humorous change and laugh." He let out a shrieking laugh, which perplexed the Yellow people, for they apparently never heard a person laugh before.

"What was that noise that came out of your mouth? Are you sick?" Uck asked.

"Who me, sick?" he said. So amused he let out another explosive laugh causing a shockwave through the room knocking several youngsters off their feet — an unexpected and unbelievable reaction, which surprised everyone, especially us. None of us knew what to make of this bizarre situation.

Ike quickly said, as not to upset them, "Please, do not be concerned. This frequently happens in their world.

"It's true. In our world, laughter is part of our lives. It gives us pleasure," Moe said, following Ike's lead.

"You mean making that unusual sound gives pleasure?" Uck asked.

"Not exactly, the sound is just the result of being joyful and feeling good. And I must say, it also takes place among Inbetweeners and others in our world," Mary added, wondering why the merchants or anyone else never brought laughter to the Yellow people.

"Feeling good? I do not know about that. This is something new to us," Ick said, beginning to exhibit a tension.

"Grandfather, is feeling good something we should experience?" Eck asked, becoming a touch more eager.

"That's right, everyone should feel good," Lucy said, as we

began to feel energized by this extraordinary challenge.

"You mean you never felt good?" I asked, to the blank looks of the Yellows. "Why, it's the best part of life. Isn't that right, Mr. Moe?"

"That's right, Johnny. Why we laugh all the time."

"It is something we have never done," a hesitant Ock said.

"I know the Yellow people have never allowed themselves to feel good about anything. Maybe the time has come for a change. Moe and the children did not come through the *Rock* without a reason," Ike instructed, leading these people to a place they had never been before.

"This is most upsetting. I do not know if we can do that," Uck said.

I speculated, "Maybe, I'm beginning to understand that change for the good is what we are supposed to make happen."

"Yes, and not feeling good is something that needs to be changed," Lucy added.

"Grandfather, I would like to know what feeling good is like."

"Child, why have you never said this before?"

"Grandfather, because it was not something we were supposed to say. We never thought about it. It is not the way things have been."

"Maybe this is truly why we came through the *Rock*? Maybe we're not only here to bring freedom, but also good feelings," Moe speculated.

"Sir, I think it is best if you to listen to them," Ike repeated, turning it to our best interests.

"I do not know if we should change our ways?" Ick said.

"Why, we come from a world of constant change. It's what comes with freedom," Moe said.

"Grandfather, are we not allowed to change? Are we not allowed to feel good? Are we not allowed to be free?"

"Feeling good? Being free? Hmm, what does it mean? However, there is no rule saying we could not." Not knowing what to think, he asked, "What do you think, Ock?"

"It is true, there is nothing against it, but it is not our way."

"Are we not allowed to question our way?" Eck asked, as her

eyes revealed a twinkle.

"In our world, we're always questioning the way things are done," I added.

"Is this truly why you came into our world, to change us?" Uck asked.

"Well, to be honest, we don't know. But, it seems to be the effect we are having," Moe answer.

"Sir, in every city we entered, change for the better has taken place, as in Bluetropolis, Dotsville, and Redtown. And the most mystifying has been the appearance of the *White Light* confirming their work," Ike said.

"Oh, The *Light*," Uck said, showing the tiniest bit of concern.

"The *White Light*! This could be a catastrophe?" Ick said, for the first time showing an emotion.

"Grandfather, maybe this is our salvation. Can we please try to see what feeling good is like?"

"Eck, if the *White Light* is involved, I am not sure."

"Sir, how does one get to feel good?" Eck asked, with a touch of excitement.

Patrued couldn't help to get involved again, "That is easy, all you have to do is to see the humorous side of things."

"What are humorous things?" a yellow child asked.

"Things that are funny and make you laugh," I said.

"Like jokes," Lucy thought.

"And slapstick?" I added.

Moe, unconsciously reflected his own shortcomings, as he said, "Even more important, things which make you feel better, to make the right decision at the right time, to do a good job, to have done a good deed."

"What are jokes and slapstick?" Another youngster asked.

"It means to say or do something funny that tickles your ribs," Moe said, not entirely sure how best to explain it.

"Tickles our ribs?" a child asked, mystified.

"Yes, that's right."

The Yellow children looked puzzled, for the words funny and tickle weren't in their vocabulary.

Patrued boldly stepped up and said, "Watch me." He placed his fingers in his mouth, pulling his lips as broad and downward as possible, with his other hand he pushed his nose sideways, crossed his eyes, and danced around in a silly manner. The Yellow children looked at him with blank expressions. In frustration, he asked, "Do you not feel something? It is not funny?"

"I do feel something strange, but we were taught not to allow it to go any further," another child answered.

"Yes, it has always been said it was not permitted," Eck said. As the Elders tried to say more, they found the words would not come out. Even though they were relaxed, they couldn't say a word or move to stop what was beginning to take place.

Ike knew something extraordinary was happening. Being stimulated, he said, "Okay, let us do it."

Mary, with the same feeling, stood and confronted the Yellow children, "Do not be afraid of allowing those deep feelings inside you to come to the surface."

"Go to it, Patrued," Moe said, encouraging him to use even greater gyrations, whirling, twirling, and contorting his face as adults do to amuse small children.

Mar was the first to laugh infectiously. Moe motioned for all of us to do the same. As we followed the lead, Moe said to the Yellow children, "Come on! Let it happen."
Mary moved around the room, having to step over the youngsters, asking, "Children, is it not funny? Let it out. Ha-Ha-Ha," as she artificially laughed.

Uncharacteristically, Moe joined Patrued in the silly behavior. Even Ike joined in as they cavorted around the room. At first, the Yellow children looked odd, almost as if they were about to vomit. Miraculously, their armor began to crack as one by one they started to cough, and amazingly their sounds began to resemble laughter as their protective shields crumbled.

Those meager sounds built, eventually erupting in a symphony with everyone in the room participating in full-blown laughter, including the Elders It felt as if an outside force was guiding us, and we trusted it was the right path to follow.

Suddenly, a blast of *White-Light* struck, which froze everyone in the room except us. A *Man in White* stood on the arm of the couch, for there was no space on the floor to stand, for the children laid there overlapping one another. He said, "Good work.

Now, it is time to leave."

"Sir, what's happening?" Lucy asked.

"Exactly what is supposed to happen, however, the *Road* is waiting."

We all had questions, but in a flash of *White Light*, he was gone. The room again was alive with laughter. All we could do was wait until the laughter subsided. It took a while until the room was quite enough to speak. Only occurring after the Yellow children exhausted themselves and flopped on the crowded floor once again.

Uck was the first able to speak, "Is laughter always so exhausting?"

"Not usually, it might be because it's your first time," Moe speculated.

"How do you feel?" Mary asked.

"I do not know. I do feel different. It is the strangest feeling I ever experienced," Uck admitted.

"I think I might feel good if I knew what that was," Eck said.

"It is most interesting. I also feel a difference, and I must say, I think it is most significant. What are we supposed to do now?" Ick asked.

Moe could only say, "I think you should just allow your feelings to come out."

"Yes, what Mr. Moe is saying is; from now on, you must not block your feelings. Not hold them back as your heritage has taught. To set a new way enabling you to be free and contented," Mary said.

Knowing they must leave, Ike addressed Ick, "Sir, it is time for us to leave."

"How will we know what to do without you?" Ick asked.

To our surprise, Patrued said, "Sir, I would be honored to stay and help you with laughter. That is if you will have me?" It was an unprecedented request, for those of a different color were not to live together. He turned to us and said, "I am sorry, but I think I was turned white for a reason, and I believe the reason was to show people how to laugh."

"You might be right," Moe said.

"One must do what one must do," Ike added.

"That's great. You are truly a clown," Lucy said, praising him with a remark only we understood.

Patrued turned to the elders and asked, "That is if you will have me?"

Ick answered for all, declaring, "It will be an honor to have you stay and help us with laughter."

"Now, with that settled, we must go," Ike said.

Moe stood and said, "Okay, Kids, let's go."

"We thank you for visiting us. Friends, you will always be welcomed in Yellowton. Our young will guide you back to the *Road*. Now, is there anything else we can help you with?" Ick asked.

Amused and with an understanding smile, Mary said, "No, thank you, you have been most helpful." We all smiled, seeing the absurdity of that exchange, for who helped whom.

Moe said, to Patrued. "Your job is cut out for you."

"Cut out for me? Ah, yes, I see. That is funny."

With a tear in her eye, Mary said to him, "Now take care of yourself."

"You have taken a most worthy job," Ike told him.

We gathered around him, as each of us each gave him a hug, still not yet fully understanding where those deeper feelings when parting were coming from. He said, "I will miss all of you. However, I must do this, goodbye, my friends." We left him in his new home.

Several yellow children escorted us back to the Dragon.

We took Eck and a few other youngsters onboard. The remaining Yellow children waved their farewells with smiles on their faces. Ike pointed out, "The Yellow people have never smiled before. Your magic has worked again."

"We did nothing much. It was the *White Light*."

"Mr. Moe, you always underestimate yourself."

"Yes, that's right, Mr. Moe," I said.

"I guess we all did it with the help of the *White Light* and the *Man in White*. A team effort," Moe said.

Lucy said, "You got that right." At the time, none of us were quite sure of what the truth was.

Reaching the *Road*, we stopped to let the children out. Eck thanked us for the gift of laughter. As the Dragon pulled away, we waved goodbye to the now giggling Yellow children.

Ike exclaimed, "Most amazing!"

Moe stepped on the pedal, and we were once again on our way.

CHAPTER 32 Sorting Out The Events

After leaving Yellowton, due to the draining effect of the confusion we felt, and not yet able to contemplate why all this was happening, it took a while before anyone said anything,

"Wasn't that something?" Mar said.

Lucy asked, "Yes, it was. Miss Mary, it's just so silly. Did they ever know how to laugh?"

"And if they did, how come they stopped?" I added.

"Remember children, in my world due to strong leaders who imposed their will on each group, people remained isolated for many lifetimes. However, I see why no strong leaders rose up among the Yellows, for leading them had little rewards. However, I wonder why their merchants never brought laughter to them? For, I think all people have the natural ability to laugh," Mary said.

"Wait! I think it was because of the unwritten rules, which never allowed the merchants to speak of other cities. They mistakenly believed it would bring order out of chaos. No one realized how damaging and suppressive it was. Perhaps, Yellowton only attracted depressed people, and that condition became the standard for all to live by, as sick as it sounds. Knowing how laughter can lift one's spirit giving hope, they had to suppress it," Moe said.

"I see the Yellow people's depression only led to more depression. Over time it caused them to withdraw never able to find contentment, which I believe dulled their senses. I imagine it was a self-imposed punishment as they never allowed anyone to pull them out of it."

"That's right, Miss Mary. I know this illness happens to individuals, but when it happens to a whole city, it is incomprehensible. And on top of it, they were so miserable it even caused their skin to change color, which, even after all I've seen, is still hard for me to believe," Moe said.

"Why did such things not occur in your world?"

"Miss Mary, I think we were able to resist that much manipulation. We rebelled against harsh controls, as is our nature. And just as important, we shared our ideas and interacted across borders. Laughter was encouraged in all places."

"But, Mr. Moe, we did split into racial groups anyway," Matt said.

"But, that was thousands of years ago, right, Mr. Moe?" I said.

"Right, however, it probably had little to do with control or the lack of it. It had more to do with developing separately in different environments. However, a set of problems did emerge after we came together, called segregation."

"Yes, and it's still causing problems, isn't it?"

"Right, Lucy, I'll have to think about that a little more."

"Mr. Moe, maybe this has something to do with the understanding you are to find, and it might even explain the reason you came through the *Rock*?"

"Miss Mary, do you really think we're here for a reason?"

"It is apparent, is it not? Mr. Moe, did you not say you were beginning to see you were to bring freedom and good feelings?"

"That's right, Mr. Moe, we've been causing change," I then realized and said. "Wait, that's it! We're supposed to learn things here that has something to do with our world, you know what I mean?"

"I think I might know what you mean," Lucy said, for once agreeing with me.

"To learn is to learn," Ike said.

"I just want to go back home," Mar said.

"So do I," Lucy added.

"So do we all," I said.

"Kids, don't worry, we'll get you there."

"Yes… Now let us concentrate on that task at hand. Ike, what comes next?" Mary asked.

"It will be Stripepost!"

"Oh! What your father said about the Striped people is troublesome."

"Yes, indeed, yes, indeed. Before I speak of it, give me a

little time to think about it." Not much more was said as the hum of the Dragon, along with our stress level, lulled us into a sleepy mode.

The next day as we drove along, Mar said, "Look over there, we must be near Stripepost," seeing the first striped people in the distance by the roadside.

Moving closer, Lucy observed, "Hey, don't they look like war-painted Indians?"

They were colored with a variety of bright stripes of different colors, about a half-inch wide running vertically, which we assumed was their skin color covering their entire bodies. It was hard to understand how their skin evolved from the Indians in our world, who only painted those colors on. It was creepy.

Our talk alerted Ike, who was dozing. Looking out the window, he said, "Yes, we will soon be there." Then he asked, "What are Indians?" as he yawned and stretched.

"Why, they're the people with whom *The Legend of The Rock of Woes* originated. They're your ancestors. Tell us again what your father said about these people?" Moe asked.

"I will. To refresh the mind is good. I think we'll be all right."

Ike, didn't your father say they were filled with a false pride? Are they good or bad?" Lucy asked.

"Do you think they'll hurt us?" Mar asked.

"My experience with them has been the same. Their pride is not always based on the facts. They are not bad people, they just refuse to have their pride questioned, believing they are superior to all others."

"That's not a good sign?" Moe said.

"Oh, my. So Ike, how should we deal with them?" Mary asked.

"When I visited here last, I did nothing to challenge what they said or questioned their pride, no matter how unreasonable their behavior was. That is all one must do."

"That sounds easy enough."

"Lucy, So far, we've been batting zero," I reminded her.

"Now, children, we will have to watch our tongues. No more batting," Mary instructed.

"We can do that, you know what I mean?" I said with a smile, knowing I used an unfamiliar expression she probably didn't understand.

"So far, we've only caused rebellions. Do you know what I mean?" Lucy responded.

"Oh, I just want to go home," Mar, pleaded.

"Come on, Mar, stop worrying we'll get you home," Moe reassured.

Shortly we were able to see the city off to the right and even sensed its vibes, which was something we were becoming more adept at, although being uncertain. For it was something close to the supernatural.

Idge described it as a city with no tall structures, only with striped cone dwellings. Moe asked Ike, "What do these people do for trade?"

"They are potters and weavers. However, they also herd food creatures and grow food plants for their use."

Moe stopped at the dirt road leading there. "I guess we'll have to turn here if we must go into the city," knowing all along it was what must be done.

"Yes, Mr. Moe, it is what the *Men in White* told us to do," Mary said.

"And we must do what they say," Lucy muttered.

"Now, Lucy, we must show respect."

"Sorry, Miss Mary, but who are those *Men* anyway?"

"Oh, I want to go home so bad,"

"Mar, calm down, we all do," Matt instructed.

"To go home is to go home," Ike added.

"I think we should stay focus on doing what must be done to accomplish that."

"Mr. Moe, you are correct," Mary said.

"Well then, let's get to it," I said as we continued to drive towards Stripepost.

CHAPTER 33 Arriving In Stripepost

Entering Stripepost, instead of seeing transports, incredibly, the inhabitants were riding on the backs of most usual striped creatures. Describing them as being a mixture of horse, camel, and buffalos, yet, there were no valid comparisons. It was amusing to see those riders undulating up and down as the creatures slowly plotted along.

Suddenly, a weird contradiction occurred to me. I asked, "If everything is blue in Bluetropolis and everything is poke-a-doted in Dotsville, and everything is red in Redtown, and everything is yellow in Yellowton…"

Lucy impatiently interrupted, "What are you trying to say?"

"Yes, what?" Moe asked.

"Well then, why do all the transports look much the same, you know what I mean?" I asked.

"I think I know what you mean," Matt said.

"You know, I haven't given that much thought." Moe said, and then asked Ike and Mary, "Where do the transports come from again?"

"They come from a city called Mechanicsburg," Mary answered.

Ike added, "Yes, they are from Mechanicsburg, which is well ahead of us. I have never been there, and from what I understand, it is far from the *Road* and unreachable. Other than that, I can add little, except to acquire a transport one must deal with traveling merchants who represent the maker and delivers them to the buyer."

"Yes, it is the way I purchased my transports," Mary added.

"How can it be unreachable if they get the transports to their customers?"

"Moe, I do not know. I have heard from travelers that it is in an inaccessible location," Ike answered.

"Do you mean we'll have to walk there?" Mar wondered.

"I hope not. I imagine the new transports are driven out in some manner," Mary said.

"Do you know how they are made?" I asked.

"No, I do not know, and I am ashamed to admit the people in my world are not curious enough to find out."

"But, Miss Mary, you have a lot of curiosity," Lucy said.

"Yes, you are the most inquisitive woman I have ever known," Ike added.

"He's right, Miss Mary," Moe agreed.

"I guess I am. Yet, I do not know why it is so? I was just always different in that way," Mary's face flushed orange, never having been praised in that way.

Entering the city, Mar exclaimed, "Hey, look! They're not buildings. They're tepees."

"Why that's right," Moe, agreed.

"What in the world are tepees?" Mary asked.

"It's what the native people lived in a long time ago. The people the *Rockers* came from," Moe answered.

"Mr. Moe, you mean the *Rockers* lived in cone houses in your world?"

"That's right. They lived in tepees," I answered.

"Tepees and Indians. So Indians lived in tepees."

"Yes, Miss Mary. The Indians lived in tepees, also called wigwams," Lucy added.

"Tepees and wigwams? That is interesting. Your world is most complicated," Mary said.

In this city, all the streets were unpaved, just dirt with all objects having strips. The Indian-like people looked all the same, for their stripes obscured their facial features. We parked in a congested area. Being cautious, we first assessed the situation, wondering what was going to happen when we stepped out.

"It looks safe enough, and it's time to get out," Moe said.

"Let us do what we must do," Ike said. He opened the door and stepped out onto the thoroughfare, followed by me, Moe, Lucy, Mar, Matt, and finally, Mary, who was a little reluctant to step out on the powdery dirt, which kicked up with every step.

When the people saw us, their curiosity caused them to stop

in their tracks and gather around. However, they stood back a bit, in silence. With a put on a smile, Moe asked, "Hello, is there a good place to eat around here?"

A voice in the crowd said, "Yes, there are many."

"Why does a voice always come out of the crowd," Lucy muttered.

Ike asked, "Where would one be?"

"Around the corner to the left," another voice answered.

"Not very talkative people," Lucy muttered.

"Careful child," Mary warned.

"Yes, let us not forget their sensibilities," Ike whispered.

"Oh, I feel something big is going happen," I said, as I tried to guess what it might be.

"Now kids, let's be on our best behavior. Follow me," Moe ordered.

With a gathering crowd following us, we came upon a patio area in front of an extra-large teepee with smoke puffing out from its top. People were sitting on blankets placed on the ground eating. As we entered the area, everyone stopped what he or she was doing and gawked at us. A man dressed in a striped apron with one feather stuck in a band around his head nervously asked, "Would you like a meal?"

"Yes, we would please," Mary said.

"How many?"

"Seven, please." Without hesitation, we were directed to an empty spot where several waiters rolled out a large blanket to accommodate us all. Those around us, including the gathering crowd at the parameter, continued to gape at us in silence. Fortunately, we were getting used to this type of attention, although it still left us with an uneasy feeling.

"I guess they don't have menus either?" Moe asked Ike.

"Do not worry. They will take care of us, be patient."

It wasn't long before several waiters carrying trays of food held high delivering one to each of us. With no tables, we had to hold the trays on our folded legs, which was awkward.

Moe, as usual, was the first to dig in, followed by Ike and Mary, and of course, we had to taste each item first. Interestingly, the trays were made of thick heavy clay and decorated with bold, colorful images of people doing things, much like the Indians in our world might've used.

When our hunger was satisfied, we relaxed and took in the surroundings. The crowd had grown as they silently watched our every move. Lucy commented, "You'd think someone would say something!"

"Lucy, let's not compare their behavior to ours," Moe said.

"Your world is your world, and our world is our world," Ike said.

Perhaps overhearing us, a man dressed in a colorful full-length leather outfit, stepped out and asked, "Darkness is descending, would you like a place to spend the night?"

Moe looked at Ike and asked, "What do you think?" even though he knew the answer.

"With only candles for light, we better find a place. If there is anything we have learned, it would be to follow the path we are led down."

"Correct."

"Yes, sir, we would like that very much," Mary said.

"It is far. It would be best to use your transport. Follow me." He led us through the crowd and back to the Dragon.

"I hope this is the right path," Lucy muttered.

"Here we go again," I said, still feeling something big was about to happen.

As we boarded the Dragon, we heard drums in the distance. The stranger pointed and said, "Go in that direction."

To relieve any tension, Mary said, "My name is Mary, this is Mr. Moe" and proceeded to introduce us all.

"It is nice to meet you. My name is Muddle."

"Hellow, Mr. Muddle," Mary said. We all acknowledged him, as always hoping to put strangers at ease, as our parents had taught us to do.

"And it is nice to finally meet all of you. We have been expecting you."

"You were expecting us?" Lucy asked.

"Yes, we have heard of your travels and know you are the *Rockers* we have been waiting for a long time."

"Ah, finders," Moe said.

"Yes, Moe, our fame travels ahead of us," Ike said. He turned to Muddle and asked, "Then you're bringing us to a special place?"

"I am bringing you to the Chiefs. They have long been looking forward to meeting you. However, we will have to wait for first light. I am taking you to a place where you can sleep during the darkness."

"Our fame travels faster than we do, for they have good finders," Ike said.

"Oh, we're famous, aren't we? I guess spies are watching us all the time."

"Mr. Moe, they have people who work to find out what is going on elsewhere. And whether you like it or not, you are famous, and their spies, as you call them, are relaying that information ahead of us."

"I didn't say I didn't like it," Moe said, to her amusement, knowing his humility."

"Turn left at the next intersection," Muddle directed, seemingly not to understand what we were talking about.

"Yes, sir," Moe said.

"Sir? Hmm."

"How far are we going?" Moe asked.

"It will take a while to get there." Impatient, Moe stepped on the accelerator as he noticed two transports following us close behind in the cloud of dust the Dragon's tires had kicked up. There were only two vehicles seen here so far. As we recalled from seeing so many western movies, we assumed the drums were announcing our arrival ahead of us. It was fun, hoping for the best.

In total darkness, we arrived at an extra-large teepee with flames on pedestals on either side lighting the entrance. Light glowed inside as seen through the thin animal hide walls. Entering it, we saw it was coming from a fire pit in the middle of the interior where several ladies were waiting. The elderly woman in charge pointed to a blanket and a pillow piled on a pad sitting on the hard ground, one set for each of us. Shown a place behind a thick hide partition to undress and wrap ourselves in one of the blankets.

Once settled on the pads, the ladies doused the fire. One instructed, "We will wake you at first light for breakfast. Have a good night's sleep."

Mary thanked them, and they departed, leaving one of them seated just inside the flap that acted as a door. It was the end of another long day. Being together allowed us to feel safe. Soon we were all asleep.

CHAPTER 34 Meeting The Chiefs

With the glow of the morning light and the stir of activity outside the tepee, the attendant stationed just outside saw Mary wake and left her post. She quietly called to Ike, waking him, "What do you think they expect of us?"

He looked around, shrugged his shoulders, and said, "I do not know."

The door flap folded back, and a succession of ladies filed in, each carried a colorful tray, one for each of us. Mary loudly called, "Mr. Moe. Children, time for breakfast."

Roused, and served a tray where we lay. Moe said, "Ah, breakfast in bed."

"I do like being waited on," Mar said.

"I hope they're preparing us for something good," Lucy said.

"I think they are. Isn't that right, Mr. Moe?"

"Right, Johnny. Ike, don't you think he's right?"

"What will happen will happen."

"Ike, I thought you said these were good people?" Mary alarmed, asked.

"That is what I said. However, traveling with you, I can only think anything could happen. What is, might not be what is."

"Now, that worries me," Mar said

"Everything will be all right, you know what I mean," I said.

"Sure, everything will be okay. Now let's eat," Moe ordered.

The woman in charge entered, followed by Muddle, with a measure of respect and a little excitement, she said, "Good morning, visitors. When finished eating, you will each be given an outfit to wear to be properly presented to the Chiefs. When ready, Muddle will take you to the clearing." Before we could ask questions, she exited, leaving Muddle with us.

"Muddle, what is the clearing?" Mary asked.

"Yes, it doesn't sound good," Lucy said.

"It is a cleared space in the forest where large events take place."

Moe, knowing better, asked, "And what large event is there today?"

"The event will be you. Everyone in Stripepost wants to see you."

"Remember, Mr. Moe, you are a celebrity. But, you know it is for us." He responded with a slight grunt and a sheepish smile, indicating he has accepted the notion of our fame.

After breakfast, each was given a pan of water to wash with. It was embarrassing when only dressed in our underwear as the ladies help us put on the provided leather outfits. However, it was cool and fun to be dressed like an Indian, as if it were one of our childish games. They even painted stripes on our faces with their fingers, relieved it wasn't over our whole bodies.

Filled with enthusiasm, yet tempered with an uneasy feeling about what was ahead. Muddle directed us in the Dragon away from the settlement into the woods. The roadway was cluttered with people headed on foot or riding those funny looking creatures in the same direction.

"Are all these people coming to see us?" Mar asked.

"Yes, they are. You are the biggest event taking place in my lifetime."

"I also have the feeling something even bigger is going to happen today," Ike mumbled.

"Do you think it will be something good or bad?" Lucy asked.

"I do not know. So far is so far."

"Do you think they'll harm us?" Mar asked.

"We're going to be okay, right, Mr. Moe?" I said.

"I would think so."

"Now, children stop thinking like that," Mary instructed.

"My people will not harm you," Muddle said.

"I hope not," Mar added.

We entered a large clearing packed with people. Muddle directed us to drive down the grassy incline to the flat spot in the center as the crowd parted, allowing us to pass. The people gazed at us with a sparkle in their eyes, perhaps as people would in seeing

Elvis in our world. It gave us a conflicting set of feelings wondering why us? Although we understood it was probably because we were different and alien to them.

Several men, who Muddle called the Chiefs, were waiting at the bottom. It was obvious who they were, for they wore elaborate leather beaded regalia with massive fancy headdress, which held a large assortment of brightly colored feathers. Without any doubt, they looked just like the Indian Chiefs of old in our world, except for the stripes.

Disembarking, we faced the Chiefs as Muddle introduced us. The head Chief, who he called Mighty, said, "Welcome, we have been waiting for your arrival for lifetimes."

"You've been waiting for us since before we were born?" Lucy asked.

"Being the true ancestors of the original *Rockers,* we seek our past."

"Sir, I do not think you are correct in that," Mary pointed out. Ike grabbed her arm quickly, shaking his head from side to side with the look of alarm warning her not to say anything challenging their pride. A little taken back, she nevertheless remembered what he said and stopped pursuing it. However, having some understanding of what they sought from us, she asked, "Would you like to know about the other side of the *Rock*? If you would, they would be pleased to tell you."

"Yes, we must know our past," Mighty said.

"Okay, what would you like to know, Chief?" Moe asked.

"Tell us how brave, strong, and proud our people are on the other side?"

"Their people," Moe whispered out of the side of his mouth, "Who does he mean?"

I said, "I think he means the Indians?"

"Hmm."

"Yes, tell them about the Indians?" Ike whispered.

"Oh… The Indians." Then said to them, "Well, if you mean the real Indians, the people the *Legend of the Rock* came from."

"Yes, tell us how mighty they are so we could share in their pride."

"Remember, pride, their pride," Ike whispered.

"What can I tell you?" Moe said, unsure of what to say.

"Tell us the truth. The truth about how powerful and glorious our people are on the other side," Mighty demanded.

"You want to know the truth... the real truth?"

Ike had a deflated feeling as he saw the grimace on Moe's face, he could only utter, "Here we go again."

"Yes, it is what we want to hear, the real truth," Mighty insisted.

"Oh my," Mary mumbled, knowing Moe could not but tell the truth. That is most of the time.

I also understood that about him. However, I gritted my teeth and said, "Let's do it. You know what I mean."

"This time, I'm afraid I do," Lucy said.

Moe began to speak, knowing caution was the better part of valor. However, he found he was unable to contain what he was about to say, "There was a time when the Indians were a proud and powerful people. However, since the last *Rockers* came through, the Indians have lost the power they once had and melted into the current population, diminished to the point of hardly being recognizable. And I hate to tell you this, but the *Rockers* were the ones the tribes rejected."

"No, this cannot be. We are the superior people. You are not speaking the truth."

Mary, unable to contain herself any longer, said, "He is telling the truth, Mr. Moe never lies, and by the way, we are also descendants of the *Rockers*."

"Me too," Ike meekly added as pandemonium broke out. They surrounded us with a scary disordered dance.

We were unceremoniously grabbed and restrained as Mighty proclaimed, "You are liars. You cannot tell us we are not superior. You cannot challenge our pride."

"Oh yes we can if it's not true," Lucy said, as once again the courage beyond her natural behavior and maturity welled up in her. She went on to say, "You fools, can't you see your pride isn't real."

Seized by the same courage, I went a step further, hoping it would calm them, "That's right. How dumb can you be? If you would've seen the *White Light*..." However, my words had the opposite effect.

Ike relaxed into a sitting position on the ground, and said, "I wasn't kidding when I said here we go again."

In a rage, Mighty exclaimed, "The *White Light* has nothing to do with us!" Upon saying those faithless words, a crack of thunder and a flash of *The White Light* struck. All were frozen in place except for us, which now included Mighty. To our surprise, in the flash of *Light*, we were miraculously stripped of those leather outfits and were again dressed in our regular clothing with unpainted faces. Undeniably, it was a supernatural occurrence, which we found not only incredible but almost too hard to believe.

Not totally unexpected, a voice came from behind, "Good, all that is left to do is to tell these people the whole truth. When finished, you must leave." Upon seeing and hearing *The Man in White*, Mighty let out a groan as he trembled in fear. We turned to look at him and then back to the *Man in White* only to find him gone.

As the people started to revive, Mary asked, "What do we do now?"

"I guess we tell these people the truth," Moe said.

"What is the truth?" she wondered.

"The truth is the truth," Ike said.

"The fact is that those pulled through the *Rock* were the rejects of a proud people, who no longer are as powerful as they once were," Lucy said.

"Yes, and we're all equal. No group is better than any other," I said, as I was beginning to understand the bigger picture.

Moe took a gulp of courage and directed his words towards Mighty, Muddle, and all the people who could hear, "If you would've seen the *White Light* and heard what was just said, you better change your ways. Being too proud is not good."

Mighty, being the only striped person to see and hear all that happened, laid there cringing, as Moe aimed his words at him, "Your pride is false. You're no better than any other people. Your pride should be about how much good you have done, not in how much you think you are better than others. Cultures come and go, and they should be remembered for how much good they left behind." Those inspired words even surprised him as they flowed out of his mouth, words well beyond his ability to express.

By the people's silence, we could see his words were having

an effect. It was as if light bulbs were going off in their heads. Seeing their reaction, Ike said, "I think our work here is done, we better go."

I wasn't quite sure I understood what just took place, but said, "Yeah, let's get out of here."

"It's about time," Lucy said, relieved.

We slowly drove off as the people scramble out of our way. We were taken by how they bowed to us as we passed, giving us the impression these people were now freed and thankful for the information they just received. With apprehension, we drove in silence until back on the *Road*.

Mar was the first to speak, "I thought we were going to die."

Ike said, "It was evident in how the magic worked. We must accept there is a greater power at work directing us."

"Yes, and we're not going to die. We are being protected," I said, hoping I was right.

Lucy muttered. "Famous last words."

"It does seem we're protected. However, we must remain on guard, one never knows, for it seems what's happening is beyond our control," Moe said.

"Yes, and this message of goodness is not coming from us, rather it appears to be coming through us. Nevertheless, I agree we must stay ever-vigilant," Mary said.

Mar couldn't help herself and asked, "You mean we might die?"

"Don't worry, we're not going to die," I said, not knowing if it would be so.

For our sake, Moe said, "You're not going to die. We're going to get you back home."

"To die is to die."

"Oh Ike, no one is going to die," Mary said, not knowing either.

"What do you think will happen to those Indians now?" Mar asked.

"I think their future isn't in our hands, we were told to move on, and we must do so to get you back home." Changing the subject, Moe asked, "Ike, where to next?"

"Purplesin."

"Mr. Moe, is that the place those purple men who caused all the trouble at the station and eating place come from?" I asked.

"I afraid so."

"Oh no," Lucy grumbled.

CHAPTER 35 The Purple People

On our way to Purplesin, Mar asked, "Miss Mary, are sure we're going to be safe until we reach the end of the *Road*?"

"Child, so far, we have been kept safe. There is no reason to believe that will change."

"But things are becoming more dangerous. It was pretty scary in Stripepost," Matt said.

"Yes, it was, like in the movies, when the Indians danced around the settlers before they scalped them," Lucy said.

"What does scalped mean?" Mary asked. Moe explained it graphically. "Oh, how dreadful!" Mary exclaimed.

"It was frightening, yet so far, we haven't been harmed. Ike, how many more cities are there?" I asked.

"As I said, I cannot answer that question. No one has ever reached the end. Therefore, I do not have an answer."

"Maybe we shouldn't keep asking the same questions? Our thoughts seem to go around in circles. Anyway, I choose to believe The *Men in White* and The *White Light* are protecting and guiding us," Moe said.

"Doesn't anyone in this world know anything more about the *White Light*!"

"Be calm, Lucy... You see, as I grew up, I was taught not to speak of it," Mary said.

"Yes, I was also told never to mention it," Ike added.

"Weren't you curious? I know I would've been. Why wouldn't you want to know what it was?" Lucy asked.

"We believed if we asked about it, there would be consequents not to our liking," Mary answered.

"Kids, remember people here think differently, that's except for Mary, Ike, and Inge. Let's just think about you getting home."

"Mr. Moe, do we think like you?"

"Yes, Miss Mary, you really do."

"Why, thank you, Johnny."

"Yes, that's right. Now, let's think about the Purple people. Ike, tell us again what your father told us about them?" Moe asked.

"And I agree with him, they cannot take responsibility for their actions, and as you have already seen, they can be most difficult. However, I do believe they are a sad people who also cannot be told they are at fault."

"It must mean they suffer from paranoia?" Moe said.

"It depends on what that term means?" Mary said.

"I guess it means they can't take criticism from others," Moe said.

I don't have a good feeling about the Purples. I think many in this world have mental problems," Lucy said.

"I just want to go home," Mar said.

"Come on, we all know you do. We all want to get back home soon," Lucy, bemoaned.

Later, Matt exclaimed, "I see it!"

"See what?" Lucy asked.

"I see Purplesin."

"Where?"

"Over there!" pointing to a purple blotch on the horizon.

"Yes, that is Purplesin," Ike said.

"Well then let's get there," Moe said, as he stepped on the accelerator taking the chance it would be safe to arrive there not long before darkness fell, eager to get on with it.

Once deep in the city, we parked and peered out the windows to see their skin was a dark effervescent purple. Their clothing, buildings, streets, and even the sidewalks were in shades of purple, which was most unwelcoming.

"We must do what we must do," Ike said.

"That's right," I agreed.

"Well then, let's get it done before it gets dark," Moe said as he opened the door and stepped out, followed by us. Again, the people stopped to look at us. Moe immediately asked, "Where could one get a good meal?"

At first, there was no response, Moe again asked, and a

reluctant man stepped out and said, "I believe I can help you."

"You know where we can get a good meal?"

"I know where you can find a meal along with some rest. We have been waiting for your arrival."

"Oh no, not again, I hope this time it is the finders," Lucy said.

"Oh, why does the same thing happen in every city?" Mar murmured.

"I guess there're spies everywhere. Kids, perhaps with all our differences, people aren't so different after all. All we can do is to follow where we are led and hope for the best," Moe said.

"That is right, our fame precedes us, and we must follow the path we are on," Ike said.

Mary asked the stranger, "Would you please tell us where that place would be?"

"You will have to drive there. If you wish, I will show you the way?"

"Okay, let's go," Moe said.

On the way, Mary took the lead in making friendly gestures to the ominous-looking man by introducing us, and then asked, "What is your name?"

"My name is Speck."

"It is nice to meet you, Speck," Mary said.

"Really?" was his stark response. "Turn left at the next intersection."

"Okay."

We arrived at a sizeable uninviting building. Inside, as usual, a group of ladies greeted us, only this time they were holding lanterns. It was evident, in this world, young women were taught to serve, and I knew Lucy and Mar didn't appreciate that fact.

Speck instructed, "They will meet your needs. I will see you in the morning to take you to our leaders. May you have a good night's rest," he politely said, giving us hope these people were not so bad.

We were treated much the same by these ladies as in the other cities. As different as the cultures were, the primary way all the cities greeted travelers was similar. I believe it had to do with the one contact point they all shared, which was commerce. In the glow of the lanterns, they served us a meal, and afterward, we were taken to rooms with soft beds.

The next morning, cleaned, dressed, and fed, Speck took us to an open field where it seemed all of the people of the city were waiting. Meeting again in an open public space, to say the least, was worrisome. There were out of proportion wooden bleachers, which were severely overcrowded with people precariously hanging off its sides wherever they could, surrounding a high dirt mound.

Trees ringed the open space that contained many people sitting up high on the branches. Some were dangerously hanging from the limbs only by the grip of their hands, much as monkeys might.

Speck led us up the steps and onto the mound. The crowd became extra quiet, as several tall, pathetically skinny men emerged from the opposite side. All dressed in peculiar-looking purple full body tights with flowing capes and wide brim hats that sat low on their heads shadowing their faces. One stepped forward and asked, "We understand you are from the other side of the *Rock*?"

"Yes, we are," Moe answered.

"And what are you doing here?"

"We are heading back to our world," I answered.

Another man asked, "And what does that have to do with us?"

"Sir, we do not know the answer to that," Ike replied.

"You are a Redman. Who are you?"

"My name is Ike. I am their guide."

Another man asked, "And, you do not know what this has to do with us. How are we supposed to know what to do with you?"

"We don't know if you are to do anything with us," Moe said.

"Are we not good enough to do something with you?" another asked.

"Sir, we are seeking your help," Ike said as he sensed trouble from their attitude and tried to smooth talk.

Lucy was fixated on the people hanging from the trees and bleachers. Suddenly, one and then a couple more of those hanging from the trees lost their grip and fell to the ground screaming in pain. Horrified, she let out a shriek, "Oh no! Look! Look!" pointing at those who had fallen.

"Wow!" I also saw what happened and exclaimed the obvious, "Those people fell from the trees!"

None of the caped men reacted, but asked, "What does that have to do with us?"

Lucy appealed, "Aren't you going to help them?"

Puzzled, those men just stood there. Ike knew what was happening and urged, "Remember, they cannot accept blame." Just then, a section of an overburdened bleacher collapsed, sending many agonizing in pain to the ground.

Horrified, Lucy questioned, "You're not going to help them either, are you?"

I also couldn't believe their reaction, and said, "Yes, what's wrong with you people, aren't you going to help, you know what I mean?"

"Yes, that's right," Moe said, perplexed.

"We must do something," Mary said.

"Here we go again," Ike mumbled.

"I'm going to help them, you're not very nice people," Lucy said.

"Lucy, if you keep accusing them, you know what might happen," Ike warned.

"Oh, my. Oh, my. Ike, we must do something to help," Mary said.

Moe and a hesitant Ike accepted there was a need to help. As we started to move, the caped men seized and overpowered us. Struggling to free ourselves, we were dragged off the mound. They were pretty strong for such skinny men, for we couldn't break free.

A large door, built horizontally right into the ground, was opened, and they forced down us into a cave-like room under the mound. Once inside, the door slammed shut. Petrified, in total darkness before torches were lit. We struggled as they placed us in straps against the wall, in vertical positions with our legs together and our arms stretched out.

Mar was crying, Lucy was angry, I was trying to get loose, Matt was frozen, Mary was horror-struck, and Moe was looking around trying to figure out what to do. Ike loudly called out, so we all could hear, "My friends, we are definitely going to need help to get out of this one."

"We always get help, don't we?"

"That's right, Johnny," Moe answered.

"These creeps need to be straightened out," Lucy said without reservation.

"How can we do that when we're all strapped in?" Mar asked.

"Yes, we are supposed to do something to cause change. It seems to be what must be done for you to get back home, is that not so Mr. Moe?"

"Right, Miss Mary. Okay, kids, let's not be afraid of these creeps, right Ike?"

"Right, Moe, we must do what we must do," as he called up his bravely the best he could.

A caped man spoke, "How dare you come into our city and accuse us?"

"What did we accuse you of?" Lucy asked.

"You accused us of not helping those people."

"Yes, but they're your people, and you didn't help them, did you?" Lucy further accused.

"Yes, why won't you help them?" Matt added.

"It is not our fault. It is not our responsibility."

"You mean it is not your responsibility to help others?" Mary asked.

"Remember Mary, these people are not able to accept responsibility," Inge said.

"That is correct, responsibility is not our responsibility," one of the men stated.

Aggravated even more so, Lucy said, "You're not only ugly but also mean and selfish."

"Yes, how dumb can you be," I said, adding to their groans.

"No, you are the dumb ones. You cannot accuse us of anything."

"Why are you unable to see your faults?" Mary's words further disturbed them.

Another said, "We are never at fault. You must pay for your accusations," to the accepting groans of all the caped men. Who numbered no more than a dozen or so.

"You're even worse than dumb. You're stupid," Lucy couldn't let up.

"How dare you keep accusing us," another angry man, said.

"I think these people need a good shot of the *White Light*," I threatened, not knowing what I was saying.

"The *White Light*, how dare you. The *Light* has nothing to do with us." Immediately, upon those faithless words being uttered, popping sounds were heard, coming from those extremely deranged men. Astonishingly, their wide brim hats began to pop off their heads caused by big black boils expanding on their faces and bald heads. Unbelievably, they started to look more like giant bugs than men. This horrifying sight caused us dread. In fact, the whole incident was most distressing in spite of our seemingly confident attitude.

The headman ordered, "Get them." Fortunately, as they moved towards us, a loud crack of thunder struck. It blew the door in, merciless pinning the leaders against the wall as the *White Light* shone, blinding us.

Suddenly, to our great surprise and disbelief, we found ourselves unshackled and standing outside among the injured people — another mind-boggling supernatural event.

The countless Purple people stood there, frozen in place. To our relief, not one of those caped bug-like men were among them. Shocked and uncertain, we looked at each other. "What do we do now?" I asked.

"We must do what we must do," Ike answered.

Not unexpected, a voice came from behind, saying, "Yes, you will do what you do."

As always, we turned to see a *Man in White*. Relieved, Moe asked, "Sir, what should we do now?"

"All you have to do is to help the injured and tell these people they are now free and must show Goodness to each other."

"What about those bug men who tried to hurt us?" Mar asked.

He pointed towards the dungeon's door. Unbelievably, where the door had been was now dirt and grass as if it never existed. He then said, "Tell these people Goodness has come, and those who oppressed them are no more." We looked at the crowd as it began to stir and focus on us. We turned back to The *Man in White* to find him once again gone.

"Oh my," Mary said.

"Wow! You know what I mean," I exclaimed.

"Yes, I know what you mean," Lucy agreed.

We did what we were told to do and aided the injured under Mary's direction. Moe, with a smile of confidence, said, "Well, it's time to explain it to them." He cupped his hands around his mouth and yelled, "You're free! You're free!" However, the crowd just stood there looking at us motionless.

"What's wrong with them?" Mar asked.

"I believe they do not yet understand what has happened," Mary said.

"Well then, let us tell them," Ike said. He turned towards the people and yelled, "Your leaders are gone. They no longer control you. Goodness has come. You are free to live your lives with goodness. You are free! You are free! Those who oppressed you are no longer here. They no longer control you. You must now help and take care of each other with Goodness."

It was evident those words were not coming from his understanding, but from a place not yet understood. We repeated those phrases in all directions, "You are now free! You are free! Goodness has come!" As Moe and Ike repeated shouting those words, the people began to stir as we continued to administer first aid and encouraged those around us to help. Amazingly, they had no concept of how to help others, so we resorted to showing them by example how to do it.

With Mary's guidance and knowledge, we feverishly helped her to set bones, stitch cuts, and whatever else was needed to patch them up. That alone was a miraculous feat. In making the Purple people help, they seemed to find satisfaction in doing so. It was something they never experienced before. Their enthusiasm in wanting to help quickly grew. Fortunately, there were no life-threatening injuries.

After a painstaking effort to care for everyone the best we could, we looked around to see the Purples comforting the injured on their own. Ike noted, "Before we came, these people would never help another. Now, look at how they are caring for each other. It is another unexplained miracle."

"We didn't do much. We only did what was expected of us, which was the only decent thing to do," Moe said.

"Moe, it does not diminish it from being a genuine miracle," Ike said.

"If it weren't for Miss Mary, it would've been impossible," Moe said.

With an orange blush, she said, "I am only doing what I know how to do."

"And Miss Mary, that's all that was necessary," Moe added.

By doing this, it gave us lots of gratification in knowing we were able to help.

Once seeing all were attended to, Mary asked, "Mr. Moe, what do we do now?"

"I don't know?" he said, as we stood up exhausted, a swirl of excitement took hold of the purple people, as cheers overtook them. I came to understand these people knew we were *Rockers* and believed we were representatives of their ancestors, which caused them to accept what we were saying as truth. Moreover, it seemed those men who were wearing those capes and hats were different creatures, and thankfully, especially for these people, none of them appeared to survive that disastrous blowout.

Ike said, "I believe our work here is done. We must move on."

"That's right, let's get going." As Moe spoke those words, we suddenly found ourselves supernaturally seated in the Dragon parked on the pebble *Road* with its engine running. As these incredible events were becoming more frequent, we were beginning to accept them as a matter of course. With a "Ha" and a big grin on his face, Moe stepped on the pedal, and off we went.

CHAPTER 36 Interpreting What Had Happened

Driving away from Purplesin, we were silent for a time until Mary asked, "Mr. Moe, do you think the Purples understood the lesson back there?"

"Miss Mary, most likely not, at least not right away. However, I believe in time they will."

"They understood what they understand," Ike said.

"That explains that. But we couldn't stay around to find out," Lucy said.

However, the four of us sensed those people's invisible chains were now broken. As dramatic as that might sound, we felt we had accomplished something good, even though at that age, we understood little.

"I can't believe what just happened. I thought we were going to die."

"Yes Mar, it was dangerous, yet wasn't it exciting to be transported from one place to another without having to walk there, you know what I mean?"

"It was Johnny. However, I hope there's no more excitement like that."

"Lucy, I am afraid there is going more ahead of us. Let us hope you will get home soon," Ike said.

"Children, if you are patient, you will get there soon enough," Mary added.

Ike said, "I never saw those men who wore those capes and hats before. They were not like any of the other Purples."

"Urk, they were like bugs," Mar said, repulsed.

"It looked like they became bugs," I added.

"Yes, they seemed to turn into bugs. I also never heard of them. And as unkind as it may be, I hope they are gone forever,"

Mary said.

"Kids, you see what I meant when I said, there were things out here you wouldn't believe. Those creatures must have developed a separate strain among the Purples."

"Could it be they mixed with bugs?" Matt said.

"Oh no, that's way too gross. I don't want to even think about it," Lucy said.

"How many more times do we have to stop in cities and find things like that?" Mar asked.

"I believe as many times as there are cities," Ike instructed.

"Isn't there anybody in this world who knows how many cities there are!" Lucy exclaimed. Ike shrugged his shoulders.

"Kids, let's hope there aren't many more."

"Children, maybe we should just concentrate on getting to the end," Mary suggested.

"That was something. First, we were in a cave, then suddenly we were outside, then we were in the Dragon. It was like magic. After that, I think we can't be hurt, and we'll get home."

"Maybe you're right Johnny, so far we haven't been harmed, and I don't pretend to understand what happened back there. I've always believed magic was just tricks. I think this was much more than magic," Moe thought.

Suddenly, a voice came from the unoccupied back seat, shocking us all. "That is a correct assumption." We turned to see a *Man in White* sitting there.

Barely able to speak, Mar asked, "Sir, do you mean we are not going to be hurt?"

"I agreed all this is more than magic," he calmly said. "You must never forget you are only human, and being human, there is always an element of danger and it being so, there is always the possibility of harm."

"Sir, do you mean we can be hurt?"

"Sir, does it mean we can even be killed?"

"Lucy, Mar, your destiny depends on your personal behavior."

"Sir, do you mean we can avoid being hurt by the way we act?"

"Johnny, you must remember, as you travel through life, you

cannot avoid being exposed to hurts even if your Goodness was perfect. It is especially true if you walk on the side of Goodness for death awaits all."

"Sir, must there be hurts and death?"

"Mary, part of being human, is living a life of doing one's best to avoid the harms humans impose on each other. You must remember death is part of life."

"Do you mean we are going to be hurt or even killed?"

"Yes and no, Mar. You must understand this; if you live your life only to avoid being hurt or killed, you're missing the very point of what life is all about. Death comes to all and should not be feared."

"Oh, Gee-Wis, how will we know when we find that understanding?" Lucy asked.

"If you seek it, you will find it. If you travel the *Road* without succumbing to the fears that would stop you, you will not only reach its end, you will gain the understanding." Upon saying that, he disappeared right in front of us.

"Hey, they really do disappear, don't they?" Mar said.

"Yes, but where do they go?" Lucy asked.

"Who knows?" Moe said.

"Who knows, knows," Ike added.

"He said, if we keep seeking, we will find the understanding," Mary contemplated.

"Yes, he also said, we must not be afraid, and at the same time, we should do our best to avoid being hurt or killed," Moe said, and then added, "Complicated isn't it?"

"I don't like this. I only want to get back home," Mar said.

"I think I'm beginning to understand. If we continue to travel on the *Road* without fear, we'll succeed in getting back home. You know, in a sense, our parents taught us the same thing," I said as I began to contemplate more things about life.

"Yes, what our parents taught us. I think you might have something there, I'll have to think about that," Moe said.

"Then, we better keep moving on," Ike suggested.

"Mr. Moe, please step harder on that accelerator thing."

"Yes, Miss Mary." As he did, he asked, "What's next, Ike?

"It will be Orangestop.

CHAPTER 37 Passing Through Orangestop

Heading towards Orangestop, Moe asked, "Okay, Ike, what's it like there?"

"I have only traveled there one time. I found them to be a secretive people. They do not allow ordinary merchants or simple travelers to enter their city, only a select few. I had to stay in the trading area at the border where outsiders stopped as they travel by or to gain permission to enter. It's most unusual how they not only restrict entry into their city but keep what they traded a secret."

"What is it they trade?" Moe asked.

"I do not know. You see, their merchants only deal with certain individual traders behind closed doors. One only gains access by using secret code words. Customers are required to keep what they purchase to themselves. I was not interested in going any further with them, for I felt there was something not right. My father also had no additional information to add to what they produced or how they lived in their city."

"What you mean to say is, you have no idea of what to expect," Lucy concluded.

"To expect is to expect."

"I guess we don't have any idea," Moe said.

"Anyway, we'll still have to go into the city, right?" I said.

"Right. Regardless of the obstacles, we're going to find out about them soon enough, whether we'll like it or not," Moe said as we sped on peddle.

In time, we approached the sizable trading area, which was a separate community in its self, Lucy asked, "How come there're no Orange people around here?"

"It is because almost all stay within the closed city. The only Oranges out here are those who service the travelers in the trading area. Those who trade with the merchants enter the city and do their business behind closed doors," Ike answered.

"If it's closed, how will we get in?" I wondered.

"I am thinking the same thing."

"Miss Mary, we'll have to wait and see, right, Ike?"

"To wait and see is to wait and see."

"I don't like this."

"We'll be all right, Mar, right, Mr. Moe?"

"Oh… Right, Johnny, we'll be just fine." He then asked Ike, "How can we enter the city?"

"As I said, I have never been in this city. If possible, I believe we must bypass the trading area and enter through the main gate to find and fulfill our purpose. We first must determine if it can be done."

"I guess so. Wait... Maybe, we should just keep driving, for I don't see anything blocking the way."

"Moe, what makes sense makes sense."

"Then that's what we'll do," Moe said, as he stepped down on the pedal.

To our surprise and relief, we drove right past the trading area and in through the main gate without attracting any unwanted attention. Was it because the Orange people couldn't see us through the tinted windows? Although, it was weird that the Dragon itself didn't draw any attention. Perhaps, it might've frightened them.

"It is unbelievable how simple entry was. I guess people have been too afraid to even try to enter before," Ike said.

"I guess if you don't try, how can you know what could be done," Lucy said.

Moe said, "How true that is."

Once in the bright orange city, I expressed a, "Wow!"

Moe laughed, then asked, "Now, where would the center be?"

"Wouldn't it be where the most activity is?" I concluded.

"Well, I see some taller buildings way over there," Lucy said.

"Good, that's the place," Moe said.

Reaching that point, we parked and observed the people as they passed. The inhabitants walked in an upbeat manner and wore flashy clothing with a broad range of flamboyant styles, although the only color was orange. There was something strange about them, as evidenced by their hyper-mannerisms.

"They don't look like bad people," Lucy said.

"As they say, you can't judge a book by its cover," Moe said.

"I know we have to do this. Mr. Moe, please lead the way," Mary said. As usual, the people were startled as we exited the Dragon. Close up, the first thing we noticed was their large round eyes, which hardly blinked. Their eyes were like a doll's eyes, which at first was unsettling, although fascinating.

A man asked, "Are you suppose to be here?" Moe reflected, then said, "Yes, we're supposed to be here." Wondering if he would get away with that less than truthful answer.

"Are they really supposed to be here?" A woman asked.

Another said, "If they say they are supposed to be here, then they are supposed to be here."

Another man turned to the crowd and asked, "Do you not agree?" Not knowing what to think, they agreed.

"To be here is to be here," Ike said.

"They're a pretty trusting people," Lucy muttered.

Curious, the crowd closed in around us, asking questions wanting to know who we were and why we were here. Moe, never sure in how much to reveal, immediately asked, "Where could we get a good meal?"

Several answered at the same time. In the confusion, a young man exclaimed, "We will show you!" Before we could say anything, a couple of them jumped into the Dragon. We quickly got back in fear of losing control. Several more young Oranges crowded us in, while more jumped on the sideboards and more even climbed on the roof, Moe could only say, "Show me the way." The strangers quickly discussed among themselves where to go. Deciding on a place, the young men directed them, "Turn right at the next corner."

"You got it," Moe said, as he drove slowly in fear of someone falling off the roof.

"My name is Mary," and she introduced the rest of us. Then asked, "And who are you?"

The one who was directing us answered first, "My name is Ham."

"My name is Rose," a young woman said.

"My name is Beef," the second young man said.

"My name is Daisy," the second young woman said.

"My name is Potato," the third young man said. It didn't include the others standing on the sideboards and those hanging on the roof, for they couldn't hear us.

At first, we wondered, with those names, could they be farmers or something like that.

Mary said, "We are glad to meet all of you."

With a smile, Moe stated, "I'm getting hungry." Mar giggled.

"Please, Mr. Moe," Mary said.

"Turn left here and stop where it says Obsessions," Ham ordered.

Parked, they led us into the establishment to find an expansive smoke-filled restaurant/bar/dance hall type room. It was filled with men and women engaged in excessive loud chatter while puffing on what looked like oddly shaped cigarettes, cigars, pipes, and other weird-looking paraphernalia.

Waiting to be seated, Mary asked, "What are they doing?"

"They're smoking," Lucy said, with a frown on her face.

"Smoking, why would they want to do that? She thought and then asked, "Are they cooking their insides?" as she put her hands over her mouth and coughed, inhaling the smoke.

"No, although it does seem so, doesn't it. However, in our world, smoking is a widespread habit, and some even claim it's an addiction. Others believe it's life-threatening. I never took to it myself."

"Mr. Moe, life-threatening, and what is meant by the word addiction?"

"It means they get hooked on it. It means they can't help themselves. It means they can't kick it," I said, trying to explain it, with the little understanding I had.

"My, hooked, kick it, it seems most complicated."

"It's pretty simple Miss Mary; when one smokes, they inhale chemicals, causing them to become addicted. Meaning, they cannot help but desire more. They become hooked on it. Meaning, it takes them over, so they aren't able to stop smoking to kick the addiction out of their system."

"Moe, you said, it can kill them? Why that sounds awful," Ike said.

"Yes… Yet, youngsters seem to think it makes them appear to be grown up and glamorous or something like that. I guess that's what immaturity is all about," Moe explained.

"This might be the reason they are so secretive?" Ike said.

"In our world, people fight openly for the right to smoke," I added.

"Your world is most peculiar," Mary said.

"Mr. Moe, didn't the Indians smoke peace pipes?"

"That's right, Lucy. Hmm, since there's little peace here, that tradition must have stopped when they came through the *Rock*. Except those here seem to have taken it to the extreme. However, I have the feeling these people aren't looking for peace."

"Mr. Moe, I never heard of smoking. Have you Ike?" Mary asked.

"No, never," he answered.

Ham left us to speak with a ruffled heavyset man who we guessed was the Maitre d' or the guy in charge. After some discussion, he came over a little distraught. Nevertheless, he said, "My name is Pork. This way, please." With the help of a few waiters, they pulled several tables together to seat all who came with us in the Dragon, which numbered twenty-three. Then he asked, "May I order for you?"

Seeing the complication of asking for a menu, Moe said, "Okay!"

"Thank you, would you please," Mary said

As we waited for the food, we observed what was taking place around us. Everyone was energetically partying, although they didn't seem to be enjoying themselves. Along with smoking and boisterous conversations, some were dancing wildly by themselves within the crowd to discordant music coming from somewhere unseen. They also were guzzling down orange drinks in one quick swallow.

As our eyes adjusted to the smoky haze, most conspicuous were colorful large advertising signs hung from the ceiling and along the walls depicting the different smoking choices and the drinks they were having. Then to our dismay, we clearly saw, hung right out in the open, pictures displaying hand-drawn men and women doing unmentionable intimate things with each other. Pictures, up to that point, I'd only seen when mischievous boys brought them to school and showed them in secret.

Moe understood, and said, "Okay, I see what they're up to. No wonder these creeps keep it a secret. Kids don't look at those pictures." However, because of their sheer size, it was impossible not to.

Mary, being overwhelmed by the pictures, asked, "What's going on, Mr. Moe?" Moe shook his head in despair.

A waiter delivered those same drinks to our table, which contained about a half-inch of an orange liquid. Moe and Mary look at each other with the same feelings we all had that something was wrong or even hazardous in this place.

Foolishly, Lucy sipped her drink and exclaimed, "Hey isn't this alcohol!"

Moe smelled it and then took a sip. Making a face, he instructed, "That's awful stuff, it tastes nasty. I think this is more than alcohol. Kids, this place, is like a bar, or even worse, like an opium den or a house of ill-repute, don't drink anything." At that age, being quite naïve, we couldn't even imagine the full extent of what he meant.

"Oh my, what's going on?" Mary asked.

"What's alcohol?" Ike asked.

"It's what makes you drunk," I explained, knowing little more than that.

"What does drunk mean?"

Mary and Ike looked to Moe for a definition. He said, "It means if you drink too much of this stuff, you might lose control of your behavior in a way that might be embarrassing or make you sick or even worse."

"My parents always told me getting drunk could lead to unpleasant things," Mar added.

"Yes, we were told if we drank too much alcohol, we could get into trouble," Lucy said.

"Some of our friends got drunk and wound up doing stupid things, like getting into serious car accidents or even worst, you know what I mean?" I said.

Lucy said, "Yes, I don't even want to talk about that."

Ike sniffed his drink and asked, "If I took just a sip, would I get drunk?"

"I don't believe so. No, I don't think you would if you only wet your tongue," Moe said.

Ike trusted him and carefully wet his tongue, assessing it, he said, "It tastes like what we call libation in Redtown, only it is stronger and has other flavors I do not recognize. We sometimes sip libation after a meal."

"I know of libation. As a youngster, I was told not to drink it. I now understand why," Mary said.

"I believe there are stronger drugs involved here, not just alcohol and tobacco. Let's not drink anything, for we're going to need our full senses. They must grow and distill this stuff themselves, which I believe enhances those behaviors depicted on the posters," Moe concluded and then said, "As I remember, the people you are descended from didn't do well with alcohol, although I believe they did use drugs that gave them visions."

Ham was listening to our conversation while smoking what looked like a fat cigar, only it had an irregular and twisted shape. Along with guzzling down the drinks, which noticeably caused his large round eyes to glaze over, he urged, "Come on, have some fun!"

Mary stiffened and said, "No, thank you, Mr. Ham. We're just fine."

"Where the (f*# %& @) do you come from?" he said, using profanity we clearly understood, shocking us.

Outraged, Moe said, "Ham! Don't say that word in front of Miss Mary and the kids."

Surprised, Ham asked, "What word?" as several waiters arrived with our meals.

"The third word you said. We don't use words like that in front of kids and ladies where we come from," Moe said with firmness. Ham, now in a dazed condition, didn't know what to make or cared about Moe's strong reaction.

"Mr. Moe, I never heard that word before, what does it mean?" Mary asked.

"Trust me, it's, just not a nice word. Maybe we should just

eat." Seeing his discomfort, she stopped her questioning.

"Yes, words are words," Ike added.

Although hungry, Moe carefully sniffed and sampled the food before allowing us to touch it. Doing his best to make sure it was not spiked, after which he said, "It's okay kids, dig in," trusting he knew what he was doing, which might not have been so.

Rose, Beef, Daisy, and Potato hadn't overheard what we had said, as they began to discuss the meal and other things using a wide vocabulary of foul language. Some words we knew and others not, although the tone was unmistakable. "Kids, don't listen to what they're saying. Let's eat and get out of here," Moe strongly suggested.

"I just want to go home," Mar said.

"Maybe we should just leave," Mary wondered.

"I do not think our purpose here has been fulfilled," Ike speculated.

"I wish we knew what that was," Lucy said.

"I think it's for us to deal with whatever comes our way," Moe said.

"Here we go again," Ike said.

"Oh, my. Oh, my."

"Can't we just get away from these silly people," Lucy said.

"Careful Lucy," I warned, knowing her temperament and limitless big mouth.

Halfway through the meal, Rose and the others had gulped down several of those drinks, which the waiters kept bringing to the table. The drinks seemed to be most potent, and as a result, the Orange's had become inebriated or more likely drugged to a high.

Rose said to Daisy in a slurred voice hard to understand, "I think that A#@&* Johnny is cute."

"He is, and that A#@&* Matt is too," Daisy added. I must say, in spite of the language, Matt and I were oddly flattered with their attention, for they were cute, yet it made us uncomfortable not knowing how to react in this unwholesome environment.

Not believing the outright flirtatious, Mary said, "Now girls, mind your manners."

"What are c#@&* manners?" Rose asked.

"Young ladies, it simply means, to be good, to be courteous

and to be polite."

"We're all *#%&@ good here," Ham said. "Come on, Mary, drink your drink and let's have some *#%&@ fun."

"Mr. Ham, what in the world does that mean?" Mary indignantly.asked.

Rose stood and said, "Come on, Johnny, let us have some i*#%&@ fun," then collapsed back down into her chair, laughing hysterically.

"You silly l@#$," Daisy said. Both Girls were well beyond the power to control their behavior, as their large round eyes were now glazed over no longer able to focus.

Moe wasn't only taking in what was happening at the table, but what was going on in the rest of the room. Concerned, things were out of control, for people were doing things that should only be done in private. Any decent person could see things had gone too far.

Protective of Mary and us, he became so indignant one could almost see smoke coming out of his ears. Compelled by a force deep inside him, without fear, he jumped up on the table and yelled, "Stop this, you degenerate people. Stop what you're doing! And for heaven's sake, keep your clothes on!" Everyone in the room stopped to look at him. There was a scary uneasy silence.

Courageously, I followed Moe's impulse and jumped up on the table alongside him, shortly followed by Ike and Matt. We now compounded Moe's strength and outrage, as he yelled, "You think you're having fun? Do you really think smoking, drinking, and whatever else you're taking until you can't control yourself and acting like fools, is fun? Do you think using foul language is fun? Do you think being indecent and obscene is fun?"

"Hey, don't you stupid people know being good and decent is the way to be?" Lucy yelled as she joined us up on the table.

"Yeah, I'll bet you don't even know what she means?" I added.

A voice called out from the crowd, saying, "Who are these people?"

Another said, "They are not even Orange," which was evident from the beginning, although no one seemed to have noticed.

Other voices followed, "Who are they to tell us how to

behave?"

"How, did they get in here anyway?"

"I saw Ham bring them in," a voice accused.

Ham denied it and proclaimed, "No, I don't know who they are," as he slithered away, followed by Rose, Daisy, Beef, Potato, and all those at our table disappearing into the crowd.

"Oh, my. Oh my," Mary uttered, seeing a possible unpleasant outcome.

"It'll be all right, Miss Mary," Moe reassured as he reached down, helping her up onto the table followed by me helping Mar up.

Ike also saw the danger and spoke to the crowd, saying, "You better watch out. These people are *Rockers*" to gasps.

Infused with even greater courage sprinkled with my innocence, I said, "That's it. We're here to teach you about decency and goodness."

Moe whispered to me, "Good job, Johnny." He turned to the crowd and added, "Can't you see your faults? Can't you see you're not having real fun?"

"How do you know we are not having real fun?" a voice called out.

"How do I know? Well, because… Because…

Mary seeing his hesitation, quickly whispered, "Mr. Moe, because you know what real fun is."

Without further hesitation, he yelled, "Yes. Yes, because I know what fun is." Then he whispered back, "Miss. Mary, do I really know what fun is?"

"Of course, you do, Mr. Moe."

A voice called out, "Do people on the other side of the *Rock* know how to have real fun?"

"We do, and what you're doing is not really fun," Lucy added.

"What do you mean by that?" a confused voice called out.

"I'll bet you don't feel very good when you get home after you've been out drinking, smoking, and whatever?" Moe said.

"And just look at your eyes, why you drugged up dummies," Lucy said.

"Afterwards, I do feel ill, and usually, my eyes burn along with my head aching," a female admitted, followed by a cough almost choking.

"What does it matter when you are having fun?" a man said as he coughed.

"It looks like you're having more pain than fun," I said.

"And, why do the other things you are doing called fun when you do it in public?" a troubled Moe asked.

"What other things?" another voice asked.

"Well, it's. It's…

"Say it. Say it, Mr. Moe," Mary urged, with a blushed look of embarrassment.

"Okay, Miss Mary. It's; Sex! Sex!" he quickly exclaimed and took a gulp of air.

Mary boldly asked, "Do you care for the ones you are having sex with?" Moe was startled in hearing that coming from her.

"Why should we care for others if we are having fun?" a voice asked.

Mary couldn't contain herself, "Why! Well, because you are missing the most important thing of all. How foolish of you."

"What is more important than fun?" many voices echoed.

"Why, of course, it's caring, I mean loving, being concerned about others, can you not understand that?" Mary said, exhibiting more knowledge than she ever thought about in her sheltered life.

"What is this caring and loving you are talking about?" More than one asked.

"Why, the things life is all about. How dumb can you be?" Lucy said, even though she hadn't yet experienced such intimate things.

"Lucy!" I exclaimed, alarmed not being any more experienced than she was.

"It's all right, Johnny," Moe said, turning to the crowd, "Yes, how dumb can you be? Don't you understand the meaning of love?"

"Sometimes, I want to feel something other than just having fun. The truth is, most times, after having fun, I do not even remember what happened," a woman admitted.

"You do not have to remember anything to have fun," A man shouted.

"Come on, girls, do you really think getting sick and not even remembering what you did is having fun," Mary said.

And what about getting pregnant?" Lucy asked.

"Lucy!" Matt exclaimed, unsettled, not believing Lucy was capable of saying anything like that.

"Yes, and when we get pregnant, we are sent away until we have the baby. Then we are brought back, leaving our babies with others to become pregnant again," another woman said.

"Why, ladies, that is no fun at all," Mary said.

"Yes, it is not fun at all. I always thought we were just being used," another woman accused.

"Girls, you know you want to have fun," A man said.

"We are aware most men do not care for us," a woman responded.

"Yes, ladies, do not give any man fun unless they love and care for you," Mary instructed.

"These strangers are trying to ruin our fun," a man accused.

"Wait, maybe they have a point," another man said.

"I think I would like a girl to care for me," another man said.

"And I would like a man to care for me," a woman added.

Standing against the far wall where a bunch of unprincipled types, one of them yelled out, "You are just trying to ruin our fun. Boys, let us get them out of here." As they started to move towards us, suddenly, some of the women jumped on them, attempting to stop them from reaching us. Then to our further amazement, there was a welcomed and satisfying sight as some men came to the aid of those women. Anyway, bedlam broke out.

However, a couple of those troublesome men were able to work their way up to our table. But, as the first one touched us, the *White Light* suddenly struck, and everyone in the room, except for us were frozen in place. A *Man in White* stood at the door. He said, "Good, your work here is done. It is time to move on." Just as suddenly, everyone was unfrozen, and he was gone as the confrontations continued.

Fortunately, the good people among them were now restraining those men from reaching us. Rose and Daisy reappeared, having come to a sobering realization and implored us, "Come with us. We will guide you out of here."

"Kids, grab your food," Moe ordered as Rose and Daisy led us out a side door and back to the Dragon, guiding us to the edge of the city.

They both thanked us for telling them to follow their true feelings, something they never heard of or even knew existed. Daisy admitted, "I always felt there was something more for us, but did not know what it was,"

"I still think Johnny and Matt are cute," Rose said.

"Now, ladies, you deserve to have a special man who really loves and cares for you, do not let them use you just for fun," Mary instructed. They asked if we could stay and help them learn more about their true feelings. Mary explained our situation and said, "Ladies, only act on those feelings that come from deep inside your heart and stop drinking, smoking, and taking any of that awful stuff they push on you. Above all, stop giving yourself away just for fun.

Although disappointed in us leaving, they were inspired to do better in their lives from the seed of love rejuvenated in them this day. As we bid our farewells, we noticed their eyes seemed focused as we hoped they were now able to see things more clearly with their hearts.

CHAPTER 38 Troubles in Greenhinge

Speeding towards the next city, still filled with bizarre images of the Orange people, only added to our apprehension. "Miss Mary, will we ever reach the end of the *Road*?" Mar asked.

"Oh child, we will get to the end. Everything has an end. If one takes care of what is happening at the moment, the end will come soon enough," Mary could only say to reassure her.

"The end is the end," Ike added.

"Kids, sometimes the end seems so far away, yet it could be right around the corner, be patient. Haven't you kids noticed how fast the *Men in White* are moving us along, not wanting us to stay very long in each city? I believe they want us to reach the end as much as we do."

"All I want is to go home," Mar could only say.

"We'll get home, you know what I mean?" I said.

"I'll know what you mean when we get there," Lucy quipped.

"Ike, what is next?" Moe asked.

"It will be Greenhinge."

"Tell us about Greenhinge?"

"I hesitate in saying anything. I was so wrong about the Orange people. How could I be right about anything else?"

"Ike, you were not wrong, you just did not know their true character, for it was hidden," Mary said.

"Please, tell us about the Green people?" Lucy urged.

"Ike, the more we know, the better prepared we'll be," Moe appealed.

"Hmm… I know the Orange people showed outsiders their better face. Maybe, the Greens do the same."

"One can only make judgments on what they see," Moe observed.

"Mr. Moe, that's so profound."

"Really, Miss Mary?"

"Yes, really, Mr. Moe."

"Ike, please tell us what you know?" Lucy again urged.

"Hmm… Considering they might have also fooled me. However, I do believe they are not bad people. They seem to be most concerned about their health. They are always running and exercising."

"There are people like that in our world, too," I said.

"Yes, there are, and some of them make me barf," Lucy added.

"Barf?" Mary asked.

"I'm sorry, forget that remark."

"She means, it makes her throw up," I clarified.

"Oh my, how awful," Mary reacted.

"If the people in Greenhinge are like them, they would be exercising and watching what they eat all the time," Ike said.

"That's like them," Lucy said.

"Maybe, then, we shall not have any trouble," Ike added.

"Again, famous last words," Lucy muttered.

"Ike, is it not so that the Greens make and supply health potions to all the cities?

"Yes, Mary, it is what they do."

"I remember Mr. Right took some of those potions when he became ill, which was most helpful."

"So did McCloud, yet they both died."

"They did. However, potions are their primary source of trade," Ike replied.

"Interesting?" Moe said.

Even knowing we've not been harmed so far, we drove towards Greenhinge with an outlook salted with fear. In time, Ike said, "There it is," seeing it the distance. "We will be there soon. Moe, take the next left turn."

Once in the city, we saw the inhabitants jogging along the streets. I knew Lucy felt a knot in her stomach as she said, "Oh no, not joggers."

"Joggers? Is something wrong with joggers?" Mary asked, not knowing what it meant.

"No, she just doesn't like healthy people, they make her sick," I said.

"That's not true. I just don't care for those who work at it so hard."

"Oh, I think I understand."

"Thank you, Miss Mary," Lucy said with satisfaction as she smirked at me. I jokingly I stuck my tongue out at her when Mary couldn't see. Lucy just gave me that look of conquest and settled back, knowing she won that one, however small it was.

Reaching the center of the city, it wasn't getting any easier for us to confront the people. However, knowing we must do this, we stepped out onto the street. When the joggers saw us, they stopped one by one, asking who we were and where we came from?

Again, strangely, they weren't alarmed by our color, which seemed most peculiar in a world based on color segregation. We didn't hesitate to answer their questions, but again didn't mention the *White Light* or the *Men in White*, at least not until we could judge if it were necessary to do so. Finally, Moe asked the important question, "Is there a place we can get a good meal around here?"

"There is, we will take you there," A Green answered, as several of them jogged off, stopping they beckoned us to follow,

"Come on. We'll show you, it's not far."

"They want us to jog there? I do not think I can do that," Mary said.

"Neither can I," Moe added.

As the Greens jogged in place, one of them urged, "Just follow us."

"See what I mean. Let us just walk fast. I believe they will wait for us," Ike said.

"Well, I hope it is not too far," Mary said. We followed the Greens as they jogged in circles around us in order not to get too far ahead.

It wasn't long before Moe and Mary were breathing heavily. Moe stopped and bent over gasping for air and said to the joggers, "You'll have to wait a minute. I have to catch my breath."

As the Greens jogged in place, one said, "You are not very healthy," stating the obvious.

"Sir, your health is most impressive, we can only dream of being as healthy as you," Ike said, as not to offend them, as he thought Moe might do in seeing the look on his face.

"You can if you exercise and eat the right foods. We are taking you to a place that has the right foods. As soon as you are able, we will continue."

"Thank you, Sir," Mary said.

When ready, we continued the fast walk. A little farther along, we stopped again to catch our breath. It was comical in seeing how the uncomplaining joggers stopped and jogged in place three times before we arrived at the destination. And as they said, it wasn't very far. It was a building with large plate glass windows, surrounded by a vibrant green lawn with a number of green statues of people posed in different exercise positions guzzling down a liquid from little bottles. Plainly, it was their way of advertising what they produced.

The building contained one large room looking more like a gymnasium than a restaurant; it had rows of long tables. Each of which stretched the full length of the chamber, where many people were eating. Finding a place to sit the lead man explained a meal would be served to us."

"Thank you, Sir. What is your name?" Mary asked.

"My name is 'Sixty Two Thousand, Eight Hundred, and Twenty Seven." Seeing the expressions on our faces, he said, "They call me Six."

After Mary introduced us, Moe picked up Mary's lead and said, "Glad to meet you, Six." Several waiters delivered the meals. And to Moe's bewilderment, there were less than a dozen tiny pieces of food spread across a small plate. He had to restrain himself from saying something negative.

Mary saw his expression and said, "Mr. Moe, I am not sure, but I think we better follow the path we are being led along without question."

"Yes, Miss Mary. I'll do my best." Using our fingers, it took only seconds to finish the meal. Than Six, along with others, led us down to a large room below the restaurant filled with people exercising. They placed us in line with others where we were expected to exercise in unison. Mary, Moe, and even Ike were unable to keep in sync with the Greens, which I must say was a sight to see.

Before long, the three of them were on the floor, exhausted. The four of us did better, but also eventually ended up on the floor. Six and others helped us go outside to catch our breath. "It is going to take a while before you will achieve health," Six said.

Leaving us alone lying on our backs on the lawn, the joggers headed back into the building to continue their exercising.

"These people are crazy."

"I have to agree with you, Mr. Moe. What are we to do?" Mary asked.

"We must do what we must do, and I am afraid I no longer know what it is," Ike added.

"Even though we are different, they don't seem to know or care who we are," Lucy said.

Mar asked, "Can't we just tell them what we're looking for?"

"You know anything could happen then," I warned.

"These people don't seem to be too swift," Lucy said.

"Mr. Moe, What do you think?"

"Well, Miss Mary, maybe we should go along with them a little longer to see where it'll lead. Can we all do that?"

"To do is to do," Ike added.

"I can. It's kind of fun trying to keep up with them. You know what I mean?" I said.

"This time, I really don't know what you mean," Lucy said.

"Don't we have to tell them what we're doing here, sooner or later?" Mar asked.

"It might be so, but first I need to rest," Moe said, as he dropped his head back down on the grass and closed his eyes.

"We should all rest. We will need our strength," Mary instructed. Exhausted, it wasn't long before we all dozed off as darkness fell.

The next thing we knew, Six and others were shaking us while holding lanterns, "Wake up! Wake up! You must come with us for a very special dinner for the sake of your health."

"Oh, I don't want to move," Lucy said.

"We will have to use your transport to get there, to walk at your speed, we will be too late," Six said.

"I don't think I have the strength left to walk back to the Dragon," Moe explained.

"Don't worry. We will carry you there."

"Good boy, Six," Moe said and then ordered us to wait for his return." The joggers picked him up and carried him off, amused at seeing that sight, yet confused and wondering what these people wanted from us.

It wasn't long before we heard the Dragon's undoubtedly raw sound. "Good, children, let us go," Mary ordered. When it pulled up, we piled in with the help of the joggers and drove off."

After a short drive, Six ordered, "Pull up here," stopping in front of a large round gloomy-looking building void of windows and those corny statues.

"What's this place?" Moe asked.

"It is where one gets what is needed for their health."

"And what would that be?" Mary asked.

"If you come with us, you will see." Six and the other Greens jogged up the steps to the front door and patiently waited for us to amble up as fast as we were able.

"I don't like the looks of this place," Mar said.

"This time, I agree with you," Lucy said.

"I guess this is following the path, so let's do it, and I hope there's more food in there," Moe quipped.

"Let's do it," I added.

"Mr. Moe, do you think it will be okay?"

"So far, Miss Mary, every time we've gotten in trouble, we've been saved."

"I hope our luck holds out."

Correcting her, Moe said, "Lucy, I don't think it has anything to do with luck," not yet fully understanding his statement.

Entering the building, we found it contained just one large round room with continuous circular tables. It started with one large circle near the wall, and another smaller circle inside that one for ten rows, ending with a small round table in the center of the room. Four narrow paths were cut through the circles at equally divided points allowing people to enter or exit all the circles.

In the crowded room, it was hard to hear each other with the level of chatter aided by the excellent acoustics. Six directed us to sit at the largest circle against the wall, a place least noticed.

Moe asked Six, "Again, what's this place?"

"It is where we eat our sacred food, the food that gives us our health. You are fortunate to be here at this time, for it takes a long time to harvest enough for all to eat." He then moved away to talk with others who were all in a festive mood.

To be heard, Ike had to shout, "I have never heard of this activity. I wonder why they keep a secret."

"I have a bad feeling," Lucy said.

"I just want to go home," Mar said.

"Please stop worrying. We'll get there," I sternly said, hoping to calm her.

"What could this food be?" Mary wondered.

"Yes, it is strange, although I suspect it is one of their potions. Whatever it might be, I am afraid we are going to find out," Ike said, as several Greens enter carrying large trays filled with tiny plates with silver covers.

The room became silent, leaving only the noise of the clanging plates as they passed them out. We were among the last to receive one. Seeing no one touched theirs, we tentatively waited.

A man at the center table stood and began to speak in the eerily stark quiet room, "We must be humble and thankful, praising our leaders for this great honor they are giving us." Everyone began to loudly chant in unison, "Praise - Praise - Praise." The echo was so strong that one could feel those words reverberating throughout their bodies.

The man ordered, "To our health, let us partake."

All the Greens simultaneously lifted the plate covers, and with one quick swallow, consumed the one little green piece of dried food. We lifted our silver covers, and Mar exclaimed, "Oh, gummy bears!" to the loud gasp of Moe.

"What 's wrong, Mr. Moe?" alarmed Mary asked.

"They're not gummy bears. They're… They're..."

"What are they?" Ike asked.

"Why they're dried fetuses!" I blurted out, having seen drawings in our science books.

Lucy, with horror, said, "Ugh, don't touch them!"

Mar screeched, "I almost touched it." In the silence of the

room, our voices loudly rang out.

"I never heard that word. What does it mean?" Mary asked.

"It means... It means... Moe again couldn't quite say it.

"It means; they're human babies," Lucy explained, also having seen those same drawings.

"Oh, my! Oh, my." Mary expressed.

Bewildered, Ike said, "This cannot be, for our children are our most prized possessions."

Everyone in the room heard what we said. Six was the first to ask, "What do you mean?"

Outraged, Moe could hardly speak, "Why you... Why you..."

I boldly jumped in and said, "You're eating your children," as yet, not fully understanding the ramifications of it all.

"No, it is not true! It is our saving health food," Six finding it hard to accept that truth.

"You're not only murders but stupid on top of it," Lucy accused.

With all the attention on us, a distraught woman asked, "What do you mean, our children?"

Pulling himself together, Moe asked, "Where does this food come from?"

"Why it comes from us women, and we are honored to give our fruits for our health."

Bewildered, Mary trusted what we said as truth, stating, "I am afraid you are eating your children."

"Look at these little figures. Don't you see how they are shaped just like you? And there is even a piece of their umbilical cord," Lucy declared, being at the very edge of her knowledge.

Another woman observed, "They do resemble us. I always wondered about that." Now enlightened, some women screamed in horror and began to weep.

Some men yelled, not believing, "That cannot be true! It is not true!"

Taking all this in, the man who led the praise asked, "Who are these people? They are not Green. Where did they come from?" At that point, we wondered if the people in this world had selective colorblindness for our colors was obviously visible.

A finely dressed man entered with an assemblage of people following him. After a painful silence, having heard the commotion, the man asked, "What is going on here?"

"These people are telling us we are eating our children," a woman declared.

The man turned to the praise leader and asked, "Who are these people?"

"By their color, they must be those who are pretending to be *Rockers* and have been causing havoc as they travel along the *Road*."

"Troublemakers, I see. Who brought them in here?" the headman demanded. Six shriveled up as some pointed at him. The headman asked him, "And who are you?"

Quaking, he answered, "My name is Sixty Two Thousand, Eight Hundred, and Twenty Seven."

"Arrest him," the headman ordered. Six collapsed in fear.

Lucy, again unfettered, charged, "Why you murder. You bloodsucking freak."

"And who are you to even speak to me?" the headman asked.

I came to the aid of my sister, for no one could talk to her like that. Without fear, I said, "You jerk, we are *Rockers*, and all you women are allowing your leaders to tear your babies out of you," as I exhibited the same unexplained courage and knowledge just as Lucy did.

"Not only that, they make you eat them," Repulsed, Lucy added to the woeful sighs of the women.

"Silence! Arrest them," the headman ordered.

Moe, now filled with that supernatural courage, yelled, "We know the truth. Stop them from doing this to you," to more screams, wailing and fainting away of women as most of the men seemed dumbstruck.

"Get them! Get them!" the headman ordered.

As his men started to move towards us, Moe pleaded, "Would the good people in this room not allow them to get away with this evil any longer." Bedlam broke out, and to our delight, many of the good men went to the aid of the fainting women rather than approaching us.

However, as we were about to be seized by the few henchmen, a flash of *White Light* struck. All were frozen in place, except for us. When able to see again, there was a *Man in White* standing on the center table. He said, "Good, you have done well. These people's seeds have been revitalized. It is time for you to leave without delay." Another flash of light and he was gone as the people came back to life.

"Let's get out of here," Moe ordered, as the mayhem continued around us.

While heading out, Six, who was lying on the floor, grabbed Moe's leg and pleaded, "Please, take me with you. I cannot live here anymore."

Unsure, Moe said, "I don't know."

He saw the look in Mary's eyes as she pleaded, "Please, Mr. Moe."

"Yes, Moe," Ike added.

He helped Six to his feet, and we scurried out and piled into the Dragon. Driving off, Six directed us back to the *Road*. We drove away from Greenhinge as fast as the Dragon would take us.

When safely away, Mar asked, "How could they eat their children? I was afraid they might eat us too?"

"Oh, child, try to remember, we are not going to die or be eaten," Mary said, a bit frustrated, yet just as uncertain.

"Mary, was it really our children?" Six sorrowfully asked.

"I am afraid so. Mr. Moe and the children are from the other side of the *Rock* and know of such things.

"What? They always told us we were taking a very special potion."

However, remember, you did not know any better," She gently answered, trying to pacify him.

"And, you never questioned them?" Lucy wondered.

"How could we, they are our leaders, and the practice has been taking place for lifetimes, longer than anyone remembers. No one would dare question their authority."

"I would've challenged them."

"Lucy, try not to forget, we grew up free with an understanding of many more things, these people didn't have that opportunity," Moe instructed.

"Are you really from the other side of the *Rock*?" Six asked, as that fact registered.

"Yes, we are," Moe answered.

"When anyone asked about the *Rock,* we were told it was a myth. Why did you come to Greenhinge?"

"We are on our way home," I said.

"All this is too hard to believe. Please tell me about your understanding from the other side of the *Rock?*"

"Six, it simple means; one should try to understand more than they do at the moment, and not to trust everything your leaders tell you. However, we are now seeking a greater understanding of your world," Moe explained.

"A greater understanding of my world?" Six asked.

"Yes, it is something we are looking for. Would you like to join us in that quest?" Mary asked.

"Oh, yes, I would be honored to join you."

"Well then, keep your ears and eyes open," Moe said.

"Oh, I will do that. I will keep my eyes and ears open."

"That's good. Okay, Ike, what's next?"

"It will be Blackside, but Six probably knows more than I do about his neighbors."

"Oh no, all we were ever told about anyone outside of Greenhinge was that we were healthier."

"How come you were so friendly, and your leaders were so nasty?" Lucy asked.

"I do not know. Maybe, it was because we never met or even saw anyone from the outside before. I thought it would be exciting to help you to better health. Sadly, I did not know any better.

"I have always known our leaders were demanding and controlling, which I never saw challenged before. You saw what happened when you questioned their authority. I have always been too scared to have ever spoken to them. I am so thankful you took me out of there. And, I am sorry I cannot help you any more concerning Blackside."

Ike said, "It is all right. You do not have to be sorry. I cannot add very much either, for I have never been there. We will all have to learn about the Black people's character together."

However, at the time, it puzzled us in what the *Man in White* said about the Green people's seeds having been revitalized.

CHAPTER 39 Arriving in Blackside

While driving towards Blackside, Ike explained, "From what I have been told, all I can say about the Black people is their skin is dark black, they grow fruits supplying them to all the cities. They too are a secretive people. Come to think of it, it seems every city has its secrets."

"Okay, this means we'll all have to start from scratch," Moe said.

"Scratch?" Mary asked.

"It just means we'll all start from the place of not knowing anything," Lucy added.

"Ah, you have all these colorful expressions," Mary said.

"You know what amazes me is that everyone here speaks our language," Matt wondered.

Moe said, "Yes, I haven't given that much thought. But, now thinking about it, how could they have learned our modern-day language? It's not only remarkable; it's outright mysterious, even supernatural."

"Imagine how it would be if they didn't," Lucy thought.

"Boy, it would be a mess," I agreed.

"It certainly would be. If they didn't, why we'd never get home! I'm glad they do," Mar said.

"In your world, do you not speak the same?" Six asked.

"No, we speak in many different tongues."

"Tongues?"

"Sorry, Miss Mary. It just means languages."

"With all your tongues, it must be very confusing."

I said, "Actually, it's less complicated than understanding why your cities don't know anything about each other. You know what I mean?"

"This time, I even know what you mean," Lucy agreed.

"Anyway, it's cool," Mar could only say.

"Yes, it is. Okay, but now we'll all have to learn what Blackside is like from scratch," Moe said."

And to understand is to understand. I think it is best to stop and rest right here until it is light again," Ike suggested.

Visibly exhausted, Mary said, "Yes, we all need to rest."

"Mr. Moe, could I relieve you and drive the dragon for a while? I tentatively asked, hoping for a positive answer.

"Do you have a driver's license?"

"I have a certificate from Drivers Ed, and my dad taught me when I was fifteen to be a good driver."

"Why, Mr. Moe, I think that is a good idea. You need to rest too."

Having been a teacher of young people for many years, he had a sense of which students would be trustworthy. Moe said, "Well… We'll try it. However, it's getting dark now. Johnny, I'll test you tomorrow. For now, I agree with Ike, we should stop right here." We pulled off the *Road*, built a fire, and ate. After darkness fell, it wasn't long before we were asleep.

At daybreak, I woke first, excited about my chance to drive. I gathered some wood and built a fire, knowing Moe was going to be hungry. Mary woke, feeling a chill she came over the fire to warm herself in spite of the temperature being comfortable and never fluctuating much.

"Good morning, Johnny. You must be eager to drive today?" She said, seeming to be a bit frail. Both she and Moe clearly appeared to have aged in the past few days.

"Oh yes, Miss Mary, I was ready to take the driving test in a couple of days before we were pulled through."

"It must be hard for you, not knowing when you will get back."

"That's if we ever get back."

"Now Johnny, do not even think like that. You will get home."

Moe emerged from the Dragon with an armful of breakfast packages, saying, "Time to eat." He asked me to wake the others while he heated the food. After Moe had his fill, he turned to me and asked, "Are you ready?"

"Yes sir, I'm ready, you know what I mean?"

"We all know what you mean. Maybe I'll be next," Lucy said.

"Why don't you all stay here while I let Johnny drive up and down before we all get on board."

With me in the driver's seat, Moe instructed, "Now, the controls are a little different than those in the cars in our world. I will show you as we go. Now, turn the starter crank."

"I know Mr. Moe. I've been watching you."

"Good. Go ahead, turn it." I turned it with all my might. The engine kicked off with a mighty roar giving me an awesome feeling of power. "Good, now step on the clutch and put it in gear. Okay, now step gently on the fuel pedal and move out slowly."

Following his instruction, I drove a short distance, then turned around and came back, passing the group to an equal distance in the opposite direction. Turning around again, and with a burst of speed, we drove past the group and into the distance until they no longer were visible.

"I hope he doesn't wreck the Dragon."

"I am sure he will do just fine, Lucy."

"I know Miss Mary. I just don't like it when he gets one up on me."

"One up?"

"It means we are competitive. I guess we've always been so. I was told it has something to do with being twins."

"I have never known twins. It is most interesting. I only question being competitive."

"Twins are twins," Ike said.

"I wish they would come back soon," Mar said, revealing her concern for me.

They'll be back soon. I wish I could drive the Dragon too," Matt said.

After Moe had put me through several maneuvers, we drove back to where they were waiting. Speeding past them for a short distance, stopping and turning around again, we pulled up to them.

Moe jumped out and ordered, "Johnny is ready. Let's pack up and get on our way."

With all aboard, Moe asked, "Ready?"

"I'm ready, Mr. Moe."

"Then let's get going."

With a broad smile, I said, "Here we go," I stepped on the pedal, and we were on our way as Moe checked my performance carefully.

In time, we reached the side road that led to Blackside. To be safe, Moe took the wheel before we entered the city. Little else was said, for none of us knew what to expect. Before long in the distance, we saw people walking along the road, just able to make out their jet-black skin.

"Negroes," Moe said.

Lucy, sharply taken back, said, "Mr. Moe, our parents taught us it wasn't nice to say that."

"Yes. They are people just like us.

"Johnny, it's a name older people called them. I guess it's an old tradition that's hard to break. I didn't mean it in a bad way. I know the world is changing with you, youngsters. I'll try not to say it again."

As we moved closer, having better vision, Mar was the first to notice, "Hey, look! They have pointy little noses with tips of different colors!"

"And, I must say they're not Negroes at all."

"Mr. Moe!" Lucy scolded.

"Sorry, kids. The truth is they look much like us. Except their skin is jet black, looking like those seen in minstrel shows."

"Oh, Mr. Moe," Lucy retorted.

"Sorry, I'm just trying to describe them."

Look, there's a red nose, and an orange one," Mar, pointed out as we drove closer.

"And a green one and yellow one," Matt added.

"I see a blue one," I said.

"I guess I forgot to mention their noses," Ike confessed.

"That's just what we need, colored noses," Lucy bantered.

"Now, Lucy—I too now remember hearing about their noses. It is interesting, and I cannot remember why it is so. Ike, do you know why their noses are colored?"

"I believe it has to do with their status. Six, would you

know?"

"Sorry, I have no idea."

"Well, we're going to find out soon enough. I'm heading towards the tallest building. What do you think, Ike?" Moe asked.

"I think what is best is best."

Reaching it, to find it was only three stories high, Moe ordered, "Let's do it." We stepped out and waited for a reaction.

It took only seconds before a brown-nosed man stopped and asked, "Can I help you?"

"Sir, where could we get a good meal?" Moe asked.

The man asked, "Do you have credits?" Not being sure of what he meant, Mary flashed her card. Seeing it, the man quickly said, "I will take you there. Come this way."

"Can we take our transport?" Moe asked.

"We can. I will direct you." On the way, we found out his name was Lack. Reaching the destination, we park, and several assorted color nosed people besiege us. Each held a basket filled with a variety of luscious fruits waving them in our faces, as they quoted prices. "Are they trying to sell us these fruits?" Lucy asked.

"Are you going to gain something?" Lack asked.

"Not right now," Moe said. For some unknown reason, he resisted his natural desire for fruits.

"Then let us move on." The peddlers started to quote lower prices as if it were an auction. When we entered the building, they didn't follow us, remaining on the outside. Inside, a yellow-nosed attendant stood behind a counter. He asked, "How many rooms?"

"We just want to eat," Moe said.

"To eat, one must have a room."

We looked at each other distressed. Mary asked, "Would we be able to bathe in the rooms?"

"Certainly," the attendant said.

"Well then, could we have one room for the ladies and one room for the gentlemen?" Mary ordered.

"Wait, Miss Mary," Moe interrupted and asked, "What's the cost?"

"Thirty credits for each room."

"We'll give you ten."

"Twenty."

"Fifteen, and that's the best we can do."

Sizing us up, he saw how disheveled we were and noticed our different colors, which must have confused him. He said, "Done! Your cards, please, and each must sign the register."

Mary handed him her card and said, "Use mine for all of us and take five credits for yourself."

"Thank you, madam," he said with a smile.

"Can we eat now?" Moe asked.

"Yes, you can. I will show you the eating-room," Lack offered.

"Thank you, Lack. Please join us."

"Miss Mary?" Moe reacted

Lack took the lead, as she whispered, "Mr. Moe, maybe we can get more information from him. How did you know how to get the cost of the rooms down?"

"Oh. It's just something we do in my world."

"I see."

While eating in the busy dining room, Mary asked Lack, "It seems everyone here likes to collect credits."

"Likes? It is not to like. We must."

"Why must you collect them?" Moe asked.

"If we did not collect them, our system would collapse."

"You mean if you don't earn credits, your whole system will fall apart?" Matt asked.

"Earn? We just collect them."

"And, what do you do with your credits?" Mary asked.

"Are you rich?" Mar asked.

"Rich? You have words I do not know. With the credits, we give our taxes."

"Ah, tax collectors. How much do you pay in taxes?" Moe asked.

"Pay? Why we give it all."

"All! Then how do you pay your bills?" I asked.

"Bills? I don't understand that word."

"How do you get your food, your clothing, and all the things you need?" Mary asked.

"All our needs are taken care of by them."

"Who's them?" Lucy asked.

274

"Why, the White-noses, of course."

"Are the White-noses in charge?" Six timidly asked.

"In charge? If you mean, they are above us and tell us what to do, then yes."

"Do you do what those people outside do to pay your taxes? Moe asked.

"Why no, we all work in the fruit fields. Those you saw outside were trying to gain a better position by collecting extra credits."

"Hey, it sounds like slavery to me," Lucy said.

"It does, doesn't it," Moe agreed.

"Lack, could I ask what might be a dumb question?" Mar asked.

"Certainly."

"Well… how come your noses are different colors?"

"It is what marks our class level."

"You mean your noses change color when you do better?" Matt asked.

"Not exactly, when we please the White-noses by working harder and accumulate extra credits, they give us a drink which upgrades our nose color."

"And, if you displease them, what happens?" Moe asked.

"Of course, we must take a drink that degrades our color."

"I guess it's better than wearing badges or stripes," Moe jokingly said.

"Where does a brown-nose stand in your system?" Ike asked.

"The lowest grade is blue, and then green, brown, yellow, orange, and at the top is white."

"I see you've got a ways to go," Lucy mumbled.

"What does a brown-nose have to accomplish?" Mary asked.

"It is because I am very good at obeying orders."

"Ah, I think I understand," Moe said.

"It does sound like slavery," I said.

"It certainly does." Lack looked at us curiously, not knowing the meaning of the word slavery.

When finished eating, Mary ordered, "It is time to go to our rooms and refresh."

"Yes, it's a good idea," Moe said.

"I will wait right here for you," Lack said.

"Good. First, we must get fresh clothing from the Dragon. Lack, it might take a while, but when we are refreshed, we will see you. Let us go, children," Mary ordered.

CHAPTER 40 Decolorizing Blackside

When rested, bathed, and dressed in fresh clothing, we were ready to face whatever was coming, expecting something extraordinary was going to take place, just as took place in the other cities. We headed down to find Lack, for he was the only path to follow. He was napping on the floor in the corner where he said he would be. I guess his nose color didn't rank high enough to warrant a chair. Awakened, he seemed nervous and excited as he explained, "The White-noses have heard you were here and want to see you."

"Here we go," Ike said.

"I guess we'll have to go," Moe said.

"I am afraid so. We must follow the path we are led down," Mary added.

"I don't like this," Lucy said.

"Are we going to be all right?"

"Mar, we're going to be just fine. Would you please try to remember that," Moe gently scolded.

"Yes, don't worry, you know what I mean?" I said, hoping to lessen her fears.

"I want to go to this meeting even less than the ones before," Lucy said.

"Okay, where to?" Moe asked Lack.

"It is not far."

"To meet is to meet. Lack, lead the way," Ike said.

In the Dragon, Lack directed us to a building constructed of massive white stone blocks, some of which had chiseled out shapes of fruits painted in realistic colors, looking most appetizing. Lack knocked on the door. A yellow nose man opened it and waved us in.

We entered a large empty auditorium with a balcony that encircled the entire room. Skittish, Lack led us down to the platform in the center. As we moved, people filed in through the many doors. By the time we reached its center, remarkably, the room had filled with people. Of course, all were black, and since it couldn't accommodate all the people of the city, there was only a representation of each nose color.

The floor level contained yellow and orange-nosed people. The balcony included people of the other nose colors. A trap door on the stage opened, and a u-shaped table rose up with a dozen white-nose, men and women seated on its outer side.

Lack directed us to stand inside the U. When silence was achieved, a White-nose man called out each of our names, then asked if those were our names. Moe wondered why they were so formal, as he answered for all, "Yes, sir."

One of the White-nose men asked, "We have heard of your travels, and that you claim to be *Rockers*. Would you tell us why you **are** in Blackside?" Again in a formal manner, almost as if it were a trial.

"Sir, we are heading to the end of the *Road*."

"Then, why are you in Blackside?"

"We just stopped to get refreshed," Moe said, not thinking he should tell any more.

"So, you planned to use credits here?"

"No sir, we did not plan to stop and use credits, it was just the way it happened," Mary answered, somewhat suspicious.

Another man at the table stated, "It does not matter. If you enter Blackside and use credits, you must give taxes."

"Okay. How much are your taxes?" Moe reluctantly asked, not yet concerned.

"It is all you have," the second man stated.

"You must be kidding!" Moe exclaimed, not believing.

"Yes, since you are not from our world, it is all," the first man said.

"All of what? Ike asked.

"The tax for you is all you have," a woman at the table repeated.

"That's extortion, not taxation," an outraged Moe accused.

"We are *Rockers*, and we don't have to give you all of it," Lucy said.

"Yes, taxation without representation is not legal," I stated, having learned that much in school.

"We are the ones who set and collect taxes. Not being from our world, your taxes are all you have," the first man restated.

"Since we're not from your world, we don't have to pay your stupid taxes," I argued, knowing we could not allow this.

"It does not matter if you come into our city from another world, you must give all you have. Hand over your cards," the second man ordered.

Lack tentatively spoke up, "But sirs, you have never demanded that much from any travelers before?"

"Quite! Be silent if you want to keep your position."

"Here we go again," Ike said as he saw Moe building a head of steam in his frustration.

Moe turned to the crowd, especially those in the balcony, and pronounced, "These white-noses are trying to do to us what they've been doing to you, by taking all the fruits of your hard labor, so to speak," for they were fruit pickers by trade. He then accused, "Which of you gave them that right?" antagonizing the white-noses.

"You cannot question us," A White-nose woman stated.

"Why not, you're just people, aren't you?" I said.

"How did you get your White noses, anyway?" Lucy asked, remembering what Lack said about the drinks.

Moe, focused in on the balcony, and asked, "Didn't you work hard for your credits?" There was no response, so he continued, "Why are you afraid of these people whose only difference from you is the color of their noses."

"We are not afraid," a voice sharply called out from the balcony.

"Then, why do you let them take all your credits?" Lucy asked as a rumbling started up there

I could feel a momentum building, and I repeated, "Yes, why do you let them take all your credits?"

"A miracle, a miracle," Ike said. Embolden, he loudly spoke out, "You certainly look as if you're afraid. What power do they have over you?" The commotion in the balcony grew.

"Silence! Do not listen to them. You must obey the rules," the first white-nose man ordered.

"Then you must be cowards. You see how we are able to stand up to them. It's not right that they take all your credits, come and stand with us for your rights," Moe said, as he felt the fullness of himself.

Voices in the balcony were now speaking out in rapid succession, "Maybe they are right?"

"Yes, they take everything from us."

"Do we not have the right to keep what we have worked for?

"Yes, it is so, the White-noses are no better than us."

"Should we not join them?"

"Stop this! Silence!" A White-nose man yelled with panic in his voice. Then ordered, "Take their cards!" This was in spite of Mary and Inge being of their world. Several of the orange-noses, who were standing by, seemed uncertain. However, a few stepped up, and a struggle ensued in an attempt to take their cards.

To our surprise, in mass, the people in the balcony started to flow down onto the main floor looking to help us. We once again were involved in the chaos. As before, faced with danger, the *White Light* struck. And again, a *Man in White* was there, and all the people were frozen. He said, "Do you understand what just happened? Do not answer, just think about it. But now you must leave." Another flash of *Light* and he was gone, and the people were unfrozen. Amazed and pleased to see those who once served the white-noses were now restraining the twelve of them. "Let's go," Ike ordered.

Reaching the door, Lack appeared, and asked, "Are you leaving Blackside?"

"We are," Mary said.

"If you must, please let me guide you to the best way out of the city."

"That would be helpful," she said.

"Well then, let's go," Moe ordered. Once outside, we quickly piled into the Dragon and drove off.

Still shaken, Lack asked, "I do not understand what just happened? They have always been demanding of us but never treated outsiders like they did you. The most they ever demanded in taxes from travelers was ten percent."

Moe said, "Maybe, they don't like the color of our skin? Ha! However, Lack I think today you have become a free man?"

"I do not understand what being free means."

"Why it means you can live your life the way you would like, that is with goodness," Lucy added, again not yet fully understanding what she said.

"But, we have never done that."

"From now on, you are free to do what you want with your lives," I stated.

"That is as long as you do not let the White-noses take all your credits away," Mary added.

"How would we do that?"

"Why, in the way we just did, by not giving in," Moe said.

"You mean we must cause a conflict?"

"In our world, we had to fight for our freedoms," I said.

"If you're not willing to fight for your freedom, you'll never be able to keep it," Moe added, having heard that stated before, but not quite remembering where.

"And, if you're not willing to fight, I am sure if you go back, you will have trouble, and if so, you can come with us," Mary added.

"I did not think of that. I am afraid, but I cannot leave my people."

"Lack, don't you think all your people should have the same color noses?" Mar timidly asked, not entirely understanding the need for the different colors.

"I think all your noses should be just plain black as nature meant it to be," Matt added.

"Yes! That would be something. You mean we should all be equal?"

"That's it, you've got it Lack," Moe said.

"You said that a drink changes the colors of your noses?" I asked.

"Yes, but how would we get those drinks?"

"By struggling. Remember, to struggle is to struggle," Ike instructed.

"To struggle is to struggle. I will remember that."

"And remember, you'll lose if you allow fear to overtake you," Moe said. Then he noticed we were low on fuel and said, "Hey, we are going to need fuel."

"I will remember not to be afraid. Moe, if you turn right here, you will find a fuel station." We filled the tank and the extra cans. But before leaving, Lack asked, "You are from the other side of the *Rock*. What is it like there?"

"It's much like your world is going to be now that you are free."

"Oh, I cannot wait for that."

"Good. Keep up the struggle, and you'll get there," Moe said.

"I will. I will. Now, if you follow this road, it will lead to the pebble Road."

"Remember, we will always be with you," Mary said.

"You must do what you must do," Ike said.

With a sense of sadness, Lack said, "I will always remember all of you. Thank you for what you have done for us, and I will remember what you said, to struggle is to struggle."

"Don't ever let them take your credits away again. There are many more of you than there are of them," Moe warned.

We bid our farewells and drove off into the night, leaving Lack standing alone at the station.

CHAPTER 41 On The Road To Mechanicsburg

On the *Road* once again. Being concerned about the fate of Lack and the Black people, we speculated on what there was to learn from Blackside, for the *Man in White* indicated it contained a lesson. As seen in totalitarian societies, it reflected the same mentality for slavery in our past, which some think still exists. Still being naïve, we weren't sure about any of it. We fell into a period of rest, for the day was most exhausting. The short night and day cycles were taking a toll on our metabolisms.

Driving through the night, Mary suggested, "Mr. Moe, it would be a good idea to let Johnny drive so you can rest."

"I'm ready, Mr. Moe." We stopped and switched seats, and with an inner delight, I steered back onto the *Road* and sped on, imagining I was a racecar driver. I now feel a little silly about how immature I was.

Having driven well into daylight, Matt exclaimed, "Look! Look!"

"Look at what?" I asked.

"See over there," he said, pointing to the right.

"I see it," Mar said, just able to make out several wiggling hair-like white columns of what looked like smoke."

"Ah, I see them. I believe they are coming from Mechanicsburg," Ike said.

"That's where the transports are made, right?"

"Johnny, if it is Mechanicsburg, then it is where the transports are made."

"Gee, I can't wait to see it."

Our talk woke Moe, "Ah, yes. I'd like to see it too, but first, we'll have to make sure it's safe."

"To be safe is to be safe," Ike said.

I think I would also like to see it," Six said, wanting to be included.

"Males are all alike," Lucy said with a frown.

"Now Lucy," Mary instructed.

"Lucy, I'd like to see it too," Matt added.

"Oh great," a deflated Lucy said.

In time, we arrived at a turnoff, which appeared to lead to the city. Since the stories say it is unreachable, we had no idea of what to expect. Regardless, with little choice, Moe took the wheel and made the turn towards the city.

Ike suggested, "It is still far away. We will not be able to make it there before dark. I think it is best to attempt to enter it in the light of day, for I fear it cannot be reached we will not reach it."

"I agree. That's what we'll do, and if it can't be reached, it's going to be interesting."

"Mr. Moe, I also agree," Mary said. We drove until darkness began to fall, stopped and camped out for the night.

The next day, I got another chance at the wheel. By afternoon, we came to a steep hill with an incline of forty-five degrees upwards. I asked, "Wow! Mr. Moe, what should I do?"

"Look, just step down on the pedal to the floor and keep it there until we are over the top," he ordered, thinking it was the best way to make it up and over. "Everybody, tie yourselves in, there might be a big bump when we go over the top."

"Okay, here we go!" I said as I floored the pedal.

"To go is to go," Ike said, as we braced ourselves.

"I don't like this," Mar said.

The Dragon had plenty of power, and it seemed to go faster as we climbed. Upon reaching and going over the top, we found to our great horror and disbelief the road suddenly dropped off at a ninety-degree angle straight down, which left the Dragon sailing out into space, like an airplane, with all aboard screaming with all we had. We traveled horizontally for some distance, due to the momentum the power of the Dragon allowed. Terrified, we screamed with our eyes tightly closed, believing it was our end.

Later I realized none of us saw what happened. I could only speculate on what took place. Unbelievably, we sailed out for perhaps a mile before the Dragon began to descend slowly. We were high enough to pass over a second smaller hump, beyond which the road was now sixty-degrees on a downward incline. Falling, yet maintaining the powerful forward momentum. The rear bumper then touched the roadway causing a shower of sparks slowing us down. We continued forward and downward on that trajectory, the road became a forty-five-degree slope. At that point, the back wheels touched. The road continued to lose its steep angle as the front wheels touched.

Petrified, I was able to open one eye. In sheer terror, during our descent, I held the steering wheel with all my strength, with my foot inadvertently locked down on the peddle to the floor. By doing so, I kept the front wheels straight, and with the power of the turning wheels, it moved us along, preventing us from flipping over. At least that's what I figured happened.

The others didn't see the Dragon was righting itself, for they had not stopped screaming or opened their eyes in their absolute dread. The road eventually, degree by degree, once again became flat. At that point, still moving forward, Moe stopped screaming and managed to open his eyes to see we were on the road once again. As if it was a miracle, due to the gradual descent over such a long distance, we avoided making a hard landing. Moe reached over, shifting the gears into neutral and yelled to me, "Steer! Do not step on the brakes! DO YOU HEAR ME?"

I was able to snap out of my state of shock and did what I was told, screaming back at the top of my lungs, "I HEAR YOU! I HEAR YOU!"

We were traveling at such a speed it seemed to take miles after safely landing to slow down. At that point, Moe breathlessly ordered, "Now you can step on the brakes," bringing us to a full stop.

Still shaking, I was only then able to unlock my frozen iron grip on the steering wheel. After a moment of complete exhaustion, Moe untied his safety rope and suggested with a cheerful tone, "Why don't we get out and stretch our legs. I'm famished."

"We're lucky to still have legs," Lucy said.

Six, who could hardly breathe, got out and lay prostrate on the ground kissing it.

Mary started to laugh, and Lucy asked, "Miss Mary, what's

so funny?

With tears rolling down her face, still laughing, "I am just so happy we are still alive."

"Yes, I guess I feel the same," Lucy admitted.

"This time, I really— really thought we were going to die," Mar could only say.

"I'm sorry, but we made it, didn't we, Mr. Moe?" I asked, still shaking.

"We really did. Johnny, you did a great job. Let's eat?"

Mary wiping the tears from her eyes, said, "Oh yes, Mr. Moe, let us have something to eat."

"To eat is to eat," Ike agreed.

Only then did we look back up the road to see the towering cliff in the great divide we drove off, which soared up perhaps a mile high, higher than any other spot we'd seen in this world, which was now miles away and. We just stood there in awe for a long moment looking up, not able to imagine how we made it from there to where we landed.

Ike said, "I see why it is said to be inaccessible," which was the most humorous remark Ike made up to that point.

Moe examined the Dragon to find the springs were damaged, the back bumper was ground halfway down, and the tires were smoldering, burnt almost all the way through. Ahead, those several columns were now clearly recognized as smoke coming from tall smokestacks.

Later, after eating and a period of much-needed relaxation. Fearing another road catastrophe, we decided to spend the night right there to allow the tires to cool, for they were still too hot to touch and replace with the spares.

Around a fire, we reviewed the events of the day. Still bewildered and exhausted by the dramatic incidents during the trip, it wasn't long before sleep overtook us.

CHAPTER 42 Arriving In Mechanicsburg

The next morning after breakfast, we mounted the spare tires.

Lucy asked, "Mr. Moe isn't it time I got a chance to drive too?"

"So, you want to drive the Dragon? Even after you saw what happened with Johnny?" She nodded a Yes! "What do you think, Miss Mary?"

Lucy looked at Mary and quickly injected, "I can do anything Johnny can do."

"Lucy, I am sure you could. Mr. Moe, I think you should show Lucy how to drive the Dragon."

"Alright, Miss Mary," knowing Lucy was as capable as I was, he ordered, "Everyone wait here. Let's go, Lucy."

"Oh, thank you, Mr. Moe," she said as she excitedly slipped into the driver's seat and yelled out the window, "Thank you, Miss Mary," turning to me with a smirk on her face.

Honestly, I was glad she got her chance, regardless of what I might have said, for she had the same training I did and was even more aggressive than I was. In those days, I wasn't as considerate of my sister's feelings as I've become.

Moe showed her the controls, and off they went, driving back and forth, putting her through those maneuvers until he felt she was ready. With Moe seated next to her, just in case, we piled in and took off, headed straight towards the smokestacks.

Later, we approached another rise in the road. This time to be safe, Moe ordered Lucy to inch her way up to the top cautiously. Thankfully, on the other side, instead of a drop-off, it was just a steep ride down. Stopping at the top, we took in the view, which revealed the entire city of Mechanicsburg sprawled out in the valley below. It was a good size industrial-looking city, highlighted by two long narrow buildings, boasting those smokestacks puffing away.

Those two buildings resembled auto production plants I'd seen in pictures back in our world. In contrast, surrounding the city, a thick forest grew as far as could be seen. After a moment, Moe asked Ike, "That looks like the place to go, does it not?" as he pointed to a cluster of office-like buildings.

"The place to go is the place to go."

Moe took that as a yes, and we slowly drove down the steep incline into the valley. However, before entering the city, Moe ordered, "Good job Lucy, I'll take over from here. I knew she was disappointed to give up the wheel, but she quietly obeyed, knowing it was for our safety.

We saw no one until close enough to those buildings to make out people coming and going. To our surprise and relief, their skin was just like ours. Parking, Moe ordered, "Well, it's time to get out."

"Oh, my."

"Are we going to be all right?" Mar asked.

"You know we'll be all right," I said.

"So far, so good," Lucy allowed.

"It looks as if this time, Ike, Six, and I will be the ones who will attract the attention," Mary said.

"Maybe, we should stay in the Dragon?" Six said.

"Absolutely not! You have as much right to be here as we do, right kids?" Moe asked. We enthusiastically acknowledge that fact.

As usual, when we stepped out, it attracted a crowd. "Is there a place we can get a good meal around here?" Moe asked.

A well-dressed man spoke up, wearing a colorful business type suit. A suit that perhaps was in style a hundred years ago in our world. He held the hand of a woman also dressed in impressive old-fashion clothing. Noticeably, all the others were dressed in the same style, only not as colorful and rich-looking. "You are not from here?" the man asked.

"No, we are not familiar with your city," Mary answered.

Hearing that the crowd backed up a little, and I noticed a few quietly slipped away, which I thought odd.

"Is there a place to eat around here?" Moe again asked.

The woman nodded, "Yes, there is. Come, we will show

you."

The couple looked pleased, as Mary thanked them. They led us into the massive building, which revealed an expansive marble-clad open space covered by a high glass dome filled with the hustle and bustle of busy people moving in all directions.

There was a crowded open cafeteria, but they led us past it. Suddenly, several men, wearing plain dark old fashion suits, stopped our progression. One of them asked the man, guiding us, "Sir, is everything in order?"

"Yes, everything is in order. Now, let us pass," he ordered.

"Yes, Sir," one of the men said. They immediately scatter, disappearing into the crowd.

As we walked on, Mary asked, "Sir, you must be an important person?"

"Important person? Well... I guess I am."

"You certainly are, dear," the woman added.

"Let me introduce us," Mary said. She introduced each of us and then asked, "And sir, you are?"

Amused, the man smiled because he wasn't accustomed to introducing himself, for everyone in this city knew who he was. He said, "My name is Chair Number Three, and this is Mate Number Three."

"Do you have proper names?" Mary asked.

"Proper names? Ah... I know in other cities, there are different systems used to identify their citizens. Here, our status gives us our names. However, you can just call me Chair."

"Yes, status is status," Ike said.

"Here we are," Chair said, stopping in front of an ornate wood-paneled door manned by a doorman who opened it. We entered to see a small luxurious dining room.

A neatly dressed man in bow tie and tails rushed up to us and asked, "How may I serve you, Sir Chair?"

"Waiter Number One, I would like a table to sit at with our guests. Then, please serve us with the best meal you have."

We were impressed.

Waiter Number One seated us and instructed, "The meal will be ready shortly." Would you like something to drink?

"Waiter Number One, may I call you, Waiter?" Moe asked.

He nodded, he could. Moe continued, "Waiter, are the drink's alcoholic?"

"Sir, alcoholic?"

"Yes, Mr. Moe means are they an intoxicating libation?" Mary explained the best she could.

"Ah, yes, they are Madam."

"Would you have non-intoxicating drinks?"

"Yes, Madam, we do. Would you like those for all?"

"Yes, please."

The waiter asked Chair and Mate if they would like their usual. Mate responded, "No, we will have exactly what our guests are having."

"I have never had an intoxicating drink," Six said.

"Good for you. Now is not the time to start," Mary said.

"Ike, you must be from Redtown. Six, you must be from Blackside. Mary, you must be an Inbetweener. But, Moe, and the children, where are you from?" Chair asked.

"Well, to be truthful. We're *Rockers*." We tensed, waiting for a strong reaction, but none came.

"Ah, I knew something was different about you. I thought coming through the *Rock* had stopped more than a lifetime ago. Please tell us why you are here?" Chair asked.

"That's a long story," Moe said.

"There is no rush. We have the time."

Moe tried to avoid answering the question for the moment by saying, "From what we understand, you manufacture all the transports. Would you be able to show the kids how you build them?"

"First, you must tell us your long story."

"Sir, I'd really like to see how you build the transports," I said.

"Me too," Matt added.

"It could be arranged. The transport you arrived in looks as if it could be one of ours, but with changes, I have never seen?"

Mary saw Chair was plainly seeking answers to his questions, and stated, "You want to know all about Mr. Moe and the children. If you would like, we will be pleased to tell you."

Pleasantly surprised, Chair said, "That is straightforward

enough. I will be straightforward with you. For countless cycles, people have not been able to travel here over the broken road. Seeing how you drove right up to this building was quite astonishing."

"Sir, if people can't come here, how do you deliver the transports?" I asked.

"Good question. Mary and Ike must know we sell our transports through representatives, and when the orders are ready, we deliver them. An outsider has not come into the city since the road separated."

"I remember seeing your representatives in Blackside," Six said.

"Sir, why is the road like that?" Lucy asked.

"Another good question… You see, sometime after the road was first cleared, the ground began to shake and shift. It created the loudest sounds ever heard. Every once in a while, the ground shifted a bit more. That process lasted for many cycles. During those times, people thought the world was splitting apart and would soon end. However, in time, it calmed down and has remained still ever since, leaving us well below the rest of the world."

"That's interesting," Moe said.

"How do you deliver the transports up over the mountain without a way up?" I asked.

"I'm sorry son, it is a long-held secret I cannot divulge."

"How in the world did you develop the technology to build the transports? Moe asked, changing the subject.

"All of you ask many questions. Not many here ask those types of questions. It is refreshing to see you are not afraid to ask. I have never faced so many questions and will do my best to answer.

"Now, to answer your last question, when the separate cities were established, Mechanicsburg was a place where most of the talented craftsmen gathered to produce the needed hard implements. It was a primitive operation until the arrival of a *Rocker* called Mach, decades ago. He was a trained technician in making fuel engines.

"By today's standards, his knowledge was primitive. However, he was able to bring his work manuals with him, which was enough to build on. They contained all the information necessary to build transports. Even how and where to find and process the materials needed. With our talented and creative people, over the decades, our knowledge and factories grew exponentially. We continue to amass better and more efficient ways to build transports. That is how we accomplished it. Now Moe, tell us how you made it down here?"

Moe thought it was now fair to do so, so he told how it happened, as he saw it. After hearing it, Chair said, "That is amazing. Johnny, that was good driving. Moe, did you build your transport?"

"No, it was my benefactor, McCloud."

"I would like to meet him," Chair asked.

"Regrettably, he has passed away."

"Sorry, that is too bad. You must tell me what brought you here?"

Moe told the story of our quest, again excluding the *White Light* and the *Men in White*.

Being satisfied, Chair said, "Tomorrow, I will give you a tour of our factories, but for now, let us finish our meal."

"And tonight, you must stay with us," Mate invited.

"We would be honored," Mary said. We ate and talked until well after darkness fell, then retired to Chair and Mate's home for the night.

CHAPTER 43 Chair And Mate Are Told Of The White Light

In Mechanicsburg the next morning, as usual, Mary was the first to rise. With the aid of a young servant girl waiting to meet her needs, she was able to bathe and dress in fresh clothing taken from the Dragon. She asked the girl, "What are you called?"

"Madam, I am called, Servant One Hundred and Thirty-seven."

"Oh, my. What do they call you for short?"

"In this home, they call me Four.

"What does Four stand for?"

"It is because I am the fourth servant in the household."

"I see. Well Four, is it possible to get a glass of juice?

"Yes, Madam. First, let me show you to the main-room where Madam Mate will join you shortly."

The main-room was just downstairs, for it wasn't a large house. "Please make yourself comfortable. I will bring you that glass of juice."

While waiting, she looked for something to read but found all the books on the shelves that surrounded the room where work manuals. In touching some of the furniture and accessories, she discovered they were made of painted sheet metal. She thought how deceiving the finishes were in giving the impression of being soft and warm as wood would be, yet to the touched, they were hard and cold.

When Four brought the juice, Mary found the most comfortable upholstered chair and sat there sipping it. After a few minutes of relaxed thought, Mate entered and exchanged greetings sitting across from her. Mary complimented her home. She apologized for Chair having to take care of some business and guaranteed he would be back in time for the factory tour. After an awkward pause, she asked Mary, "Do you plan to go to the other side of the *Rock*?"

"Why no, this is my world.

"Is Moe going?"

"Sadly, he has nothing left there to go back to."

"I have never been outside of Mechanicsburg. I sometimes wonder what life is like beyond my city."

"I spent my entire life on the estates of my father and Mr. Right, my deceased husband. I have always lived in a protected environment, that is until Mr. Moe arrived."

"Mary, is our world not safe?"

"I am sorry to say it can be hazardous. If it were not for being with Mr. Moe, I would not have had the courage or strength to survive traveling through it."

"Does he have special powers?"

"I do not believe so. However, I do believe he and the children are under a special protection."

"Special protection? Is there such a thing?"

"If you saw the *White Light,* you would think so." Upon quick reflection, she said, "Perhaps, I should not have said that. Oh, my."

"The *White Light*! Is that not a myth?" Mate asked.

"I should not have mentioned it."

"When I was young, I heard about that myth. But we were taught it was just our childish imagination and were not to talk about it. We were to put our trust in our technology. Mary, are you saying the *White Light* exists?"

"I am afraid so."

"How do you know?"

"I should not have said anything."

"Mary, you opened the door, you cannot now shut it in my face."

"I see how that might not be fair. All right, I will tell you what we have seen." Mary proceeded to tell Mate of the incidences experienced with the *White Light*.

In hearing it, a pale Mate could barely say, "What you have said has shaken my very world."

"And it has broadened my understanding of our world too. I

now experience feelings I never knew I had. You see, I had not spent much time thinking about such things before my trips with Mr. Moe. Although I must admit, it has been exciting to experience things they said did not exist. Trying to understand things beyond myself, has been enlightening and all new to me."

Mate said, "This information is most unsettling."

Just then, a Cheerful Moe entered, "Good morning, ladies."

"Mr. Moe, you must be hungry?" Mary asked, knowing him so well.

"I am, but the kids will be down shortly. Let's wait for them."

"Yes. However, I know you would like some juice.

"Oh, I am sorry for not being a good hostess," Mate said. Still pale and shaken, she walked over to a tube sticking out of the wall and loudly spoke into it, "Four."

"Mate, are you all right?" Mary asked, motioning for Moe to help her.

"I guess I am a little faint." He helped her to a chair. She thanked him as Four entered. "Please bring three glasses of juice, and tell One to ready breakfast for nine," she ordered.

Moe quizzically looked at Mary for what might be the trouble with Mate. She explained, "I am afraid I told Mate about the *White Light.*"

"Yes, and I am confused about why it has affected me so."

"It has confused us too. We are trying to understand it," Moe said.

Hearing the energetic sound of the four of us coming down, Mate said, "I would like you to tell Chair this information, but for now, let us have breakfast." Moe, with Mate on one arm and Mary on the other, moved to the dining room for breakfast.

Shortly, Chair showed up and gave his apology for not being there earlier. Mate ordered, "Dear, would you please sit, I would like you to hear something."

"Has something happened?" Chair asked, sensing something was not right, "You look a little pallid, are you not well?"

"I am well. However, it concerns the information our guests have given me. You must hear it too." Turning to us, "Please inform Chair of what you told me."

Moe willingly told of our experiences with the *White Light*. However, Mary had discreetly signaled us not mentioned the *Men in White*, not knowing what further effect it might have.

After listening to our story, Chair sat in silence perplexed for a moment. He then said, "This is astonishing information, what does it all mean?"

"Sir, we hoped you could tell us how to understand it, you know what I mean?" I said.

"I know what you mean. I just wish someone in this world knew what all this *White Light* stuff was," Lucy said.

"Yes, is the *White Light* going to get us home?" Mar asked.

"As you see, we do not have much understanding of it," Mary said.

"Dear, explain to our guests what we understand."

"What you have told us has no equivalence in our understanding," Chair responded.

"Please tell us as much as you can?" Mary pleaded.

"Please, dear, explain it to them."

"Yes, dear." After a moment of reflection, he said, "You must understand the foundation of our culture is to believe in serving technology. We must find our place in our manufacturing plants and work diligently to glorify that knowledge. If we do this with conscientiousness, we gain our place."

"You mean if you obediently work hard, you'll be rewarded. Is that all there is for you?" Moe asked.

"All there is? I am not sure I understand what you are asking. However, on the tour of our factories, I will explain how our system works."

"I would like to see it," Moe said.

"As soon as we finish breakfast, we can start," Mate instructed.

CHAPTER 44 The Factory Tour

On the factory tour, we arrived at the narrow end of one of those huge rectangular buildings. It was massive, maybe a hundred feet wide, and of a length so long the end couldn't be determined. Large floor to ceiling windows covered the walls. Two tall smokestacks attached to its side emitted those columns of white smoke.

Having driven there in the Dragon, Chair was impressed with its power and suggested we allow his mechanics to check it over for the damages incurred by the jarring it took in jumping off the divide. Moe agreed, not wanting to take the chance of breaking down later.

The large metal door was rolled up, allowing us to drive into a beehive of activity. Large machines were stamping, turning, cutting, and even casting metals. Puffs of steam escaped here and there, and the noise made it difficult to hear what Chair was saying. He motioned us over to a small trolley-like car, about twenty feet long, with its sides and top made of glass, which allowed one to see what was taking place in all directions.

It sat on a track running the full length down the center of the building. Once inside, it blocked out the loud sounds enabling us to hear each other with ease. With a slight jar, the trolley started to move slowly along the track, being pulled by a hidden cable in a grooved slot in the floor.

As we moved, Chair described the functions of each station along the way. He pointed to and explained how leather belts drove the machines off pulleys mounted on a main shaft hung from the ceiling running the length of the building. Two boilers under the smokestacks supplied the necessary steam power.

Seeing everything was steam-driven, Moe asked, "What fuel do you use to make the steam?"

"Why we burn wood which grows in abundance around our

city. In your world, how do you make steam?"

Moe asked, "I see you don't have electricity?"

"You said electricity? I am not familiar with that word. What knowledge do you have of power?"

"Oh, electricity is what we call the power used in our world.

"Is electricity what makes your steam?" Chair asked.

"We don't use steam directly anymore. However, it's still used in many cases to generate electricity, which runs our machinery.

"Fascinating, and what fuel do you use to make this electricity?"

"Why we use water, oil, gas, coal, or anything able to drive the generators which produce the electric. And, there is a new energy called atomic, which hopefully will eventually generate all the power needed to run our world." Moe explained it the best he could from his limited knowledge.

"Many of your words I am not familiar with. It is extraordinary that you have knowledge we do not have. You must tell me more and meet with our engineers."

"Chair, I'm sorry, but I've told you almost everything I know. However, I'm willing to speak to anyone you wish."

"Good." Seeing Matt and my interest in how they made the transports, he said, "We will finish the tour, later we can talk about such things." We watched and listened with enthusiasm as Chair explained the process of making the parts as we continued along the track.

Reaching the assembly area, I whispered to Moe, "Mr. Moe, this looks like what I saw in those old movies showing how we made cars years and years ago, doesn't it?"

"That's right, Johnny," Moe whispered back as not to offend our hosts, "We've come a long way." Clearly, it wasn't like our modern factories, for each car here was being put together by hand.

"Look over there, they're painting the transports," Matt said.

"Hey, they're using large brushes to paint those designs," I said.

"Yes, our best artisans do that job. We did not paint your transport. Do you know who the artist was?"

"I can only guess it was McCloud, but I'm not sure."

"Interesting."

"Can we get out and see them work up close?" I asked.

"Sorry, Johnny. The tour trolley cannot be stopped during its run."

"That's a shame. Again, how do you deliver the transports over the hills to your customers?" Moe asked.

"As I said before, it is a good question. However, I cannot divulge that secret. Although I can say, there is a way."

"I do not like secrets," Mate said.

Ike whispered to Moe, "Good try. Secrets are secrets."

"I had a secret once," Six confessed.

"How interesting you must tell us about it sometime. There are many secrets here."

"Mate, please..." Chair abruptly changed the subject, "Now, finished with the production plant, would you like to see our recreation place?"

"We would like that. Is it so Mr. Moe?" Mary said, being cautious in seeing Mate's tension.

"Oh, yes. We'd like to see it," Moe said, picking up from Mary's tone.

At the end of the run, when we stepped out of the trolley, a man in coveralls created Chair and said, "Sir, we need to speak with you."

"Not now. It will have to wait until tonight when I am alone."

"Yes, Sir. We will meet at your house tonight."

Before leaving the building, Chair had a mechanic explain the work the Dragon would need, "Your transport could use a set of new spare tires, repairs to the suspension, steering, and the back bumper needs to be replaced."

Seeing Moe's distress, Chair said, "Do not worry, as our guest, we will fix it so it will be like new at no cost to you. That is if it is all right with you?"

"It will be appreciated. Thank you," Moe understood there was little choice, knowing the repairs were necessary.

Mary, not sure of what was going on with this welcomed generosity, added, "Yes, thank you."

"Good."

Exiting the far end of the building, Chair said, "We will drive the rest of the way in one of our open-top transports." We boarded a waiting one, and as we did, the door of the adjacent building, which had four smokestacks rose. Halfway up, to our surprise, we saw what appeared to be a camouflaged tank-type transport, with what looked like a cannon mounted on it.

Before we could be sure, as if it were a mistake, the door abruptly closed. "Wasn't that..." I started to say. Ike saw the grimace on Chair's face and quickly put his hand firmly on my shoulder, quieting me.

"Sorry, I did not see anything," Chair said, denying the obvious.

"But that was..." Lucy began to say as Mary clenched her arm, hushing her. With a grunt, she defiantly crossed her arms and sat back.

"I saw something too," Six whispered under his breath as the driver pulled away. Although we all saw whatever it was.

We approached an open field filled with people engaged in unusual activities, looking like unfamiliar sports games. I asked, "Sir, what games are they playing?"

"They are not playing games. They are doing their required recreation."

"Do they pick a side to recreate on and try to win the recreation?" Moe asked as he picked his words carefully, attempting to understand what they were doing.

"Do they keep score?" I asked.

"If you mean, we must do better, yes, we must always come out ahead."

"I never cared for that," Mate said.

"Now, dear, you know it is our way."

"I never cared for it either," Mary agreed.

"Why must someone always win?" Lucy asked, which contradicted her intense competitive spirit.

"To win is to win," Ike injected.

We drove to another building, where Chair proudly said, "You must see this." We entered a massive room filled with hundreds of people working out on what looked like exotic exercise equipment. Most of which looked familiar but more contrived and complicated as if Rube Goldberg himself designed them.

"Ah, exercising," Moe said.

"This is what we call recreating," Mate instructed.

"Yes, we must remain strong to be most productive," Chair said.

"Yes, it is our way," Mate said with a sarcastic tone.

"It was our way too," a dishearten Six said.

We were shown around the room explaining the benefits of the equipment, which was interesting but gave us no answers. When finished, Mate suggested we go back to the house for lunch. Pleasing Moe, so we headed back to the transport.

Once outside, two men, also dressed in expensive-looking dated clothing, were standing off to the side. When Chair saw them, he excused himself to join them. They had a spirited conversation as they kept glancing over towards us.

This exchange went on for a short time, after which a pale Chair came back to the transport. Mate could only express to him, "Dear..." which gave us some concern.

He ordered, "Let us go home." The driver quickly moved off.

CHAPTER 45   Coming To Terms With Chair And Mate

Back at Chair's and Mate's home, they ushered us into the main-room. Mate politely instructed, "If you need anything, please call Four over the tube. One will prepare the meal, but for now, you must excuse us. We will join you when the meal is ready."

Leaving us along, Lucy asked, "What's wrong with them?"

"I am not sure—Mr. Moe, what do you think?" Mary asked.

"It looks like something political is going on."

"Political, what is meant by that?"

"It means, what politicians do, right, Mr. Moe?"

"Johnny, something like that, however, I think it's more like what those in power do when they're threatened."

"Mr. Moe, do you think Chair and Mate are in some sort of trouble because of us?"

"Miss Mary, I'm not sure. Something was definitely going on at the factory. Those men Chair spoke to seemed upset with him. What do you think, Ike?"

"I thought you would never ask."

"Those two men looked like White-noses, so to speak," Six added.

"Yes, Six, White-noses explains it well. Ike, we are sorry, you know we value your opinion. Tell us what you think is happening?" Mary asked.

"First, tell me what you meant when you called that transport in the other building a tank?"

"In our world, tanks are weapons of war. Only it wasn't exactly like the tanks we know of, it had four wheels and was much smaller. It was closer to the Dragon than an ordinary transport; most surprising was it had a small cannon turret similar to our tanks." Moe said.

"Are cannons used to kill people?" Ike asked, beginning to see the danger.

"Yes, they are."

"Ike, did not our treaties outlaw all instruments whose only purpose was to kill? Is it not so that all the cities agreed to not forcibly interfering with each other?" alarmed Mary asked.

"Yes, but in the outer parts, there are outlawed cities who never signed the treaty. We know Warland uses weapons, although, only internally. No signer of the treaty is supposed to produce or take killing equipment across borders. For Mechanicsburg to be doing so is a total violation, which makes them outlaws," Ike added.

"I'm beginning to see what is happening here."

"Mr. Moe, you mean Chair and Mate are outlaws?"

"I hope not Miss Mary. I prefer to think they are simply victims, just doing what they're told to do without fully understanding the consequences."

"They did seem threatened," Ike said.

"I don't like being in the middle of this," Lucy said.

"I just want to go home."

"Mar, don't forget we have to learn and gain understanding to get back home," I said.

"That's right. And, the *White Light* and the *Men in White* are protecting us, right, Mr. Moe?"

"Right, Lucy... "I can only wonder how Mach was able to get all his manuals through the *Rock*, and with him possibly being a white man. It's most curious," Moe said.

"I thought back then only Indians were pulled under the *Rock*?" I asked.

"So did I? Maybe, it's time to reconsider," Moe concluded.

"But, Mr. Moe, we're white too?"

"That's right, Johnny, we are. I'll have to give that more thought."

When can we leave here?" Mar asked.

"When the *Men in White* tells us to, right, Mr. Moe?"

"Right, Johnn. But first, I think we should figure out whether Chair and Mate are the bad guys or if they need our help."

"Oh, yes, we must help them. Perhaps, we should tell them what we are thinking?" Mary suggested.

"To tell is to tell. First, we should refresh ourselves before we are called for the meal."

"I know what you mean, Ike. Let's go," Moe said.

Once refreshed and back in the main-room, Four announced dinner was served. Chair and Mate greeted us in the dining-room, giving their apologies for any discomfort or confusion they might have caused. It was a little awkward to start talking about what we thought was going on. After some small talk, Mary looked at Moe and urged, saying, "Mr. Moe."

"Yes. Yes." He cleared his throat and said, "We kind of believe we're here for a reason. Not that we understand what it might be. However, we think it might be to help you." Moe said this, perhaps not appreciating the possible danger if they guessed wrong about who the bad guys were.

"If only you could," Mate said, for the first time showing vulnerability.

"If you tell us what's going on, we might be able to," he said with unwarranted confidence.

"Moe, it is complicated. I do not know how we could be helped?" Chair explained.

"I think we should tell you everything we have experienced so far, in the hope when you hear it, it will convince you," Mary said.

"Please, we want to hear it, right, dear?"

"Yes, dear," still unsure, Chair complied.

"Mr. Moe," Mary prompted. He proceeded to tell our story again, only this time he included the appearances of The Men in White.

Astounded, Chair and Mate listened as they slowly began to realize there was more going on than they were able to comprehend.

When Moe finished, he said, "Now it's your turn."

"What do you think, dear?" Chair asked Mate.

"You know what might happen tonight. This might be our only hope. Please tell them."

Still somewhat reluctant, Chair nevertheless agreed and began to explain their situation. "I know you saw the weapon we have been making since long before I was born. The path through the mountain has been kept a secret to prevent strangers from seeing what was going on. The present and past Chairs had become extremely demanding as the orders for weapons multiplied, along with the regular production of civilian transports. It is a booming business.

"The One and Two Chairs seemed only concerned with profit, thereby overworking everyone to meet unreasonable deadlines. Production is a rather slow process, and there is a high demand for the war machines and small arms, which we sell to both sides in Warland. Over time, a rebellious mood grew among the workers. Due to that unrest, the Chairs increased harsh disciplines and penalties on anyone who questioned them."

Upon hearing this, Moe asked, "Oh... totalitarianism. But, you're Chair-Three, couldn't you do something?"

Mate said, "He's tried but has always been overruled by the current top Chairs. He is only responsible for maintaining production, not to whom or what they sell. Because of his questioning, he will never rise any higher. And tonight, our position may finally come to an end."

"What do you mean?" Mary asked.

"Yes, what do you mean an end?" Moe added.

"We do not know? No Three has ever challenged a One or Two before. And by welcoming you, Chair has questioned their authority," Mate explained.

"Can't the workers just get together and take over?" I suggested.

"Yes, that's one way to solve the problem," Moe agreed.

"We have never done anything like that. We don't know how to do such things," Chair confessed.

"There is a first time for a first time," Ike said.

"Ike, here we go again," Lucy mumbled, as he nodded in agreement.

"And, tonight, many discontented workers are coming here in secret to meet with Chair. One and Two berated him for showing you around, as you saw. Unfortunately, I believe they might want to punish us for befriending you. And I feel something terrible is going to happen," Mate expressed.

"We saw nothing wrong with showing you friendliness,"

Chair admitted. "We never had an opportunity to associate with anyone from the outside, and saw it as a good thing."

"I'm beginning to get the picture. However, we're going to have to play it by ear."

"Moe, play it by ear?"

I mean, you must trust us."

"Yes, you must do that. Mr. Moe will figure it out. You will see," Mary urged.

"To figure it out is to figure it out," Ike said.

"That's right, Mr. Moe will do it," I said.

"Yes, they helped me in Greenhinge," Six added.

"I will put my trust in you, will you, dear?" Mate asked Chair.

"Yes. I will," with some hope left, he agreed. "The workers will be here soon. I will do my best. You must show us how to deal with this."

"Yes, and we'll also do our best, but I have a question for you…"

"Moe, what is it?"

"Chair, was the dragon built in the tank factory?"

"Ah… It most likely was, although it was modified for civilian use lacking the weapons. Some of its design features are extraordinary, which I have never seen before. I can only wonder where your friend McCloud acquired that knowledge. We thought no city other than Warland could have acquired one. Do you have any idea where it came from, for it would have never been legally allowed to be sold to him."

Moe said, "I now see McCloud died with many secrets, and I can only wonder who he was. Seeing how corruption is in all things."

On that note, we paused for a moment and then continued to discuss what could be done right now. All we could think of was to wait for the next step to unfold. At that point, we realized and understood we had little foresight or control over whatever dangers were ahead.

CHAPTER 46 Taking Charge

As darkness fell, the factory workers began to gather behind Chair and Mate's house. At first, both looked so authoritarian. But now, they were visibly apprehensive looking to us for guidance.

Moe, as usual, had no clear path to follow; he just allowed his veins to fill with adrenaline. However, he was now infused with something spiritual that was well beyond him, which gave him more courage than he had a right to have.

As the workers filled the yard, Moe watched through the glass doors, suddenly he said, "Let's do it!" as he opened the door and stepped out.

Chair, said to Mate, "Yes, let us do it!"

"To do it is to do it," Ike said.

"Yes, it is time to go out and face them," Mary clarified.

As if a supernatural embodiment sparked us, we all went out. Having already been through several confrontations, we were beginning to put our trust in whatever was propelling us and were prepared to go with the flow of events.

Once among the workers, Moe whispered to Chair, "Introduce us."

"Yes, of course." He announced, "My fellow workers, I want you to meet our new friends," introducing each of us. He then stated, "They are here to help us." Upon which questions came from the timid crowd, asking who we were as if it just dawned on them that three of us were of a different color.

"How can they help us?" a voice called out.

"They understand more than we do." Seeing the puzzled expressions on the worker's faces, Chair said, "They're from the other side of the *Rock*," the workers were dumbstruck.

The silence stretched, causing a frustrated Mate to exclaim, "Moe and these children are *Rockers*! Do you not understand? Listen carefully; they are *Rockers*!"

Murmurs began, a timid voice called out, "But, can they help us?"

"I'll bet we can," I said, not having the slightest idea how to.

"First, you must tell us exactly what kind of help you need?" Moe asked.

Different voices poured out a succession of complaints; "They work us all the time."

"We have no time for ourselves."

"We cannot question anything we are told to do."

"Anyone who questions them is demoted."

"They do not allow us to do what is best for ourselves."

"They demoted those who rebel to the lowest level."

"We are not free."

"They take our children away to train them to become workers."

"Wait! Wait just a second. Did you say they take your kids away without permission?" Moe asked, with alarm.

Mary asked Mate, "Is that true?"

"Yes, most of the time, our children do not live with us, being trained to be workers," Mate said.

Stunned, Mary asked her if they had children. A tearfully, Mate admitted they had three children.

"That's not right," Lucy said.

"I can't imagine growing up without being with my parents," Mar added.

"Mr. Moe, we've got to do something," I said, again not having any idea of what that might be.

"Yes, Mr. Moe, you must do something," a horrified Mary said.

"I'll do something. Let me think… Wait a minute." As if a light bulb went off in his head, he took hold, and asked, "Is there a police force in Mechanicsburg?"

"No," the hesitant workers answered in unison, although they had no idea what a police force was.

"Is there an army?" Moe asked.

"No," the workers answered.

Lucy saw the direction Moe was going and asked, "Who forces you to do the things you are told to do?"

"No one forces us, Chair answered. It is only the chain of command headed by the Chairs. We do it because… Why I do not know, it is just the way it has always been done."

I asked, "You mean, you willingly volunteer to oppress yourselves?" With those words, we began to see an incredible change in their expressions as they started to realize, for the first time, they might be responsible for their situation. With that spark of revelation, they fell silent.

"Why in the world would you do that to yourselves?" Lucy asked, not understanding.

It was now clear to Moe, "So, no one really makes you do what you don't want to do. And I'll bet when one of you stands up and says stop this, no one stands with them?"

"Why no, it is not our way," Chair admitted.

"Well… Then you must change your ways," Moe concluded.

As this was taking place, the numbers of workers had grown from dozens to what seemed like hundreds.

"How do we change our ways?" a worker asked.

"Let me see… Okay, who of you has ever said no to them?" Moe asked. Just a few hesitant hands rose, numbering no more than seven. He then asked, "Okay, would those who held their hands up, stand." Reluctantly, one by one, they stood.

He then asked, "Are your reasons for saying no, for the good of all?" The workers agreed it was so. He then asked, "Good… Now, who is willing to stand together with these brave ones?" Uncertain, the workers were immobile. He urged, "Okay… If you'd all stand in support of these few, your no - will mean no." There was another long moment of non-movement.

"Come on, you can do it," Lucy yelled. We all joined in the urging, each in our own way.

Six couldn't help but say, "You have to stop acting as the Greens did in Greenhinge. In fact, you have to stop acting like the pathetic pinks you are."

"All you have to do is to stand together as one, and you have won. You can have your way if you stand for the rights of each other. Don't you see how easy it is?" Moe instructed.

As this information began to saturate the worker's minds, one by one, they stood, as if it were like pulling teeth. Finally, all were standing. Moe said, "Okay, it's done. You have gained your freedom." The workers began to relish this new way of thinking. We congratulated each other for our apparent success.

However, abruptly, the crowd became silent as all attention focused on the entrance to the yard, where Chair One and Two stood. Chair One demanded, "What's going on here?" No one volunteered to answer.

Chair timidly said with all the courage he could manage, taking the chance of losing everything in this one statement, "Things have changed."

"Changed! What do you mean?" Chair two asked.

"What he's saying is that the two of you no longer can oppress these people," Moe explained.

"I knew these people were going to be trouble," Chair One, grumbled, then ordered, "Three, you are demoted to a servant."

"You can't demote anyone anymore, you jerk," Lucy stated, unleashed.

"Yeah, you jerks," I added.

"You don't know who I am," Chair One proclaimed. He turned to the workers and ordered, "Get these people out of here." Still uncertain and fearful, the workers just stood there, not knowing what to do, yet having enough courage not to move to carry out that order.

Seeing this, Moe seized the moment and said, "You're no longer in charge."

"Yeah, you don't get it, do you? And what are you going to do about it?" I said, knowing they had no backup forces.

"Arrest them," Chair One ordered. When he saw no one in the crowd obeying his order, he said, "If you don't obey, I will call out the weapons."

"Would you actually harm us?" Chair asked, with alarm.

"Yes, I would, if you do not obey," Chair One said.

"That would be breaking the rules," Chair said.

"We are the rules," Chair Two declared.

"Moe said, with that same unexplained courage, "I really hate to tell you guys, but there're new rules." Turning to the workers, he asked, "Are you going to stand together and take charge now?"

"We will fight you," Chair One challenged.

"Are you going to fight the *White Light*?" Lucy asked.

"We are the leaders here. The *White Light* is a legend and has no power," Chair One said.

We expected the *White Light* to strike, but it didn't. Moe had to quickly resort to challenging the resolve of the workers,

"Are you going to stand up for your freedom. If you lose this opportunity, you'll lose it forever. Don't let them do this to you."

As if miraculously, the workers understood this could be their only chance and overcame their fears. In a surge, they overwhelmed Chair One and Two, lifting them over their heads and unceremoniously carrying them off. As they did, the strike of *White Light* finally struck, everyone froze except us, which now included Chair and Mate.

Lucy said, "It's about time.

A *Man in White* stood in the crowd. He said, "Yes, it was good work, you can rest here tonight. But tomorrow you must be on your way. We do not want time to run out, do we?" Another flash and the workers were once again alive, and the *Man in White* was gone.

Chair and Mate were not only astonished at seeing the *White Light* and the *Man in White* but speechless. With Chair One and Two removed, powerless, and dumped into oblivion in the factories trash heap, humiliated and dethroned forever with no recourse. The workers began to celebrate their victory, which continued late into the night. Mate appealed, "Must you leave? You must teach us about the *White Light* and the *Men in White*."

"As you heard in what was said, we must leave. Anyway, you already know as much as we do. We must get the children back home," Mary said.

"Yes, of course. Let us go into the house." We talked for a time giving Chair and Mate as much information and encouragement as we could. Mary understood our need to get some sleep and ended our evening, although the people's celebrating continued.

Once in bed, it took a while for our adrenaline to dissipate enough to allow us to fall asleep as another exhausting day ended.

CHAPTER 47 Getting Back On The Road

The next morning in Mechanicsburg, at our last breakfast with Chair and Mate, they expressed uncertainty in what they would be able to accomplish after we left.

Chair, being exhausted from the night before, said, "I think I should step down and once again become a worker."

"I must say, we believe that would be a mistake," Mary said as she glanced at Moe. "Mr. Moe, you can explain it better than I."

Moe feeling their success spoke with certainty, which came from that place well beyond him. "Yes, Miss Mary. From what I understand, people need leaders. Not leaders who oppress, but rather those who defend all the people, who understand equality, justice, kindness, caring, and above all the freedom to be Good."

"Freedom is to be good? Hmm, is that what freedom is?" Mate asked.

"Without any doubt, One and Two had their freedom but used it to oppress others. They used their personal liberty in the wrong way. It was not true freedom. If freedom isn't for all, it's a false freedom, it's a lie. It is only fulfilled when one restricts their behavior to acting with goodness that benefits all."

"Is he not marvelous?" Mary couldn't help but say. She didn't say it merely out of her fondness for him but marveled at seeing the change in him, which was greater than himself. It reflected an understanding she saw blossoming in him, at least for the moment filling him with a knowledge people in her world hadn't yet understood.

"Yes, he is," Mate, agreed, to Moe's embarrassment.

"I do not think I could live up to that," Chair confessed.

"Yes, you can, dear. You are the kindest person I know."

"Chair, Mate is correct," Mary said.

"Remember, whether you appreciate it or not, you are the only one who can bring this brand of freedom to Mechanicsburg.

You have been chosen to lead."

"Moe, do you really think I have been chosen?"

"Yes, we all think so. Why do you think you were able to see the *White Light* and the *Man in White*?"

"Ah, I am beginning to understand. Yes, maybe I must lead."

"Dear, I am so pleased," Mate, added, as we all spontaneously applauded him.

"To lead is to lead," Ike said.

Six tentatively asked, "Chair, may I ask you something?"

"Yes, of course."

"I know I am a Green, but, could I stay here and work for you?"

"You are a free man, and since we now have freedom, you can make that choice yourself." Then with sensitivity, he said, "However, I am going to need assistance in the new freedom. Will you stay and assist?" Again the rules of segregation were being broken.

"Sir, I would be honored to assist." Then he hesitantly said, "Sir, there is one more thing?"

"Yes, what is it?"

"Since I am the only Green man here, would it be possible to be called One instead of Six?"

"Certainly. From this day on you will be known as One the green man." The newly ordained One brimmed with pride. We all bathed in the humanity of the moment, understanding the goodness of what just took place.

Moe said, "That's great! Now that everything is settled, it's time to leave."

"Yes, it is. Come along, children," Mary ordered.

"We will never be able to thank you enough. The Dragon is like new and full of fuel waiting for you. Please be careful when you pass through Warland. And, since you cannot drive back over the divide, I will send an escort to guide you around it," Chair said.

"Wow," I expressed.

"But, what about keeping the secret?" Moe asked.

"Everything is different now. There are no more secrets," Chair said.

Mate said, "Yes, you have changed everything for the better, and we will miss you. If you come back this way, please stop, all of you will always be welcomed. Goodbye, Mary, goodbye Moe, goodbye Ike, and children may you get back to your home safely."

"Take care. Six. I mean One," Moe said.

Once again, we experienced those deep emotions when parting, which we still didn't understand. As tears flowed, we piled into the Dragon and pulled away.

"To leave is leave," Ike said. There were crowds to wave their goodbyes all the way out of the city.

Guided to a spot along the road, before reaching the divide, which looked no different from any other spot. One of the guides jumped out of his transport and ran over to the woods and grabbed a small tree pulling it down like a lever. Suddenly, a portion of the woods swung open like a gate wide enough for the Dragon to pass through. I let out another, "Wow."

After driving through the opening, the man lifted the tree allowing the little patch of land with its trees, bushes, and grass to swing closed, concealing the entrance. We moved up an incline along a snake-like road, which made the steep climb easier. A canopy over the path formed by the branches of the surrounding trees hid the road from the mountaintop above.

After driving for a time, we stopped at the base of the divide. Again, a tree lever was pulled, which opened a hidden, camouflaged door. We drove into the mountain, up and around on a spiraling roadway until we reached daylight and another door. Exiting, we found we were back on the road, only now on the top of the mountainous divide. Now Moe expressed a, "Wow!" At that point, the guides left us. Once again, we were on our own, heading back to the pebble *Road.*

Still surrounded by the dense woods after driving for an uneventful day, we realized we wouldn't reach the next city before dark. We stopped for the night, built a fire, ate, and relaxed for a time contemplating the universe.

"I still can't believe what's happen to us?" Mar lamented.

"Before I met Mr. Moe, I never really thought about what

was beyond my little world. The only responsibility I ever had was to make sure my Slops did their work properly. How shallow my life was," Mary pondered.

"But, Miss Mary, you did all that reading."

"I know Mr. Moe, but all those books were fantasies with little relationship to what was taking place in the world around me. I existed only in a little corner of my sheltered world."

"Mary, our way has always been to repeat what was done before us. Not to question, you only did what was expected of you, the same as I did," Ike added.

"Miss Mary, that's what you were taught. There's no shame in that," Moe added.

"Mr. Moe, our parents, always taught us to try to make things better," I said.

"Yes, not to just go along with things if they weren't right."

"Right, Lucy, but our world is a different place," Moe said.

"Why is my world so different from your world? Why can we all be the same?"

"I don't know Miss Mary. I guess it's just the nature of things."

"I think I'm beginning to understand all this, yet, not sure if I can express it, you know what I mean?" I speculated.

"I think I might know what you mean," Lucy agreed, surprising me.

"Ah, me too. Things are getting interesting. Let's sleep on that. We're going to need all the rest we can get to face what comes tomorrow," a weary Moe ordered.

CHAPTER 48 Approaching Warland

Moe and Mary were the first to wake the next morning. While eating in front of the blazing fire, Moe attempted to verbalize a feeling, "Miss Mary, I spent some time thinking about…"

"Thinking about what, Mr. Moe?"

"Well… When I was young, I just wanted to be a normal person with hopes and dreams, much like anyone else," He lamented.

"But you are that. In fact, you are the most rational person I have ever known."

"No, Miss Mary. Maybe in this world, I might seem so, but in my world, I never fitted in. I always felt out of place. Come to think of it, I don't quite fit in here either."

"Mr. Moe, I think you fit in very well."

"I'm sorry, Miss Mary, but you're the only one I ever felt comfortable with."

"Then, why are you feeling sad?"

"Miss Mary, it's just that the understanding we're to understand still isn't making much sense. Even the kids understand more than I do."

"Is that what's bothering you? Why I think you are gaining a great understanding. And, have you thought, maybe gaining it is just for the children to help them get back home?"

"Maybe you're right, Miss Mary. I'll have to think about that."

Ike appeared, stretching as he sat by the fire and helped himself to the warm food. Moe asked him, "What do you think is waiting ahead?"

"I have never traveled out this far. Except for my father, I know of no one else who had, and he went no further than this. Sorry, but I know little about what is ahead. However, without a doubt, I am afraid we are now about to enter Warland. A place I secretly read about when I was a child in forbidden books, although I believed it was only a myth."

Mary added, "And, that is all I know. What I know comes from my husband behind closed doors, who never traveled this far."

"Ike, what did the myths say? Can you guess what is ahead?"

"I read there were two groups, the establishment, and the dissenters. One side was called the Ins, and the other was called the Outs. Those in power asked much of the people. However, lifetimes ago, a rebellion against the establishment grew, causing the banishment of the dissenters. They were pushed out and away from the others."

"It must have been awful for them, and it seems it is still going on."

"Clearly it is Miss Mary since Mechanicsburg is still selling weapons to both sides. However, I'm afraid we're going to find out the truth soon enough. I think it's time to wake the kids and get going."

Later, as we drove, we no longer were surrounded by the forest, having passed more grasslands, barren lands, among others. We reached a desert-like area with a growing number of tall bushes, at least twelve feet high. In time, both sides of the *Road* were covered with those dense bushes sprouting large flowers of assorted colors.

Moe suggested we stop to stretch our legs and change drivers. The bushes were enticing, so we examined them up close. So far, we hadn't had the time to stop and enjoy the wilderness and smell the flowers.

Mary, observe, "Be careful children, there are sharp thorns. However, the leaves have the sweet smell of honey, and the flowers smell even nicer."

"It's so quiet here," Mar said.

"And everything's so still. Can anything live around here?" Lucy asked.

"It doesn't look like anything could survive in these thickets. But it's wondrous how life can adapt to extreme conditions," Moe said.

"I don't like this place," Lucy said.

"Wait—listen!" Mary alerted.

Listening, I said, "I don't hear anything."

"Listen!" Mary ordered as she cupped her hands around her ears. Listening, within seconds, we heard a low humming sound, which increased in volume sounding like the hum of an idling engine. We looked up and down the *Road* and into the air over our heads, not seeing a thing.

Then suddenly, an object darted by in the air just above our heads. It disappeared in one direction as another one zoomed-in from another direction. We ducked to avoid being struck.

"Get in the Dragon!" Moe hollered. Horrified, as panic set in, climbing over each other as we all scurry into the Dragon. Watching from inside the safety of the Dragon, objects slammed into the windows and fell to the ground, apparently trying to attack us.

"They're bugs!" Lucy exclaimed.

"Yuck, they're gross!" a repulsed Mar cried out.

"Oh, my. What are we going to do?" Mary asked, horror-stricken.

"Moe, this must be Insecticide, we better get out of here while we can," Ike ordered.

We drove slowly, for the *Road* could hardly be seen through the flying swarm as the wheels crunched over crawling bugs. The winged creatures looked similar to giant wasps with wingspans more than two feet across, looking quite fearsome and were most aggressive. The wingless ones looked like enormous cockroaches, more than a foot long, creating a most ghastly sight. We huddled together, hoping they wouldn't break through the windows.

"Keep going, Moe," Ike ordered.

"Yes, keep going, Mr. Moe," Mary added.

"I am Miss Mary. I am."

"Are we going to die?" Mar couldn't help but say.

Under the stress, I blurted out, "We're not going to die. Would you please stop saying that, you know what I mean?"

"I hope you know what you mean," Lucy responded, in her panic.

"We must break clear, keep going, Moe," Ike said. We continued driving in spite of the bumping, slamming, and crunching taking place around us.

After an intense ride, we finally emerged into the clear. Mar looked back and said, "Those crawling bugs are dragging away the dead ones."

"I think it's their food, isn't it so, Mr. Moe?"

"Johnny, It might be so. They probably eat whatever they can."

"Johnny, I'm sorry," Mar, tearfully said.

"About what?"

"About asking if we were going to die again."

"Oh, that's okay. Forget about it. I understand."

"And I am sorry too. I had forgotten about Insecticide. I believed it was only another myth. I have never seen a bug before. If we had not stopped, we would never have known they were here. Moe, do you have those creatures in your world?" Ike asked.

"We do, but most of them are just tiny little things which are more of a nuisance than a threat. This these is creepy. When do you think we'll be out of their territory and safe?"

"I think we will be safe when the terrain changes," Ike said.

"Mr. Moe, would you please speed up as fast as you can go." He sped up to top speed as the mangled pieces of the bugs flew off the Dragon.

After driving some distance beyond Insecticide, we felt safe enough to stop for a hot meal. The terrain was now desolate, filled with massive boulders scattered around as far as could be seen. Many were as large or even larger than the Dragon. There was no wood to burn, so we had to eat the food cold. While eating in the stillness, we felt a slight ground tremor under our feet. "What' s that!" Mar exclaimed.

"I fear that is what my father described. I believe it is coming from Warland," Ike said.

"Yes, I believe it's the results of munitions?" Moe said.

"Is there a chance we could be hurt?"

"Oh, Mar."

"I'm sorry, Johnny, I'm just so afraid."

"I know you are, we all are, but you must be brave and have courage."

"I'll try. I'll try Johnny," Mar tearfully said.

"Yes, Kids, I'm sorry to say, as you know, weapons are dangerous. However, we have to do our best not to let it frighten or discourage us from our goal. Only our fear can stop us now," Moe said.

"Oh, my. What are we going to do now, Mr. Moe?"

"Miss Mary, all we can do is to go ahead as we must. Ike, it'll be dark soon, maybe we should stay right here for the night."

"We should. It might take a whole day to find the center of Warland, and it wouldn't be wise to drive in the dark in this place."

CHAPTER 49 Captured By The Soldiers

At first light, we said little in anticipation of what was ahead. No reasonable person with any sense would go into Warland with the dangers it posed. However, determined to reach the end of the *Road,* we had to pass through that zone. "Do we have to go through Warland?" Mar asked to affirm the obvious.

"We do. Remember, the *Men in White* said we must go into every city," Matt said.

"To go into is to go into," Ike said.

"Yes, I think the time has come to go into," Moe said.

We piled into the Dragon with the same trepidations soldiers might feel just before entering a combat zone for the first time. We sped along on the pebble *Road.*

Later in the day, we began to see a scattering of fragmented boulders, as if a giant hammer had struck them where they stood surrounded by a maze of potholes in the sandy soil. From his personal experience in the army, Moe knew it was the result of cannon fire.

"Miss Mary, it's been days since we came through the *Rock,* do you think we'll ever get home?" Mar asked.

"Child, I do think you will. We just have to follow the *Road* to its end."

"Everything has to do with following the *Road,* following the path, follow, follow. What does it all mean? Would someone explain to me, are we following, or are we being pushed out front?"

"Lucy, that is an interesting question, following or being pushed? Could they be the same, what do you think, Mr. Moe?" Mary asked.

"I hadn't given it much thought. However, I would think, to follow is the responsibility of an individual, and to forge out ahead is the responsibility of the leader."

"To follow is to follow and to lead is to lead," Ike said.

"I'm glad that's cleared up."

"Now Lucy… I think this might have something to do with the understanding," Mary instructed.

"I'm sorry. I'm only trying to understand what's going on."

"I think I'm beginning to see things differently."

"Johnny, that is fascinating. What's different in what you see?" Mary asked.

"It's the way things are done that causes change for the better."

"Is that what we're supposed to do—make changes?" Lucy asked.

"It seems everywhere we go in this world, things change for the better."

"That is true, Johnny, at least I hope so. And it always happens with the help of the *White Light* and the *Men in White*," Ike added.

"So, with their help, we are change-makers."

"Lucy, it might be so," Moe said.

Suddenly, out of nowhere, the whistling of an incoming projectile sounded and landed well ahead of us, erupting in a loud explosion. Moe stepped hard on the brakes, jarring us. Then he sped up, hoping to get away as another landed even closer. Braking hard again, Moe brought the Dragon to a firm stop.

"I think someone's shooting at us!" I said.

"They are, aren't they," Moe said.

"Moe, back up. Turn around," Ike ordered.

Unfortunately, the abrupt stop stalled the engine. Under stress, Moe tried to start it without success. Another explosion hit closer yet. Near-total panic, yet understanding the Dragon was the target, Moe yelled, "Quick, everyone get out and away from the Dragon." He led us far enough away to feel safe, picking a spot between two boulders large enough to hide behind.

Thankfully the shelling stopped. As we caught our breath and calmed a bit, Lucy asked, "What now?"

Mary looked for a hopeful sign in this direr situation and pleaded, "Mr. Moe!"

"I don't know. Wait, let me think, Miss Mary." After a

moment, he peeked over the boulder in the direction of the Dragon. He quickly dropped down to sit in a fetal position.

"What?" Lucy asked.

"Are we going to die? Oh, I'm really sorry about that."

"Mr. Moe!" Mary again exclaimed.

"Miss Mary, I think we have a problem. Ike, look, what do you think?"

He looked and then sat down next to Moe and said, "A problem is a problem."

"What's going on?" Mary asked as several blue-uniformed soldiers appeared holding what looked like antique rifles pointed at us. Fortunately or not, they had the same pink skin as ours.

"Oh, my. Oh my," Mary said.

"Moe, I think you better explain who we are," Ike suggested.

"Here we go again," Lucy said.

Standing up, he cleared his throat, and with that unnatural courage, said, "Hello. My name is Moe." His friendly gesture were met with blank looks. He went on, "We're travelers on the *Road*." With no response, he asked, "Who's your leader?"

A soldier stepped out from behind a boulder dressed in what appeared to be an officer's uniform and ordered, "Come with us." Marched away from the *Road*, to where there were several of those tank-like transports hidden behind large boulders. We were loaded into one of them and driven off.

We drove passed several wrecked and rusted shells of war transports as we zigzagged around the boulders. I would guess we drove for a mile or more before reaching the first of a series of tiered built-up man-made ridges running parallel to the *Road*. On the far side of the ridge were dugout fortifications safe from a direct hit by incoming artillery.

Stopping, the officer disembarked and entered a bunker. We were unloaded and waited with anticipation wondering what was in store for us. Around us were entrenched cannons pointed towards the *Road* that ran in a depression at the center of the boulder-filled valley. The officer came out accompanied by an older and higher-ranking officer, who asked. "Who are you, and where do you come from?"

Moe stepped forward and stood at attention as if he were a

soldier and said, "Sir, my name is Moe, and we're from the other side of the *Rock*." His answer shook the officers. The older one whispered in the ear of the younger one who ordered us back into the transport and drove us deeper into their territory.

Another mile farther in, we reached the top of the next ridge. From that elevation, we were able to see the other side of the *Road,* which was a mirror image of identical man-made ridges, one a little higher than the one before it, like steps. Undoubtedly, the other side was enemy territory. The only difference was on the other side, there were red blotches seen along the ridgelines.

On this side sat many armed transports strategically parked and manned by soldiers in blue. We assumed all the equipment on both sides was built in Mechanicsburg.

Over the third ridge, we saw tents sprawled out, filling the entire area. We stopped in front of a large canvas tent where the officer went inside.

In a moment, he came out and ordered us inside, where several elderly blue-uniformed officers sat at a table facing us, one asked, "Who are you?"

We looked at Moe. He took a hard swallow and again stood at attention, answering, "Sir, my name is Moe, and we're from the other side of the *Rock*."

Noticeably made uneasy by his answer, the officers whispered to each other, the same officer then asked, "What are you doing here?"

Before Moe could answer, another officer pointed at Ike and asked, "He is a Redman, and the woman is an Inbetweener. Who are they?"

Moe answered, "Sir, they're friends helping these kids to travel to the end of the *Road* so they can get back to their world."

"No person has ever made it to the end," an officer stated.

"Sir, just because it hasn't been done doesn't mean it can't be done," Lucy said.

The oldest looking officer at the center of the table, spoke, "Most courageous." He ordered the soldiers who brought us in to get chairs for us. Once seated, the apparent leader, asked, "Would you please tell us how you got here and what the other side of the *Rock* is like?"

"Sir, why did you shoot at us?" Lucy asked

Child, we did not shoot at you—it was the Reds, who are our enemies. They shoot at anything that moves out there. They are not friendly people. We sent a patrol out to pick you up and give protection."

"Oh…" Thinking things might be okay, Moe asked, "Sir, what would you like to know?"

"First of all, how did these children get into our world? I thought it was no longer possible?" the Leader asked.

Moe told them him how we got there as they listened with wonder. Another officer asked, "Do you have peace in your world?"

"Sir, right now, we do, but like you, at times, we still have wars."

"You mean you start and stop wars?" another officer asked.

"Sir, yes, we do. How long has your war been going on?"

"Why it has been going on for countless lifetimes," the leader answered.

"Sir, Why are you at war?" Lucy asked.

That question caused a rustling among the officers. The leader explained, "Because we want to be free to live our lives the way we see fit."

Another officer added, "We do not like to be told how to think, how to act, and our only duty was to serve the Chief."

"Your Chief, asks that of you?"

"It is not us—we are the Blues. It is the Reds, our enemies. We do not live under the rule of a Chief."

"Sir, in Redtown, it was thought they were called the INS, and you were the OUTS?" Ike asked.

"Yes, that was once true because our people no longer were willing to do all the things the Chief demanded of them.

"Ages ago, a Chief started to persecute those who wanted to be free, and as they did, our resistance grew, however, we had to keep it a secret. Over time the INS, those obedient to the Chief, began under his orders to uncover and cast out the disobedient ones. That is why we once were called us the OUTS.

"In those early days, within a lifetime, half the people remained on their side, and the other half was forced out across the *Road* to our side. It split our society in two, it divided families in two, some stayed, and others had to go. Brothers and sisters split, husbands and wives separated, and children and parents split.

"However, since then, we became as powerful and equal to the INS. We no longer consider ourselves the OUTS. This land is as much our land as it is theirs. Now, because of the color of our uniforms, we are called The Blues, our enemies are called The Reds."

"Most interesting," Ike said.

"You mean you've been at war all this time?" I asked.

"Yes, son. In the beginning, they tried to overrun us, to disperse us, thinking it would make us disappear. We fought them with sticks and stones, and people crossed back and forth at will, for we all looked the same without uniforms. It remained so for lifetimes until the knowledge of firearms and the wearing of uniforms came. The Reds started to shoot at those who were moving between the two camps, and we shot back.

"You began to kill each other?" Matt asked.

"At the time, the weapons were not accurate, most of the time they missed their intended targets or regrettably once in a great while the guns exploded in the faces of the shooters, only to kill themselves.

"It was frightening, which caused most to stop freely crossing between the two camps. However, since then, with better weapons, they shoot at those who try to cross over to us, and we shoot at those who attempt to stop the defectors so they can safely make it over here."

"And you keep killing each other?" Mar asked.

"We try not to kill anyone. It is a rare misfortune when one loses his or her life by our hands," another officer said.

Moe asked, "Sir, what's the purpose of continuing the war?"

"It is to hold the line as not to be overrun. We hope someday all our people will come over to our side, leaving no one on their side, except for the Chief. Until then, we will protect ourselves and those who want to cross over."

"Will the war ever end?" Mary asked.

"I imagine someday it will. Until then, we must hold that line."

"Sir, what else do you do?" Moe asked.

"What else? What do you mean?"

"Sir, I mean, where do you get your food, clothing, and pay for the weapons?"

"Ah, yes. You have not yet seen our way of life. We grow our food, we make our clothing and whatever else we can, but most important is the mining and processing of mineral rocks to trade for everything else, including our weapons."

"Sir, where do you do all this?"

"We will show you where it all takes place, and there is no need to call me Sir, I am called, Commander. Now, you must tell us about the other side of the *Rock*."

We spent some time answering their questions to their keen interest and fascination. When their questions were exhausted, Commander asked if we'd like to have a meal. Moe was famished and immediately accepted the invitation. Commander and his general officers accompanied us to the eating tent where a substantial meal was served.

During the meal, we explained how we found out Mechanicsburg was supplying their weapons. Commander seemed unconcerned, we knew. However, we didn't mention the flow of firearms might stop if Chair decided to do the right thing.

CHAPTER 50 Learning About Warland

Upon finishing the meal, we boarded an open-top transport along with Commander. Driven to the top of the next ridge away from the *Road* to see a vast number of canvas tents sprawled out, filling the area between that ridge and the next one in the far distance. Commander explained this tented area was out of range of the Red's cannons where the soldiers lived with their families in relative safety in a domesticated way.

Every man was a soldier who rotated from being on the front lines to be a farmer, a skilled worker in the necessary trades, and all did their share of work in the mines. Driven to the top of the next ridge, a spectacular sight greeted us. It was a flat plain stretching as far as one could see. It was partitioned into large parcels, each perhaps a quarter-mile square.

There was a lot of activity taking place. Small truck-type transports were moving along the roads that surrounded each partition. As we drove past the squares, Commander explained the purpose of each one. There were many cultivated squares used for the planting of grains, corn-like plants, melons, spices, and fruit orchids, among other strange crops. Also, there were squares with penned in domesticated animals, sadly waiting for slaughter.

He further explained that most of their creatures lived in herds, grazing in the vast distant pasturelands until needed. Most of this abundance was for their use. We past squares with large tents where the processing and storage took place. Others had food drying racks, for there was no refrigeration. There were tents where the uniforms and other soft goods were made. It was a sizable well-oiled operation to fuel their city.

However, beyond all those squares, there was an extra-large square, more than a mile across. He explained it was where their mining operation took place, which was excavated out of one big hole, perhaps a mile deep, although, their measuring system was different than ours.

It took lifetimes for the enormous hole to be dug out by hand, as they loaded the material in huge buckets hoisted to the surface. That was until recent times when engine power was utilized. On the surface, gigantic piles of rocks were waiting to be processed and hauled off in trucks for trade.

It was extraordinary, for we assumed what was taken from that one hole was most likely iron, copper, aluminum, coal, lead, or other common minerals. However, unbelievable and mind-boggling, we were told besides all those minerals, it also contained gold, platinum, silver, diamonds, rubies, sapphires, and other gems. Imagine that! All dug out of this one hole. In our world, it would be impossible and beyond belief, which only proved this was definitely not our world.

They used this abundance of wealth for trade with other cities, mostly for weapons. Because they hadn't signed the treaty agreement, all illegal trading had to be kept a secret, for it was against the rules of others to deal with them. Therefore, they operate clandestinely, for only the leaders of the cities they traded with knew of the arms and other war-making commodities. For the riches were immense for those who broke the rules simply because of the exorbitant profits they received.

Even more remarkable, the Reds had similar operations fueling their side, which continued the stalemate. Sadly, most of their wealth was spent on the war effort, not to enrich their people's lives. As daunting as these activities were, the way they operated seemed primitive to us.

"What do you think?" Commander asked.

"It's most impressive," Moe said, not wanting to take the chance of offending these people by giving that simple answer. But, it seemed risky for them to tell us how they operated. They were either naive or fearless? Anyway, Moe decided not to get into it and changed the subject, "Since you are self-sufficient, why continue the war?"

A bit taken back, Commander answered, "Because, half our people are still under the Chief's control. His oppression has kept our people in bondage. We want all our people on both sides to be free and to come together as a family once again."

"I see your point," Moe said.

"Yes, it is most commendable," Mary said.

"How old is the Chief? I mean, when will he die?" I asked.

"From what I understand, he is very old. Oh, I see what you are getting at. The Chiefdom is a rank passed down from father to son. There will always be a Chief. That is until we end their reign."

"You mean the Chiefs won't let you live in peace?" Mar asked.

"Chiefs do not believe in peace."

"But aren't you free now? I mean, the Blues?" Matt asked.

"We cannot be free until the war is over. Because of it, we live under military control. If not, we would be overrun, conquered, and forced into submission. Our dream is to build houses and not live in tents, able to move around as one would like. Our only business is war."

"You mean you have never known real peace and freedom?" Lucy asked.

"No, never, we must win the war first."

"Have you tried to negotiate a peace?" Moe asked. "To end a war in my world, that's what must happen. That's unless the leaders are killed or captured first."

"In my lifetime, I have never seen or spoken to a Chief. The end of the war will only occur when all the Reds have defected and become Blues or dreadfully visa-a-verse."

"Do you have any idea what their Chief is thinking at this time? Mary asked.

"What we know is only through defectors who have come over. Since only a few Reds have defected in recent times, I do not know his thinking at this moment, and since none of the blues have ever defected to his side, I do not believe he knows what we are thinking.

"Why don't you just attack them?" I asked.

"Attack them? If we attempt to cross the valley, we will be bombarded by their many cannons. It will cost too many lives."

"Why don't you outflank them?" Moe suggested.

"Outflank them?"

Moe saw the blank look on Commander's face, and explained, "Perhaps, by going around them and surprising them from the rear."

I never thought of that. It seems it would not be moral."

"Is it moral to allow half your people to be oppressed?" Lucy asked.

"I have never thought of that either. Is that the way you wage war in your world?"

"Yes, it's one way."

"Most interesting? Please, will you tell us all about the wars in your world?"

"Yes, I'll tell you all we know, which is not very much, if it'll help you gain your freedom."

Once back in Commander's tent, we discussed war and other matters well into the night until Mary explained we must get some sleep, for we had to leave in the morning.

"Could you not stay and help us?"

"I'm sorry, but we must get the kids back to their world as soon as possible. Their parents must be distraught by now," Moe said.

"Of cause, you are right. Will you come back later if you are able?"

"If we are able, we will," Mary said.

Commander ordered subordinates to take us to a sleeping tent and bid us goodnight

Exhausted, soon, we all were asleep.

CHAPTER 51 Captured By The Reds

The next morning in the Blue encampment, we woke early, eager to get on our way. Commander ordered a small force of well-armed soldiers to escort us to the Dragon, which included two mechanics to help start it, if necessary. We bid our Farewells to all those able to see and hear. Finally, we were on our way.

Speeding off, headed towards the Dragon was a rough and bumpy ride. Arriving alongside it. We knew it was kept from being molested by the Blue's cannons aimed at anyone who might've approached it. Along with the mechanics, we got out, leaving the armed soldiers standing in their personnel carrier peering in all directions.

As Moe opened the Dragon's door, Mar let out a gasp of horror. We were overwhelmed by a force of Red-uniformed soldiers who emerged from behind the surrounding boulders. It was a well-set trap using the Dragon as bait.

The Blue soldiers were vastly outnumbered, leaving them with little choice but to duck down in their transport and speed off as the Reds shot at them. Fortunately, most of the bullets flew wildly, bouncing off the surrounding boulders. Those few that hit the carrier just bounce off its armor as they disappeared out of sight leaving us helpless. The Blue's cannons were of no use. If fired, they indeed would've hit us.

The Red soldiers coldly order us to march off. Taking us, along with the two mechanics, to their war transports cleverly hidden behind the boulders. The only difference between the Red and the Blue transports was that the Reds had little red flags, and the Blues had little blue flags. All were manufactured exactly the same in Mechanicsburg.

In a convoy, we drove off holding on for dear life during another bumpy ride. Traveling Over a couple of ridges, we arrived in front of a large tent with a massive Red banner over it.

Separated from the two mechanics and led into the tent, we found a similar setup as in the Blue's command tent. Except those here wore fancy red uniforms. All had impressive large sparkling gold stars on their shoulders in contrast to the Blues who used only simple cloth patches. Most had one star, a couple with two, one with three, and the one in the middle had four even larger stars. All had high, wide-brimmed hats with red feathers fanned out on the right side, the more stars, the more feathers.

The three-star officer, sitting to the right of the top ranking one, asked, "Who are you, and what were you doing with the Blues?"

Moe stood at attention and stated, "My name is Moe, and we're from the other side of the *Rock*."

Shocked and flustered, the officers shuffled their papers, apparently not knowing how to react to that information. We waited for the next move as they chaotically directed whispers to each other towards the one in the center, whom we assumed was the Big Chief. He calmly sat there as the officer on his right whispered in his ear. The right-hand officer asked, "What do you mean you are from the other side of the *Rock*?"

The way they reacted to Moe's statement, we saw a weakness and again felt that incredible courage in us, especially Moe as he calmly answered, "It's simple, we are from the world on the other side of the *Rock*, the place where all your ancestors came from."

The Chief's spokesman whispered in the Chief's ear, then asked, "No one has come through the *Rock* recently, what were you doing with the Blues?"

Lucy said, "They were the first to greet us when we came into your valley, as others were shooting at us." I could see she was beginning to have trouble containing her thoughts.

The Spokesman cut in, "If you are really from the other side of the *Rock*, what is your interest in Warland?"

"Our only interest is in getting these kids to the end of the *Road* and back home," Moe answered.

"Are you not spying on us?"

"We told you, we are from the other side of the *Rock* and are trying to get back home." We hoped if we took a strong posture, it would keep us safe. As we moved from situation to situation, we'd come to believe nothing bad would happen. Choosing to feel so, in spite of what the Men in White indicated concerning being harmed.

"No one has ever traveled to the end of the *Road*," the spokesman said.

"So!" Lucy responded.

"If you are going to the end, tell us how far it is?"

"We didn't say we knew how far it was," I said.

"Then how do you know there is an end?"

Moe went all the way and said, "Sir, a *Man in White* told us there was."

"A man in white told you, that is impossible," he responded. From their reaction, it seemed they had no idea who a *Man in White* was. As weird as it might be, for we found no one in this world knew of them. He whispered in the Chief's ear, and then asked us, "Where do you really come from?"

Lucy, increasing irritated in seeing the way they communicated, asked, "Why can't the chief ask his own questions?"

"You cannot ask that question!"

"Why not, is he unable to speak?" I added, backing my sister.

"No one is allowed to speak to the Chief."

"Sir, can't he speak for himself?" Moe asked, seeing what Lucy saw.

"The Chief is the one we serve. You are not worthy of being spoken to by him."

As we talked, the Chief sat there unconcerned and disconnected from the conversation. We could see there was something odd about his strange behavior. One could sense our minds clicking in unison.

We don't serve your Chief," Moe said. We braced for a harsh response from that challenge, but none came. The officers just sat there with confused looks, apparently not knowing how to deal with us.

"Yes, we don't serve your Chief," I restated.

Followed by Lucy, saying, "I don't think he can speak for himself anyway."

Moe without fear pressed harder. "Is he an idiot?"

"What does that mean?" The spokesman asked.

"It means, is he a nitwit, an ignoramus, a nincompoop, an imbecile," Lucy added, in a way only she could.

"Lucy!" Mary exclaimed, horrified.

"It's all right, Miss Mary. I believe Lucy has stumbled on something. I don't think the Chief is in charge here, is he; Mr. three-star General!"

Befuddled, he sat there for a moment, then whispered to the other officers, only this time, he totally ignored the still unconcerned Chief. After some discussion, he admitted, "You are correct, I am in charge."

"Why don't you just become the Chief?" Lucy asked.

"It is not possible because to become the Chief, one must be of their bloodline."

"That's smart. You keep him around so you could be the Chief without being the Chief," Moe said.

"How clever you think you all are."

"If you're the Chief behind the Chief, why don't you stop the war and bring peace?" I asked.

"Peace! Why would I want peace? War is what gives us power."

"What about the suffering of the people?" Moe asked.

"You do not understand, do you? People need to suffer. They are not smart enough to have peace. They need to be controlled. Without our leadership, they are worthless. War is what keeps them busy."

"What you really mean is you keep the war going just so you can have the power over the people," Lucy stated.

"Remember Lucy, he's never known peace," Ike said.

"Correct, war is our lives."

"Then we'll tell your people you're just a phony," Mar threatened.

He said, "I do not think so." as he ordered his men to put us in chains.

"You can't get away with this, we are free people," Moe said. In spite of his statement, they shackled us as we struggled, unable to break free.

"There is no more time for talk. I must get on with the war," he ordered, "Away with them."

Forcibly we were taken to a tent with twelve-foot high walls fortified with chain link fencing tightly wrapped around the cloth exterior. Inside was barren with no furniture. Left alone, a tearful Mar asked, "Is this a jail?"

"No child, it is not a jail. Do not worry. No harm will come to us."

"Miss Mary is right, we've not been harmed so far," I said.

"So far," Lucy said.

"So far is so far," Ike added.

"I know we're not going to be hurt, you know what I mean?"

"No, what do you mean?" Lucy said.

"Now kids, let's see if we can find a way out of here. Spread out and look for tears in the walls to see what we can see." Being shackled made it challenging to move around. Through the holes, we saw guards standing every few feet around the outside perimeter. After appraising the situation, a dejected Moe sat on the dirt floor and suggested, "I guess we'll have to wait for an opening or if we're going to be helped."

"That's right; we'll get out of here one way or the other, you know what I mean?"

"Isn't the *White Light* going to save us? Mar asked.

"I hope so."

Mr. Moe, I still don't understand why they're fighting this war?"

"Lucy, in seeing both sides, it seems to be the old battle of *Good* against *Evil,*" he said.

"You mean the Blues are the good ones, and the Reds are the bad ones?" Mar asked.

"It certainly looks that way."

"Mr. Moe, how can we be certain who the evil ones are?" Mary asked.

"Isn't those who fight for the freedom of all, the good guys?" I said.

"It seems so, but I don't think in our world it has always been that simple. It's hard to know what any group of people have in their hearts, let alone the unintended consequences of war," Moe said.

Ike said, "That is right, Moe…"

All of suddenly, a voice came out of nowhere, startling us.

We turned to see a *Man in White* sitting in the corner on the ground.

Relieved, Mary asked, "Sir, how can one know who the good ones are?"

"Mary, that is simple. Those who use their freedom to do good by protecting the innocent without reservation are the good ones. Those who use their freedom to do as they please no matter whom they harm are yielding to evil. One must judge a person not only by what they say but by their actions. When it comes to the city against city, the leaders and their followers must be judged by the goodness they collectively foster, not in how much they are able to gain."

"I see," Mary said.

"Sir, what do we do now?" I asked.

"Yes, how do we get out of here?" Lucy added.

"You must be patient. Rest, for now, for you will need your strength when things become clear." Suddenly, a flash, and he was gone.

"I wish I could disappear from this place, too," Mar said.

"What comes now?" Lucy asked.

"What comes is what comes," Ike said.

"That's great."

"Now Lucy, let us do what we were told, which means to rest for now," Mary instructed. We complied without question, finding comfortable spots to stretch out on the hard ground the best we could.

CHAPTER 52 Finding Freed

Darkness had fallen in Warland, as we tried to sleep on the floor of the holding tent, we couldn't help but to be discouraged, not knowing what to expect next.

However, in the middle of the night, a muffled ground tremor woke us. Suddenly, surrounding the tent were sounds of turmoil. In spite of the shackles, we struggled to get to our feet to see what we could through the holes. As the sound of bugles filled the air, we heard troops chaotically rushing around. In the distance were the unmistakable sounds of gunfire. In a shrill voice, Mar asked, "What's happening?

Cannon rounds landed close, instilling fear. Moe, sarcastically observed, "It sounds like a war going on."

"I think Mr. Moe is right, you know what I mean?" I said.

"It seems obvious, doesn't it!"

"Now Lucy, remember what the *Man in White* said, let us be patient, and things will become clear," Mary instructed, in spite of her own fear.

"Clear is clear," Ike said

The sounds of battle became louder until we could hardly hear each other. Fear had its way with us as we gathered in the center of the tent. Mary, Lucy, and Mar sat close together in fetal positions as Moe, Ike, Matt, and I clustered around them in a protective mode. With great apprehension, we hoped things would soon become clear.

The gunfire and shells landed closer yet. We feared it was going to be our end. However, finally, after a horrendous period, the threatening sounds began to subside, until all we could hear was the hurried footsteps of troops around the tent.

Abruptly, the tent flap flew open, and the silhouette of a man waving a sword entered, followed by several others. Mar screamed in horror. Just then, a soldier entered, holding a lantern illuminating their blue uniforms. It was Commander standing there in all his glory, although looking every bit his age, wearing a blue cape and helmet holding a sword. "Are you unharmed?" he asked.

"We are unharmed, and I must say we are so glad to see you," Mary said.

"And I am glad to see you are uninjured."

"I thought we were going to die," Mar said.

"I was concerned if we attacked that might be so."

"What happened, I thought you weren't willing to attack?" Moe asked.

"When we found out you were taken by the Reds, I knew a bold action was necessary. We could not allow your capture. Therefore, as you suggested, we outflanked them, which took the day to sneak around them, and under cover of darkness, we were able to take them by surprise. And thanks to you, by telling us how to accomplish that, maybe now we can end the war."

"Good for you!" Mary said.

"Yes, good work, my man," Moe said.

You're a hero," Lucy added.

"No, I am just doing my job. Now, I must go and finish the war."

Moe stopped him, "First, you must understand the second one in command is the one in charge."

"What is meant by this?"

"It seems the Chief no longer has his wits about him," Ike said.

"Yes, and the second guy with three stars took over," I added.

"You must capture him to end the war," Moe explained.

"I see... I will do that. Now you must relax. My men will protect you until I return, for it is not safe yet."

"To finish is to finish," Ike said.

"Yes, the war must now be finished," Moe, said

As Commander left, he ordered his men to remove our chains and take us to a more comfortable place. They took us to a luxurious tent, which probably belonged to the Chief.

Moe asked the soldiers if it was possible to get some food. Served all the food we could eat and feeling safe, exhausted, we soon were asleep while waiting for Commander's return.

The following morning, still in the Red encampment, we slept until better rested in an attempt to catch up with the eight-hour days and nights. By midday, after consuming a sumptuous meal, we were led through the flurry of activity in the encampment to be with Commander. Who we found sitting in an open-top transport. He asked, "My friends, would you come with me, there is something I would like you to witness?"

"Sir, it will be our honor to go with you," Mary said.

"Good. Get in." Driving along, we saw the Blue soldiers cleaning up the results of the battle. Groups of Red soldiers, with their hands held on their heads, were being led to a holding area. We stopped on top of the ridge overlooking the countless prisoners.

Surprised and pleased to see the false Chief and his Generals stripped of their gold star and in shackles standing among the ordinary prisoners. He looked at us with the most hateful expression we ever saw, which I must say was most gratifying.

Commander stood in his transport as the hustle and bustle quieted down. Holding up a cone-shaped megaphone, he spoke to the mass, "The war is over. We can now establish peace and freedom. Peace is something we know little about. We must reunite and learn to reconnect as a free people to become one again. We must first put down their weapons.

"Next, the stripe of our new friend's skin color will bind together our red and blue stripes on our new flag. Those who join us will be free. Those who want to continue the war will face banishment. Our land will no longer be called Warland, from this day on, our territory will be known as Peaceland."

The throng listened intensely as we saw a process begin as the prisoners, especially the non-commissioned ones, slowly came to the realization the war was finally over, and freedom was something they might welcome.

Switching from a war footing to a peace footing is a difficult task, even in our world. We watched as that magnificent transformation began to take place right in front of us as a cheer rose up until the roar was deafening.

We thought it was imaginative of Commander to represent us with a stripe on the new flag, making us proud as we thanked him. Self-satisfied, he ordered the driver to move on to the Blue encampment surrounded by an armada of still armed transports.

On the Blue's side, we were met by a small number of women and children who had come in from the hither lands to wait for the return of their husbands, fathers, sons, and brothers.

Commander's wife of many years, greeted him smiling and excited as they hugged. He introduced us to his wife Sue, "I am so glad to meet you and see you are all safe. I was so worried," she said, as she got into the transport.

"Thanks to Commander, we are safe," Mary said.

"It was your idea on the way to attack them, and the credit is yours."

"No, dear, you are also a hero," Sue said.

"Sir, you are a hero," Lucy added.

"Yes, Commander, you are, for your bravery has proven it whether you accept it or not," Moe encouraged.

"Well, then, we are all heroes. Now, we must work for peace," Commander said, as we drove on.

Over the far ridge were the numerous remaining women, children, workers, and remnants of the soldiers who greeted us, for the main army was still in the Red encampment. Parked in the center of the throng, Commander stood with a megaphone in hand and addressed them, "We have victory," the people cheered. He calmed them and continued, "Now, with the war over, we must work to bring peace and freedom. Today we will rest; tomorrow we will form a new government." As the cheers rose, he ordered the driver to move on.

Later after dinner, in the privacy of Commander and Sue's tent, it was our first chance to discuss the events of the day freely. Obviously fatigued, Commander began to unwind from this most stressful day of his life. He asked, "My friends, what do you think?"

Mary looked at Moe, "Mr. Moe, please tell us what you

think."

Also wearied, Moe perked up and said, "Yes, Miss Mary, I will... I think today, you did exactly what you had to do. Because you made the hard decisions, we believe you saved our lives. You did what most do not do. You did the right thing with courage, overcoming your doubts and fears." (It struck me, if Moe could have only applied those same words to himself, he might have become something great back in our world.)

"Yes, yes, but did I do it in the best way?"

"Dear, of course, you did it correctly," Sue said.

"Dear, I know whatever I do, you will stand behind me. Nevertheless, today, there were some people injured, and a few even gave their lives because of my orders. This troubles me."

"Sir, you saved us from who knows what," Lucy said.

"Sir, we might have been killed today," Mar added.

"And most important is that you freed all your people, what can be better than that." Moe offered.

"See dear, you did much good. The war is over at last," Sue said.

I guess I did do good."

Mary urged Moe, with subtle eye and hand motions to see if he could further encourage Commander, as she said, "Mr. Moe, tell us what you really think."

Moe, still picking at the food, understood the need. He cleared his throat and said, "I'll say what I think from what I've learned on the other side of the *Rock*. Now, for you to keep the peace might be as hard as continuing the war."

"So far, you have told us how to win the war, now you must tell us how to keep the peace."

"Commander, I'm not sure we are the ones who can help you. In our world, we haven't solved that problem either," Moe said.

"You are the only ones who can help us now."

"Yes, you must help us," Sue pleaded.

"Mr. Moe. You must help my world," Mary urged.

"To help, is to help," Ike said.

Moe pondered for a moment... He then realized there was an untapped resource. He turned to us and asked, "What do you think kids? What about peace?"

Lucy thought, and said, "Isn't peace about; we must love each other?

"That's right. Isn't it about caring for each other?" I said.

"That is most interesting," Commander responded.

"We do care for our people," Sue said.

"I think that's it. However, you must now also care for the people who were your enemies."

"I am not sure I understand what kind of caring you are talking about," Commander said.

"Mr. Moe, tell us what is meant by that kind of caring?"

"Oh boy, Miss Mary, it's the most important question one could ask, and maybe the most difficult to answer. If the answer were easy, our worlds would be different places."

"Isn't it about what we learned in Sunday school?"

Moe said, "That's right, Lucy. I'd almost forgotten that."

"Lucy, please tell me what you were taught," Commander urged.

"Sir, we all were in Sunday school."

"Children, then tell us what you learned," Mary ordered.

"They taught us we must not only be good but must also do good," I stated.

"I didn't always understand what the teaching meant," Lucy admitted.

"I had trouble understanding it too. Although, I did understand it has to do with Goodness," Mar added.

"To be good, and to do good. Hmm? Do you mean the leaders must be good, or do you mean the people must be good?" Commander wondered.

"I think to be good is for everyone, especially the leaders."

"Mr. Moe, good is a general term which covers a broad range of feelings," Mary offered.

"Does it mean we must have good feelings? Commander asked, attempting to better understand.

"I think it has little to do with the way we feel. It has to do with the way we behave towards each other." Having trouble finding the right words to describe *Goodness*, he turned to us again.

"Okay, kids, let's find some words to explain it?"

"Doesn't it have to do with having laws protecting each and

every person," I said, having learned that in school.

"That's right. What else?"

"Doesn't it have to do with being kind to one another?" Lucy said.

"That's right. What else?"

"Doesn't it mean we must not hurt each other?" Mar added.

"That's right. What else?"

"Doesn't it mean to love each other? Matt said.

"That's right."

"Wait, I think I am beginning to see what you mean. I must now make sure our new government has laws protecting the rights and freedoms of all the people. Above all, we must take care of each other. Leaders must not oppress but give equal value to all. That must be what is meant by the word love. A word the Red Chiefs never used," Commander said.

"I think you've got it. If you care for someone, you will take care of him or her in the right way. Those in power must make sure all the innocent are protected from evildoers," Mary said.

"It's where the Red Chiefs went wrong, for they only cared about their power. They used the people to serve their personal needs, keeping them enslaved," Moe added.

"I see. We must now care for all the people, whether they are Blue, Red, Pink, White, or any other color." Sue said.

"To care is to care," Ike said.

"Moe, tell us the best way to accomplish this?" Commander asked.

"Well, I would think the first thing to do is to write a list of rules to be followed by all. Rules, which are fair, just, caring, giving all the people equal freedom, and most important would be the same rules that apply to the people the leaders must also follow."

"You mean, they must write something like our Bill of Rights?"

"Matt, that's it."

Energized, Commander stood and called out, "Sentry! Sentry!" A couple of soldiers entered. He ordered, "We need to write a document, get the Recorder." One soldier rushed out. Pleased with himself, Commander sat and turned to us and stated, "I am sorry, I cannot wait until tomorrow. We must do this right now," exhibiting a youthful energy, which inspired us all.

Shortly after, the soldier returned with an officer carrying a portable tabletop desk. He placed it on the table and opened it, taking out paper and a quill a pen which he dipped in a bottle of ink encased in the desk, indicating he was ready.

Remembering from our history class, I asked, "Don't we need witnesses?"

"Yes, witnesses are required," Moe, agreed.

Commander called out, "We need witnesses in here!" A soldier stuck his head out of the tent flap and called in the eager men and women who had been hovering around the entrance, including the general offices. The Commander ordered the recorder. "Write this down." He then looked to us for approval and direction.

"Good. First, what will you call it?" Moe responded.

"Well? Yes, how about calling it; The New Blue, Pink, and Red Bill of Rights?"

"Why that is wonderful, dear," Sue said.

"What fits, fits," Ike said.

"This is most exciting," Mary said, feeling the energy filling the room.

"Kids, did you ever think you would be a part of the formation of a new nation?"

"No, Mr. Moe, I never even thought about it. You know what I mean?" I said.

"I never thought about it either, just as I'm still finding it hard to believe we're in a different world, but isn't it great."

"It is great, Lucy," Moe said.

Commander ordered the recorder to write the title down.

We went on to discuss the finer points. When all agreed on a Right to be included, it was written down. We all did the best we could. It was a short, concise document with not many wasted words, perhaps written with a naive idealism and from a youthful frame of mind. Moe understood more than any of us and was pleased with the choices made comparing it to our *Bill Of Rights*.

When the document was finished, all felt the air of a new birth, so to speak. With the newly-penned document in hand, Commander turned to us and asked, "Well?"

"Don't you need signatures?" Matt thought.

"Signatures?"

"Yes, signatures of the people who participated and will back up what was written," Moe explained.

"Everyone here who agrees with what has been written and is willing to stand behind it, please sign," Commander ordered. As the signing started, he said to us, "You must sign it too."

"Oh, it's not necessary," Moe said.

"You must. If it were not for you, this would not have been possible."

"Mr. Moe, we must honor our host," Mary said.

"Right, Miss Mary."

"To sign is to sign," Ike said.

We all signed the document, knowing this was something extraordinary.

Later, after a time of celebration and congratulations, we were once again alone with Commander and Sue.

"Tomorrow, we will survey the land," Commander said.

"Mr. Moe?" Mar pleaded.

"Oh, yes. I'm sorry, Commander, but we must complete our mission and get the kids back to the other side of the *Rock*."

"Yes, I want to go back home. My parents must be really worried by now," Mar said.

"We all want to go home," Lucy added. Although I realized when and if we did, we could not help but miss the excitement of this adventure.

"Yes, of course, you must get back home," Sue said.

"I am sorry I have been selfish. Although I regret you must leave, it must be done. However, you must stay this night and rest tomorrow. Then we will help you on your way."

"Thank you, Sir, you are most kind," Mary said

Once in our sleeping tents, exhausted from this most extraordinary and historic day, we soon fell asleep for another well-deserved night's rest.

CHAPTER 53 Hoping To Reach The End

The following morning, we were taken by surprise and elated when Commander volunteered to escort us to the far border of the newly named Peaceland. He feared dissenters might try to do us harm. However, he explained he could go no further than that point due to the legends that did not permit his people to cross over their border in the direction the *Road* was headed.

Regretting not being able to help us beyond that point. He explained, how over time, their legends became superstitions, and he could not ask his people to go against their beliefs by crossing over the border, for they feared supernatural punishment.

However, we assured him it wouldn't be necessary to take us any further, in spite of our trepidations we successfully concealed.

After breakfast, a large number of soldiers, along with women and even children climbed onto an armada of transports, which now sported little new blue, pink, and red flags. How they were able to produce those flags overnight was unbelievable. It was a sizable caravan, for so many wanted to be involved.

It took a full day to reach the well-marked border where a simple sign arched over the pebble *Road* read, "End of Warland - No Trespassing." Immediately a group of workers began to paint over the word Warland, replacing it with Peaceland. It was amazing.

On this side was filled with extra-large boulders. Abruptly on the other side was an extremely flat barren land under a darkened sky without any sign of life or anything else. We stood there speechless, taking in the starkness ahead of us. Moe asked, "What is this place called?"

Commander said, "It has no name, it is said; it was not to be given a name."

"I know in this world that is done, but it is still strange, isn't it, you know what I mean?" I said.

"Is there anything out there that will harm us?" Mar asked.

There was no response to pacify her fears, for it looked most daunting.

"Who said it couldn't be named?" Lucy asked.

"A long time ago, a voice came out of the *White Light*, which once glowed out there, declaring; do not name this land for it is not for you to know," Sue explained.

"Sue!" Commander interrupted.

"Dear, we cannot hold back information that will help them succeed," Sue instructed.

"Yes, dear, you are once again correct. Forgive me."

"Sue, we believe the *White Light* is what it's all about?" Moe said.

"My friends, that is what we understand," Commander said.

"Well... what else?" Lucy asked, urging him to explain more.

"I am sorry, Lucy. You see, we were taught never to discuss it," Sue said.

Commander interrupted, "Dear, if there is any punishment for talking about it, let it fall on me."

"Oh my, we do not want any harm to come to you," Mary said.

"No, Mary. Moe and the children have changed our lives forever. We must do all we can to help the children get back to their world."

"We appreciate it. Commander. Please, tell us what you can about the *White Light*?" Moe asked, still desperately trying to find the understanding.

"My friends, dark is falling, we will set up camp for the night. Later we can relax and talk about such things." He turned to his people giving orders to set up an encampment, then excused himself and Sue to supervise the operation.

Provided with folding chairs, we sat and watched as the camp was set up with the hustle and bustle of activity swirling around us. Fires were built; tents were erected as we peered out over the barren land, wondering what possible dangers were lurking out there waiting to snare us.

Later, when the encampment was completed, we joined

Commander and Sue in a tent and were served a hot dinner cooked over one of the many fires. "Can we talk about what you told us earlier?"

"Absolutely, Lucy."

"Good, I'd like to hear more about the *White Light*," I asked.

"Is The White *Light* protecting us?" Mar asked.

"Now children, Commander will tell us in his own time," Mary instructed.

"It is all right, Mary, we understand their eagerness," Sue said.

"Yes, I just want to go home," Mar, bemoaned.

"We'll get you home. Try to remember that," Moe said.

"Then we must tell you all we know," Commander added.

"Now, children, let us listen."

"Yes, Miss Mary," Mar answered for all.

"I am not sure where to begin. As adults, we never spoke of these things."

"Commander, tell us about the *White Light*?" Moe asked.

"We always knew of the *Light*. However, as children, if we asked about it, we were told not to speak of it. However, in our youth, we secretly exchange legends from one child to another through the ages, which I imagine is still going on."

"Yes, as children, we talked about it in secret. It was exciting, and at the same time frightening, however, as we grew older, we learned to be silent," Sue said.

"Please, what was so frightening?" Mar asked.

"Ah, it is not easy to explain. You see, the only *White Light* we ever saw were bright flashes coming from far out there in the distance beyond this point. Flashes were once visible even from where we lived. Perhaps, it took place at the end of the *Road*, maybe not, for where the end is; is not known. All we know is that it happened out there in the direction the *Road* is headed," Sue said.

"That doesn't seem to be very frightening. In our world, we have lightning storms all the time," I said.

"What is a lightning storm?" Sue asked.

"Don't you have storms with rain and thunder?" Lucy asked.

"What is rain and thunder?" Commander asked.

"I'm beginning to understand. Since I've been here, it's

never rained, and I've never heard an ordinary crack of thunder either," Moe reflected.

Commander looked puzzled and asked, "Please explain what you are talking about?"

We all started to answer at the same time, causing confusion. Moe said, "Kids, maybe I should explain it." He spoke slowly and carefully, "In our world, it rains, meaning; water falls from the clouds in the sky and is accompanied by a loud sound called thunder caused by lightning strikes similar to the flash of the *White Light,* only it's not the same."

"Oh… And what are clouds?" Sue asked.

"Clouds are made of vaporized water floating in the sky around our world, and when certain conditions are just right, the water they contain falls to the ground."

"Water floats in the sky? Do you get wet when it falls?" Sue asked, a little befuddled.

"We do if we don't get under cover," Lucy said, amused.

"It sounds most untidy," Mary thought, also amused.

"Sir, where does your water come from?" I asked.

"Why, it flows in the many rivers. What you are telling us is most interesting. And what is thunder?" Commander asked.

"It's a loud sound similar to your gun explosions, only louder. I never fully understood how it works," Moe said.

"I see your world is entirely different and more complicated than ours."

"It sounds frightening. Is it not?" Sue asked.

"No, not really, we just think those things are natural occurrences. What's frightens you about the *White Light*?" I asked.

"It is not in seeing the *Light* but rather in what we were told about it," Commander explained. "As children, we were never allowed to question it. Even now, it makes us nervous to speak about it. However, we realize we must tell you because you seem to have magic traveling with you."

"We have no magic or power."

"Mr. Moe, you must admit, the *Men in White* and the *White Light* have been saving us. It does seem like magic and has lots of power."

"Miss Mary, I guess you're right, but I don't understand it."

"Please, sir, what was so frightening about the *White Light* here?" Lucy asked Commander again.

"Our Legends tell us; at the beginning, our ancestors, men, and women alike came through the *Rock* from your world. At first, the flashing *White Light* was all around. Over time as we multiplied in great numbers, the conflicts among us became so fierce, the powerful White Light began to strike down the worst and most arrogant of our leaders, causing them to disappear. In fear of that punishment, the new leaders who survived from each faction decided to separate into like-minded groups and never to challenge the *White Light*," Commander related.

Sue added, "And, the Legends also told, the *White Light* was judgment, and if one spoke of it disrespectfully, they would be judged and punished by being struck down by it. Therefore, when we became adults, we kept silent in fear of that punishment. However, as time went on, the *White Light* receded to rarely be seen, only by a few from afar. It is believed to be at the end of the *Road*. Since people stopped speaking of it, some have come to believe it was only a myth."

"I guess that explains why every time we needed help, or the *White Light* was challenged, it struck," Moe concluded.

"Hey, Commander, how come you weren't struck down for being at war?" Lucy asked.

"That is most interesting, I do not know? We have always been at war. I never gave any thought to why we were not. We just went along with what has always been," he said.

"Yes, it is interesting. I had also been thinking of why my world was allowed to do those dreadful things. That is before Mr. Moe, and the children arrived?" Mary said.

"And, I've never figured out why I'm here, and I don't understand why the kids are here. In my world, I was less than normal."

"Now, Mr. Moe, You are very special. You are just going to have to accept that fact," Mary said.

"Mary is right, Moe. If it were not for you, we still would be at war," Sue said.

"I don't know? What I do know is the kids must get back home."

"I want to go home so much," Mar yearned.

"Mar, we'll be home soon, you know what I mean?" I reassured her.

"This time, I think I know what you mean," Lucy added.

Commander said, "Tomorrow, we will send you on your way. I cannot tell you what is out there, for no one I know of has ever gone beyond this point."

"Dear, wasn't it so, in the beginning, some of our ancestors traveled past here?"

"Ah... Yes, that is true, Sue. I had forgotten. But, they were never seen again to confirm anything. People assumed they were lost forever and were never to be spoken of."

"Then some may have already reached the end," Moe said.

"It might be so, and if anyone can do it, it will be you helping the children. We have told all we know in the hope it will help you succeed."

"To get there is to get there," Ike said.

Commander concluded, "There is nothing out there as far as could be seen. We will give you extra water, fuel, and whatever else you think you might need,"

"You have been most helpful and brave to have spoken the unspeakable. It is time for us to get some sleep, we must depart early in the morning," Mary urged.

"Of course," Sue said. She snapped her fingers, and a soldier entered. She directed him to bring us to the sleeping tents, bidding us goodnight.

CHAPTER 54 The Hot And The Cold

The encampment began to stir early the next morning. The fires were stoked before daylight, shortly the smell of breakfast was in the air. Moe awoke suddenly as if the smell of food told his brain it was time to wake and eat. He stuck his head out of the tent and asked the two soldiers standing guard if it was possible to wash up. They nodded a yes, as one of them scurried off.

He returned shortly with other soldiers, carrying towels, washcloths, and soap, along with four small basins and buckets of heated water. Moe thanked them as they quietly placed it all in the tent. Pouring some water into one of the basins, Moe washed the best he could. When finished, he woke Ike, Matt, and me, telling us to wash up and meet him wherever the food was as soon as possible."

Passing Mary's tent, it looked dark and quiet inside. He assumed they were still asleep. Although he noticed a bucket and a used towel sitting by the door, guessing but not sure, he went on hoping she was ahead. Directed to the eating tent, as expected, he was pleased to find Mary waiting. Greeting her, he asked, "Miss Mary, have you eaten yet?"

"No, I've been waiting for you."

"Miss Mary, you knew I would head here."

"Mr. Moe, I know you better than you think I do."

"Yes, Miss Mary. Then let's eat."

She asked one of the women to wake Lucy and Mar for breakfast. She waited for Moe to ingest enough food to allow him to sit back and relax before she expressed her feelings, "Mr. Moe, it is possible we might not make it to the end of the *Road*. This frightens me."

"Miss Mary, it is frightening. Maybe, it would be better if you stayed here."

"Mr. Moe, Do not even think that. We agreed I would stay

with the children until they crossed back over. You cannot change that agreement."

"Miss Mary, I've not changed anything. I just thought you might want to reconsider."

"No, Mr. Moe. No!

"Yes, Miss Mary."

Shortly we all arrived for breakfast. Moe joined us in having another full plate. When everyone had eaten their fill, the time had come to leave. Commander and Sue led us to the Dragon, which was waiting with its nose on the borderline. Also waiting were all those that came along in the caravan.

He spoke out so all could hear, "We know you must leave. I hope you understand why we cannot go with you."

"Commander, you are needed here to build and maintain peace and freedom," Moe said, trying to help him feel better about his limitations.

"Yes, you cannot leave, and you must understand it is only for us to go," Mary added.

"I do understand. We are sorry we are unable to tell you anything more about what is ahead."

With a tear in her eye, Sue said, "Yes, and we will miss you more than you can imagine. Please remember, if you come back this way, you will always be welcome." The tears flowed as we continued to experience those strong unfathomed bonds when we parted from those we befriended.

At long last, we climbed into the Dragon. Moe ignited the engine, and we slowly drove off, waving goodbye in a gloomy silence. Once over the border, Moe stepped on the accelerator, and we sped away, leaving the saddened crowd behind.

Driving as fast as the Dragon would go, we traveled across the barren land, only stopping to rotate drivers or refuel from the spare cans. Not even stopping to eat, for there wasn't a scrap of wood to be burned.

There was no change in the extremely flat, hard-packed desert-like landscape as far as could be seen. The only marker to follow was the lavender pebbles covering the narrow *Road*, which led straight ahead like an arrow.

After darkness had fallen, we continued to drive in the glow of the Dragon's headlights hoping to get as far as possible before having to stop. During my turn at the wheel, I noticed little white crystals forming on the side-view mirrors. I softly called out, "Mr. Moe, Mr. Moe." Seeing the crystals, he ordered me to stop. When I stepped on the brakes, the Dragon went into a skid as if the wheels lost all traction.

"What's happening?" Mar shrieked, as the Dragon spun wildly to our screams of horror. It lasted only seconds, although it seemed a lot longer. When we stopped, it took a long moment for us to recover.

Lucy spoke first, "Johnny, what did you do?"

"I did nothing!"

"Wait," Moe said, as he opened the door and slowly stepped out, and as he did, his feet slid out from under him. If it weren't for him holding on to the door handle, he would have landed flat on his back.

"Mr. Moe!" Mary cried out.

"I'm good, I'm all right," he quickly answered and pulled himself back up onto the seat. He looked to where the headlights lit the area.

"Mr. Moe, what is it?" Mary asked as she saw the confusion on his face.

"Why, the ground is covered with a sheet of ice."

"Oh, my. Oh, my. Mr. Moe, what is this I am feeling?"

"It's only a cold temperature, Miss Mary. Don't be afraid, it won't harm you," he said as he shut the door.

"So, this is what cold feels like? Burr... I do not like it, it is most unpleasant," Mary said.

"I also have never experienced cold before," Ike said. "It is a strange sensation. I don't like it either. Urr..."

"What now, Mr. Moe?" Lucy asked.

"I don't know?" Due to the engine having stalled in the skid, he tried to turn the crank handle, but it wouldn't move. "It couldn't have frozen so fast," he said, worrying.

"Are we going to be all right?" Mar asked.

"We will, child... Mr. Moe, what do we do now?" Mary

asked.

"If I could only start the engine," Moe said, as he again tried to move the crank without success. He concluded, "We might have to wait until first light. Till then, let's put on all the clothing we can, and maybe get into our sleeping bags."

"I don't like this. Not at all," Lucy murmured.

"We'll be all right, you know what I mean?" I said.

"Oh! Really?" Lucy responded.

I also tried to turn the crank unsuccessfully. Moe warned, "I think the engine is frozen, it has no anti-freeze. If we keep trying, it might snap something. We better wait for morning."

We squeezed into all the clothing we could. Mary suggested, "Now children, let us have something to eat, we are going to need all the energy we can get," as she handed out the now almost frozen packets of food. "Are people in your world really able to live in cold weather?"

"Yes, they are, although I never liked being cold myself," Moe said.

Once in the sleeping bags, we held the food next to our bodies to defrost them enough to chomp on. We huddle together, trying our best to keep warm as it continued to get colder.

(They slowly became numb, closing their eyes and dozing off into an unconscious state with ice crystals forming on their faces. Was this their end?)

Moe's eyes suddenly popped opened, to find it was daylight, and to his delight, the ice and cold were gone. It was normal again. He yelled, "Wake up! Wake up!" We hadn't any idea how long we were out. However, we were so joyful things were normal again, with a renewed hope we jumped out of the Dragon and danced around, and even kissed the now warm ground.

We peel off all the extra clothing. Mary, Moe, and Ike just smiled, much relieved. Moe turned the crank, the engine immediately flared up to our cheers. He suggested, "Let's eat."

Once our stomachs were satisfied, we got back on the pebble *Road* and sped on our way.

Later, we began to notice it was getting warmer. As we

drove, it continued to get even warmer. We removed as many pieces of clothing as we could and remain modest. Fearful, Mary whispered to Moe, who was driving, "Mr. Moe, I do not like this.

"I don't like it, either Miss Mary. It doesn't look good. All I can do is to drive on in the hope of getting out of this place."

"Yes, Mr. Moe"

The temperature climbed, "Why is it getting so hot?" Lucy lamented.

"What's going on? Are we going to be all right?" Mar pleaded.

"Don't worry; we're going to get out of here, right, Mr. Moe?" I asked, even though we all knew we were in trouble.

"Right. Kids drink all the water you can," Moe said, not at all being sure of anything.

Steam began to shoot out from under the hood. Moe stopped, knowing if we continued, the engine would indeed burn out. He said we must wait until the engine cools down and ordered me to get a couple of jugs of water.

With a rag in hand, he carefully loosened the radiator cap to allow the high-pressure steam to escape. The pressure was so explosive it blew the cap out of his hand and high in the air. Fortunately, he was not injured. We watched the cap, as it flew up and away to where it landed as not to lose it.

The four of us went out to pick it up while Moe slowly poured water into the radiator. However, it immediately boiled away. We couldn't cool the engine, and it was getting hotter. Distressed, hoping for relief as it drained our energy, we laid down on the ground just off the *Road*, for the pebbles were too hot to touch. We grew weaker to the point of passing out.

(They all passed out and just laid there to be cooked alive. Was this their end?)

Once again, Moe's eyes popped opened, waking him from a coma-like state to find everything was normal. He yelled with great excitement and relief, "Hey everyone, we're okay! Wake up! Wake up!"

Each of us came to our senses and assessed our condition. We were fine, although totally exhausted. Suddenly, a *Man in White* appeared from behind the Dragon.

The first to see him, Lucy asked, "Sir, what's going on?"

"Sir, will we be all right?"

"Mar, there is something you must all understand. Whether you will be all right, depends a great deal on whether you stay in the limited space your body can survive in. Even more important is to travel on the straight and narrow *Road* where good character lives and grows. It is up to you if you will be all right."

"Sir, I think I understand, but what are we supposed to do now?" I asked.

He walked around the Dragon, saying, "At this point, it is for you to figure out." Out of sight, he disappeared in this barren land, adding to our frustration.

After a moment, Moe said, "All right, we're okay now, no time to waste. Let's see if the Dragon is working." He checked the radiator's water level to find, in spite of the water having boiled away, it was now full. Amazed, he yelled, "It's okay." He turned the crank, and once again, the engine flared right up to our joy. He said, "Let's get going." We piled in and drove on.

Driving for a time from the spot we encountered the *Man in White,* we remained silent. Lucy broke the silence, "First we were frozen, then we were almost boiled. What's there not to understand about that?"

"If it is to be taken at face value, it does seem simple," Ike said.

"At face value, it is obvious. What do you think, Mr. Moe?" Mary asked.

"I think it's much more than being too cold or too hot."

I added, "I'm thinking it's about staying within the limitations of good behavior. The *Man in White* compared the limitations of living with hot and cold to the limitations of living on the straight and narrow, didn't he? Wait, isn't that what our parents taught us." I said, as I unwittingly realized, I was beginning to understand the things our parents instilled in us. It's what they wanted us to learn, and with that simple foundation, my outlook was now actually maturing. Under these conditions, having to grow up so quickly was a strange feeling.

Lucy said, "Limitations have limitations," imitating Ike.

"Yes, it makes sense, apparently we're only able to live in a narrow zone," Moe said.

Ike wondered, "I am not sure I understand, for, in my world, the temperature remains the same at all times and in all places."

"Lucky you," Lucy said.

"I remember we were taught in school about the narrow habitable space we live in. But, how does the temperature connect with the straight and narrow?" Matt asked.

I realized, "That's it, yes it does. Just as in our world, we must have air, food, and a comfortable temperature in a small habitable space; we must also live within a straight and narrow zone of goodness to survive."

"That's right, he did indicate we had to stay on the straight and narrow, or there would be consequences that would harm us," Lucy said.

"Kids, you might have something there. To remain good, one must stay in a zone. If you step out of the zone of goodness and do something not good, there'll be consequences, just as we must stay in a temperature zone. Wait, just like in the legion, when those people didn't behave correctly, they suffered the consequences."

"Mr. Moe, you mean the consequences were to be pulled into my world. Do you think that is what this is all about?" Mary asked.

"It might be, Miss Mary. It might just be that simple."

"Oh, my."

"As Lucy said, limitations have limitations," Ike said, apparently gaining a sense of humor.

Being a bit self-satisfied and exhausted from this horrendous day, we sat back in silence, trying to get some rest as we drove on in the hope nothing else would go wrong.

Stopping only to refuel from the cans of our diminishing supply and rotated the drivers so all would get the rest needed. However, this whole adventure continued to take its toll on us, physically as well as mentally.

CHAPTER 55 To Step Off The Cliff

As we traveled, in time we spotted what looked like a white cloud in the far distance that appeared to be sitting on the ground. Just able to make it out, it looked like it covered the entire area from left to right and as high as could be seen. There seemed no way around it. With the cloud still in the far distance, Moe stopped and stepped out of the Dragon. "What in the world is that?" He said.

"Mr. Moe, it looks like a cloud."

"I know Johnny. I guess I should've asked was, why is that there?"

"Mr. Moe, why is that there?" Lucy asked.

Mary smiled and said, seeing the humor, "Oh, Mr. Moe," followed with a soft chuckle. Mar followed with a giggle, and I joined in as Ike wondered what could be that funny.

Lucy, not catching on either, asked, "What's funny?"

Moe grinned, seeing the absurdity of it all, "Lucy, come on, it's funny." she thought about it, and then let out a snigger.

"Funny is funny," Ike said. We all laugh together, which relieved some of our tension in this barren place.

Mary regained her composure and asked, "Mr. Moe, I have never seen a cloud before, what do we do now?"

"Miss Mary, I think we just keep going. Ike, what do you think?"

"The end of the *Road* is in that direction, and the end is still the end."

"Well, then. Let us go," Mary ordered. Moe climbed back in, and off we went.

The cloud remained in the far distance. Refueling from another can hoping the fuel would last until we reached the end or at least to where we could find more fuel. We drove faced only with the barren land and the cloud ahead, which only exasperated our anxiety.

As darkness fell, hungry and drained, we decided to stop to eat and rest until the light came again. Realizing the only wood remaining were the clubs, yearning for a hot meal, we built a fire with those once valuable items to heat the food.

As always, the temperature was mild enough to camp out. We decided to stay right in that spot for the night. We crawled into our sleeping bags, filled with thoughts of what might be lying ahead until sleep overtook us.

At first light, still faced with the same depressing emptiness, we ate breakfast cold, and with quiet anticipation, we drove on.

Later, with Lucy at the wheel, she stepped hard on the brakes bringing the Dragon to a full stop tossing everyone forward, waking us out of our dozing state. I exclaimed, "What happened?"

"Yes, Lucy?" Moe asked.

"The cloud!"

"What about the cloud?"

"It's here! I mean, we're there." She exclaimed as she pointed straight ahead.

"Well, look at that," Moe said.

"Oh, my. Oh, my."

"The cloud is the cloud," Ike said. We disembarked and walked right up to it, which was sitting on the *Road* like a flat brick wall.

We stood there in wonderment, I asked, "What in the world?"

"Yes, what in the world?" Mary repeated.

"I don't know?" Moe wondered.

"So this is what is called a cloud," Ike asked.

"Well, not exactly. A cloud in our world floats in the sky. This is more like a fog, although I'm not sure what it is?"

"A fog? Mr. Moe, why are things in your world so complicated?"

"Miss Mary, it does seem so, doesn't it?"

"What are we going to do now?" Mar asked.

"Yes, Mr. Moe, what do we do now?"

"Well, Miss Mary, we do what we've been doing. We go ahead."

"Well, then let us do it." Before we did, we poured in the remaining fuel to the last drop, hoping it would be enough to take us to the end, for fear of running out of it was high.

With Moe at the wheel, he said, "Here goes nothing," not knowing what else to do he inched the Dragon ahead, hoping the mist was just a thin wall.

Amazingly, as the bumper touched the mist, miraculously, a tunnel-like opening formed, just big enough for the Dragon to fit in. Bravely, Moe slowly drove in. It was bright inside. However, all we could see was just enough of the *Road* to stay on it, all else remained hidden in the mist.

"Be careful, Mr. Moe."

"Yes, Miss Mary." Only able to travel fast enough as not to lose sight of the *Road*. We drove for the longest time, wondering if we would ever emerge.

Driving for some time, almost reaching the point of discouragement, something appeared in the distance. Lucy asked, "What's that?"

"Are we going to be all right?" Mar asked.

"Stop worrying, you know we'll be all right, you know what I mean?" I said, not at all being sure.

"I wish you knew what you meant," Lucy said.

"Now children," Mary scolded

We approached the object to find it was a big square sign fastened to two thick posts firmly planted in the *Road* blocking our way. Closing in on it, the Dragon consumed the last drops of fuel, as we rolled to a stop only inches from the sign, fearful we sat there for seconds in silence, just staring at it.

Lucy slowly read it aloud, "*The-End-of-the-Road*."

"What does it mean?" Mar asked.

"I think The End of the Road means - The End of the Road," Ike said.

Somehow, we expected to be joyful and excited when we reached the end. Believing there would be something more elaborate than a dreary sign to greet us. "With no more fuel, we felt demoralized, Mary could only ask, What are we going to do now?"

"I don't know," Moe said, as he stepped out and walked beyond the sign, followed by us. The smog or mist or whatever it was, again blocked our way.

Figuring we had to walk the rest of the way, Moe stuck his right foot into the mist and took a step. He let out a yelp and fell back to a sitting position. Horrified, Mary exclaimed, "Mr. Moe!" She knelt by him, "Are you all right?"

"I'm good Miss Mary." A little bewildered, he stood and said, "There's nothing there?"

"Nothing there?" Lucy repeated.

I laid on the ground and stuck my arm in the cloud and reached way below the level of the *Road* as far as I could. "There's nothing there," I repeated.

"The end must be the end," Ike said.

Baffled, Moe wondered, "What to do? Oh, what to do now?" He bravely stuck his head in the cloud and looked around, trying to see what he could. Withdrawing it, he said, "I can't see a darn thing in there, it's too dense."

"If there's nothing there, we can't just walk off the end, can we?" I asked.

"I'm afraid," Mar stated.

"I don't know kids. What do you think, Ike?"

"As you know, no one has ever reached this point. If nothing's there, we must still either go ahead or turn back."

A voice came from behind startling us, yet it was a welcomed relief to see a *Man in White* standing there. "He is right," he said. "You must either go ahead or turn around and walk all the way back."

"But Sir, there's nothing there," Lucy said.

"In everyone's life, there are times when one is faced with taking a step in faith in order to move ahead. In those circumstances, if one has the courage, they will take that step ahead. If not, they will remain behind."

"Sir, if we step off the end, we might get hurt or even killed.

"Mar, that is true. In your world, if one steps off a cliff, they would certainly be hurt or killed. I would not try it in your world. But remember, out here at the end of the *Road* is not your world.

Here the symbolism is prominent. However, it will take a deep faith to have courage enough to move ahead." He turned and walked off, disappearing into the cloud.

Bewildered, we stood there, silent for a moment. "What do you think, Miss Mary?" Moe asked.

"We have come this far, I believe we must go on."

"The Man in White walked into the cloud, didn't he? I believe we can do anything he can do, right?" Lucy said with unwarranted confidence.

"What do you think, Ike?"

"To go ahead is to go ahead."

"What do you think, kids?"

"If we're going to get home, that's the direction," I said.

"I want to go home," Mar said.

"I agree," Matt added.

I stated, "Well, then let's do it." This move was extraordinary, for most people wouldn't step off a cliff into the unknown without knowing if it were safe. We were forced to face the eternal question of what was the right thing to do. However, we felt that unnatural empowerment and trusted to move ahead was the right thing to do, however unreasoned.

At the same time, we understood it would be a stupid thing to do in our world. But, as The Man in White said, this was not our world, and in a sense, we believed since he entered the cloud, he was leading the way, giving us permission to move ahead.

"Okay, kids, if we're going to do what he did, let's do it all together. Let's hold hands and take that step in faith on the right foot all at the same time." We lined up, clasping the hand of the one next to us with our noses almost touching the cloud.

Moe orchestrated, "Okay, at the count of three and go. Ready; One... Two... Three and go," we simultaneously stepped off the end on our right foot and were hurled head over heels into a chasm screaming in absolute terror.

CHAPTER 56 In The Cloud

Tumbling while falling at an accelerated rate into the abyss, which seemed boundless. We held hands with an iron grip screaming all the way to the point of pain. We felt for sure it was our end. However, miraculously, we gradually slowed until moving in slow motion ending in upright positions, or so it seemed, floating in the dense cloud.

As we caught our breath, our hands unlocked from our power grips, which was undoubtedly more any of us could have managed in our own strength.

Lucy exclaimed, "What in the world!"

"I thought for sure this time we were really, really going to die," Mar said, breathlessly.

"Wow! I believe we 're going to be all right, you know what I mean?"

"Johnny, I know what you mean," Mary said, catching her breath.

The light in the cloud intensified to the extreme, overwhelming us. In the stark silence, a sense of warmth circulated around us, having a calming effect. Almost overwhelmed, the light softened, we saw an uncountable number of *Men and Women in White* embedded in the cloud floating all around us. They looked at us with angelic smiles. Oddly, it was creepy, although seeing them, gave us a feeling of safety. However, we didn't know what was happening or what to expect next.

A soothing voice punctured the silence, "Welcome, well done, you have made it to the end of the *Road* and beyond." The sound of the voice surrounded us. We looked up and down and all around, trying to see where and who it was coming from. Unseen, it said, "Relax. You are safe now." A gentle peace filled us; our trepidations disappeared, which allowed us to ask questions without hesitation. Our thoughts came out of our mouths unfiltered.

"Sir, where are we, and who are you?

"Moe, you know our name cannot be said. However, right now, it is not as important as *The Why*? That is the question to be asked."

"Sir, are we really at the end of the *Road*?"

"Mar... Marla, you know you are. As I said, you must now understand *The Why*?"

"Sir, are we allowed to ask questions?"

"Johnny, questions are at the center of understanding. You must never stop asking them."

"But Sir, so much is not clear?"

"Moe, the answers which come from us are always clear. It is your understanding or acceptance as seen through a man-made maze, making clarity difficult for most."

"Sir, how are we to understand something we cannot clearly see?"

"Good question Lucy. It has to do with a vision, not people's version of it, but the original vision. There have always been those who diligently keep impairing or even blocking that vision in the minds of men. It is the vision, which works through Goodness. The Goodness, which emanates from us. It is the quality which separates humans from all other living entities."

"Sir, I've sought to understand who we are. Why have I only found confusion? Is that the vision you are talking about?"

"Moe, we are aware you have sought the vision, and you are commended for that effort."

"Sir, then why haven't I been able to find the understanding you speak of?"

"Sir, if you knew of Mr. Moe's confusion, why, have you not given him that understanding?"

"Mary, that confusion resides in all mankind. In the first world, where Moe, Johnny, Lucy, Marla, and Matt come from, people were not only given free will but also received the knowledge of *Good and Evil*. Because of the powerful force that knowledge contains, it burnt an unintended hole in people's ability to understand. It has been difficult for mankind to manage the type of free-will choices necessary to repair that hole."

"Sir, why must it be so difficult?"

"Marla, it has to do with the complexity of free-will. We gave it as a gift, not knowing exactly how it would manifest itself, for it has to do with individual choices. We knew we should not control the choices one makes, for it would cancel the intent of free-will.

"It has been interesting to see the path it has taken. You must understand each choice one makes sends one in a different direction. Each of the trillions of choices humanity makes daily creates infinite possibilities. Yet, in truth, there is only one perfect choice."

"Sir, may I ask, what does this have to do with us coming into this world and us getting back home?"

"Ha, another good question. Lucy, each encounter you experienced along the pebble *Road* contained a key to understanding; a vision, a shadow, an example of correct and incorrect behavior, which you will now carry with you, to effect change for the better. What you unwittingly learned in each situation will be the guiding force for the rest of your lives.

"Sir, are we going home now?"

"Dear Marla, let us not jump ahead of ourselves. Understanding is achieved one step at a time, and you must learn by taking the first step."

"Sir, what is the first step?"

"Good Johnny, that question is the first step, which is to seek."

"Sir, what's the second step?"

"Lucy, Lucy, let us finish the first step first."

"Sorry, sir.

"Sir, it seems I've been taking first steps all my life and have gotten nowhere. Am I stupid? Am I a fool? Am I crazy?"

"No Moe, you are not stupid, you are not a fool, and certainly not crazy. It is that you are human."

"Sir, do you mean we're all flawed?"

"Sir, do you mean, no matter how hard we try, we're doomed to fail?"

"Moe, Mary, not at all, it simply means, one must work at seeking that understanding. Goodness, in the full sense of the word, is an acquired skill fostered through the original seed placed in each of us, which must be nurtured for it to grow."

"Sir, I've been working on it all my life and still failed."

"Moe, you only think you have failed. The only failure you had was not putting the steps in proper order."

"Sir, how come Mr. Moe was unable to, as you say, put the steps in order?

Mary, the reason you are all here is to answer that question. Many people live their entire lives without seeking answers to the most fundamental questions, which leads to that understanding of Goodness. Life is a quest to find one's purpose if one wants to experience life to its fullness. The challenge life presents is to complete a successful journey up *The Road of Understanding*. It is a trip all too short, for it only lasts one's lifetime. Due to how brief it is, it must be traveled one-step at a time and in the correct order. If too many missteps are made, one will not have the time to redeem what was lost."

"Sir, when do we get started?"

"Sir, Yes, when?"

"Lucy, Johnny, you have traveled the pebble *Road* in the other world. Again, now the time has come to understand; *The Why.*"

"Sir, when do we get to go home?"

"Oh, Marla, you are jumping the steps again."

"Sorry, sir."

"Children, I think we will get there if we take one step at a time."

"Wise Mary… Now, let us finish step number one."

"Sir, do these steps apply to my world too?"

"Yes, Ike, they do. It is for all mankind, no matter where or when one lives, or the color of their skin."

"And step number one is?"

"Ike, it is to understand life has a purpose, and one must find that purpose. It is a tragedy if one does not discover the purpose they were given. We created *Goodness* for the fulfillment of all. If you listen to the seed in you and allow it to grow, you will gain the understanding, which comes from us. Do you all understand what I have said so far?"

"I think I understand," I answered.

We all indicated we thought we understood, except for Moe,

who admitted, "Sir, I'm not sure I understand?"

"Moe, you have always understood. However, I know I will have to describe it to give it authority. You are still too timid to declare it aloud. Your purpose is the same as it is for all others. Although, the way one goes about accomplishing it is unique to each person. One's purpose is fulfilled by taking care of each other through your actions. One's unique individual actions.

"To love is not only to emotionally care for others; it is also to physically take care of others as well as yourself. This kind of love is what pleases us and glorifies our *Goodness*. If we are pleased, so shall you be. The tragedy is that humanity keeps missing that point.

"To work is not only for maintenance and survival as it is for all other living entities. Neither is it only for accumulation, which has become all too popular. It is not just to be concerned about self, but also to be concerned for others. Human life was not created for the I, but for all to join together in strengthening our *Goodness*. All must learn, when adrift in the sea of confusion mankind allows; one must deny the things which do not come from us."

"Sir, it seems I've always denied myself."

"Moe, with all the pressures and confusion the world places on one, it has become a much-misunderstood action and difficult for most to comprehend."

"Sir, I'm confused, you know what I mean?"

With a slight chuckle, the Voice answered, "Johnny, I do know what you mean. The denial we speak of is when one denies oneself for the sake of others."

Sir, do you mean we are supposed to deny ourselves everything?"

"No Lucy, of course not. In fact, it is to the contrary, if you want to gain everything *Good*, you must first learn self-denial."

"Sir, now I am getting confused?"

Mary, have trust, and confusion will leave as your understanding grows."

"Sir, do you mean we're to be good all the time?"

"Lucy, is there anything better to do, then to be good? Which means to take care of others, as well as yourself, and pass on your seeds as life was mean.

"You must learn, our free choice has two sides; one is to do the right thing by making good choices; the other is to do harm by making bad choices. It is no more complicated than that. You must learn to deny the types of lust, greed, and selfishness, which tempts you away from Goodness.

"If all could accomplish that simple task, life would be full of Goodness. A condition we should all seek, although it is continually denied by most."

"Sir, are you saying our true purpose is to serve one another?"

"Moe, you already understand that. To meet one's needs, one must also take care of the needs of others."

"Sir, I was taught to be respectful of others. But, our primary purpose in life was to take care of others? Why have I never heard that clear teaching before?"

"Mary, you and Ike are the only ones that have heard this teaching from us."

"Sir, have you spoken to those in our world about this?"

"Ha, good Johnny. Yes, we have spoken to your world about our *Goodness,* and quite loudly. Yet, too many times, humankind only hears what they want to hear, attempting to fit us into their changing images, although we have remained unchanged."

"Sir, I never heard of you in our world. Who are you?"

"Correct Lucy, it is because in your world we were manifested in a different form. Moe, Johnny, Lucy, Marla, and Matt; you not only know who we are, you already have a deep relationship with us. That is the 'Why' you were chosen. You see, we are already in your hearts."

"Sir, do you mean you are…

"That is correct, Moe, although our *Goodness* remains beyond human comprehension. Our original message given in your world has been twisted, mangled, and fragmented to deceive." As we listened to these revelations, we were astonished. Being so young, it was almost too much for us to absorb.

Moe was hardly able to speak as he squeezed out this question, "Why, Lord, haven't you revealed yourself in Miss Mary's world?"

"Interesting question. You see, the people who entered her

world through the *Rock* were expelled because of their unruliness and defiance. So we decided to see what would happen if we did not give her world any guidance leaving them only to rely on our seed, which we gave to all whether they accepted it or not."

"Lord, Miss Mary, Inge, and Ike turned out to be good people."

"That is true, Moe. The isolated cities created different societies with people whose actions ranged from being good to being downright evil, much as it is in your world. However, we inseminated everyone with the same seed, which allowed the same options to choose from. The only difference was, in Mary's world, it was not explained.

"Remember, those ejected from your world had already denied us, especially those who took leadership. However, many individuals were most courageous and allowed the seed to germinate in them."

"To be good is good."

"That is correct, Ike. The troubling factor is things on the other side of the *Rock* are not much better. People have not yet understood that living in *Goodness* is the most rewarding behavior for one to gain fulfillment.

"To end wars, killing, hatred, jealousy, envy, poverty, and all the harmful acts humans inflict on one another; Goodness must come. Although regrettably, Evil is still well and alive until the day it will be banished. The struggle will continue until *Goodness* comes and gathers all those who qualify to live on together in peace."

"You mean we'll end up just floating in the cloud, like these people around us?" Lucy asked.

"Let us not jump ahead. However, there are a great deal more exciting things going here than you are able to see, which you will learn about when your time comes."

The light intensified, a warmth embraced us, leaving us speechless for a time. I believe our spirits received fortification during that intense warming sensation as a peaceful calm again saturated us. It was an uplifting experience, which filled us with a sweet mystical aroma.

CHAPTER 57 The Farewells

We shortly came out of a momentarily suspended state and were able to speak again, Lucy asked, "Lord, please tell us again *The Why's* we were chosen?"

"Lord, and to do what?" I added.

"As I already said, you were chosen to take on this quest because our message is already deep in your hearts, although there are many like you, you are the first Chosen in today's battle. The Chosen are the frontline combatants in this war. It is not a war fought with guns and swords, but with *The Words of Goodness* given by us. However, the truth being, there will be times when force must be met with force, but it must be remembered, only when the innocent are to be saved. The rewards given for doing this work will be beyond anything you can imagine right now."

"Lord, all I want is to go home."

"Marla, we know at first this is difficult to understand. But be reassured, all we ask of you is to realize your true purpose. Now, to help you grow in understanding, you must take something with you."

"We must take something with us?"

"Yes, Marla, from this moment on, you are to become teachers."

"What would or could we teach?"

"Do not worry, Lucy, you will be instructed."

Listening to all this, Moe confessed, "I'm too tired and old now. I once hoped to make a better world, but I failed. I no longer have the strength or desire left to go back and accomplish anything."

"Yes, Moe, but in your own way, you have achieved a great deal more than you think you have, especially in the other world. However, your time has come. We invite you to join us where you can bathe in our *Goodness* beyond all understanding."

"Yes, I'm worn out and need to rest. It makes me sad I

wasn't able to live up to my hopes. I would've liked to see how things unfold, but I just don't have the will anymore." As he spoke, an even great peace came over him, accepting his fate.

"Yes, Moe, it is time to say your farewells to your friends." In that blissful state of acceptance, he turned to say goodbye.

However, Mary suddenly let out a loud cry and pleaded, "No, you cannot leave me alone!" She crumbled, grabbing his right leg to our alarm.

Moe, utterly taken by Mary's showing of devotion, for he never fully understood why he was worthy of her friendship. Finally, he had to accept the fact she cared for him and, in many ways, had become dependent on him, as he did on her. His back stiffened, he turned with Mary dragging from his leg to focus on a rotating spot above, "I cannot leave Miss Mary here alone. Can't she just come with me?"

"We are sorry, Moe, but that is not how it works. There are rules. It is not Mary's time."

Moe was never able to say no to Mary, he powerfully said, "Sir, if Miss Mary can't go, then I'll just have to stay here with her."

"Moe, there might be consequences if you do not come willingly."

"Sir, consequences or not, I can't leave Miss Mary alone. Anyway, didn't you say we must take care of each other?" That spot in the cloud swirled, speeding up in an erratic pattern.

After several swirls, it slowed down, and the Voice once again spoke soothingly, "Moe, are you willing to give up everything to take care of Mary?"

He answered with authority, "Yes, I am. I must take care of the ones I care for."

"That is quite noble of you. I see your understanding has grown. Mary, are you not fearful of what might happen to you if you come now?"

"There could be nothing as bad as being left alone for the second time. It was bad enough with Mr. Right the first time. If Mr. Moe leaves me, it will be unbearable."

"You can see, I cannot leave her."

"This is most unusual. To treat people of both worlds, exactly the same is new to us."

Lucy said, "But, I thought this is what you wanted us to understand, to take care of each other?"

"Lucy, we have never been challenged in this way.

"So!" she responded.

"I see… Moe, do you understand the rules cannot be broken?"

With a tearful Mary still hanging on to him, he stated, "Yes, I think I do. However, I cannot abandon Miss Mary."

"Moe, the rules cannot be broken... However, with a little effort, we can bend them a bit. Mary, you are from a different world than Moe. You still have a life to live there, are you willing to give it up to be with Moe?"

"To be left without him would be no life at all."

"To be willing to possibly give up everything for the sake of devotion to another is something we cannot allow to go unrewarded. I believe we are all learning. Mary, you are welcome here.

Moe and Mary physically collapse as they hung in the air, exhausted from the stress they just experienced. (Whatever force was behind The Voice, it had the power to do as it wished. However, fortunately for Moe and Mary, that force was not looking to exercise absolute control over them. It was not what it wished.)

The Voice took on a tone of authority, "Moe, Mary, it is time to bid your farewells."

As they floated to an upright position, I pleaded, "Mr. Moe, you're not going to leave us, are you?"

Lucy, with tears in her eyes, said, "You both can't leave us now?"

"Children, Moe, and Mary have successfully reached the end of the *Roads* in their worlds. Let them go, you still have many years left to travel."

"They're not going to be harmed, are they?" Mar asked, with tears in her eyes.

"No, they are not going to be harmed, ever again. The time has come for them to join us. Do not be concerned, for they are going to a much better place where harm does not exist."

"Kids, don't be concerned, we'll be all right, and not to worry, you'll be okay too. When you're back in our world, don't forget us. Goodbye for now."

"Yes, children, remember we will always be with you. Goodbye, we are all going into the unknown, be brave," Mary's voice echoed as they floated off arm in arm, disappearing into the cloud. With tears in our eyes, we experienced those deep feelings of separation more intense than ever before.

After Moe and Mary had left, we were overwhelmed for a time as the cloud embraced and massaged us softening our deep sorrow.

CHAPTER 58 Heading Home

Shortly, snapping back into the moment, Lucy asked, "Lord, what's going happen to us now?"

"Are we going home now?"

"Yes, Marla, however, first you must understand how to finish your trip here."

"Isn't the trip finished it yet?"

"Lucy, you have completed your trip on the pebble *Road*. However, you are just starting on your journey up *The Spiritual Road of Understanding*, which exists in your world. It is not a tangible road as it was there; it is a straight and narrow spiritual one, which is not a visible manifestation."

"You mean we must continue to drive on?"

"No, Matt, your trip in the Dragon is over. The trip is now within you. A journey filled with *Truth* and *Goodness*. It is a never-ending trip for humankind, one which has existed from the beginning and will continue until it is completed."

"Will we do this back home?"

"Yes, Marla, but first, let us finish the work here. Now, you are to receive *The Golden Book of Goodness*."

"*The Golden Book of Goodness*?" Lucy repeated in wonderment.

"Oh Sir, please give it to us, you know what I mean?"

"Soon enough, Johnny, but first, I must explain a little more. You must understand that your countries Bill of Rights was written by the free will of men. *The Book of Goodness* was written by us."

"Is there something wrong with our Bill of Rights?"

"Matt, when written, it was as good as mankind was capable of. However, under the circumstances, like most things in your world, humans will find or create loopholes that unfortunately developed twists and turns, which at times serve those who oppose *Goodness* by corrupting the original intent.

As you know, the opposite is Evil. You must learn to recognize only the original goodness in your Bill of Rights. *Goodness* surrounds you, and you must learn to separate it away from *Evil,* which has entwined itself in all things in your world."

We marveled at what we were being told. "Children, this is all about *Good and Evil.* It is about *Truth.* It is about *Justice.* It is about *Purity.* We selected you to be the first charged with this renewed quest, this journey, this mission out of the multitudes who qualify."

"Sir, you said we're to be teachers?"

"Yes, Johnny, but not what you think a teacher is supposed to be, but rather to be examples."

"Why just us?"

"Good question, Lucy, it is not just you. In the past, we have sent out others. Moreover, it is open for all who are attracted to join in securing our *Goodness.* You must remember we have seeded all people to be good, yet many do not allow our seeds to grow while few intentionally cause them to die. You are just the first Chosen for this new mission because of your innocence, purity, and spirit, in spite of your obvious flaws, for all people are inflicted with imperfections. From now on, you are to be soldiers fighting *Evil,* which continuously works to overtake us. Our seeds are dying and must be watered."

"Lord, are we to save the world or something like that?"

"Johnny, each act of *Goodness* saves the world. No good deed goes unnoticed. In your world, not long ago, your society came to a pivotal point in its development, as it has in times past. In today's world, people have the choice to take a step forward on the path to real *Goodness* or to remain on the man-made path of self-destruction, where deceivers destroy.

"Because people have free will, the masters of misleading convinced many it is better to travel down the road that leads to destruction. A devastating action not fully understood by most. Those two divided paths are in opposition to one another and are a matter of choice. *Goodness* grows out of selflessness, and the *Evil* of self-gratification grows out of selfishness. Before acts of *Evil* are put to an end, there is much work that is to be done to stop the killing of the innocent."

"Sir, I think this is beyond anything we could do."

"Lucy, do not worry, for you are just starting on *The Spiritual Road*. You will gain a greater understanding as you travel farther along. Remember, from this moment on, you are among the Ones Chosen."

"Wow! I guess we are?" I said, as we all began to envision and marvel at this incredible prospect, it's so much more empowering than we could've ever imagined in any of the unreal games we played in the park.

"Back in our world, how would we gain that understanding?"

"Good. Lucy, you are asking the right questions. It is why we are giving you *The Golden Book*." Suddenly, a *Man in White* floated up to us holding a gold-bound book, and as he did, we heard calming music in the background. (It was a good touch.)

"Johnny, take the Book. It will be your guide." I took the Book.

"Who do we give the Book to?"

"No, no Marla, the Book is for you to study, a workbook. I am afraid when you get back to your world, no one will accept your story of this trip. If you tell anyone about it, it will make your quest more tricky, so you must remain silent. "Now, take the Book back to your world, relax, study it, and as you do, your understanding will grow, and your mission will become clear.

"Remember, the understanding of fundamental truths is not open to different interpretations. It will become apparent, and you will understand what there is to do. It will be like the *White Light* flooding the dark side, peering into every dark corner, not allowing darkness to give cover to those who lie, cheat, and kill. People have always interpreted books, but our Book is so clear it cannot be misinterpreted unless one is corrupted and convinced otherwise by the deceivers, who are quite clever."

"Are we going home now?" Mar timidly asked.

Before she got an answer, Ike, who was taking all this in, meekly asked, "Sir, what about me?"

"Ike, not to worry, you are not forgotten. There is a Book for you too. Take it with you and share it with your friend Inge and all others who want to understand. It is for you and Inge to act on its words, strengthening our *Goodness* in your world." A *Woman in*

White floated over to him with a silver-bound book as the same warming music was heard. "Ike, take the Book and bid your farewells. It is your guide, you will drive the Dragon up and down the full length of *The Road of Understanding* spreading our *Goodness*."

"I will, Sir. I will, Sir. Ha! I finally get to drive the Dragon."

"That's great," I said.

"Go, Ike!" Lucy cheered him on. Through tears, hugs, and those strong emotions, we exchanged our goodbyes. Then, to our overwhelming surprise and astonishment, the Dragon flew in with its wings extended out, looking very much alive, although it was still a car. It was incredible.

The voice instructed, "Ike, the Dragon is your friend, and it will take you wherever you direct it to go." With his arms wrapped around the Silver Book, he got in. Seated in the driver's seat with the biggest smile on his face. He waved goodbye and screeched with joy as the Dragon flew up and away, disappearing into the cloud.

Only then did I realize it wasn't me, but the Dragon who saved us as we flew off the divide in Mechanicsburg? Maybe, that's why McCloud kept it a secret. I then wondered who McCloud really was.

Clasping *The Golden Book* against my chest, we huddle together. The Voice said, "Now your turn has finally come, remember the quest is yours. May your faith stay strong for it is your closest friend. Freewill could lead you astray, away from *Goodness*, just as it brings you into it. "From this moment on, you are soldiers fighting not with guns and swords, but with words and your lives to make a better world. You are destined to become true superheroes. For all those who work only within the boundaries of our *Goodness* are the real superheroes. Farewell, our children, we will always be by your side."

We started to spin, and as we did, we rose up and away. The spinning accelerated to a furious rate. Within seconds, we were tossed and rolled out on the grassy knoll. As we collected ourselves, we realized we were at the mouth of the cave under the *Rock*, and everything was as it was on graduation day, even our clothing.

At first, we thought it was all a dream? But when we saw *The Golden Book* still clenched in my arms, we understood it wasn't. We were so excited we raced down the zigzag path, with The Book in hand, to the park where we came across several classmates still dressed in their graduation robes. I quickly slipped the Book under my shirt, as a girl classmate asked,

"Wasn't the graduation great?"

Mar, still a little disoriented, asked, "What graduation?"

"Why, our high school graduation silly," the girl answered.

"What time is it?" I asked. When told, I realized not one second was lost while in the other world, and all things were as if we were never gone. Ecstatic, we screeched sounds of joy as we raced to our families, who we hoped were still picnicking in the park.

CHAPTER 59 What The Future Holds

It's been twenty-two years since our return from the other world. Now I'm called John. Every year since, Lucy, Marla, Matt, and I gather at the mouth of the cave under the *Rock* on the anniversary of our high school graduation. We celebrate by ritually retell the old original Indian legend at the *Rock,* not able to tell the story of our great adventure to anyone, not even our children who now includes my children, Johnny, who we call Junior, and Sarah, along with Lucy's children, David, and Paula.

On this particular anniversary day, Junior was the first of our kids to graduate high school. Consequently, we decided, since all our kids were now teenagers and have reached an age of responsibility, the time had come to tell them the story of our great adventure.

As we sat by the *Rock* telling it, our children were mystified, and at first, found it almost impossible to believe. Junior asked, "Dad, you mean you actually didn't lose any time while on the other side of the *Rock*?"

"Son, I know it's hard to believe, but that's the way it happened."

"Mom, is this story really true, or is it a graduation joke?" Paula asked.

"Now, dear, this is no joking matter," Lucy scolded.

"Sorry, mom."

"Dad, what happened to the book?" Sarah asked.

"Dad, is that what you keep in the safe behind the picture in the study?" Junior asked.

"Oh... We didn't realize you knew about the safe. I guess secrets are hard to keep. Yes, son, it's there."

"Dad, was that where you got the ideas for reforming the educational system?"

"Yes Junior, in learning from the *Book,* gaining more understanding, we saw where improvements were needed. Fortunately, as you know, through our hard work, we acquired influential positions, allowing us to cause changes to take place by using the principles from the *Book.*

"It took years to distinguish ourselves after our return. With me now being the Lieutenant Governor and both your mothers having become prominent citizens in civic affairs, including Matt being successful in academia, we have gained considerable clout. This enabled us to be effective in our mission, causing changes to take place, although there is much left to do.

"Wow! When can we see the *Book*?" Junior asked as the others were speechless.

"Kids, you're not only going to see it, but we'd like you to learn from it and gain the understanding as we have."

"Is that why, when we were small, those people caused you so much trouble?"

"Oh, you remember that... Exactly, Junior, it's been a great struggle. Many people cannot understand it's best to be good.

We have tried to communicate, in the years since our return with those who rebel against *Goodness.* It has been difficult for they fight to turn our society upside down.

"It has taken time to get some basic principles of caring through *Goodness* into the schools of today. Dreadfully, the pretenders, in their ignorance, fool themselves and many others as they claimed to be good while becoming most resistant to accepting true *Goodness.*

Your mothers have published many children's storybooks about *Goodness.*

"We had to endure many strange and extraordinary things, which we've not been unable to tell anyone about," Lucy added.

"Yes, those forces are still working diligently to squeeze *Goodness* out of our lives. We painfully learned the forces of *Evil* were just as influential on our side of the *Rock.* Getting the teaching of how corruption affects us into the community has been difficult.

Mar said, "Now, children, you cannot tell anyone of the existence of the *Book,* for there are still those who lay in wait to discredit its teaching."

Junior let out another, "Wow!"

"It's been hard to keep this secret from you, now you'll learn all about it. It's difficult to change the minds of those who don't abide by the rules in *The Book*. It is why we became so close to one another for our love for each other grew, and Marla and I married."

"Yes, and why Matt and I married," Lucy added

Paula couldn't help but say, "Cool."

"Wow, dad, then you are truly superheroes... When can we see *The Book*?"

"Okay son, but let's take it a little slow, you'll have a lifetime to learn from it. We've only been able to make a few strides since our return. It's been harder than we could've ever imagined. You see, the people in our world are not much different from those in the other world. We've learned that many in our world are more resistant to *Goodness* because of their free-will and were given the knowledge of *Good and Evil*.

"However, You will accomplish more than we were able to. I hate to say this, but it is going to take a lot longer before *Goodness* comes. You'll have to learn how to deal with those who want to obstruct that process."

"Dad, do you mean we are going to have to continue the struggle."

"Sarah, I'm sorry to say the struggle is far from over. In fact, the battle is just beginning to heat up, and I must say, it's been exciting, and I think you'll find it quite challenging and stimulating. Fortunately, you'll start from where we are today and not to start from the beginning as we did.

"However, let's not forget, today is a day of celebration, it's not only Junior's graduation day, but it's also the rite of passage for all of you. Today is to enjoy; tomorrow will be faced in due course."

Lucy ordered, "Yes, and it's getting late. It's been a long day, and it's time to head home."

I couldn't help but say, "Yes, and tomorrow will be the first day of your new superhero status."

"Wow, dad!" Junior expressed, as all the kids reflected their excitement and enthusiasm.

All their lives, we've taught them about *Goodness* without being able to tell them why. Now the time has come to break free and tell them all.

Suddenly, a most unexpected and supernaturally voice came from the mouth of the cave under the *Rock* as it lit up, "Kids, you're doing just fine."

With great excitement, I recognized the voice, and exclaimed, "Mr. Moe, is that you!"

"Kids, you can bet the *Rock* on it."

"Now, Mr. Moe."

Lucy, with tears of joy in her eyes, asked, "Miss Mary is that you?"

"Yes, dear Lucy, it's us."

With uncontrollable tears rolling down our cheeks, I asked, "Mr. Moe, are you coming through the *Rock*?

"No, Johnny, I'm sorry we can't do that. However, we've been watching how much you have grown in true *Goodness* in your mission. And kids, would you believe McCloud is here.

Mary added, "Yes! Mr. Right is here too. And Janis and Samuel will soon be joining us. However, we must go now."

"Please don't go!" Marla pleaded.

"We must. Remember, children we'll always be with you, and we'll be watching as we peer out from under our *Rock*. Children until we see you again," as her voice faded, A bolt of *White Light* struck.

When we were able to see again, an understanding Matt said, "Lucy, it's time to go home."

With tears rolling down her face, she said, "Yes, okay. Children, let's go home." With our children's roles now delineated, we all headed home with peace and a clear mission in all our hearts ready to face whatever tomorrow will bring.

The End

www.ingramcontent.com/pod-product-compliance
Lightning Source LLC
Chambersburg PA
CBHW060346260626
47160CB00006B/2222